The Tomorrow Heist

JACK SOREN

WITNESS
IMPULSE

An Imprint of HarperCollins Publishers

Excerpt from *The Monarch* copyright © 2014 by Martin R. Soderstrom.

EPub Edition NOVEMBER 2015 ISBN: 9780062365200

Print Edition ISBN: 9780062365217

10 9 8 7 6 5 4 3 2 1

For Tasha

No one longs to live more than someone growing old.

SOPHOCLES

Tomorrow is never what it's supposed to be.

BOB DYLAN

Prologue

Houston
July

IT WAS THE strangest kidnap and recovery mission Hoyt Randall had ever accepted.

Hoyt peered through the binoculars down at the cookie-cutter industrial plaza, a place that looked like it had been designed by an architect with a Lego obsession. Five businesses resided within the repetitive tan stucco frontages, accented by a burgundy saw-tooth pattern and identical bushes in front of smoked glass doors. The lights in the empty parking lot provided just enough illumination to discourage amateur thieves but not enough to dissuade a professional. Nothing moved. All was still.

Dressed all in black and wearing latex gloves, Hoyt fingered some notes into his forearm-mounted computing device before he put the binoculars away and pulled a black balaclava down over his face. He double-timed it down the hill, coming to rest behind the sign that said "Crystasis Foundation."

Arlo Perez, the man who'd hired Hoyt to retrieve his daughter, said Crystasis specialized in freezing the recently dead. Hoyt had heard of cryonics, of course, and most people knew the stories of Ted Williams and Walt Disney supposedly having their heads frozen after death so they could be thawed out in the future.

Hoyt found it all creepy as hell. Personally, he couldn't think of anything worse than waking up in a world where all of your friends and loved ones had been dead for a hundred years. Or worse, waking up inside a robotic body.

Linda Perez, Arlo's daughter, had been diagnosed with pancreatic cancer a year ago. The prognosis gave her a year to live, at best, with the final few months holding incredible pain and suffering. Six months ago, Linda committed suicide. Or, more to the point, a team from Crystasis had assisted her in their facility. Immediately after death, the team prepared her body and froze her, with the goal of waking her sometime in the future when her condition could be treated. Her parents, who had been vehemently against the procedure, wanted her back. They had plans for her body more in line with their religious tenets than the tiny hope of more life in the future. Hoyt was pretty sure he believed that. He also believed Mr. Perez was interested in the $200,000 that Linda had stolen from him to give to Crystasis.

He checked the area one last time, then jogged across the parking lot continuing around the back of the plaza. Hoyt bypassed the alarm system, then picked the lock on a service door. Inside, Hoyt let his eyes adjust to the minimal lighting before checking the floor plan on his forearm device. The entranceway was unmonitored, but his notes said there was video surveillance. He eased up to the corner and took out a small mirror on a telescoping metal antenna. He extended it and had a look around the corner. His notes were right; there were video cameras mounted high on the wall, but he could also see that the network cable wasn't connected to the unit. Hoyt figured the unit was under repair, and he'd just lucked out. He moved to the next room—the video surveillance there was disconnected as well. Now cooking inside his mask, Hoyt pulled it off and wiped his eyes before stuffing it into his waistband. A few corridor turns later—each with another disconnected video camera—he arrived at his target, two large metal doors which gleamed even in the low light.

Hoyt pushed through the doors and felt like he'd walked into a science fiction movie. The room, about the size of a small basketball court, had a dozen large, shiny, chrome tanks lining its perimeter. A weird hiss and hum throbbed from the ten-foot-tall cylinders.

"Jee-zus." Checking his forearm computer for the serial number he was looking for, he walked down the line and found a match near the back on one of the shiny cylinders. Linda—or what used to be Linda—was inside.

"And how the hell do I get you out of there?" Hoyt said, rapping his knuckles on the cylinder. A solid *thud-thud-thud* sounded. The pressure gauges on the outside of the tank, along with the cabling and tubing, were far more complicated than expected. The temperature gauge read -320 F.

Then Hoyt noticed an extra device on the canister. And the cylinder next to it. And the one next to that. Unlike the cryonic hardware, these he recognized from experience—magnetic, timed charges. And with the amount of C-4 packed inside each, someone was trying to put this place on the moon. The red digits on each device were synchronized and counting down.

8 . . . 7 . . . 6 . . .

Hoyt turned and ran. He was only ten feet away when the rockets launched. The blast wave slammed him through the doors, metal shards from the destroyed canisters slicing him to ribbons before what was left of his body slapped into the far cinder-block wall with a wet crunch.

SHE HAD NOT stopped him from going to his death.

Death was a necessary part of life. Stopping someone from dying would be the greatest irony for her.

Once the explosions subsided, and flames began to lick out of the windows broken from the blast, she stepped from the shadows dressed not unlike the late Hoyt, save for the bright red hair that peeked out from her black hoodie. She hurried to the front of the building, pulling a can of orange spray paint from her pack and shaking it in her gloved hand, the sound like a rattlesnake's warning. When she was done—sirens just starting to sound in the distance—she tossed the can aside, took out her phone, and dialed.

"It's done," she said in Japanese. "Moving on to the next."

She put her phone away as she ran back into the bushes. She wheeled her black Ducati motorcycle out of its hiding place. Straddling it, she lowered her hood and shook her flaming hair free before pulling on her gleaming black helmet. She revved the motorcycle's engine a few times and sped off into the night. Behind her, the flames illuminated what she had written:

"Dead Lights."

North Pacific Ocean
August

DR. ERIC NORRIS, head of the Dead Lights Project, edged out farther along the massive ship's railing. He wanted to get as far from the door leading back inside as possible, at least far enough to ensure he was out of earshot, but he knew he only had so much time before they came looking for him. Staring into the night sky, he pressed his cell phone against his ear and waited for a voice to come back on the line and break the silence. The ocean spray was cold and felt good on his face. It had been a long time since he'd been topside. He licked salty drips from his mouth and looked down into the black ocean forty feet below him, not at the surface but past it, at something far below.

He was on the line with the UK's Secret Intelligence Service—known to insiders as the SIS, but better known to the world as MI6. He'd already told his story—or as much of it as he was willing to tell without guarantees—three times. Everyone he spoke to had started off apathetic, but either his story or the angst in his voice managed to convince them he was on the level, and they'd tell him to hold before passing him up the chain. Small successes, yes, but each new voice asked him to tell the story from the beginning again. He didn't have time for this. If the old woman, or worse, that black limey bastard heard him revealing their secrets to a government agency, things would get real hairy, real fast.

"Come on, come on," he urged.

"Something I can help you with, Dr. Norris?" A British accent not unlike Norris's own said from behind him. He spun around, hiding his phone behind him like a child caught with a cookie.

Oh no.

"Just . . . just getting some air. You know, it can get kind of stuffy down there," Norris said, proud of his quick thinking. He slipped the phone into his back pocket.

The man was dressed impeccably in a three-piece suit and trench coat, the collar pulled up against the ocean mist, his dark-skinned face almost invisible. Norris didn't know his name and didn't want to. He had seen the man with the old woman on several occasions, and there was just something about his bearing, his presence, that made Norris's colon tighten up. The man lit a cigarette, momentarily illuminating his features. Norris thought his expression was one of—bemusement.

"Sure, darling," the man said. He eyed Norris quietly as he took a long drag from his cigarette before sending a wide plume of smoke into the world. After what seemed like minutes: "Well, don't dawdle. You wouldn't want to miss your ride." Without waiting for an answer, the man flicked his cigarette into the black water before turning and walking silently away.

When the man had disappeared around the corner, Norris exhaled, turned back to the railing, and took the phone out of his pocket. He saw that in hiding it, he'd inadvertently hung up. He had to start all over again.

"Damn i—" Before Norris could finish cursing, a hand gripped his throat from behind as another stripped the phone from him. He fought for breath, but the assailant pinned him against the railing.

"Who are we calling, darling?" the man said.

"Just . . . just some friends on the mainland. Nobody—"

The man had hit the redial button and put it on speakerphone. *"SIS. How may I direct your call?"*

"MI6, Dr. Norris? Now why would you do that?" the man hissed into his ear.

"It . . . it's too dangerous," Norris said.

He was trying to convince the man that he was talking about the project and what it could mean for the general public, but if he'd really cared about any of that, he never would have signed on to the project in the first place. No, what Dr. Norris was really worried about was what would happen to him now that his work was complete. Norris had lost touch with half his team already after they went ashore and never came back, and he was scared he was next. Or worse, they'd start doing to him what they were doing to Dr. Reese, someone who had been stupid enough to fail the old woman.

"Well, darling, I guess you should have thought of that before you took all that lovely money."

The knife blade shoved up through his neck only hurt for a moment, then Norris felt nothing even though he was still fully aware. Suddenly, he was flying, the spray blinding his unblinking eyes. He hit the water like a sack of dirt, the slap echoing across the waves. Panic spiked through him, but not for long. Soon his thoughts were as black as the water. And then they were gone.

Dead Lights

Dead Lights

Chapter One

London
Thursday
12:15 P.M. Local Time

Jonathan Hall hadn't been home in almost two years. Not that he hadn't had a place to live during that time. As a matter of fact, Jonathan had lived in some extravagantly opulent locales—a penthouse in New York, a yacht on the Aegean Sea anchored off Mykonos Island, even an abandoned palace in Thailand. But none of those were home. The last home he'd known was a tiny, run-down house in Tallahassee, Florida. But it hadn't been the building that had made it home. It had been the company.

Now, as he sat in a café in London, watching the crowds pass by outside in the midday September sunshine, oblivious to the magnificence of the Thames and London Bridge, Jonathan thought of his daughter, Natalie. Not that his thoughts were ever far from her. He hadn't seen her in person in almost a year. And the year before that he'd only managed to see her a few fleeting times. These were important years for her, and he was missing them. The same way he'd missed the first five years of her life. He hadn't even known Natalie existed back then, but it still bothered him.

He wished Natalie's mother was still alive. That's what a thirteen-year-old girl needed, a woman to explain all those things she was feeling and experiencing as she became a teenager. Not a father who, when he was around, put her life in danger. A father who had no idea what he was doing. A father who had been an art thief for the past eighteen years.

Jonathan squeezed a napkin to ease his tension as the waiter drifted by. He ordered another chai tea. The waiter nodded and took the old cup away. It was Jonathan's second.

He checked his watch. Their contact was over half an hour late. But he wasn't giving up just yet; Fahd was skittish as hell and in all likelihood was pacing back and forth up the street trying to decide what to do. In the end, Jonathan knew he'd show. It wasn't hubris speaking, it was pragmatism. Fahd needed the money that was weighing down Jonathan's black leather jacket, making it hang on the back of his chair at an odd angle.

Jonathan had found Fahd the same way he found all their jobs these days: through the Dark Web. Using a special Web browser that protected his identity, Jonathan could access Web sites and discussion forums where normal search engines couldn't go, with no fear of being tracked. He still had to vet his contacts carefully before actually meeting them—law enforcement agencies around the world were well aware of the Dark Web, and stings were becoming more and more common—but after all these years, Jonathan had become quite skilled at knowing who was and wasn't on the level.

As the waiter brought his beverage, Jonathan took the opportunity to scan the room again. He avoided direct eye contact—

especially with the hulking man sitting by the window, hunched over a plate of pastries and a giant, ridiculously sweet coffee, his long duster coat hanging over the back of his stool. The man was Lew Katchbrow, Jonathan's longtime partner and about the only person in the world he trusted. Jonathan nodded thanks as the waiter left again, confident that the scattering of patrons were oblivious to him.

He sipped his tea as his thoughts drifted back to Natalie. She'd just started high school last week, and he hated that he couldn't be there. But it was for her own good. Because of him, her life had been in jeopardy twice in the past two years. He wasn't going to let that happen again. No matter how difficult it was.

The first year Natalie was away at boarding school in British Columbia, Jonathan had tried to stay away, but he'd given in to his emotions and slowly started visiting her every few months. Then it became every few weeks. She'd been mad at him for sending her away at first, but she soon came around.

Then the unthinkable had happened. They'd found her. He didn't have any proof, but he was sure it was because of his visits. Canton George, an industrialist with a score to settle, had sent men to take her and to find Jonathan and Lew any way they could. It was only by sheer dumb luck that Lew had been with Jonathan on that visit to her campus when Canton George and his men came. Several tense hours later, George was blind in one eye, his men were dead, and Natalie had been forced to once again abandon her life. Sadly, George had managed to get away.

A new identity and a few months later, Natalie was enrolled in another boarding school. This one in Switzerland. And that was the last time Jonathan had seen his daughter in person. Even their encrypted Skype calls had started to make him nervous.

As painful as it was, he'd stopped taking her calls and instead paid the school's headmaster to keep Jonathan updated on his daughter's activities through a series of back channels, again on the Dark Web.

The bell over the café door rang, shaking Jonathan from his memories. It was Fahd, his contact, a guard at a local museum. Jonathan waited for a small crowd of patrons to finish leaving before he motioned to Fahd. The caramel-skinned, slight, black-haired man nodded and moved toward the table, furtively scanning the room as he approached. As he did, Jonathan's phone, resting on the table, buzzed. He looked down and saw Natalie's picture displayed on the screen.

He swore under his breath and swiped the reject button as Fahd sat down. The waiter drifted over and asked Fahd for his order, but Fahd, who kept wiping sweat from his brow with a napkin, tried to just wave him off. Jonathan smiled, apologized for his "friend" and ordered an espresso for him. Though as the waiter left, Jonathan thought more stimulation was the last thing this guy needed.

"You're late," Jonathan said flatly.

"I almost didn't come," Fahd said in a British accent that said he'd been schooled well despite his position at the museum. Jonathan knew the story behind that though not from Fahd himself. Fahd had been expelled from school after only two years for running an illegal poker game out of his dorm. A position as a guard at a local museum was the best he could do with that track record. It was one of the reasons Jonathan had decided to deal with him in the first place. He was motivated by money even more than most people.

The job was a small one, as far as their jobs went—a stolen set of rare books. But lately that seemed to be the rule of the day. Not that there weren't bigger opportunities out there, but Jonathan had become selective, taking lower-profile jobs, which, of course, meant lower pay. But if they could stay off the radar of their usual vindictive-billionaire targets, maybe it would be safe to reconnect with Natalie. Still, their resources were starting to feel the pinch, and Lew was starting to notice the pattern.

Sometimes Jonathan wondered what it would be like to sell the works he and Lew stole instead of settling for the finder's fee from the original owner or museum. Even though what they did had never been about the money.

Jonathan took the envelope from his jacket pocket and placed it on the table. Fahd, his nervousness gone at the sight of the fat envelope, reached out and tried to take the money, but Jonathan kept his hand on it.

"The name," Jonathan said when Fahd looked up at him, confused.

"Oh, right," Fahd said, licking his lips and appearing to weigh responding against letting go of the envelope. "Jacobson. Peter Jacobson." Jonathan hesitated for a moment but then took his hand away. Fahd yanked the envelope off the table and held it in his lap under the table, peeking inside.

"The address?" Jonathan asked.

Fahd told him the address, practically giggling as he pocketed the envelope. The name and address were new information for Jonathan, but he'd already met briefly with Fahd and knew that Peter Jacobson was another guard at the museum. One with even fewer scruples than Fahd.

"Nice doing bus—"

"Sit down," Jonathan said, his tone slamming Fahd's already rising butt back down on the uncomfortable wooden chair.

"Why'd Jacobson tell you he has the books? You're obviously not friends."

"I honestly don't know. He doesn't really have any friends that I've seen. He's, well . . ." Fahd seemed to be looking for the right words.

"He's what?"

"Well, he's weird. Has conversations with himself. Only wears half his uniform sometimes. He'll sit down across from you on break, stare at you, and never say a word."

This Jonathan didn't like. It made his ultimate target unpredictable. And that meant dangerous. He also figured something else out from Fahd's subtext.

"So he didn't tell you. You just heard him talking to himself," Jonathan said.

Fahd looked like a kid caught swiping a sweet from the local Tesco.

"Relax," Jonathan said. "You can keep the money. Assuming this pans out. If it doesn't, you'll be the one your coworkers are calling weird." It was a vague threat, which Jonathan found worked best.

"Can I . . ." Fahd said, nodding toward the door.

"Yeah, beat it," Jonathan said. He thought about stopping Fahd and making him pay for the espresso just for kicks but let him go. He knew from past experiences with guys like Fahd, the less you had to do with them, the better.

Jonathan watched as Fahd stumbled his way back out of the café. The second he was out the door, Jonathan grabbed his phone. His anxiety eased when he saw that Natalie had left him a voice message. He was about to dial his voice mail when Lew dropped down into the seat Fahd had just been in.

"Twitchy give us anything good?" Lew asked, still chewing on a pastry.

"How are you not a thousand pounds?" Jonathan asked as he watched Lew inhale the rest of his "snack." Jonathan had eaten with Lew more than he had anyone else on the planet, even Natalie, and the amount of food Lew consumed was always amusing. Especially since Lew was six feet tall and over 220 pounds, but only about 10% body fat. Jonathan was jealous. He had a thinner body type than Lew, but the past couple of years he'd had to really work to stay in shape. And he couldn't remember the last time he'd let himself have anything resembling a pastry.

"Clea' libbing," Lew mumbled through a mouthful of dough. "So what's up?"

"Talie called," Jonathan said.

"Yes! I knew it. Told you, didn't I? What did the little squirt say?"

"I don't know. She called just as Fahd got here."

"No, don't tell me . . . you rejected her call? For that sleaze? That's messed up, man," Lew said, shaking his head.

"We got the name and address," Jonathan said, ignoring Lew's jabs. After all these years, he'd gotten good at that. "We'll go tomorrow. Make sure you get some sleep tonight."

"Yes, Mom." Lew drained his coffee. "Still can't believe you didn't answer the kid's call." He stood up, the chair creaking a sigh of relief. "I'll come by your place in the morning. Call your kid."

"Want some company?" Jonathan said, standing up and throwing a few pounds onto the table. Lew furrowed his brow and looked at him. Jonathan knew why; they'd made a habit of not being seen in public together. Just in case.

"Uh, sure. Anything specific you want to do?" Lew asked, donning his Ray-Bans.

"Just walk," Jonathan said.

They stepped out into the afternoon and headed east toward St. Paul's Cathedral. They didn't talk for almost an hour. They were as close as brothers, and their silences were never awkward. Sometimes it was just good to be around someone who meant that much to you. After getting a couple of ice cream cones, they ended up leaning against a railing and watching the afternoon river traffic.

After a while, Lew turned around and leaned back against the railing, watching the crowds. Tourists and businessmen strolled by in the September sunshine. But Jonathan knew Lew wasn't people watching; he was making sure there were no threats about.

"You gonna tell me what's on your mind?" Lew said without taking his eyes off the crowds.

"We're running out of money," Jonathan said. The smaller jobs had taken their toll. Paying off Fahd had actually made Jonathan worry about making his rent this month.

"I know," Lew said.

"You know."

"Sure, but this is what you do."

"What I do?"

"Every now and then you get all freaked out about drawing too much attention, and you only set up smaller jobs for us. But you get over it; and then we're flush and back to normal. I have to admit, it's gone on longer than usual this time, but you'll come around. You always do," Lew said.

"You seem awfully sure of yourself," Jonathan said, trying to roll with what he'd just heard. He'd had no idea he was being so transparent or that there had been enough of these times for there to be a pattern.

"I do, don't I," Lew said, looking at Jonathan over his Ray-Bans.

The look Jonathan could take, it was the shit-eating grin that went with it that got under his skin. "It must be annoying."

"Hang on," Jonathan said. "Why are you so calm about this?"

"I'm not calm."

"You seem calm."

"I don't know why I'd seem calm."

"Maybe because you're calm."

"Huh, maybe."

"Well?"

"After your last spate of cut-rate jobs, I figured it was time to add a little cash to the bugout bag in my closet."

"A little. How little?"

"About fifty grand," Lew said.

"Jesus."

"You can borrow some if you want."

"I can?"

"Sure. All you have to do is ask."

Jonathan sighed and braced himself. "May I borrow some money."

"What's mine is yours, *amigo*. But you know there's a way we can make sure this doesn't happen again."

"Uh-huh. How's that?" Jonathan asked, but he was pretty sure he knew what was coming. Lew took off his glasses and looked Jonathan dead in the eyes.

"Let's be The Monarch again."

Jonathan knew Lew had never minded being The Monarch. Liked it, in fact. Especially the big payouts. They had started all of this because they'd been fed up with the system—Lew with the army and Jonathan with intelligence. Both had felt they were doing more harm than good. But then a chance meeting in Bogotá,

Colombia, had set them on the path to make a difference. Though there was a big distinction between returning some rare books stolen by a delusional security guard and finding a lost Rembrandt the world had thought destroyed. As The Monarch, they were preserving culture and history, but there was a big price to pay.

"What about Natalie?" Jonathan said. She wasn't just Jonathan's daughter, she was Lew's surrogate niece.

"We can figure something out," Lew said, sounding like a kid trying to convince his dad to take him to a ball game.

"'Figure something out,'" Jonathan said flatly. "Jesus, you thought harder about which pastries to eat back at the café! Natalie isn't something *to figure out*. She's all that matters."

"And I don't know that?" Lew said, getting defensive. "I'm just the fucking idiot muscle."

"I didn't say that," Jonathan said. Then after a minute: "But there are times—"

"Fuck you," Lew said, pushing off from the railing. "If I'm such a mouth breather, get your own fucking money." He roughly put his glasses on, swung around, and marched off, his coat swirling in his hurry.

"Lew, don't be like that. You know what I meant," Jonathan said, but Lew kept walking. "Lew! Are you coming tomorrow?"

Lew spun around and walked backward. "Sure! You might need me to lift something. Ladies and Gentlemen, Jonathan the giant brain. Give him a hand," Lew said to the people around him, waving his arms like a circus ringmaster. Then he turned and disappeared into the crowd.

Sometimes I can be such a dick.

Jonathan didn't believe for a minute that all Lew brought to the table was his physicality, but it was a button he could push to make

Lew drop The Monarch nonsense. In retrospect, Jonathan knew he was lucky Lew hadn't knocked him on his ass. He had to apologize, but when Lew got like this, you just had to leave him alone for a while. The only person who could cut through his moods was Emily, his on-again, off-again girlfriend.

But as far as Jonathan knew, they'd been off for a long while. Ironically, for the same reason Jonathan was staying away from Natalie. Not that Lew would admit it, of course. Jonathan actually wished they could work things out, but he knew Lew could be a lot to take on a constant basis.

She was probably better off without him.

Chapter Two

North London
3:00 P.M. Local Time

EMILY'S HEAD ROCKED back from the masked man's slap, blood and spittle flinging across her living room. White flashes exploded in her head, and her ears rang as she distantly felt hands push her back down into the chair. She coughed and spit more blood as the white faded, and her two captors came back into focus, one beating her while another stood back a little holding a gun even though they'd duct-taped her hands to the arms of the chair.

"Where are they?" an electronic voice with a South African accent demanded. It came from the iPad sitting on her coffee table beside her. A man with deep black skin and an eye patch peered out from the screen: Canton George. She'd met him before, only then, *he* had been the one being beaten for information. That scenario had ended with George's being locked in his own vault and his ill-gotten mansion explosively spread across half an acre.

He'd been hunting Jonathan and Lew ever since.

She wanted to scream and cry—to give in to the fear and pain—but that was exactly what George wanted. And to be honest, after searching for her for so long, she was a little insulted that he was phoning it in though she was pretty sure she knew why he wasn't there in person. George had found Natalie in her British Columbia boarding school about a year ago, and he'd tried to take on Jonathan and Lew in person. It had not worked out well, as his eye patch and the scar peeking out from under it attested.

"They're right outside your compound, Georgie. I'd start running if I were you," she said. She knew she was going to pay for the lie, but the look of fear on George's face, even though it only lasted a second, made it worth it. His remaining eye widened, and he disappeared from the screen, apparently gone to make sure she was lying. When he returned, with a very different look on his face, Emily was laughing harder than she had in a long time. Her face still felt like it was on fire, and the teeth on one side of her mouth felt loose when she touched them with her tongue, but this little victory made her momentarily forget the danger under her sofa.

"Again!" he shouted, his anger throwing spittle onto the screen.

Emily's laughter was abruptly cut off by a powerful right cross from one of the masked men. This time she did lose a tooth, and she was pretty sure her nose cracked. She spit out the tooth and tried to put on a brave face and laugh some more, but it came out as mewling.

She was forcing herself not to look under her sofa. Her cell phone was under there, dimly glowing its existence, but to Emily it felt like a spotlight. She'd been on the phone with Natalie when the masked goons had burst in through her door. The door had hit her from behind, and the phone had gone flying, luckily ending up under the sofa. It was encrypted, but she hadn't had time to lock the screen. All they had to do was look at her call log, and they'd track Natalie down in a matter of minutes. She just prayed the connection had been severed. If Natalie was still on the line listening to this nightmare—she shook that idea away. It was too horrible, and she needed to concentrate on coming out of this alive so she could warn Jonathan and Lew.

"Miss Burrows, be sensible," George said, his voice quieter as he feigned compassion.

No one had called her that name in over a year. It was her pen name back when she was a writer though her only work had been about The Monarch, Jonathan and Lew's abandoned alter ego.

"If I were sensible, I would have put a slug into your psychotic brain when I had the chance," Emily said. This enraged George again.

"Another!" he shouted. The masked man wound up and hit her again, this time with a closed fist. He hit her so hard, her slender frame was knocked right out of the chair, and one of her hands tore loose of her taped bondage. Lying on the floor, the chair still attached to one hand and on top of her, she fought for breath, coughing. She felt something in her mouth and spit it out. Another tooth landed on the carpet beside the first—right beside her phone.

"Pick her up, idiot," George barked from the screen.

The man crouched to pick her up but hesitated. He reached past her head and under the couch.

No!

Up on her knees, she swung her free hand, knocking the phone from his hand. Then she gripped the arm of the chair in her still-taped hand, looking into the eyes of her assailant. It only took him a second to realize what she was going to do.

"Don't—"

She swung the chair at him with all her strength. The hardwood legs slammed into his face and raised arms. As he howled, and before the other man could react, she drove one of her long legs into the wounded man's midsection. With an *oof!*, the masked brute fell back against her bookshelf, howling. She tried to get to her feet to smash the phone, but the wounded hood's partner swung his gun at her. She caught his arm and used her weight and the swing's momentum to pull him down onto the floor with her, slamming her knee into his throat. Before she could do anything else, the first man picked her up from behind and tossed her and the chair through the air against the same bookshelf. Excruciating pain burst out from her side as she fell to the floor in a heap, the chair smashing to bits. She fought for her breath, every inhale now a stabbing pain. Lew had taught her how to defend herself, but in the end she was just too slight.

The man who'd thrown her picked up the phone while his partner lay motionless where she'd left him. She wanted to jump up and run away, but the pain was just too much. She could feel her consciousness starting to swim. But through all of that, the worst thing she felt was the grief.

Emily had almost been responsible for Jonathan's and Lew's demise two years ago, but she'd made amends, and in the end, she'd not only helped them, she'd had a torrid love affair with Lew. But it was all for naught. She was right back where she'd been at the start, responsible for their impending deaths. All because she cared.

She'd felt sorry for Natalie, being left alone. She understood why Jonathan had severed contact with her, but that didn't mean she agreed with his actions. Despite her promise to him, she'd been calling Natalie on a regular basis, keeping her up to date on her father and her uncle Lew. Not that Emily's motivations would matter if George got ahold of Natalie.

"I've got it, sir!" the masked man exclaimed. "His daughter's phone number."

"Please! She's just a—" Emily's pleas were cut off by a kick to her side.

"Bring me the girl."

"What about Burrows?" the underling asked, looking at his partner. "I think she might have killed Neill."

George didn't even hesitate. "Kill her." The screen went blank. George was gone, along with Emily's chances of saving Natalie.

And that was it. It was over. The sin she'd committed years ago returned in full.

The man pulled out a gun and turned toward Emily.

At least I'll be first, she thought. Standing by and watching it all go down again was something she just couldn't take.

Emily closed her eyes and braced herself for the shot. A crash reached her ears, and she flinched before she realized it wasn't a gunshot. She opened her eyes and saw that her front windows had shattered into the flat; two ropes were hanging on their sills, left behind by the two new masked men standing before her. These men looked different—more professional. They were wearing body armor, and each held an automatic weapon, red beams slicing from their sights. They instantly targeted the other masked man and the one on the floor, efficiently putting a staccato hail of bullets into each one's head.

"Clear!" one of the men shouted after checking the entire flat.

"We're clear, sir," the other one said, even though he wasn't wearing an earpiece.

Her front door opened, and a well-dressed man with incredibly shiny black shoes walked over to where Emily was huddled and crouched beside her.

"Can you hear me, Miss Denham? Are you all right?" The man said, using her real name.

Before she could answer, the murkiness grabbed her and pulled her down into unconsciousness, the idea of Jonathan and Lew— mostly Lew—being safe allowing her to let go. She pictured Lew's face one final time before everything was gone.

Chapter Three

Houston, Texas
12:02 P.M. Local Time

THE HELICOPTER SWUNG in from the east. Per Broden stood by his rental car dressed in a tan-wool trench coat over a matching three-piece suit and perfectly knotted brown bow tie. He held his briefcase in one black-gloved hand, his other hand hung, un-gloved, by his side as he waited.

His journey had started over thirty-six hours ago in a place where his attire made more sense. Stockholm, Sweden, his home since he was a boy, was almost fifty-one hundred miles from the spot where Per was currently rooted. At fifty-four, he still called it home though in all those years, he'd traveled the world several times over.

The helicopter was only fifty feet off the ground when it stopped its arc above the scrub grass that stretched as far as the eye could see. It rocked for a moment, then descended to the desert floor, blowing Per's thinning dirty blond hair from its perfect side part down over his round-lensed spectacles, dust following the wind and peppering Per. He remained still.

When the chopper finally came to rest, Per reached up with his free hand and swept his hair back into place.

A man in jeans, a blue-checked button-down shirt and black cowboy hat stepped from the chopper. Holding his hat in place and bending slightly to avoid the rotor blades, he jogged to where Per was waiting.

"You Broden?" he said with a thick Texas accent.

Per took a business card from his inside vest pocket and handed it to the man: "Per Broden, International Investigations."

The man read the card, shrugged and handed it back to Per, who pocketed it.

"Name's Green. Hank Green," the man said, wiping sweat off his brow with one forearm. "Jesus, you must be hotter than a four-balled tomcat in that getup. I work for Mr. Harcourt. He's waiting up at the main house." Hank eyed Per's briefcase. "Mind if I take a look?"

"Yes, I do," Per said, the first words out of his mouth in almost two days.

Hank jerked back slightly at the refusal. "Look, *amigo*. Either you let me look in that case and frisk you, or this meeting ends before it starts."

"I understand," Per said.

"Good. Now if you'll—"

"Good day," Per said as he turned and opened the car door.

"Whoa, hang on," Hank said, grabbing Per's arm. Per continued into the car as if nothing was stopping him. Hank looked surprised that Per wasn't as weak as he appeared. It was a look Per was well acquainted with.

"Tell Mr. Harcourt I hope he solves his mystery. Now please back up," Per said.

"All right, all right," Hank said. "I won't look in it. Can you at least leave it in the car?"

"Yes, that would be acceptable," Per said. He placed his briefcase on the passenger seat and rejoined Hank.

"Should I bother to try to frisk you?" Hank asked with a smirk.

"It would not be wise," Per said flatly.

"Huh. You're an odd one, ain't cha?"

"That would be an accurate assessment, yes."

They climbed into the helicopter, buckled themselves in, and, a few moments later, they were airborne. Per sat straight in his seat, neither looking out the window nor avoiding the view. He simply wasn't interested in it. What he was interested in was why his new employer hadn't been here to meet Per himself.

"Mr. Harcourt doesn't leave the house much these days," Hank said, apparently anticipating Per's question. "He's taking these attacks personally. But you can't really blame him."

Per nodded slightly and waited for more information.

"To be honest, he thinks someone is trying to kill him. Figgers the words left behind is just a smoke screen to draw him out."

Per raised an eyebrow and turned to look at Hank. This was why he was here.

"And what do you think, Mr. Green?" Per asked.

"Me?" Hank said, surprised. "Hell, I ain't paid to think!" He slapped Per's shoulder as he laughed a loud, hacking laugh.

Per believed him.

Thirty minutes later, a large, ranch-style house appeared on the horizon, surrounded by a barn and a corral filled with horses. They landed in the front yard as workers fought to control the spooked horses. Per followed Hank out and up to the front door.

Hank started to open the door, but then stopped and turned to Per, concern in his eyes.

"You have to help him, Broden. It was all I could do to get him to meet with someone. He's a real mess. I may work for him, but he's the best friend I ever had, and it kills me that I can't do nothin' for him."

Per waited, then realized they weren't going to pass through the door until he responded verbally.

"I'll do what I can, Mr. Green," Per said. It was the truth. Per was actually incapable of doing any less. But truth be told, he couldn't care less about a rich Texan's sudden phobias. He was here for one thing and one thing only—the puzzle.

As a child in Stockholm, Per's brother Peter had been kidnapped by a serial killer. The killer taunted Per's family for weeks with riddles and unsolvable clues. In the end, his brother was killed. Per had thought at the time that if he'd just been smarter, more clever, better at puzzles, he could have saved Peter. Despite reassurances from his parents, the authorities, and several therapists over the years, Per still blamed himself for Peter's death.

Since then, he'd spent his life solving puzzles; first for the police and now freelance as an investigator. Per would never let himself feel that way again. He'd rather die than fail.

Every time Per solved a case, he felt like he'd made an atonement to his murdered brother. A drop in a bucket that would never be full.

Per followed Hank into the house, and he suddenly felt like he was only a few kilometers from home. Despite the mansion's exterior, the interior was decorated in classic European designs rather than what one expected of a Texas estate. The space was immense, easily fifteen meters high with an expanse more like an auditorium than a living room. The floor was cream-colored marble, brown diamond shapes inset where the large tiles met. The furnishings were green and gold and crimson. Staircases ran up the walls on both sides of the room, large paintings resting on the wall wherever a landing occurred. Against the far wall was a fireplace with more furniture arranged around it. In the corner was a grand piano just a few feet from a dining-room table covered in a deep red tablecloth and surrounded by fourteen chairs. In the center of the room was a large plant on top of a working fountain, gurgling away.

They walked to the fountain, and Hank asked Per to wait. He went up one of the staircases and was gone for almost half an hour, his absence accompanied by echoing shouts. Finally, he returned, and asked Per to follow him upstairs. At the end of a long corridor, they entered an office bigger than Per's entire house.

The office was decorated as extravagantly as the rest of the house, but a foggy sheen seemed to obscure the brilliance. The leather sofa against the wall held rumpled pillows and a blanket, and there were more than a few empty beer bottles along the floor beside it. From the smell, Per doubted that Harcourt had left anytime recently.

At the end of the room, slumped behind a wide desk covered with food trays and open books, James Harcourt sat dressed in a green-plaid bathrobe. Per could see a shiny silver .44 Magnum revolver lying in front of Harcourt along with a mostly empty bottle of Jack Daniel's and several half-empty bottles of pills.

Harcourt was a big man with a wild, unkempt beard. Even seated, Per could tell that Harcourt was taller than he, but since he was only five-nine, that didn't say a whole lot.

"Mr. Broden, this is James Harcourt," Hank said before fading into the background. Per stepped in front of the desk and waited for his host to speak. Or, to at least acknowledge he was there. Five minutes later, he got his wish.

"Jesus! Where'd you come from?" Harcourt slurred, grabbing his gun and pushing back in his overstuffed brown-leather office chair. The only thing that kept Per rooted to his spot was that despite his antics, Harcourt had yet to point his gun anywhere but at the floor.

"He's the Swedish detective," Hank said, floating into the scene again. "You sent for him, Jim. Remember?" Hank looked at Per apologetically.

This was not what Per had expected. When the first cryonics facility had been bombed, and the first occurrence of the enigmatic "Dead Lights" phrase had been scrawled onto the pavement, Per had read about it on the Internet. He'd immediately contacted Harcourt with an offer to investigate. After several more bombings and even more e-mail exchanges, Harcourt had finally acquiesced and invited Per for a meeting. But the man Per had communicated with online had been articulate and wary. Not the self-indulgent, ready-to-surrender figure before him.

Harcourt looked at Hank, then back at Per. A long moment stretched out as the big man's eyes fought to focus.

"Right. Right," Harcourt said, seeming to just now notice that he was holding his gun. "Jesus, sorry . . . Broden, is it?" Per nodded as Harcourt put the gun back on the desk before swallowing down more pills with the whiskey. "Sit down, sit down."

Per obliged. Harcourt shook his head and grunted, apparently trying to clear his head.

"The pictures, Jim. Show him the pictures," Hank said before taking a seat against the wall, holding his hat in his lap.

"Uh. Right, the pictures."

Harcourt picked up a stack of eight-by-ten photos from his desk. He looked at them before turning his attention back to Per.

"It started a few weeks ago," Harcourt said, handing Per one of the photos. Per took it from him. It was a picture of what had once been a building, now half-missing and all burned. On the remaining brickwork in front of the structure were the words "Dead Lights." It was from a different angle, but this was the image Per had seen on the Internet that had first drawn his interest to the mystery.

"What am I looking at?" Per asked, willing to play whatever game Harcourt was selling. To a point.

"How much do you know about me, Broden?"

"Not much," Per lied. If he hadn't known everything there was to know about Harcourt, he never would have gotten on the plane to come here.

Harcourt had made his money like most millionaires in Texas—in oil. But he'd gotten out of the black-gold business years ago. Since then, he'd been interested in one thing and one thing alone—life extension. In every capacity.

Toward that interest, he had created the Crystasis Foundation. The rumors in the life-extension chat rooms Per had frequented before coming here were that, in truth, Harcourt was only interested in finding ways to extend his own life. Per thought it made sense that someone who was business savvy wouldn't experiment on himself but find a way to experiment on others until he found what he was looking for. And Per thought the influx of capital from people willing to pay hundreds of thousands for even a shot at more life wouldn't hurt either. But the facilities where Harcourt stored frozen corpses with the hope that one day they could be thawed and cured of what killed them was just part of his longevity empire.

"Look around you, Broden. It looks like I have everything a man could want, doesn't it?"

"Some men."

"I've been lucky. I have enough money for several lifetimes. The problem, of course, is that I don't *have* several lifetimes. Like everyone else, I have just one. I can't change that. But I can make the one life I do have long. Really long." He took a long pull on the bottle and wiped his mouth with his forearm.

Per just looked at him.

"That used to be one of my life-extension facilities. There used to be seven of them around the world. Here, South Africa, Europe . . . even had one in Russia. Most of them are just repositories, but I've got a research lab up in Toronto too."

"You *used to* have seven?"

Harcourt tossed three more photos on the desk in front of Per. "Over the past few weeks, there have been bombings at three of my facilities. No warning, no explanation. Just that goddamn message on the bricks in front of the ashes.

"I've beefed up the security at my other facilities, but I don't want to just be safe. If a coyote is taking your herd, you don't build a bigger fence; you kill the mongrel."

Per looked at the photos for a while longer, then put them down in a neat pile on the desk. He leaned back and brushed some hairs from his suit.

"The only leads we've got are this man and this security camera picture." Harcourt handed Per two final photos.

Per examined the first photo. It was of a thin, bearded man in a lab coat. The word "Crystasis" CRYSTASIS was embroidered across the lab coat's breast. Beneath was a name tag: "Dr. Reese." He put the picture with the others.

"Up until six months ago, Dr. Chris Reese worked out of my lab in Toronto on special projects," Harcourt said.

"What happened six months ago?"

"He just up and disappeared. Poof. He didn't resign or, as far as my inquiries could tell, take a job anywhere else. He emptied his bank account and walked away from his house. No mortgage payments or other bills have been paid since then. A few months later, the attacks started."

Per turned his attention to the final picture. It was dark, the only source of light the flames from the burning building in the background. He squinted and could just make out a figure on a motorcycle. The shape of the skintight leather and the hair splaying back from the rider's helmet told him the rider was female, and probably young.

"That was taken by a warehouse security camera just up the road from the first facility that was attacked minutes after the alarm went out to the fire department. We enhanced the photo as much as we could without washing out the details. Afraid that's the best we could do."

Per put the photo down on the pile, looking up at Harcourt. He examined the man for a few long moments, Harcourt seeming uncomfortable under Per's gaze. If not for the booze and pills, Per would have probed the discomfort further.

"Why me?" Per asked, finally.

"I heard what you did in Spain last year," Harcourt said, glancing at Per's one gloved hand. "You're the man for the job, all right."

Per understood why Harcourt had looked into his past, but he didn't like it. There was too much there to find.

"As I said in my correspondence, my fee is one hundred thousand dollars and expenses. Deposited to this account," Per said, holding out a business card with his bank account transfer information on it. Harcourt just looked at it. Hank got up and took it from Per before returning to the sofa.

"I'll need full access," Per said.

"You'll have it," Harcourt said. He reached in a drawer and took out a passcard. He tossed it to Per. "This will get you into all my facilities. And this should take care of your expenses." Harcourt tossed another card onto the desk. This one was a credit card. It was black. "No limit. And you can use it at any ATM for as much cash as you need. Passcode is L-I-F-E. 5433," Harcourt said, taking another drink.

"You are being very trusting, Mr. Harcourt," Per said. The implication was, *how do you know I won't rob you blind?*

"As I said, Broden, the one thing I do have is money. And my horse sense. You hold your cards pretty close to your chest, but I can tell I can trust you."

Per simply looked at him, wondering what the drunk would say if he knew that Per had no intention of killing anyone for him—unless they got in his way, of course. Per would solve the Dead Lights mystery—what it meant and what the bomber was trying to achieve—and then move on to his next puzzle. The answers were all that mattered to Per. All that would ever matter to him. He'd trade his life for those answers—his and anyone else's.

Per stood up, pocketed the cards, and picked up the photos.

"I'll solve your riddle, Mr. Harcourt," Per said.

"You misunderstand me, Broden. I don't care what the meaning is. I want you to find the coyote and put him down."

Per had expected as much.

"Of course. There could be . . . collateral damage," Per said. The last thing he wanted was his new employer's reporting him to the authorities because he didn't approve of his methods.

"Do what you have to do, Broden. I don't care what it costs. It's self-defense. And in Texas, that can be bloody."

Not just in Texas, Per thought.

HANK GREEN ASKED Per to wait outside while he finalized things with Harcourt. Per obliged without a word and left the opulent office. After he'd closed the door, Hank turned to face his boss.

"You didn't tell him Reese was our man," Hank said, moving toward the desk.

"Judgment call," Harcourt said. "Tracking Reese will lead him to the old woman, but it can't be too easy. Broden isn't just cagey, he's incredibly perceptive, from all accounts. He needs to work for it." The slur was gone from his voice. Harcourt was sitting up straighter now too. Hank knew that Harcourt had intended to act helpless, so Broden wouldn't fully know who he was dealing with. Hank also knew that Harcourt was deluding himself. He might not have been as confused as he'd acted, but he was far from in control. He hadn't left his office in weeks, and if Per had taken a closer look at the beer bottles by the sofa, he would have seen they were full of piss.

"But what if he doesn't figure it out? What if Reese isn't a big enough clue?"

"Then he's not the man for the job," Harcourt said.

"What do you think he'll do if he finds out Reese didn't disappear but that you sent him to work for Tenabe?"

"Nothing good, I'm sure. Don't be fooled, Hank. His demeanor is deceiving. This is not a man to be fucked with."

"If you don't trust him, don't hire him. We'll get someone else," Hank said, sitting on the corner of the desk.

"He's the man for the job, all right," Harcourt said. "But he's a control freak. If he knows we're going to be looking over his shoulder the entire time, he'll never take the case."

"Why him?" Hank asked.

"You heard me mention Spain?"

Hank nodded.

"Last year, the high-speed train service in Spain was having a problem with theft. Jewels were going missing on almost every trip despite the fact that they were locked inside a train going almost two hundred miles per hour. The company operating the service spent thousands putting undercover security on the train, installing cameras, you name it. Nothin'," Harcourt said as he got up from behind his desk and shuffled over to the sofa.

"Then they called Broden?"

"Broden called them. He rode the train endlessly for weeks. Even when his employer told him to give up and cut off his money, he kept buying tickets with his own money and riding the train over and over. The guy's a bulldog."

"He solved it?" Hank asked.

"The company's pretty tight-lipped about what actually happened, but yeah, the thefts stopped. Most of what I know I heard through rumors and cobbled-together police reports," Harcourt said, seeming to lose interest in what he was saying, staring at the whiskey in his hand.

"And?" Hank prompted.

"Huh? Oh, right. The most common theory is Broden figured out it was an inside job, after all. Couple of guys on the security crew, backed by some local organized crime. But that wasn't good enough for him, he wanted the whole picture, and a couple of tight-lipped bag men weren't going to give him that. But here's where the real conjecture comes in—they found one of the security guys tied up in the baggage section. Almost every bone in his body was broken."

"Jesus. Broden?"

"Broden. Looks like he worked him until he talked. Maybe a bit after too. The inside men would gather the jewels during the trips while passengers were sleeping, then put it all in a special case they had constructed that looked just like a normal traveling trunk. About the size of my desk. Some padding and struts inside to keep the hauls from getting destroyed."

"Destroyed?"

"When the train went through the Sierra Morena mountain range, it would slow down because of the curves in the track. Somewhere in there, they'd launch the loaded case out the bottom of the last car. After the train was gone, and the case had stopped bouncing, their buddies would pick it up."

"Sheesh. So what did Broden do?" Hank asked.

"He got in the case."

"He . . . holy shit. How fast was the train going?"

"Somewhere around a hundred twenty-five miles per hour."

Hank whistled and shook his head. "And he survived without getting hurt?"

"Not quite. The guy's tough but he's still flesh and blood—or at least he was back then. He was messed up pretty bad, and his arm was so crushed he had to have it amputated later at the hospital. But the really amazing rumor is that he still climbed out of the case and killed the three armed guys waiting for their score."

"Jesus," Hank said. Then he realized what Harcourt had really said. "What do you mean 'back then'?"

Harcourt laughed before continuing. "I can't believe you didn't notice. This is why we need his help. If he makes it to Tenabe's ship, he's going need that arm to stay alive, never mind kill that Tatsu bitch."

"Wait. He had it amputated? But he has both . . ." Then Hank remembered that Broden wore a glove on one hand. "Son of a bitch. I didn't even notice it was fake."

"Ain't fake. Robotic. It's very advanced and works just like a normal arm—if a normal arm were made of titanium and had the strength of a trash compactor. Or, so the rumors go." Harcourt smiled and winked, which made Hank even more uneasy. He kept thinking what would have happened if he'd tried to forcibly search Broden back at the car.

"Still, like Broden said, it's a lot of trust."

"I'm not a fool, Hank. Despite the talk," Harcourt said. "He's not going to have as much freedom as it appears."

"How so?"

Harcourt took a cell phone out of his pocket. The screen displayed a local map with a single point blinking on it. It was a map Hank was very familiar with. A map of Harcourt's ranch. And the blip was about where his front door would be.

"I didn't just give him that card so he could get in and out of doors," Harcourt said before handing the phone to Hank. "But that's not my ace in the hole."

"What is?"

"You. You're going with him."

Chapter Four

London

8:00 P.M. Local Time

JONATHAN ENTERED HIS galley kitchen and set about making himself a cup of tea. As he waited for the water to boil, he thought about Emily. Or rather, the tea made him think of her. It was a green tea and bergamot blend that she'd introduced him to awhile back and it had quickly become his favorite. Now, every time he made a cup he thought of her; how they'd met and how Emily and Lew couldn't seem to make things work on a permanent basis. It seemed a consequence of their lives that relationships were few and far between.

As the kettle whistled, Jonathan found himself thinking about Sophia for the first time in weeks. Jonathan had met her at the same time Lew had met Emily. They'd hit it off, but before they became more than friends, they'd followed their own paths, and nothing ever came of it. But he thought about her often. When money was good, he even thought about grabbing a flight to Sri Lanka, where Sophia was heading up a research team at the university. But that was his loneliness talking.

Jonathan took his tea into the living room and popped a copy of *The Fifth Element* into his entertainment system. He settled back in his recliner with his tea and watched the movie for about the hundredth time, trying to slow his frenetic mind with the sights and sounds of the wisecracking Bruce Willis, but he kept finding himself focusing on Milla Jovovich's outfits. Before he could follow through on the idea to turn it off, a power nap grabbed hold of him and wrestled his consciousness to the ground.

When he opened his eyes, the credits were rolling up the screen and his cell phone was ringing. He turned the movie off and grabbed his phone, hoping it was Lew so he could apologize. He knew if he tried to call Lew, he'd never answer. Not yet, anyway.

It was Natalie again. He thought about what Lew had said in the café but rejected the call anyway. Jonathan was starting to doubt his decision to stay away from Natalie, but he wasn't quite ready to throw in the towel just yet. Then he decided what he really needed was a little time off the grid. He put his phone on vibrate and dropped it into the bowl by the door where he kept his keys.

He got changed into his workout clothes and spent an hour burning off frustration more than fat in the home gym he'd set up in the flat's second bedroom. The exertion and rush to get from set to set without letting more than thirty seconds pass was just what he needed. His mind wasn't given the chance to wander as he moved from squats, to push-ups, to dips, and so on. But when he got to the cardio part of his workout, the treadmill let his mind drift again. He tried to focus on the job tomorrow, but his mind kept recalling other jobs they'd pulled over the years. Especially the ones where he brought a lost treasure back from the dead and delivered it to its rightful owner. And while it was usually Lew who was crass enough to point out the paycheck, Jonathan also found himself thinking about the finder's fees.

As he showered, he thought about Lew's crazy idea: *Let's be The Monarch again.*

Jonathan smiled as he rinsed the final remnants of shampoo out of his hair and wiped his eyes. He chuckled, shaking his head, as he turned and let the water pelt him in his well-exercised shoulder blade.

As the rhythm of the water droned, Jonathan's conscious mind drifted far away, recalling his favorite moments from some of the jobs he and Lew had pulled over the years. When he finally snapped back to the present, his shoulder was tingling from the extended massage. He turned off the water and toweled himself dry in the tiny bathroom.

"He's crazy," Jonathan said. Someone needed to say it out loud.

Chapter Five

Jirojin Maru
1,100 km East of Tokyo
7:00 A.M. Local Time

UMI TENABE, CEO of the Tenabe Group, drank her breakfast tea while the *Jirojin Maru*'s steward stood by waiting for her assessment of his efforts. Umi thought he looked tired but knew he had only been awake for an hour. Umi, as usual, had been up since 4 A.M. tending to paperwork and international phone calls. She had been running her multinational group of companies—or *Zaibatsu*—from her superyacht for months now. While difficult, at first it had been legally necessary. Now, it was just nostalgia—this was where she'd spent her last moments with her husband as he died.

Before she'd inherited her father's company over seventy years ago, Umi had believed she would follow the path that most of her contemporaries had taken—marrying and disappearing into the identity of her husband. But her father's sudden passing had changed all of that. At thirty-two years of age, she became—for all intents and purposes—a man. It was 1945, a difficult time in

Japan. Her father was an important and very rich man at the time. But after bringing a morning meeting to order in an office building in Nagasaki, her father's life was ended and Umi's path forever altered in a brilliant flash of light.

She continued to sip her tea, watching the steward squirm in her peripheral vision. Now at a hundred and two years of age, Umi still enjoyed torturing the men in her life. There had only ever been one man she hadn't felt that way about. But Mikawa, her husband of only a dozen years, had been murdered six months ago. While his death had released Mikawa from the cancer ravaging his body, Umi could not bring herself to abide the act. Her every moment since that day was in the pursuit of a single, solitary goal: revenge.

About to send the steward back to the kitchen for a "better" cup of tea, Umi changed her mind when her computer screen announced she had an incoming call. Especially when she saw who it was from.

"*Ike,*" Umi said, telling the steward to get out. Then she added that he'd better bring a better cup of tea for lunch, or he'd be out of a job. When the door was closed behind him, she answered the video call.

"Tatsu, it's so good to see you," Umi said, slightly surprised that she actually meant it. "Where are you, now?" Umi leaned in toward the image of her great-granddaughter on the screen. She was a striking young Japanese girl, dressed in black leather, her red hair splayed out across her shoulders.

"Hello, *Obasan,*" Tatsu Koga said, sounding just as pleased. "I'm at JFK Airport, in New York, waiting for a connecting flight."

"How are things going? I haven't heard from you since Texas."

"Things are going well. I've taken care of two more cryonics labs."

"Excellent. And you made sure to leave the name at the scenes?"

"Yes, in spray paint just as you asked."

"Good. I knew I could trust you. That's why I picked you for this assignment. When your mother left you in that terrible place, I knew she'd made a mistake. You just needed . . . direction," Umi said. "You've proved me right a hundred times over, Tatsu. I'm so very proud of you." It was true, but Umi was well aware she was using the praise as a tool.

But then, isn't everything a tool?

Tatsu wasn't technically her blood, but Umi treated her like she was. After Tatsu had beaten two bullies to death in Osaka's Kamagasaki district—Japan's biggest slum—for brutalizing her brother, Tatsu's parents took the opportunity to admit her to a psychiatric hospital. From what Umi knew of them and their situation, it was probably more to reduce the number of mouths they had to feed than save Tatsu from jail.

That's where Umi had found her while touring the facility several years ago, trying to decide if she should fund their research facility. In the end, she hadn't provided the money they wanted, but she had made a smaller contribution for the freedom of a young girl who had garnered her attention. At the time, she'd had no idea what she'd use her for, but Umi was always stockpiling things on the off chance she'd need them.

Back then, Tatsu had had natural talent but was like an unpolished gem. Over the years, Umi had arranged training for her. She'd learned judo and karate in the early days, advancing to disciplines that involved knives and swords. By the time Tatsu was eighteen, Umi began sending her out into the world.

Tatsu had lacked conviction, though. While she'd had the skills, she'd lacked the heart of an assassin, which was the real reason Umi had rescued her from the facility and honed her skills. But if there was one thing Umi was good at, it was finding someone's motivation and using it to her own ends. Umi found Tatsu's motivation when she remembered why Tatsu had killed in the slums. Bullies. Tatsu couldn't stand bullies. Once Umi understood that, motivating Tatsu to do her bidding had just been a matter of concocting the right story—again, something at which Umi excelled.

"I'm so glad," Tatsu said. "I'm headed home. I should be there by tomorrow afternoon." Umi could almost feel the girl's need for approval through the screen.

"Excellent. We'll need time to prepare."

"Yes, *Obasan*." Tatsu preened. Umi had given her what she wanted, but there would be a price.

"But . . ." Umi feigned indecision. "No, never mind. You've done enough, child."

"What is it? Please tell me."

"If you're sure."

"I am!" Tatsu said, before turning to apparently check her surroundings after speaking so loud. "I mean, I am."

"Well, all right," Umi said, stifling her smile. "There may be a new problem. But this isn't like anything you've faced before. He's . . . experienced." She'd only just received the reports from the bugs she'd had planted in Harcourt's mansion back when Reese had come to work for her, but she needed to be ready.

Per Broden wasn't a pudgy executive stealing from the company coffers, or a politician keeping Umi from getting what she wanted. She knew what she was asking, but there wasn't any choice. She had no doubt Tatsu had what it would take to do the job, but skilled as she was, she had never faced anyone of this level before. And there was a very good chance she wouldn't be victorious.

But at the very least, she'd delay him.

Umi gave Tatsu her new instructions and ended the call. Almost immediately, she received another call. This one from not quite so far away.

"PLEASE, BE REASONABLE!" A bearded, disheveled man in a dirty lab coat said from the other side of the screen. He was in a lab of some sort though all of the stations behind him were empty. He seemed to be very much alone. Still, he kept looking back over his shoulder as he spoke. "It's been weeks. You have to let me go!"

"I have to do no such thing, Dr. Reese," Umi said in perfect English. Though she could speak almost ten languages perfectly, the number she could manage to struggle through was a mystery even to her. Reese was Canadian by birth and spoke English and a hackneyed version of French. He was disappointing in so many ways, Umi thought.

"Please, just . . . just let me out of here," Reese said, the tone of his voice revealing his abandonment of hope. "Just let me come up to the surface for a little while. Let me breathe some actual air!"

"If you didn't have air, you would have died a long time ago." And Umi definitely didn't want that. Not yet, anyway.

"You know what I mean," Reese whined, putting his face in his hands and rubbing his eyes until they were even redder than usual.

"We had an agreement, Dr. Reese. You didn't deliver on your part of the contract. Why should I deliver on mine? No, you'll stay where you are. Now if you'll—"

Reese suddenly grabbed the camera and shoved his face up against it.

"It . . . it keeps watching me," he hissed, furtively looking around. "When I try to sleep, it sends things to . . . to *touch* me! Please . . ." Reese trailed off like he'd realized there was no point in continuing. Umi watched a tear track down Reese's hairy cheek. It was under her orders that Reese was being prevented from sleeping. And despite his deserving the punishment, she was finding the results fascinating.

She reached out and ended the call, the conversation failing to hold her interest. She took a sip of her tea and thought about which call she should make next. She closed her eyes for a moment as she swallowed.

It really was the best cup of tea she'd ever had.

TATSU KOGA—NOW DRESSED in loose-fitting pajama pants, Converse sneakers, and an oversized hoodie that said "WHAT THE FUKshima" across the front—sat against the base of a pillar using her duffel bag as a pillow. The white earbuds that snaked out from under her raised hood plugged into her phone, but it was all for show. Her phone's games and music were silent. She'd learned a long time ago that this was not only the best way to be left alone but also the best way to listen and watch the world around her. It made her invisible and unapproachable, which was best for everyone concerned.

Her flight had landed at JFK Airport over three hours ago. That was expected. But now, as her connecting flight taxied out onto the runway to take off for Tokyo International Airport, she was still sitting in the passenger waiting area.

She was posing as just another student traveler waiting for a long-delayed flight, but in truth she wasn't booked on any flight yet. Umi's instructions had been to study the files she had sent to

Tatsu's phone and wait for her to call with Tatsu's new destination. Tatsu didn't know where she was going next and might not for quite some time, but she knew what she was going to have to do once Umi knew where Per Broden would be long enough for Tatsu to connect with him. She really wanted to be back by Umi's side for the coming event, and she might still make it, but that would have to wait for now.

Umi had rescued Tatsu when she was young and lost, and she would do anything for the matriarch. And she had already proved it, time and time again.

Tatsu pulled up Per Broden's picture again on her phone's screen and examined it, memorizing every detail.

He was a funny little man on the surface, but his files told a different story. According to the reports, he was intelligent, perceptive, tenacious and, as of late, dangerous. He'd spent most of his life in law enforcement in Stockholm; first for the police, then for the Swedish Security Service. He excelled at puzzles and had an incredibly high success rate, almost as high as his IQ. Though apparently as the years went on, the violence associated with his cases had increased. He'd finally retired five years ago and now worked as a kind of international private investigator, still picking and choosing the most enigmatic cases he could find. And apparently Tatsu's recent work had caught his interest. She smiled slightly when she imagined the little man trying to figure out what "Dead Lights" meant.

Tatsu closed her eyes, turned on her side, and tried to calm her mind. But as had happened for the past few weeks, when she closed her eyes, she saw the face of the man she'd killed in the Houston bombing. She didn't feel remorse, exactly, but she continued to wonder why she hadn't delayed the attack. The bombs that had leveled the building were on timers, and she'd had a kill-switch app in her phone. All she would have had to do was tap her screen, and the timers would have stopped. When the man was done whatever he was doing in there that late at night, dressed the way he was, she could have restarted the timers and still have completed her mission. But she hadn't. It hadn't even occurred to her at the time.

She knew there were a lot of good reasons for not stopping the timers, of course. If the man had noticed the stopped timers and fiddled with them or reported them, the mission would have been in jeopardy. And for all she knew, he'd been sent there to stop her. But that last part was a stretch and doubtful.

Of course, he wasn't the first person Tatsu had killed and wasn't even the first person she'd killed for Umi, but he was the first person she'd killed because he happened to be in the wrong place at the wrong time. She was aware that he might actually not be the only one. She hadn't done a full search of the other facilities she'd bombed in the past few weeks, but she'd always been assured that the premises were vacant. Of live people, anyway. But there was a difference when you actually knew, when you'd looked a person in the eye—albeit through binoculars—watching as his life stopped.

Tatsu's thoughts were dragged away by voices nearby. While she was only pretending to be waiting for a delayed flight, there were large groups of people scattered around benches and tables throughout the airport who were doing it for real. At a bench across from her, a couple of girls in their teens sat with backpacks in their laps looking down at the busy concourse several meters below, their demeanor plainly showing that traveling was something new for them. Behind them, three young men in their early twenties laughed to themselves. Every now and then one of them would step forward and harass the girls for a bit before stepping back to shoulder punches and nods of approval from his compatriots. And each time they did it, they got more brazen.

Throngs of people still streamed by, but they either didn't notice the scene or were pretending not to. If it continued, Tatsu knew where it was headed. She had been like the girls for a short time early in her life, before she'd learned to push back. Naive or not, the girls' wide-eyed, frightened looks said they knew what was building as well. She thought about closing her eyes again, but she couldn't get the bullying out of her mind.

Eventually, she sighed, took her silent earbuds out, and shoved her phone into her duffel bag. She casually got to her feet and, with her generation's signature slumped shoulders, walked around a set of benches so she was coming up on the men from behind. As she did, she slowed her pace so she could time reaching the men just as one of them made another incursion into the girls' space. She'd accidentally bump into him and send him over the railing, slamming down onto the marble floor below. Then she'd dissolve back into the crowd that would gather to witness the terrible accident.

But before she could reach the men, someone called to them from down the concourse. The bullies said one last thing to the girls before turning and hurrying to meet up with their waiting friends. Apparently, their flight was finally boarding. Without missing a step, Tatsu swung around the pillar just past the girls before heading back to her bag. She took out her phone, sat down, and was "asleep" again moments after putting her earbuds back in.

She dreamed of the little man who stood between her and her family. For the moment.

Chapter Six

London

11:35 P.M. Local Time

LEW SAT IN The Stag's Horn pub around the corner from his flat, a place he went so often he didn't even have to verbally place an order. He'd just sit down, and pints would appear on his table. It was the kind of magic Lew liked. He'd been there longer than he should have with a job staring him down in the morning, but "should" rarely entered Lew's vocabulary.

He was still pissed about the argument with Jonathan earlier though not at Jonathan. He was pissed at himself. The fact that Jonathan had wanted to walk with him in public meant his partner was feeling a little lost, and he'd tried to take advantage of that.

Lew spun his cell phone on the table in front of him with one hand and gripped a Guinness in the other like he'd fall down if he let go. He was trying to decide who he should call—Jonathan or Emily.

He knew he could just show up at Jonny's in the morning, and they would pretend nothing had happened. Which was probably what he was going to do. But he knew the class act would be to call him and apologize, or at least confirm he was going to show. Not that Jonny needed him for this one. Or any of the jobs, lately. Which was kind of the point. Lew missed the excitement and challenge—and the paydays—of being The Monarch, but more than that, the types of jobs they'd been pulling lately was making Lew feel . . . unnecessary.

On the other hand, he knew he shouldn't call Emily. He was trying to stay away from her to keep her safe, but he was having trouble with the follow-through on that idea.

"Don't do it, Lew," he said to himself.

He'd had Emily's contact info up on his phone's screen for a while now. He kept swinging his thumb toward the call icon, but then he'd argue with himself and end up dropping his phone onto the marked-up table where he'd spin it some more. With each attempt he had to argue harder, and for the past two beers the argument had moved out of his head and into actual speech. He knew he kept getting side glances from the few patrons left at this hour, but he also knew no one would approach him. Lew had spent most of his life fighting in one way or another, but the ironic thing was his size and body language meant he usually didn't have to.

He didn't think it was a booty call. Well, he hoped it wasn't, but he hadn't seen Emily in months, and lately, he'd been having trouble getting her out of his head. Jonathan didn't know it, but Lew and Emily's romance had never really ended. They weren't a couple anymore, but they still had a connection, unlike anything either of them had ever experienced in their lives.

Lew downed the remainder of his dark brew and waved for another. While he waited, he picked the phone up again. Just like all the other times he swung his thumb over the call button, but before he could swing it away this time, his phone buzzed and rang. It startled him and he dropped it on the table again. He smiled and grabbed it, sure Emily had been feeling the same way and was actually calling him. They did that a lot, had the same idea at the same time. But when Lew turned the phone over, he saw a face he hadn't seen in a year. He pressed the answer button.

"Shrimp?"

"Uncle Lew!" Natalie's voice screeched. He knew it was her, but in just a year she was already sounding different. He missed being "Unca Lew," even if she wasn't his actual niece.

"What the hell are you—"

"Oh my God, I've been dialing and dialing. I musta called like a thousand numbers. I didn't think I'd ever find you!" Natalie's words ran together like spaces weren't something she could afford.

"You've been what?" Lew said, trying to force himself to be more sober. Though not so hard that he didn't nod a thank-you to the barkeep for bringing him another Guinness. "Um, how exactly *did* you get this number?" As much as Lew had wanted to give Natalie his number, he'd known how Jonathan would react if he ever did.

"Emily gave it to me months ago, but my art supplies leaked all over the notebook I wrote it in. I only had the first half of it."

Lew had accused Emily on several occasions of calling Natalie, but she'd always denied it. Being right didn't give him any pleasure. He did smile at the idea of Natalie's systematically dialing all the possible numbers until she found him. She was a lot like her dad that way.

"Why didn't you just call Emily and get the number again?" Lew asked, a bad feeling stirring in his gut.

"That's the thing, Uncle Lew. It's Emily. She's . . . I think she's hurt. Bad."

The shock raced through Lew's system faster than the Guinness. He fought to breathe against the squeezing in his chest. His knuckles turned white on the glass in his hand, and he forced himself to put it down before he crushed it.

Natalie told him what she'd heard through the phone hours ago. When the phone had been knocked from Emily's hand and under the sofa, the connection had continued and Natalie had heard every word, every punch, and every shot.

"I knew it was him. I'm sorry, I tried to call Dad like a billion times, but he wouldn't answer. I'm so mad at him! You've got to find her, Uncle Lew. You just have to."

"You knew it was *him*? You knew it was who?" Lew was still reeling from Natalie's detailed description of what she'd heard, and he needed to hear the name, but he was sure he already knew.

"That terrible man that wants to hurt you guys. George. Canton George."

WHEN JONATHAN AND Lew had decided to settle in London, they'd deliberately gotten flats not only close to each other, but close to where Emily lived. With Canton George still out there and after them, it was a safety issue. They were also close to all the London museums and galleries, and less than five hundred miles from Natalie's boarding school. That was all well and good, but all Lew cared about was that he was only a ten-minute cab ride from the only woman he'd ever loved.

Lew got out of the cab a few blocks from Emily's place in Tufnell Park, the cool night air helping to sober him up as he ran toward her place. Though it was more of a stagger as he simultaneously ran and dialed Emily's number over and over.

This can't be. It just can't. She's too smart for that prick to find—

Lew rounded the corner, and Emily's flat came into view—or what was left of it. She lived on the third floor. Sometimes Lew would walk by just to see her pass in front of the windows— windows that were now just boards decorated with yellow police tape. His breath was coming in pants, and he was having trouble making his legs move toward the building. His eyes fogged, and he had to blink the moisture away to see what he didn't want to see. Then it started building in him, quietly at first, but rising.

"...no, no, no, No, No, NO, NO!" And then he was running, his powerful legs slamming the ground with a thwack they could hear all the way back at The Stag's Horn. Wind buffeted his long duster coat out behind him as he practically flew through the night's light rain. He pulled out the key Emily had given him and raced up the stairs. He shot down the hallway and didn't bother with a key when he saw the door was similarly covered in plywood and police tape.

Lew raised one leg and smashed his boot into the plywood. The flimsy material splintered under his force, and he was inside. The smell of gunfire and blood was still heavy in the air.

"Emily! EMILY!" Lew called as he searched every room, but he was the only one there. Back in the living room, he flipped on the lights, and his anxiety doubled. Blood was everywhere—on the walls, the floor, even the broken bookshelf. Lew walked over to it—the shelf he'd made for her—and saw a tuft of hair snagged in the wood grain. With a shaking hand, he pulled it free and twirled it between his thumb and forefinger. It was Emily's. He'd know her hair anywhere. The last time he'd seen it was hanging in his face as she straddled him, smiling and telling him that she hated how much she loved him.

And that broke the spell.

Lew howled and started smashing things. First what remained of the bookshelf, then the plywood over the windows. He slammed his meaty fists into the wood over and over, until blood splashed from his knuckles, mixing with Emily's blood on the floor. Exhausted, he fell down on the ground, his breath coming in hitches. When he'd calmed slightly, he managed to pull out his phone and dial, fighting for control.

"Hello?" Jonathan's sleepy voice said. "What time is—"

"J-Jonny. She's gone, man. It was George. That fucker took her. I . . ." Lew fought for control, pressing the index finger and thumb of his free hand against his eyes, forcing the tears out so he could see. "I think she's dead."

Jonathan managed to get most of the story out of Lew as he calmed him down. Lew knew that part of his state was from the drink, but that didn't help.

"Natalie?" Jonathan said when Lew told him about the phone call. "What the hell was she . . ." And then Jonathan abruptly stopped talking.

"Jonny?" Lew said, getting up and shaking his head to try and clear it.

"Where are you, Lew? Please tell me you're not in Emily's apartment."

"Uh, well I can tell you that, but—"

"Jesus, Lew, get out of there!"

"Relax," Lew said. "There's no way the cops would be—"

Ding.

With the door destroyed, Lew heard the elevator clearly from where he was. And then he realized what Jonathan was getting at. If Canton George's men had found Emily here, it stood to reason Lew or Jonathan would be somewhere nearby. And if they sat on the place, they might just . . .

Lew heard footsteps coming toward the flat. A couple of sets. Heavy footprints, with no talking. And then Lew was in the moment and moving. He told Jonathan to meet him at his place and hung up. Lew knew he was in no shape to take anyone on, not without damaging himself. And if Emily was alive, he needed to be at full capacity to find her. With fight out of the question, he turned to flight.

Lew grabbed the corner of one sheet of plywood over the window and yanked. The nails squealed but eventually let go, wind and rain washing over Lew's face. It was too high to jump all the way down, but the overhang above the entrance was only two stories down and looked fairly solid. Lew braced himself, took a few breaths, and slipped out the window. He hung down as far as he could, then let go. As he dropped, he turned so he could see where he was landing, and realized he was going to miss the overhang. He ran through the parachute training he'd had as a soldier, and as he touched the ground, crumpled and rolled.

He'd knocked the wind out of himself, but otherwise he was unhurt. After gathering himself, he headed around the side of the building before running in the opposite direction of his flat. He'd circle back once he was sure he wasn't being followed and head home.

But something told him it wasn't going to be home for very much longer.

Chapter Seven

Las Vegas, Nevada
8:17 P.M. Local Time

BARELY TEN MINUTES from the Strip, where tourists were staggering, players were strategizing, and young men and women were doing things that would stay in Vegas, Per and Hank sat in their rental car watching a nondescript building surrounded by a nine-foot chain-link fence topped with razor wire. The fence had been there before, but the razor wire was new, a security measure implemented after the bombings started.

Despite the crowds on the Strip, this street was quiet and seemed practically deserted. The building they watched wasn't the only unmarked structure in what looked like a typical industrial section of town, but while the contents of the others contained massage parlors, VIP clubs, and sex shows, this building contained nothing but the cold dead.

It was the last intact cryonic repository Harcourt owned in America. What Per wanted to know was why. Why was this building spared? Was there some significance in that, or was there some other reason it hadn't been attacked like the others, perhaps a timetable Per had yet to discover? Had the bomber been on her way here but something had happened to her? Was the pattern interrupted because of something as pedestrian as a traffic accident? Per's exterior might have been silent and calm, but inside he was a roiling ocean in a storm.

"Y'all ever been to Vegas before?" Hank asked from the driver's seat.

"No," Per said flatly, his eyes never wavering from their target. It was the fifth time Hank had tried to engage Per in some sort of conversation in the three hours they had been sitting there, and every time, Per had responded with a single, monosyllabic answer. He was regretting not leaving Hank at the motel or leaving him for good and continuing on his own.

"Hell, I remember the first time I was here," Hank said, launching into another of his one-sided conversations. While most of Per's attention was on the building, part of him was fascinated by Hank's inability to endure quiet. But he knew that was a common personality trait in Americans. Silence let them think, and if nothing else, America was a nation of distraction. In another time, it was something that Per would have enjoyed investigating and dissecting. But not now. He slowly put his gloved hand on Hank's forearm and squeezed with a just few percent of his artificial arm's capacity.

"I'm going to need you to sit quietly for a little while, Mr. Green. Can you do that for me?" Per asked without taking his eyes off the building.

"Y . . . yes. Yes, sir," Hank managed. Per released him and put his hand back in his lap, barely noticing Hank panting and rubbing his forearm.

"Good."

When another hour had passed—in silence—Per had gathered

everything he was going to from his proximity to this puzzling structure. He wasn't going to find any answers here, but he had known that before they had come. He was here to build his question database, to enrich the space where the answers would go.

"Tell me what you know about Dr. Reese," Per said abruptly in the car's quiet, finding no amusement in Hank's flinch. He knew the scientist had disappeared four months ago and what was in his file, but Per wanted more.

"Uh, Reese? I only met him a few times. He worked out of our research facility in Canada, just outside Toronto. Nice enough guy, I guess. Crazy smart. I mean, genius smart. Couldn't make heads nor tails out of what he was saying when he talked about his work. He'd been with us almost five years before he . . . disappeared."

"Yes, that's all in the file, Mr. Green. Tell me what's not."

"Not? Okay, let's see. He liked fancy cars. He didn't have one, he just liked them. He'd go on and on about the new BMW or Aston Martin. His desk was always covered in car magazines too."

"I see," Per said. "Go on."

"He was married for a while. Didn't work out, though. Got divorced a couple of years back. Apparently she took him to the cleaners too."

"Anything else?"

"Listen," Hank said, turning in his seat to face Per. Per obliged the silent request and took his eyes off the building for the first time to look at Hank. "I know what Jim—Mr. Harcourt—said, but I don't think this Reese thing is anything. We investigated a little when he disappeared, but there didn't appear to be no foul play or nothing. I'd just move on to something else if it were me."

"Thank you for your counsel," Per said, turning back to the building.

Hank started to say something else but then apparently thought better of it and just turned around in his own seat.

"Take me to the airport, Mr. Green," Per said abruptly.

"We ain't going in?"

Per answered him by leaning back and closing his eyes.

"Where we headed to now?" Hank asked after a few minutes of driving.

"Toronto."

Jirojin Maru
1:52 P.M. *Local Time*

LESS THAN FIFTEEN minutes after Hank had booked a flight out of McCarran International Airport, Umi's Internet sniffer—a computer code designed to search constantly for information all across the World Wide Web—sent a report to her office computer. Ten minutes after that, she called Tatsu and gave her the details.

"Toronto?" Tatsu said from the computer screen.

"Is there a problem?"

"No, *Obasan*, no, of course not. It's just—never mind."

She knew Tatsu was tired, and rightfully so. She'd been working hard these past few weeks. But if they didn't take care of everything—every last thread, especially now—then it all would have been for naught. She was sure Tatsu knew that, but then again, she was young and wild and very far away.

"There's a flight out in less than an hour. I should go," Tatsu said.

"Excellent, little one. Call me when you land, and I'll give you more instructions. And don't worry; if all goes well, you'll still be here in time," Umi said. She was about to cut the connection, but then added: "It wouldn't be the same without you."

Tatsu smiled and seemed to become reinvigorated by the false compliment. Though Umi wasn't a hundred percent sure it was false. Her feelings for Tatsu were starting to complicate her clear vision. Not enough to endanger things but enough to be annoying. She hit the disconnect button and leaned back in her chair. She didn't think she was showing it, but Tatsu wasn't the only one tired from the past few weeks. And the illness ravaging Umi's body, despite her medication, wasn't helping things. Umi was keeping that hidden from everyone, as well. She'd even kept it from Mikawa as his illness had triumphed over him.

"She seems unsure," the woman standing just out of sight of the webcam said. She spoke with a slight British accent. Her name was Maggie Reynolds, an ex-MI6 operative with a checkered past. Now she was Umi's head of security and had only recently taken the position. Umi knew her loyalty only went as far as the money given to her, but in her experience, Umi found the simplest motivations were often the best. Umi's money had lured the British spy away with very little effort. But after spending over twenty years in intelligence—ten of those in a Russian gulag—it really hadn't taken much convincing.

"Let me worry about Tatsu, Ms. Reynolds, you worry about your end. Has everyone been vetted as I requested?" Umi asked. She had let Maggie know that Tatsu was abroad on an assignment associated with the coming event, but she hadn't revealed any details, and she had no intention of sharing them now.

Umi still routed all security concerns through her head guard, Mr. Morgan, and had instructed him to keep Reynolds out of the loop. Umi had only wanted Reynolds for her recent MI6 credentials—credentials that would help convince certain guests that it was safe and viable to attend the conference. The "vetting" was another ruse, simply meant to put Reynolds's face and credentials in front of the right people.

"About eighty percent, so far. The rest should be—"

"Ms. Reynolds, you assured me that you could handle this. I could have hired several younger agents for what I'm paying you." The dig wasn't necessary, but it made Umi feel better. She'd expected the disgruntled agent to be a lot easier to manipulate. But Umi supposed that was her mistake since her experience with other MI6 operatives on her payroll was not all that different.

"I am handling it. Perhaps we'd be done by now if the security staff you saddled me with didn't spend most of their time elsewhere, and you didn't keep changing the guest list," Maggie said. Her tone was even and matter-of-fact, but Umi got the message. Her new security chief wasn't like the rest of her staff. She didn't cast her eyes down when Umi passed or stumble over herself in an attempt to please her.

"I'll keep your limitations in mind, Ms. Reynolds," Umi said. She took pleasure in the effect the words had. Reynolds didn't say anything, but the smolder in her eyes was plain.

"I'd best get back to work if there's nothing else," Reynolds said after a long silence. "Oh, I almost forgot, Captain Tanaka wants to see you on the bridge. Something about the defense system."

"Thank you, when I have time I'll—"

"And I wanted to ask you about Crystasis," Maggie said, stopping in the doorway as she tapped on her tablet computer.

Umi's scalp tingled at the mention of Harcourt's company. *She can't know.*

"What about them?" Umi asked, her external demeanor unchanged. After a few more taps on her tablet, Maggie looked up.

"Most of the guest list is very specific—scientists, venture capitalists, et cetera, but Crystasis seems to have a blanket invitation to the conference. Everyone from lab assistants to administrative staff. Was that an error?" Umi searched Maggie's features but could see nothing veiled there.

"Jim—Mr. Harcourt, Crystasis's CEO—is an old friend. He's made his resources available to me for some special projects over the past year. As a favor, I extended the invitation to all his employees, as a kind of company vacation. Now, if there isn't anything else, perhaps you could worry less about my work and more about yours."

It was all a lie made up on the spot. Umi had gone to great lengths to keep her name from being associated with the conference for just this reason. If Harcourt had even suspected for a moment that she was involved, he wouldn't have allowed a single member of his staff anywhere near the *Jirojin Maru*.

Maggie looked like she wanted to reply, but Umi busied herself with paperwork on her desk. After a few moments, Maggie left. When the door closed, Umi dropped her pen and took a few deep breaths. The second Ms. Reynolds had fulfilled her purpose, she had to go.

In more ways than one.

MAGGIE COULDN'T REMEMBER the last time she'd met somebody who could push her buttons like Umi Tanabe. Of course, she was a thousand years old, so she'd had lots of practice, Maggie thought. The humor did little to lighten her mood. And it wasn't the first time she'd felt like this. There was only one thing that was going to let her shake off the anxiety, so she could do her job. Well, two things really, but only one could be done on the *Jirojin Maru*, Tenabe's leviathan of a ship.

She checked her watch and saw that she had just enough time before the next round of vetting interviews. She hurried back to her cabin and put on her running clothes, grabbed a bottle of water, and headed for the lower decks. They were the least frequented parts of the ship, she'd found, and perfect for some stress-reducing laps. Tenabe had the third largest yacht in the world, so a quick 2K run meant a mere eight laps. She put in her earbuds, surfed on her smartphone to her music, and started a shuffle of fast-beat jazz songs. The driving snare drums and smooth-legato piano practically moved her legs for her.

With each lap, the urge to grab Umi and shove her out a porthole lessened a little more. There weren't enough laps in a day to completely remove the desire, but Maggie was used to keeping her emotion off her face. The trick had kept her alive in environments where others would have perished. Literally.

With that thought, images of her time in the Russian prison flooded back into her brain, as they usually did when she left a crack for them. She shook her head and ran faster, trying to drive the images and the memories away. It had almost worked when she rounded a corner and suddenly faced three men in strength-multiplying exo-skeleton suits carrying a huge crate and blocking the corridor.

"Whoa!" Maggie yelled as she skidded to a stop, falling backward, her phone shooting out of her sleeve holster and clattering against the wall, the soothing music—and mood—abruptly gone. But the run had done the trick, and she laughed at the near miss. "Sorry, guys."

The men just stared at her, still holding the crate, which must have weighed a ton if it took three men wearing those suits to lift it. She remembered the first time she'd seen the suits. A handsome young man named Nagura, who she saw now and then on the ship, had explained that the suits were basically wearable robots, increasing the wearer's strength and stamina.

Maggie looked around and spotted her phone against the wall. She bent over to pick it up and while down there, looked back at the upside-down men—now with very different looks on their faces as they stared at her fit derriere and put the crate down.

Ah, shit.

She stood up and faced the trio as they made comments to each other in Japanese and laughed, the tone recognizable in any language. Maggie could tell they were working up their courage, taking small steps toward her.

"Take it easy, guys," Maggie said even as she realized they probably had no idea what she was saying. She'd picked up a little Japanese in the past few months, but nowhere near enough to say *Hey, don't rape the pretty blond lady.* And after exhausting herself with her run, she wasn't sure she could take on these three brutes all at once—especially with those damn suits. At least, not without getting hurt herself.

She tried to move back the way she'd come, but one of them stepped in her path. Reflexively, she gave him a rabbit punch in the nose and pushed him away, old habits from her time in the Russian gulag kicking in. His bulk didn't move, and she only managed to push herself closer to the two men behind her. The man touched his smacked nose and seemed to growl. He tried taking a swing at Maggie, but she easily brushed it aside and smacked him two more times in the nose, harder this time. A little blood trickled out one of his nostrils.

This is bad, she thought, turning and squaring off against all three. But before she could ready herself, the other two grabbed her by the arms. She struggled to get free, but it was impossible while they were wearing those suits. It was like trying to pry open a bear trap.

"Don't!" Maggie said, slight panic working its way into her chest.

"Is there a problem, Ms. Reynolds?"

Maggie looked past the man in front of her and saw Umi's small form standing in the hallway. She winced at the irony, noticing that even in English, the old woman's words had an effect on the men. The two behind her immediately let go and moved back behind the crate.

Maggie was more concerned about the brute in front of her. With his bloody nose, he didn't seem as easy to dissuade and appeared to be trying to decide what to do.

Umi barked something in Japanese and after a long stare at Maggie, the man finally moved past her to join his comrades.

"And I suggest you get back to work as well, Ms. Reynolds, if you're finished with your playtime."

"Yes, Mum," Maggie said, bowing her shoulders and walking past Umi. The honorific had just slipped out, but her embarrassment wouldn't let Maggie try to explain before she left.

It was much later—when she was showered, dressed, and back in front of her vetting computer—before her pride let her think clearly about the scene belowdecks. She kept wondering what had been in that huge crate. The area was technically off-limits, and equipment was stored in a completely different hold at the other end of the ship. But more importantly, what was Umi doing down there?

The next scientist's face popped up on Maggie's computer for his vetting interview, so she put the questions aside, but not before she decided to go back down there later. This time, though, she was leaving her earbuds in her room and bringing her gun.

Chapter Eight

London
Friday
8:00 A.M. Local Time

AFTER SPENDING TWO hours calming Lew down to the point where he didn't want to grab a couple of grenades and run back to Emily's flat, Jonathan had finally lain on Lew's couch and stared at the ceiling for another two hours before he gave up on sleep altogether. He'd tried to call the headmaster at Natalie's school, but no one answered. Lew had assured him that Natalie wasn't in any danger when she called him, and had only been worried about Emily. Jonathan wanted to think that was the reason he hadn't tried to call Natalie, thinking there was no need to wake her up, but he knew a bigger part of it was the fact that he hadn't seen or spoken to her in so long. Regardless, he would have to call her in the morning to get to the bottom of this.

After making a few phone calls, he slipped out and left Lew snoring under the influence of his beers, anxiety, and a fistful of sleeping pills. When he got back, carrying a couple of large coffees, Lew was up and waiting for him. Most people would have been out cold for another half day.

"How's the head?" Jonathan asked.

"I'll tell you once the paramedics bring me back to life," Lew said, rubbing his temples. Jonathan handed him a coffee before taking a long drink of his own. "Where have you been?"

"Getting this," Jonathan said, pulling a few stapled pages out of his jacket pocket. "Preliminary forensic report."

"From Emily's?" Lew asked, the bleariness seeming to almost completely fade from his eyes.

"Yep."

Jonathan had pulled some strings from his old life in the intelligence community to get an early copy of the forensic report from Emily's loft. A lot of people owed him favors, especially in the UK, where his agency had run joint missions back in the day. His contacts had gotten him the report in under an hour. Which had surprised even him.

"What's the verdict?" Lew said.

"There was a lot of blood at the scene," Jonathan said, wishing he'd started somewhere else when he saw Lew's face fall. "The good news is that while there was some blood at the scene that belonged to a female, it was only trace amounts. Most of the blood was male. Enough for a couple of corpses."

"Corpses? She killed them?" Lew asked, hope obvious in his wide eyes.

"No idea. And it was enough *blood* for a couple of corpses, but no bodies were found at the scene. And while the place was riddled with bullet holes, most of the brass and slugs had been cleaned up. But they were in a hurry and missed a few. Looks to be P90 fire. From the bullet trajectories, at least two shooters."

"What the hell did she get herself into?" Lew said. "Wait, the good news? What's the bad news?"

"Well, just like the corpses, Emily was nowhere to be found when the locals got there. I'm guessing whoever took out the attackers and cleaned up must have taken her with them when they Casey Jones'd out of there."

"Shit. What else?"

"They found a cell phone and a computer tablet at the scene. Both have already been sent to computer forensics for analysis. It's a good guess that the phone is Emily's. Did she have a tablet?"

"No idea," Lew said. "I guess we better make that call now."

Jonathan knew he was talking about Natalie. "Yeah, I've been thinking about that. I'm not sure we should. I mean—"

Lew marched over to Jonathan, reached in his pocket, and pulled out his phone. He took Jonathan's hand and slapped the phone in it.

"Call her, or I'm going to make you look like I feel," Lew said. Jonathan thought about saying something clever like "oh yeah?" but gave in and dialed his daughter's cell phone. He wasn't as worried about endangering her now as having to face her anger for not calling sooner. When it started to ring, he pushed the speaker button and put the phone down on the table between him and Lew.

Jonathan took a deep breath and was getting ready to say "Hi, Baby," when she picked up the line and immediately took a strip off him. For the first minute, she cursed more than Lew on a bad day, but even as her boil seemed to slow, he could feel her wrath coming through the line.

"If it wasn't for Emily and Lew, I don't know that I'd ever talk to you again, Dad. I'm serious. I mean, a year? Don't you care about me at all anymore?" That last was punctuated with a crack in her voice. It hurt, but it was also the best thing Jonathan had ever heard. She was hurt more than mad. He was starting to think about ways he could fix things between them but remembered that that would have to come later. There were other priorities right now.

"I'm sorry, Natalie, I really am, but we—"

"Don't call me that," she said abruptly.

"Call you what? Natalie? Uh, that's your name, honey."

"Not anymore. Everyone here calls me Nina now. That's my name."

Jonathan looked at Lew and mouthed *Nina?* Lew shrugged and nodded.

"Fine, Nina, just try to remember everything you heard—"

"I don't have to. When the phone banged to the floor, and I heard the men yelling, I started recording the call. Hang on a second, and I'll play it for you."

Despite the name nonsense, which Jonathan would deal with later, he felt pride at his daughter's ingenuity. A moment later, muffled voices emanated from the phone. His skin prickled when he recognized Canton George's voice demanding to know where he and Lew were. Then the convincing started, and Jonathan saw Lew wince with every smack that echoed from the speaker.

Then, with a wooden crash, the fight was over. Emily begged for Natalie's safety and a male voice said he thought Emily had killed someone named Neill. Lew actually clapped his hands at that. But his attitude fell when George ordered the man to kill Emily. The few seconds of silence that followed seemed to last forever. It was finally broken by a tremendous crash. And gunfire. Even without the police reports, Jonathan would have recognized the unmistakable sound of P90s' rapid firing. Again, silence stretched out, and Jonathan and Lew held their breath and waited.

Someone yelled "Clear!" and then a strange man's voice was heard.

"Are you all right, Ms. Denham?"

"Yes! She's alive!" Lew shouted, jumping to his feet.

"Lew!" Jonathan chastised, trying to listen to every sound.

"Sorry," he said as he sat down with a huge grin on his face.

"She's out."

"What's her condition?"

"They worked her over pretty good, missing a couple of teeth and definitely some broken ribs, but I think she'll recover."

Lew seemed to have trouble catching his breath as they heard the prognosis.

"Get her patched up, then I'll meet you at the Gallery. I've delayed the locals, but not by much. Get a move on."

"Yes, sir."

"Gallery?" Jonathan and Lew said at the same time.

After some rustling, the room grew quiet. Then the man spoke again, but it was loud and clear, unlike before.

"If you've listened to this, you know we saved Ms. Denham. We have her, but she's not a prisoner. We are making sure she gets the care she needs. You just need to come and get her."

A tingle started at the base of Jonathan's spine and slowly scampered up into the back of his skull. Realization was setting in.

"Yeah, like we're just going to walk in there," Lew said.

"Lew."

"What? Why the hell would we trust this guy?"

"Lew!"

"What?"

Jonathan took a deep breath and leaned down toward the phone.

"Where do you want to meet?" Jonathan prayed he was wrong.

Hoped against hope that "Nina" would get on the line and start chastising him again.

"What are you—"

"The Sandstrom Gallery. I'm texting you the address. I look forward to meeting you, Mr. Hall. You too, Mr. Katchbrow. Oh, and come unarmed."

The line went dead.

And so did Jonathan's hope.

"I KNEW WE should have killed that guy instead of just locking him in his own vault," Lew said.

Lew's head was spinning with all the revelations in the past few minutes. Not to mention the thumping hangover. But what he did know was that Emily was alive. Or, at least, she had been after the attack at her flat. Regardless, it was a hundred times better than all the scenarios that had been rifling through his brain since seeing the blood on her floor last night. On the other hand, Natalie was now an unknown. Which made Jonathan an unknown. They'd tried to call Natalie back after the voice had hung up, but the call wouldn't go through.

"You're right about that," Jonathan said. He walked to the window and pulled open the bench where Lew kept his weapons stash. He took out one of the Beretta 9mms, pressed the eject button, and examined the clip.

"Uh, what are you doing?" Lew asked, though he knew.

"The same thing you should be doing. Getting ready," Jonathan said as he slammed the clip back in the gun's grip. He took a shoulder holster out of the window seat and slipped it on.

"He said no guns," Lew said. He had to find a way to manage Jonathan, or he was going to blow this thing, including Lew's chance to get Emily back in one piece. Not to mention Natalie, whom he loved like a niece. Lew knew he was no good at this kind of stuff. This was usually Jonathan's forte, but right now, Jonathan was doing a pretty good Lew impression.

"I think I gave you too many pills last night," Jonathan said, staring at Lew incredulously. "Even if you buy what that guy was selling, we have no idea what happened to Natalie. I hesitated last time, and it almost got her killed." Jonathan shoved the gun into his holster, then took another Beretta out of the window seat and held it out for Lew. "I won't make that same mistake again."

"No, you're making all new ones this time."

"Lew, think about it. How the hell did that guy get to Switzerland and find Natalie so quick? Hell, how did they find Emily just in time to save her from George's men? And if they know where we are, and they have Emily, why wouldn't they just bring her here?"

"Well, because . . . because—" Why the fuck, indeed.

"It's a ruse," Jonathan said. "Hell, he probably works for George! I'm not sure of all the fine points, but I do know we have to go in hard, or we're not coming out."

Lew hated to admit it, but Jonathan was making sense. And walking into traps seemed to be their specialty lately. After a few more moments rationalizing, Lew sighed and grabbed the weapon. "You know those were P90s we heard in the recording. Why do you think these peashooters are going to be of any use against machine guns?"

"Because we're going to be Han Solo this time," Jonathan said.

Lew just stared at him blankly.

"Han Solo. You know, *Star Wars*?"

"How I became best friends with a nerd is beyond me."

"Whatever. The point is, we're going to shoot first."

"Now that reference I get."

Chapter Nine

Toronto
4:30 A.M. Local Time

HANK HAD NEVER actually been to the Toronto research facility and was fairly dazzled by the building when he walked Per in. The Crystasis Foundation's main laboratory was housed in what had once been a steel mill on the outskirts of Toronto. The smelting hardware and blast furnaces had been replaced with state-of-the-art labs. Several levels of catwalks still ran along both sides of the vast, football-field-sized main chamber, but now they were painted a gleaming white and washed down several times a day to avoid contaminants. Along all the catwalks were floor-to-ceiling glass walls with offices and small labs clearly visible. The center of the room was still wide open and almost a hundred feet from the floor to the peaked roof. Where the blast furnaces once used to run hot for months at a time, spraying molten metal high into the air, showpieces now sat—modern art and sculptures to impress investors.

The lab was a poster child for excess and spoke to the man who had created it. A man who, ironically, couldn't bring himself to leave his home to visit his monstrosities. He had to settle for pictures and webcams showing him the daily routine of his workers. Who, unbeknownst to them, all toiled for a single reason—to extend the billionaire's life. Indefinitely, if possible. Oddly, even at four in the morning, it hadn't been that difficult to find someone to take Per on a tour of the facility. Though it was partly because of the company-wide memo that had gone out telling everyone that when they were speaking to Harcourt's newly hired investigator, they were speaking to *him*.

Hank let Per go on the tour alone and snuck into one of the upper offices to use his cell phone in private.

"I think we made a mistake," Hank said into the phone, his back to the door. Per was several floors down, but even at that distance, Hank found himself lowering his voice. There were no shades of gray; Hank was terrified of the man.

"What are y'all talking about," Harcourt said. "You've barely been gone a day and a half. Give him a chance."

"Listen, I'm telling you he's not right. In the head," Hank said, checking over his shoulder. "Or anywhere else, neither."

"Jesus, is it the arm? Get ahold of yourself. It's . . . well, let's face it, it's weird. But it's just a prosthetic. Other than that, he's just—"

"It ain't the arm!" Hank said, louder than he meant. He took a second to get himself in check. "It's not his arm. His arm is about the most normal thing about him. It's the way he talks, or worse, the way he don't. And the way he looks at stuff. People too. When he looks at me I feel like . . . like he's pulling me apart and trying to figure out what all my bits are for."

"Look," Harcourt started, but Hank knew if he let him speak, he'd end up talking Hank out of what he wanted. He always did.

"No, I don't want to do it no more. Get someone else. You got a couple of hundred people on staff here. Get one of them to do it. Or better yet, just fire his ass. I can get you a dozen investigators a day for half of what we're paying this guy."

"Wait a second," Harcourt said, his voice sounding confused. "A couple of hundred people? Jesus, you took him to Toronto?"

"Uh, yeah. You told me to take him wherever he—"

"I didn't mean there! Christ, Hank, don't you get it? That's where Reese worked. If someone there knows that Reese didn't just disappear—"

"Oh, shit," Hank said. He hadn't even thought of that.

"Listen and listen good, Green. You get his ass out of there, and I mean *now*. You understand me?"

"Uh, yes. Yes, sir. But about accompanying him—"

"Just get him out of there and babysit him for a few more hours. I'll make some calls and get someone else there to take over. I don't want Broden running around on his own. And for God's sake, don't tell him what you're doing. He doesn't seem like the kind of fella that takes kindly to people's making decisions about him."

"No shit," Hank said. "Thanks, Jim. And sorry about this." Hank hung up, took a deep, breath, and headed out of the office.

How could I have been so stupid? Well, just get him out of here, and you're done in a few hours. No big deal. A few more hours won't kill me.

Distracted by his screwup, Hank walked out of the office just as someone grabbed his arm, wrenching it up behind his back. The pain was instantly replaced by fear as he felt cold metal press against his carotid artery.

"Take me to Per Broden. Now!" a woman with an Asian accent hissed into his ear. Hank, could see her reflection in the glass. The woman was just average height, but incredibly strong—though nowhere near as strong as Per's robotic arm. He couldn't see her face because she was wearing a black hoodie, but what he did see was the glint of the knife against his throat.

"Sweetheart, I don't think that's such a great . . . AH!" Hank yelped as the knife slit into his flesh. He felt warm blood drip down onto his clavicle.

"Jesus, all right, all right. He's down there, lower level. But we'll never get all the way down there like this." Hank saw the reflection of the hood tilt down as she looked where they had to go. There were only a handful of people between here and there, most in lab coats, but the lab's open concept meant Hank and the woman would be on display the whole time.

The woman said something in a language Hank didn't understand, then, "Fine. Then we make him come to us." She turned Hank and pushed him back into the office he'd just come out of.

"We'll do it any way you want. You're the boss."

As Hank stepped into the room, he pushed her arm away from his throat and spun around to shut the door on her, but she was fast. Like lightning. Before he'd moved the door an inch, she'd plunged the knife into his abdomen. He clasped his hands to the wound as pain ripped through his stomach muscles, and he fell back onto the office's carpet. His attacker hung on to the knife as he fell, and more pain assaulted him as the blade slid out. Then he was being dragged across the floor, behind the desk, every bump like his guts were being scooped out. He distantly realized she was hiding him.

Afraid of more pain, he couldn't bring himself to lift his head or call out. He carefully raised his hand up so he could see the blood on his fingers as he gasped for breath. It was dark, almost black. A lifelong rodeo rider, Hank knew about puncture wounds.

Every rider knew that if you were gored and the blood was black, your liver was hit and you were done.

He carefully put his arm back down and stared at the white lift ceiling tiles above him as his life slowly spilled onto the carpet. He heard the door close, then the woman knelt beside him. He winced as she ripped the sleeve of his shirt off, balled it up, and pressed it against the wound. "Press here. Hard," she said.

He didn't see the point and just lay there, a numbness starting to take him. It eased the pain, but he knew he was going into shock. She took his hand and pressed it against the make-do bandage when he didn't respond. She sat back on her heels, looking at him. "Why did you do that? I wasn't going to hurt you."

"My . . . my neck begs to differ, sweetheart."

"That's a scratch. Nothing. You would have—" She stopped talking as Hank started laughing, then coughing. "What are you laughing at?"

"I thought *he* was going to kill me. I just made arrangements to get away from him. If I'd just stayed with him, I probably would have lived to be a hundred."

"No one's going to live to be a hundred anymore," she said with a faraway look.

"What?"

"Never mind," she said, getting up and taking her hoodie off. She made a pillow out of it and eased it under Hank's head. She was young, Asian, and had flaming red hair.

"Jesus, you're a kid."

"I haven't been a kid for a million years . . . what's your name?"

"Hank."

"I'm Tatsu," she said, and he knew she thought he was going to die too. He felt her pat his pockets until she found his cell phone. She took it, got up, and moved out of his view. When she came back, she was wearing a lab coat she must have found in the office. "Look, just keep pressure on that. I . . . I don't think I hit anything vital. Somebody will find you and . . . you'll be fine."

"You're a terrible liar, kid," Hank said before another coughing fit began. The room was starting to swim.

"I . . . I'm sorry," Tatsu said. She left his view again, and a moment later he heard the door open and close.

Hank tried to stare at the ceiling again, but he couldn't get the tiles to come into focus. Then he realized he was about to die in a building devoted to extending life, and he couldn't help but laugh again. It was the last thing he ever did.

PER WASN'T SURE if Dr. Reese's disappearance was connected to the bombings, but in his experience, coincidence was rarely unremarkable. And the harder it was to get an answer out of anyone, the more sure he became. Of course, what he really cared about was the enigmatic words left at each bombing. If he managed to find out what "Dead Lights" meant, the continuance of the attacks meant nothing to him. He'd already decided to dump his babysitter when they were done here, wherever Green was.

The technician finally returned to the office Per was waiting in. The man's face told Per all he needed to know.

"I'm sorry, Mr. Broden, she wasn't in either," the technician said. "Like I said before, most of the head scientists and their assistants are already en route to that conference I mentioned." Apparently there was some kind of longevity conference happening this weekend on a yacht off the coast of Japan. The entire lab had been invited—free of charge—and that was reason people were still working at such an ungodly hour. When they completed their assignments, they could all fly out.

Unfortunately, Per was finding that because of the conference, no one who had worked with Dr. Reese seemed to be on-site. Still, Per refused to believe that *every* scientist was out. Especially when the catwalks were rife with people in lab coats. Though the technician before him—Darrell something—had already explained they were all just technicians and engineers.

"And there's nothing you or any of the other technicians can tell me about Dr. Reese's work? Surely, you must be able to do that, at least."

"It's just not that structured, here. Everyone helps everyone, but there's not really a way to—" Darrell stopped talking as something in the hallway caught his eye. "Just a minute." Darrell stuck his head out the door and called: "Mark! Mark!" Darrell waved for someone to come over.

Per stood up. A young blond man came over, and Darrell put his arm around his shoulders and ushered him into the room.

"What's up?"

"This is Mr. Broden. He's doing some work for Mr. Harcourt, and I was hoping you could help us out since everyone else has already left for the conference," Darrell said. Per noticed that at the mention of Harcourt's name, Mark's demeanor seemed to change. Not much and probably not noticeably to most people, but Per caught it loud and clear.

"I'm trying to discern what Dr. Reese was working on before he disappeared," Per said. The change in Mark's behavior this time would have been noticeable to a blind man.

"Disappeared? Oh, I mean, no, I don't know what he was working on," Mark said quickly. Per tilted his head and stared at the man.

"If Dr. Reese didn't disappear, then where did he go? I'm going to assume that you had more than a working relationship with him, and that's why Darrell brought you in here. That being said, and a given, you do not seem particularly concerned considering that your friend disappeared without a trace. To be honest—Mark, is it?—you should be asking me questions right about now."

"Uh, what?" Mark said after a moment.

Per just looked at him. The air in the room seemed to slow down and thicken. Per observed everything in great detail—the man's Adam's apple bobbing up and down as he swallowed, his labored breathing, the sweat suddenly trickling down his temple. And then, just a microsecond too late, Per realized something.

He's going to run.

Mark shoved Darrell at him and launched himself out of the room. Per ducked Darrell's pinwheeling arms and let him crash into a desk before hitting the floor. Per vaulted out the door and looked up the catwalk past several people in lab coats. It took him a second to eye his prey. Mark was already halfway to the stairs. Per knew he could never get through the throng of bodies in time to catch him.

The catwalk had a railing that was three inches wide, plenty of room for the human foot. Per jumped up on the railing and without even a glance down at the cement floor twenty feet below, he ran after Mark. People turned at the clanking of Per's shoes on the metal railing and threw themselves back against the glass office walls as he passed.

Mark had reached the stairs and gotten about two steps down them when Per maneuvered around the bend in the railing and launched himself into the air. Mark looked up just as Per slammed into him. The two men rolled down the stairs and came to a stop on the landing. Per easily got the upper hand, but he knew he only had moments before others got to them. He put his robotic hand around Mark's throat and squeezed only slightly, until Mark gasped for air.

"Where is Dr. Reese? You have two seconds to tell me, or I'll crush your windpipe and search your home. The choice is yours." Per eased up on Mark's throat so he could talk.

"I . . . I don't know where he is," Mark said when he stopped coughing.

"As you wish," Per said, and started squeezing again.

"Wait, wait! I don't know where he is, but I know someone who does!"

Chapter Ten

TATSU COULDN'T BELIEVE she'd missed her chance. Per had run right by her on that railing. All she'd had to do was push him off, and her job would have been complete. She would have been headed to the *Jirojin Maru* with plenty of time before the conference started, and Umi launched her attack. But the sight had shocked her along with everyone else, and she'd just stared. She knew her hesitation had to do with stabbing Hank, who was no doubt dead by now, but knowing that didn't help her. And worse, as they walked back to the room, she'd heard them mention Dr. Reese.

This was bad.

Tatsu had met Dr. Reese months ago on board Umi's ship. She'd been there when he'd, for all intents and purposes, killed Mikawa, Umi's husband. She knew better than anyone why he was now imprisoned on the ocean floor. But if Per knew about Dr. Reese, he might know about Nagura. She had to find out what else they knew. There was a good chance she was going to have to forfeit her safety, but if it kept Umi safe and gave her time to finish, Tatsu was more than willing to do that.

Crystasis security was all over the place, now. If she made a move, she would likely end up killing more innocents—or she'd end up dead herself. But how could she get the Crystasis staff out of there? As she thought, she looked up, but before her gaze reached the massive skylight overhead, it stopped on the top catwalk. She looked at the office she'd been in a few minutes ago—the office where she'd just killed someone.

"YOU'RE SURE YOU don't want me to call the cops?" the security officer named Hastings asked Per.

"I'm quite sure, Mr. Hastings," Per said. The last thing he wanted right now was the involvement of the police. "I just need to have a conversation with our friend here. And some privacy."

"Whoa, don't leave me alone with this freak," Mark said. He was seated on a stool in the same room where Per had first met him, but this time his hands were bound behind him with a plastic tie.

"Put a cork in it, buddy," Hastings said. When Per had identified himself, Hastings had made it plain that he'd received Harcourt's memorandum. He wasn't going to do anything unless Per said it was all right. But there were limits.

"Hastings," a voice sounded from the radio affixed to Hastings's collar.

"Go," Hastings said after pressing the mic's button.

"You better get up here, Dr. Canard's office."

"Why's that?"

"There's a dead body up here. Stabbed. Blood everywhere, man." And then after a pause, "It's somebody named Hank Green."

Per, as was his nature, kept his reaction to the news internal. But he was torn. The chances that an irate employee had stabbed Hank was slim. More likely, someone knew they were poking around the Dead Lights attacks. Per would have loved to run up and see if they weren't too late to find the assailant, but he had to deal with Mark first. And that would only be easier without the audience.

"There's a wha . . . I'll be right there," Hastings said. "What the hell is going on here, tonight? You okay if I leave, Mr. Broden?"

"I'll be fine, Mr. Hastings," Per said. Hastings left, and Per slowly turned and looked at Mark, whose eyes were wide and confused.

"What are you going to do?" Mark asked, as Per moved between him and the door to prevent the need for any further chases.

"I'm not going to do anything," Per said. "On the contrary, it is you who are going to do something. You're going to tell me who knows where Dr. Reese is." Per sat on the corner of a metal desk with his hands in his lap.

"Look," Mark said, seeming to relax a little with Per not hovering over him. That was the intent. "I was scared. You were choking me. I would have said anything to make you stop. I don't know where he is."

Per didn't have time for this. It wouldn't take them long to determine that Hank had arrived with him and to turn their investigation to him. Those were questions—and time sinks—that Per wanted to avoid.

He stood up and took off his glove. Per displayed and flexed his robotic hand. While shaped like a human hand, it was obviously artificial. The palm and jointed fingers were dark black metal, and his fingertips were white, molded-rubber nubs. As he flexed, the carbon nanotube filaments were visible between the joints.

Mark, whose Adam's apple bobbed up and down—no doubt thinking about the appendage being around his throat a few minutes ago—was having trouble breathing.

"What the fuck are you, man?"

Per made a fist and, using a small portion of the strength available to his arm, punched through the top of the heavy metal desk.

"The name," Per said, as if he were asking Mark to pass the potatoes.

"Nagura. His name is Nagura. He's got a restaurant in Tokyo. Nagura's Emporium. That's all I know, I swear."

Per would have liked to work Mark some more, to be sure he wasn't holding back any information, but he was pressing his luck with Hank's body upstairs. But what about Mark? Per didn't like the idea of leaving him behind to reveal what he'd told Per. The last thing he needed was someone's tailing him all the way to Japan.

Then, like someone had heard his thoughts, Mark's life ended with a thwack and a gurgle. A knife handle sticking out of his throat, Mark worked his mouth as if he were trying to speak, blood bubbles the only thing to come out.

Per spun around and saw a lab-coated figure with flaming red hair on the far walkway, easily thirty meters away. The fact she'd hit Mark from that distance with such accuracy was only part of what concerned Per. She was cocking her arm back to throw again, and Per had no doubt who her target was. Her arm flew forward at incredible speed, the knife rocketing across the expanse between them. Per barely had time to raise his robot arm to protect himself. The knife, which would have hit him right in the heart, tinged off Per's metal hand and changed trajectory.

He'd only barely managed to deflect the weapon, but the knife sliced his forehead just above his eye. Reflexively, Per turned away. By the time he turned back, the assailant was gone.

Per touched his forehead with his human fingers and looked at them. Blood. It wasn't deep enough to need stitches, but he'd carry the mark for a long time. Slipping his glove back over his metal hand, Per thought about the last picture Harcourt had given him. A young woman on a motorcycle with flaming red hair.

PER MOVED MARK'S body out of sight and closed the office door as he left. Then he headed up to the highest walkway, where employees stood, desperately trying to see into the murder scene. Hastings was clearing everyone off the walkway and sending them away. Per looked through the glass wall but could only see Hank's feet sticking out past the desk and a pool of blood seeping out from under it. Another security officer was standing behind the desk, making notes.

"I secured him in the office," Per said when Hastings asked where Mark was. "Have you called the local authorities?"

"Yeah, but we're out of the way, here. It'll be awhile before they show up," Hastings said.

"I've had some experience with this kind of thing," Per said. "Want me to take a look?"

"Uh, sure. Mr. Harcourt will probably want as many reports on this as possible. It's obvious he trusts you," Hastings said, stepping aside. Per went in.

"Campbell," the other security officer said, extending his hand. Per shook it.

"Broden."

"Yeah, Hastings told me about you."

"You can barely see him from the walkway; how'd you know he was here?"

"Someone called and told us he was here," Campbell said.

"Someone?"

"A woman. She didn't identify herself."

Per nodded, realizing the call had likely been meant to get Hastings out of the office downstairs.

Per moved around, examining the body. A single stab wound to the abdomen and the color of the blood said Hank's liver had been hit. Death would have been rapid. At least he wouldn't have had time to say anything to any witnesses, Per thought. He noticed that someone had ripped Hank's sleeve off and put it on the wound. Curious.

"You mind?" Per said, kneeling beside the body and holding out his gloved hand to indicate he wouldn't contaminate the crime scene. Campbell shook his head and returned to writing in his notebook.

Per checked Hank's pockets and, when he was sure no one was looking, took the car keys from Hank's pocket, also noticing that his cell phone was missing. Then he looked at the makeshift pillow under Hank's head.

"Was that there when you found him?" Per asked, pointing at it.

"Yeah."

Using his gloved hand, Per gently pulled the pillow out and set Hank's head down on the floor, his authoritative manner keeping the rent-a-cops from complaining about a contaminated crime scene if they even knew to make such complaints. He unrolled the material and saw that it was a black hoodie. With his back to the two security officers, he stood up and put it on a chair against the wall. He checked the pockets, and when he felt some paper in one, he surreptitiously slipped it out and into his pocket.

A few minutes later, Per apologized that he couldn't be of more help and excused himself to go call Mr. Harcourt. Hastings and Campbell both asked him to make sure he mentioned their diligence to their boss. Per promised he would. Then he very calmly walked downstairs to the lobby and exited the building.

Inside the car, dawn still a few hours away, Per flicked on the interior light and unfolded the paper he'd taken from the hoodie—a motel receipt.

Per had seen more than his share of murder scenes, and this one was odd. The killer—obviously the woman who had killed Mark and put a slice into Per's forehead—had tried to help Hank stop the bleeding but hadn't wanted him calling for help. Then she'd put what seemed to be her hoodie under his head for comfort.

She was the most curious killer he'd come across in a long time.

Per looked at the receipt in his hand. He called ahead and booked his flight to Tokyo, but he needed to make a stop first—the Lakefront Motel. There was only one flight out in the next couple of hours, but he couldn't pass up a chance to question the Dead Lights bomber herself. Though he doubted she was the mastermind behind whatever this all added up to. He checked his watch as he started the car.

He'd have to make this quick.

Chapter Eleven

London

11:00 A.M. Local Time

WHEN JONATHAN AND Lew pulled up in front of the address the voice on the phone had given them, Jonathan thought they must have the wrong place. He checked the note he'd made during the call and confirmed they were where they were supposed to be. His stomach fell like he'd just been dropped.

"What the fuck is this?" Lew said from the passenger seat.

It was a gallery, all right, but it was about the size of a New York bodega. It didn't look like it could have hung more than a handful of paintings, and it certainly wasn't the HQ of the mastermind who had tapped into their call last night and saved Emily from George. The windows had some kind of foil on them and nothing could be seen beyond the facade. That was disconcerting, but worse was the block they were on. Run-down didn't even begin to describe it. Whatever businesses had once been there left long ago; nothing but boarded-up doors and windows remained. And the "gallery," of course.

"We've been scammed," Lew said, voicing what Jonathan was

thinking. He highly doubted they were going to find any answers here.

Jonathan tried calling Natalie again. No dice. The lines were acting like the phone didn't exist. Like it or not, the only possible place for an answer was in there.

"Come on," Jonathan said, opening his door.

"Whoa, hang on," Lew said. "You're just going to walk in there? What happened to being Juan Solo?"

"Han," Jonathan corrected, never taking his eyes off the dirty window with the simple word "Gallery" etched into it.

"Whatever. There's nothing in there, Jonny. If we haven't been scammed, we've been set up. Emily and Natalie sure as shit aren't here." Lew put his hand on Jonathan's shoulder. He turned and looked at his partner, who was making an incredible amount of sense. "Jonny, it's New York all over again. The little hairs on my neck are screaming for us to get out of here. Now."

"What about Emily?" Jonathan said, knowing he was trying to play Lew. "This is the only lead we've got. If we walk away from this, we've got nothing."

The men looked at each other for a long time. They both knew what the other had to lose. Finally, Lew puffed air between his lips and took his gun out, sliding a bullet into the chamber. "Fuck it. Let's go."

"Keep that down," Jonathan said. "Remember the conditions."

"Roger that," Lew said, slipping the gun into the pocket of his long duster coat. He got out, walked around the car, and waited on the sidewalk. Jonathan joined him. They took a moment to look up and down the block again. Nothing. No people, no movement. The only cars were wrecks abandoned long ago. It was like the rest of London had forgotten this street was even here.

Ding-ding.

The bell over the door clanged as they entered. The inside of the gallery added little to their calm. A single row of chairs sat against one dirty wall. A few makeshift paintings were hung here and there, but Jonathan was sure Natalie could have painted better ones in her sleep. And most of them hung askew.

And that was the entire gallery. There were no other doors, no way in or out besides the door they'd just come through. It didn't make any sense.

"Right corner," Lew said quietly, keeping his hand in his pocket, but Jonathan had already spotted the security camera when they first came in. No light glowed on it and, from the angle, it didn't appear to even be functioning, but you never knew. Jonathan was just noticing the speaker on the opposite wall when it crackled to life.

"Gentlemen. Please take a seat."

"Like fuck," Lew said. Jonathan could tell the whole situation was creeping Lew out, and he knew they'd be lucky to get a few minutes before he pulled his gun.

"Where's my daughter? Where's Emily?" Jonathan demanded, not sure if he should look at the speaker or the camera. If there even was a microphone.

"Your daughter?" the voice said sounding genuinely confused. "I would assume she's right—" The voice was replaced by muffled voices, like he was talking to someone. "Oh, I'm sorry. Just a miscommunication, I'm afraid. The block should be off her phone now. But we really don't have time."

Jonathan ignored him and quickly dialed. The call got through, rang once and a frantic Natalie picked up. "Daddy?"

"Baby, are you all right?"

"I'm fine, what happened to you? The phone just went dead last night. I've been trying to call you guys all night. Is Uncle Lew okay?" Jonathan knew this wasn't the place or time, but he needed to say something. With the vibe he was getting from their current situation, he didn't want to risk something's happening before he had a chance to let Natalie know something he should have said a long time ago.

"He's fine, baby. Listen, I—I screwed up. I was just trying to keep you safe, but I never should have cut you out like that." There was a silence, and Jonathan wondered if he'd been blocked again, but then a squeak and a sniffle told him what was happening. She was crying.

"I . . . I understand. But I was starting to think you just didn't want me around. Like I was—"

"No, baby, never. Don't ever say that," Jonathan said. He looked up at Lew, who was smiling. "We need to talk. A lot. But I'm still taking care of things here. With Emily. I need to go, but I'll call you as soon as I can."

"All right," Natalie said. She sounded disappointed, but he knew she understood.

When he was off the phone, he felt like a thousand pounds had been lifted from his shoulders. But he knew Lew only felt mildly better knowing that Natalie was all right.

"Now, as I was saying, please take a seat, gentlemen. We have a lot to do and not much time."

"Time for what? Where the fuck is Emily!" Lew shouted. His fuse was going to go, and if that happened, Jonathan knew from past experience that even he wouldn't be able to stop him.

Again there was muffled sounds on the speaker.

"Lew. Lew, I'm all right," Emily's voice said. "I'm here with them. I'm fine. Well, relatively fine. They patched me up. They saved my life, really. They're proper heroes."

"Them?" Jonathan and Lew said at the same time.

"Just take a seat, and we'll get started," the voice said again. Jonathan could tell by his strain that the voice's owner was starting to get perturbed at all these interruptions.

Lew took a few steps toward the speaker. "Look, pal, I ain't sitting nowhere. Let's just—"

"Christ! Fine, have it your way," the voice said angrily. The speaker clicked like it had been turned off.

"Have it our way? What is he, Burger Ki—"

Metal shades slammed down over the windows and the door. A red light snapped on, making everything look like the inside of a submarine. Then a hum started, and the floor began to shake. Jonathan and Lew put their arms out for balance.

"Ah, crap," Lew said just before their stomachs dropped, and the gallery walls began to get very, very tall. Jonathan grabbed onto Lew's shoulder for extra balance, knowing it would take a lot to knock his bulk down.

"An elevator," Jonathan said.

"Ya think!" Lew managed. The noise was getting louder and louder, and the floor was falling faster and faster.

Jonathan looked over at the chairs, which were sitting stationary and calm in all the turmoil around them. They were obviously bolted to the floor, and right now, Jonathan was wishing he was sitting in one of them.

"Brace yourself!" Jonathan shouted.

"For what?"

"At this speed, when the brakes catch, we're going to—"

As if they'd heard him, the brakes caught, and both men were hurled to the floor. Thankfully, the noise was gone. Unthankfully, Lew had fallen on top of him. Jonathan was pretty sure one of his balls was up around his throat.

"Jesus, how much do you weigh?" Jonathan said, panting and wincing as he waited for the pain in his stomach to subside.

"As much as a man is supposed to, lightweight," Lew said, fumbling his way back to his feet. He helped Jonathan up.

The wall under the speaker clicked and rose, spilling harsh light into the gallery. Both Jonathan and Lew squinted against the sudden brightness. As it subsided, a man flanked by four armed guards entered. The red light clicked over to white again and showed his smiling face. He had a small build and caramel skin—and Jonathan had just sat across from him a day ago in the café along the Thames.

"Fahd?"

As the lights came up, they showed that while Lew had been scrambling around on the floor, the gun had fallen out of his pocket and was lying on the ground before them.

"GUN!" Someone appeared from behind Fahd, grabbed him, and hurried him away.

The four guards came to life, pointing their P90s at Jonathan and Lew, red dots from their laser sights dancing on their chests. Jonathan and Lew raised their hands.

"Oops," Lew said.

"ARE YOU SURE, sir?" a guard asked Fahd a half an hour later, when Fahd instructed him to remove Jonathan's and Lew's cuffs.

They'd been rushed into an interrogation-style room deep in the mysterious maze a couple of stories under the streets of London. Jonathan figured it was some kind of shelter built back during the war, but that was about all he could surmise from their current situation.

"Yes, it was just a misunderstanding."

"Funny, I was thinking it was called kidnapping," Lew said, holding his wrists up for the guard to unlock. Jonathan knew being handcuffed always made Lew grumpy. And he wasn't in such a great mood, himself, despite knowing that Natalie was safe. The guard released them and left.

"Well, maybe I can make up for that," Fahd said, as Emily limped into the room.

"Jesus," Jonathan said. She was a mess. Her eyes were blackened, her arm was in a sling, and when she smiled, he could see that she was missing some teeth.

"Babe," Lew said, his voice cracking when he saw her condition.

"I'm okay, Lew. Really. I should probably be dead. If it weren't for Fahd."

"I'm just sorry we didn't get there sooner. She should be fine in a few weeks, though. I'm taking her to our dentist tomorrow."

Jonathan could tell Lew hadn't heard half of that. He'd slowly gotten up and was gently holding Emily. It was the softest Jonathan had ever seen him.

"Sorry I'm not much to look at right now," Emily said to Lew.

"Are you kidding? You're the most beautiful thing I've ever seen in my life," he said as he gently kissed her.

"Yes, well, if you'll take a seat, we can get started."

"Who are you people?" Jonathan asked.

"I'm afraid the Cliff Notes version will have to do for now; we don't have much time."

"Time for what?" Lew asked, sitting after he helped Emily into a chair.

"Introductions first, Mr. Katchbrow."

"Lew," Lew said.

"Thank you. Lew," Fahd said. "In a way, we're kindred spirits. My name is Fahd Qureshi. As you've no doubt guessed, I'm not a museum security guard. I like to meet new members undercover, as it were, before I indoctrinate them. It gives me a better picture, sometimes, than all the background checks in the world."

"Members of what?" Jonathan asked.

"The Custodians," Fahd said, reverently. He seemed to be waiting for a reaction that didn't come.

"Am I supposed to know what that means?" Jonathan asked.

"No, not really," Fahd said. "We've gone to great lengths to ensure that the public doesn't know we exist. Even though the public is the reason we exist."

"Who came up with that name? You?" Lew said.

Fahd smiled. "No, far from it. I wasn't a founder, by any means. In fact, ten years ago I was just a thief in Riyadh. My companions at the time and I broke into the National Museum. Successes had filled us with hubris. It was a disaster. Most of us were killed. But as I sat in custody, waiting for the police, someone very different showed up and took me away."

"Someone like you, now," Jonathan said.

"Yes. They asked if I'd be interested in using my skills in a very different way. Well, I knew my choices were to say yes or end up with my hands in a bag, so I went along with this stranger, determined to escape at my first opportunity. He indoctrinated me, took me into a world—a global subculture—that I didn't even know existed. It wasn't long before saving my hands was the least of the reasons I stayed."

"Fascinating," Lew said dryly. "But how exactly are we 'kindred spirits'? We've never robbed a museum in our lives."

"No, that's true," Fahd said. "I was referring more to the reason

I became a thief in the first place, but again I didn't really understand what you were all about back then. The Custodians helped me understand, though."

"And what are we all about?" Lew said. Jonathan wished Lew would shut up. For all they knew, he was confirming things Fahd didn't know yet. But just like Fahd's choice years ago, they didn't really have an option now. It was either sit and listen to Fahd's story or face the automatic weapons in the hallway.

"It's all in her books," Fahd said, nodding toward Emily. Jonathan closed his eyes and sighed, knowing they were blown. Jonathan and Lew had first met Emily because of the book she had written, *The Monarch's Reign*, which documented and theorized about who The Monarch actually was. Once they'd met—and Emily had helped to rescue Natalie from her kidnappers—Emily wrote another book aimed at protecting The Monarch, as opposed to outing Jonathan and Lew. At the time, it had seemed to work, but Jonathan knew there was always a chance of someone's seeing through the subterfuge.

"You didn't rob museums, Lew," Fahd said, as he got up, picked up a remote control, and pointed it at the screen on the wall. "But you did work *for* museums. You and Jonathan, both. As The Monarch." Fahd pressed a button, and the screen snapped to life, a single image displayed—two symmetrical curlicues on either side of a flattened vertical oval, looking for all intents and purposes like an insect.

Like a butterfly.

Even though he'd sensed it was coming, the image shot electricity through Jonathan's nervous system, his legs twitching slightly. They still didn't know how much The Custodians knew, but his hopes of keeping some secrets were quickly fading.

"But I'm getting ahead of myself," Fahd said. "The Custodians were—and are—about more than protecting Art. Much more. They protect entire cultures, science, languages—the list is almost endless."

"Well, aren't y'all special—" Lew started to say.

"Shut up, Lew," Jonathan said without looking at him, then to Fahd, "Why us?"

"As I said, you inspired me, even if I didn't get it at first. But I wasn't the only one. The Custodians were well aware of you even before I joined them. Apparently, it's gone back and forth over the years whether to approach you for membership, or to eliminate you."

Jonathan and Lew exchanged a look.

"Do The Custodians make a habit of eliminating people?" Jonathan asked.

"Of course not," Fahd said. "I probably shouldn't have mentioned it." Jonathan doubted anything that Fahd was saying was by accident.

"But you did mention it," Lew said.

"Please, don't read too much into it," Fahd said. "The Custodians have a council who decide everything. That motion was tabled a few times but never got anywhere near the majority vote it would have needed to be passed and put into action. Let's stay on point."

Jonathan exchanged another look with Lew, and he decided to let it go, for now. Lew appeared to agree. He could feel Emily staring at him, but he didn't have the bandwidth to deal with her, right now.

"Proceed," Jonathan said.

Fahd pressed another button, and newspaper clippings appeared on the screen, then faded one after another:

"Monet's Charing Cross Mysteriously Resurrected"

"British Museum Finds Raphael Amongst Forgotten Inventory"

"Degas Daughters Returned Under Shroud of Secrecy"

And on and on, all reports covering various jobs The Monarch had been associated with over the years.

"And just when we agreed unanimously to approach you, you disappeared," Fahd continued. He used the remote again, and the screen displayed a blackened, still-smoking island. Jonathan, Emily, and Lew all leaned forward. The last time they'd seen Tartaruga Island, they'd been flying away from it as fast they could on a stolen helicopter.

"Shit," Lew said quietly.

"You hit the radar again two years ago, and once more the decision of what to do about you has set off a difficult debate."

"I'm assuming you ended up on the side to keep us alive, seeing as we're still breathing," Jonathan said.

"It gets better," Emily said, her speech a little mumbly because of her missing teeth. "Can I tell them?" she asked Fahd. He seemed genuinely disappointed, but nodded.

"They want you to be The Monarch again!"

AFTER FAHD SAID he'd leave them alone to talk it over, and Jonathan had closed the door behind him, he spun around so fast he almost fell over.

"Are you crazy?" Jonathan said to Emily, denying the rush he'd momentarily felt at the idea.

"Tell me you were joking," Lew said. But Jonathan knew from yesterday that Lew was feeling the same rush of adrenaline at the idea of being The Monarch again.

Emily looked like someone had just told her Santa Claus wasn't real. "But I don't get it. You're already pulling jobs again. What's the—"

"We haven't used the symbol in two years," Jonathan said. "And if they want us to be . . . *him* again, you know that's what they're going to want."

"I still don't get it. What's the difference if you use the symbol or not?"

"Look in a mirror, baby," Lew said.

"And think about what I've gone through with Natalie. The symbol makes people nuts, and it puts everyone we love in danger. What do you think George will do if he hears about the symbol's being used somewhere?"

"Wait, you love me?" Emily said to Jonathan. Lew laughed.

"What? No, I mean . . . well, yes, but not like—" Emily walked over and put her uninjured arm around Jonathan. Lew just sat, smiling like his cheeks were trying to get into his eye sockets. "Would you please say something?" Jonathan said to him.

"Oh, I love you too, big guy. How's about a kiss?"

"If you take one more step, I'll suffocate you with your stupid coat."

Emily stepped back from her assault and looked Jonathan in the eye, putting her hand on his cheek.

"Jonathan, I love you too. And we all love Natalie. Don't you know I'd never do anything to put any of you in danger? But if you're going to continue, you need help. And protection. Fahd and The Custodians can do that. They can find the jobs, and more importantly, they can *fund* the jobs."

"I hate to say it, but she's making sense, Jonny," Lew said. Jonathan knew this is what Lew had been wanting for a long time.

Could The Custodians really keep Natalie safe? Was this the answer they'd been looking for all along? While he disliked The Monarch label, mostly because everyone seemed to only see the butterfly symbol, not what it was meant to represent, he missed the impact their work used to have—for culture, for history, and for him. And maybe it was time to stop overthinking everything and go with his gut. Look at what trying to use his head had done to his relationship with Natalie. He let himself think about becoming The Monarch again—really think about—and the flutter in his stomach told him what he should do.

"I can't believe I'm saying this, but I'm in," Jonathan said. Emily jumped and squealed. Lew shook his head, but smiled. "On two conditions: We take care of George first and get Natalie safe before we do anything else."

"I may be able to help with that," Fahd said from the doorway. Jonathan hadn't even heard him return. Fahd reached out into the hallway and pulled someone into the room. The person's hands and feet were in chains, and there was a bag over their head.

"No way," Lew said, getting to his feet.

"My gift to you," Fahd said as he pulled the bag off and revealed a blinking Canton George.

When he saw Jonathan and Lew, George's one good eye looked like it was trying to run away from his face. Both Jonathan and Lew started toward the author of every misfortune that had befallen them in the past two years, but Fahd held up his hand like he was stopping traffic. Jonathan would have kept moving, but the guard behind Fahd pulled the slide on his P90, locking and loading it. The sound froze both him and Lew to their spots.

"I don't get it," Lew said. "You bring him here and we can't—for fuck sakes, look at her!"

But Jonathan understood why. He stepped in front of Lew and fought to get his attention. "Lew. Lew!"

"What?" Lew finally said when he stopped trying to go around Jonathan.

"They're taking him to the authorities. They're going to lock him up. Legally."

"That's right," Fahd said.

"Are you kidding? He's a billionaire who hires other people to do his dirty work. He'll bring in a hundred lawyers and walk away. Just like always," Lew said.

"The buffoon is correct. Release me now, or I'll sue you so hard your grandchildren will still be paying for your insolence," George said.

"Not this time," Fahd said. "We've had all of you under surveillance for weeks. How do you think we knew Emily needed rescuing? We've got her assault on video. Including George's ordering her death. It's airtight."

"Fools, I'll destroy you all," George managed, but his body language betrayed his true feelings. He was terrified.

Jonathan had been wondering about the timing of Emily's rescue. He wasn't crazy about having been watched, but it seemed to calm Lew down. Emily joined Jonathan between Lew and George, putting her hand on his shoulder.

"Get him out of here," Jonathan said. Two of the guards came in, and each took one of George's arms.

"Unhand me, *cuiters*!" Jonathan didn't know what the South African word was, but he knew it wasn't gentlemen. "This isn't over! I'll have my revenge! I'll kill your families and make you watch, *Bliksems*!"

They took George away as he continued to spew empty threats at them.

"Tell it to Bubba in the showers, Georgie," Lew said.

"And my daughter?" Jonathan said, George's shouts still echoing in the hall.

"She's been protected for longer than we've had all of you under surveillance. We found her first. Her geography teacher took sick a few weeks ago and was replaced with someone a little more—useful."

"One of yours, I take it," Jonathan said. "But just one guy?" Though, he realized, with George on ice, there was no immediate danger. He hoped.

"This isn't our only facility. There are dozens of similar installations around the world. One is less than ten minutes from your daughter's school. She's safer now than she's ever been in her life, trust me."

Trust. That was something Jonathan didn't throw around very much, especially in the past few years. But there was something about Fahd. Not authority, exactly, but something disarming. There was a lot that Jonathan still wanted to know, but to his surprise, he actually did feel like he could trust Fahd. Maybe.

"Okay, what exactly are you offering us?" Jonathan asked.

"And what do you want for it?" Lew asked. Fahd nodded and gestured toward the chairs around the table. Everyone sat down again.

"First off, we're not just a ring of thieves. Our membership is made up of many different types of experts—scientists, analysts, law enforcement—but we all have the same goal. Preservation."

"How many members are there?" Jonathan asked.

"I'm afraid that's classified. And it's constantly changing. But I can tell you that there are very few permanent members. Most are freelancers. That's what we want from you. From time to time, a situation will come up where we think your unique skills are needed. Between those times, you can function however you like. But if you agree to become The Monarch again for us, we'll expect you to be The Monarch only when you're working for us.

"And if we contact you about a . . . situation you're currently involved in that we think would be better handled by someone else or simply aborted, we'll expect you to comply with our wishes."

"You don't ask for much, do you?" Jonathan said.

"You still haven't told us what's in it for us," Lew said.

"Any profits are split seventy-thirty. Seventy for us."

"Seventy?" Lew said.

"As you can imagine, there's a bit of overhead on our side. You'll also have access to all of our resources—intel, safe houses. Even equipment. And, of course, on or off assignment, we'll provide protection for you and your immediate family. I'm afraid that's about as close as we get to stock options," Fahd joked. Nobody laughed.

It was an incredible offer. Jonathan evaluated what Fahd had said. Whether they accepted it or not, he had a feeling their lives would never be the same after leaving this room.

But if they agreed, they'd basically be handing over all the work they'd done over the years and entrusting their creation to The Custodians. It was a lot to ask, but then again, they were offering a lot.

Jonathan was prepared to accept, but he wanted to make sure Lew was still on board. Neither one of them was asking what would happen if they said no. Something Jonathan pretty much knew was bouncing around Lew's head as much as it was his, but when someone has just said they were debating on whether or not to kill you, there were certain questions you didn't want explicitly answered.

"What about Emily?" Lew asked. "She's not immediate family, and she's not part of The Monarch. How does she fit into all this?" Jonathan saw Emily take Lew's hand under the table.

"We've talked to her a little bit about this. She spent a few years at Interpol in an administrative capacity, managing their Web site, mostly. Once she's regained her health, we'd like to train her in computer security and send her back to Interpol."

"Computer security. You mean you want to train her to be a hacker for The Custodians and have her spy on Interpol," Jonathan said.

"It's a good opportunity for me," Emily said.

"What about your writing?" Lew asked.

"The only thing I've ever written about is The Monarch. Somehow, that doesn't seem like it has much of a future," Emily said.

Jonathan looked at Emily. After she smiled reassuringly, he looked at Lew. He didn't seem so assured, but after a moment, he sighed and nodded.

"Okay, we're on board. Now, what's this about there not being much time?" Jonathan said.

"We've got your first job lined up, but there's a time factor. We have to leave. I'll have a car take you home, so you can pack a bag. I'll brief you on the plane."

"Plane? What, you mean now?"

"Wheels up in two hours."

Chapter Twelve

THE *JUROJIN MARU*'s bridge decor was a melding of science fiction tropes and the Old West, making half of it look like it belonged on the Starship *Enterprise*, and the other half look like it belonged on an episode of *Bonanza*. Umi, who had a special place in her heart for both genres, had designed it like that deliberately though she'd never admit it to anyone.

The captain was seated in one of the two expensive, barbershop-like chairs bolted to the hardwood floor. Dressed in a crisply pressed white short-sleeve shirt, white shorts, and black belt, Captain Tanaka seemed bored. Which was understandable; the ship hadn't gone anywhere in months, and if Umi had her way, it would never move from its current spot again.

"Captain," Umi said, leaning against the empty chair. The trip to the lower decks and back up last night, not to mention the stress of the last few months, had taken their toll, meds or not. Her illness aside, she was fitter and more resilient than most eighty-year-olds, but the fact was she was a hundred and two, and some days that was exactly how old she felt.

"Ma'am," Tanaka said, jumping up from his chair when he saw Umi. He came over to take her arm. She let him.

"You wanted to see me?" Umi said, as Tanaka led them to a butterscotch-colored leather bench on the whiskey bar side of the bridge.

"I could have come below, you didn't have to come up here," Tanaka said as they sat down.

"I'm here now. So why don't you tell me why I'm here." She said it pleasantly, or at least pleasantly for her.

"We've got some weather coming in. Just a tropical depression right now, and it's not headed right for us, but they can be unpredictable."

She'd spent the past few years living on the *Jurojin Maru* and didn't need a weather report explained to her.

"Normally, I'd advise a relocation. Especially with our guests about to arrive. If the storm turns for us, even if it doesn't intensify, the choppers could have trouble ferrying our guests from the mainland."

"I appreciate your concern, Captain, but we're not going anywhere. Keep me advised on the storm, though," she said, standing up.

"Yes, ma'am."

Just then, Maggie Reynolds came rushing onto the bridge, both Umi and Tanaka turning toward her. She looked out of breath.

"There you are, Mrs. Tenabe," Maggie said. She looked at the captain for a second, seemingly unsure if she should speak openly in front of him. "We've . . . we've got a situation."

MAGGIE HELD THE door open for Umi as they headed below. The situation was a frantic call from Tatsu. She had been trying to call Umi, but when she couldn't reach her, Tatsu had called Maggie for help. Whatever Umi had her doing in Toronto had gone tits up, and when Maggie had spoken to her, Tatsu seemed to be having something close to a panic attack. Since relaying the information to Umi, Maggie had never seen her act so concerned.

What do you know, Maggie thought. *She really cares for the kid.*

"Is she all right?" Umi asked.

"She's definitely shook up, but she seems all right. She wouldn't tell me much. Just wanted me to come and get you." Maggie thought about probing Umi on what exactly Tatsu was doing in Toronto but decided against it. Her mission—both for MI6 and her cover as head of security—was activity on the ship, inquiring about anything off ship would only bring attention where Maggie didn't want it. And she was starting to feel like she'd exceeded her quota of innocent questions.

They reached the junction between Umi's office and Maggie's quarters. Umi stopped. Maggie already knew what she needed to say. "I'll get back to the vetting. Something tells me Tatsu wouldn't be as comfortable talking to you if I were there."

Umi was nodding, but before she could concur, Maggie left for her quarters.

Maggie wanted Umi to get comfortable with the idea that she'd learned her place in this little drama. Fighting her at every turn wasn't going to accomplish that. She was thinking about the scene down in the bowels of the ship again when she entered her quarters. A familiar scent of 1970s cologne and cigarette smoke assailed her as she closed the door.

Oh, God, no.

"About bloody time you showed up," a man's voice said from a darkened corner. Maggie just stared as the tall black man stepped out of the shadows, smoke swirling around him like he was wearing it. His immaculate suit looked like he'd just stepped out of a shop on Savile Row in London—during the Thatcher years. His tightly cut curly hair was heavily salt and peppered, and he seemed to have even more crow's-feet in the papery skin around his eyes than the last time she'd seen him if that was even possible.

"Alex? What are you doing here?" Maggie demanded. Though she knew. Not specifically, but she knew what his presence meant. He was from the old school. The really old school. Only a few of them were left around the MI6 offices, like a bunch of derelict James Bonds who had lost their way and just refused to call it a day. The Home Office sent them out on harmless "overseer" missions with agents who were on their way out themselves. Missions that were deemed to have zero risk. It kept the old farts busy and provided object lessons for agents who didn't realize their own time was up— "Don't let this happen to you!" So, if Alex Corsair was here—

"Sweating my bloody bollocks off, mostly, love," Alex said, stubbing out his cigarette in a saucer left over from Maggie's breakfast. He stepped toward her and planted a too-long kiss on her cheek. She swept away from the smoky cologne and tried to put some space between them.

It wasn't her first encounter with the famed Alex Corsair. In his day, he'd been the real James Bond. In every way. And he obviously still had some skills to be able to get on board without anyone's noticing. But spy craft aside, he'd been trying to get her between the sheets for the past ten years. He seemed to take her refusals as a challenge.

She'd feel sorry for him if she wasn't so busy at the moment feeling sorry for herself. If the Home Office had sent him here, it only meant one thing—they believed she'd overstayed her welcome, something she'd sworn to herself that she'd never do. Since being released from captivity twelve years ago, she'd spent most of her time trying to prove herself—to the agency and to the part of her mind that kept screaming she was past her prime. She hadn't even seen this coming.

IN HER OFFICE, Umi sat at her desk and hit a button on her keyboard. Tatsu's image appeared on her screen. She looked terrible. She was damp from sweat and seemed to keep checking the window beside her. From the decor in the background, she was in a very basic motel room. But for some reason she was wearing a lab coat.

"What happened?" Umi asked, genuinely concerned.

Tatsu told her about the events at the Crystasis research facility. With each part of the tale, Umi's mood darkened. She was positively sullen when the story was finished. Umi knew she'd been pushing Tatsu hard. Too hard. And this was the result. The resource she'd nurtured all these years was spent. Any feelings she might have had for the girl were secondary. Umi was an expert at putting her feelings aside. The difficulty now was mitigating the damage. If nothing else, she had to make sure Tatsu stayed out of the hands of the local authorities. Nothing could endanger the schedule. Another day, and it wouldn't matter. But they were at a crucial time. And in today's world, it would only be a matter of seconds for an e-mail or phone call to derail everything.

In another time, Umi thought. Not so long ago, it would be weeks before word could get across the globe. In those days, there would be nothing to worry about. In another time. Then Umi had an idea. A terrible idea. An idea that could solve everything.

Umi's thoughts were interrupted by a sound she had never heard from Tatsu. The girl was crying, her head hanging down so that her flaming red hair hid her face. She could tell that even in this untenable situation, Tatsu was worried about disappointing Umi, even if just by showing her weakness of emotion. It was like she'd regressed back into that little girl Umi had first met so many years ago.

"O . . . *Obasan*," Tatsu managed. "There was a man. A kind, simple man. I . . . I killed him. And I just left him. Like . . . like he didn't matter."

"Little one, there there," Umi said, as if she were stroking the girl's hair. "It's all for the greater good. You know better than anyone what we're trying to accomplish. What we must accomplish. You saw what happened."

Tatsu's sobbing eased, and she nodded, keeping her head down. And then Umi was putting her idea into play before she had time to think about it too much.

"Sometimes I wish the old ways still had meaning," Umi said, deliberately sounding more like she was talking to herself than Tatsu. She waited for a reaction and was soon rewarded.

"Old ways?" Tatsu said quietly, wiping tears from her eyes.

"Yes, they made so much more . . . sense. I can feel your pain, little one. Pain that nothing in this world can take away. The dead are dead and will stay that way forever. Pain lives on in today's world. But in the past, when a Samurai had dishonored their code . . ." Umi pretended to be overwhelmed and fell silent. Though, in reality, she was letting the idea work on Tatsu.

Umi knew with all the training Tatsu had undergone and mastered, she would know exactly what Umi was referring to. Along with the skills she had learned with her body and weapons, Tatsu had been taught disciplines and codes. And the one that applied here was the ritualistic suicide known as—

"Seppuku," Tatsu said quietly. Umi resisted the urge to smile at her accomplishment.

"Yes," Umi said. "In a different time, of course. No senseless pain. Only honor."

"Honor," Tatsu said, sounding defeated.

"Wish me luck, little one," Umi said after a long silence. "I know you'll be here . . . in spirit."

"*Sayonara*," Tatsu said. Umi cut the connection.

She picked up a tissue with a shaking hand and dabbed at her damp eye, surprised at her reaction once she knew she'd achieved her goal. The plan was safe. Tatsu was a hero. And soon, she'd be a martyr.

Toronto
7:45 A.M. *Local Time*

TATSU PUT THE phone down and squeezed her eyes shut, trying to draw calm from the silence, but all she saw were the faces of those she'd harmed. Opening her eyes, she took a deep breath and emptied her pockets onto the table. She had very little: a small knife, a few dollars in bills and change, her cell phone, and the phone she'd taken from Hank. And her wallet. She went through her wallet and pulled out the only picture she had of her brother. He'd been dead a long time, but to her it was like yesterday.

Tatsu wiped the tears from her eyes. Then she pulled off the lab coat and her shirt, picked up the knife and placed it against her naked flesh, between her breasts. She closed her eyes again, this time to try to calm herself.

Honor. It's what Umi wants, and you owe her so much.

But before she could drive the blade home, she heard a beeping noise, and opening her eyes, she noticed the red light blinking on Hank's phone. She assumed it was some sort of preset alarm and was going to ignore it, but the rate it blinked seemed to be increasing. She picked it up and activated the screen, displaying a map with a single moving point. Using her thumb and forefinger, the map image zoomed out. As it did, some place-names appeared on the map, including the Lakeview Motel.

She watched the red dot move faster and faster—directly toward her room.

The red dot moved faster.

The beeping echoed faster.

They synchronized. Faster and faster.

And then . . . they stopped. The dot merged with her motel on the map, and the beeping fell silent. Tatsu looked up at the door. Deafening silence was all she heard. Everything was still except for the dust dancing in slow motion as the early morning light spilled into her room through the edges of the drawn curtain. She held her breath, the only sound the pounding of blood in her ears.

Then, tentatively, she got out of the chair and reached her hand out toward the curtain.

CRASH!

The sound of splintering wood shattered the room's quiet. Tatsu tried to understand what she was seeing. A black-gloved fist was sticking through the door, into her room.

That's impossible, Tatsu thought, as the fist turned at an unnatural angle, grabbed the chain lock, and ripped it off the door. Then she remembered the file she'd read on Per and seeing the glint of something metallic across the walkway back at Crystasis's research facility.

Before the door could swing open, Tatsu collected her belongings, shoved them back into her pockets, and grabbed the knife she had been about to end her life with. She didn't hide but stood directly where he would see her. As the door swung open, and Per took a first step into the room, he hesitated just for a moment.

At least part of him is human, Tatsu thought as she took advantage of the hesitation and drove her knife into Per's leg. A second later—with no screaming, she noted—Per knocked Tatsu through the air. She hit the bed and rolled off it, out of sight. Lying on the floor, Tatsu grabbed her shoulder and winced, sucking wind through her teeth. She'd only taken part of the hit with her shoulder and had thrown herself so she'd be hidden, but her shoulder still tingled like she'd been hit by a truck.

Don't let that thing hit you again.

"Come out," Per's voice commanded. He was smart, she'd give him that. If he'd been dumb enough to look over the edge of the bed, her poised thumbs would have gouged his eyes out.

"I think I'll stay right here, thank you," Tatsu said. "But feel free to let yourself out."

"Stop being foolish and come out of there. And cover yourself." The last was said as Per threw the lab coat over the bed. It landed beside her.

"Sorry, I thought you liked girls," Tatsu said. She had to do whatever she could to keep him from thinking he was running the show.

From the sound of his voice, he was still standing by the door, blocking her exit. Then she heard footsteps leading away and outside. *Is he leaving?* A moment later she heard a car trunk slam and footsteps approach again. She hated being trapped like this, but what could she do in such tight quarters with that arm of his waiting for her?

"This is your final warning. Come out and tell me about Dead Lights. I don't have time for this."

He doesn't have time? Why not? Because his plan has a schedule? Or maybe the schedule isn't his.

"There are plenty of flights out, today. You went to all the trouble of tracking down the Dead Lights bomber, and you're just going to leave? What's the rush?" Tatsu said, taking a shot in the dark that the schedule belonged to a commercial airline. If she was right, she had a bad feeling of where that flight would be headed.

"I am not interested in *finding* the Dead Lights bomber. I just want to know *about* Dead Lights. If you are not going to tell me, I will assume that is because you do not know. And I will go talk to someone who does know. That is the only rush. Now, come out!"

Someone who does know? Before Tatsu could ponder that any longer, something splashed all over her.

"Hey!" Tatsu shouted, instantly recognizing the pungent smell. Gasoline rained down on her from the doorway. *That's what he got from his car. Oh, God, he's going to burn me!*

"Last chance." His voice wasn't raised or excited or laced with any kind of emotion. It was eerie. Then she heard the sound of a road flare igniting, a hiss and a glaring light coming from Per's position in the doorway, making the shadows on the wall elongate and dance.

Tatsu grabbed the lab coat and wiped as much of the gasoline off her as she could, then she dipped it in even more of the fuel that was on the carpet around her. She counted to three before jumping up and tossing the lab coat at Per and the burning road flare. The coat ignited with a *whoomph!* as it fell onto Per. While he fought with the fiery coat, Tatsu jumped over the bed and dove at the curtains, crashing through the window and landing in the parking lot. She rolled and was back up on her feet in seconds. Per came out of the burning motel room, the floor and bed on fire now. Tatsu took a squared-off stance and raised her fists. The invitation to him was clear.

Per saw Tatsu standing there, waiting for him. He was a sight. What little hair he had left was scorched on one side, his glasses bent, and his leg bleeding where the knife still stuck.

"If you were smart, you would have run while you had the chance," Per said, approaching her.

"And if you were smart, you'd get that knife wound looked at instead of wasting your time flying all the way to Tokyo. You won't find any answers there, you know," Tatsu said, baiting him as they circled each other.

"I believe I will see what Nagura has to say for himself before I decide Tokyo is a waste of time. And if he does not feel like talking, maybe I will see how many knife wounds *he* can endure."

"NO!" Tatsu shouted as she stopped circling, her breath catching and electricity rifling through her arms and legs at the thought of Nagura's being hurt.

The corner of Per's mouth went up in what might have been a smirk, and instantly Tatsu saw her mistake. All this time while she thought she'd been playing him for information, he'd actually been playing her. Anger—at herself and at him—mixed with the fear already rising in her for Nagura's well-being. She fought for control, knowing if she was going to triumph, her mind and body had to be clear and focused. She needed to act, not react.

If I can get close enough to get my hand on that knife, I can end this in a hurry.

She ran at Per before he could get his bearings—or thought she had. With no trouble at all, he turned and blocked her attack.

He swung that arm of his, but she easily ducked it and swept his legs from under him, sending him to the pavement. As he hit the ground, he swung his arm at her again. She had to jump backward, arching into a back handspring to avoid it. Then she saw the hole in the ground his arm had made. All he needed was one solid connection with that thing, and she'd be dead.

People were starting to gather outside their motel rooms and someone yelled, "I've called the cops!"

Tatsu was still going to fight it out, but without a remark, Per got into his car and drove away, leaving Tatsu standing there half-naked, her motel room in flames. Sirens sounded in the distance. Tatsu looked at the crowd staring at her, some of them using their phones to take a picture. She grabbed the curtain from her motel room off the ground, shook the glass out of it, then wrapped it around her shoulders, covering herself. Without a second glance, she hurried out of the parking lot.

A few blocks away, thankfully without running into anyone, she got to her motorcycle. She unlocked the seat's trunk and took out her rain slicker, tossing her curtain shawl away. With her steed between her legs, she felt better. She took out her phone and checked the flights to Tokyo. There were a half dozen throughout the day, but the next flight actually had an hour and a half stopover in France. The flight after that was nonstop and got into Tokyo almost an hour before the first flight. Hopefully Per's rush to get to Tokyo made him take the first flight. Either way, she'd have to be careful.

Chapter Thirteen

London
1:00 p.m. Local Time

JONATHAN STOOD BACK from the window of his flat, peering out through the sheers at Fahd's men, who had driven him there and were now waiting for him and the bag at his feet. Packing wasn't the first thing he did when he got home, though. That honor had gone to finding the bugs and fish-eye cameras strategically placed around his apartment. It hadn't taken him long to find the devices, but he wondered more than a little about not having noticed them before. What else had he missed?

There had been a time when if a crumb was out of place when he returned home, he would have noticed it without effort. Was he getting lazy? Or worse, old? He'd certainly been through a lot since those days, but he'd thought he was still on his game. Even though his game was now stealing stolen art rather than covertly taking orders from a government. There were parts of that old life that he missed, but the paranoia was not one of them. Not that he'd shucked that little feature with The Monarch.

The Monarch. While he felt excitement at the idea of getting back to what he was sure he was meant to do—him and Lew—part of him was screaming that he was crazy and should slip out the back and take a cab to anywhere but here. Lew could take care of himself. Lew could even be The Monarch without him, couldn't he? But Jonathan knew from experience that that wasn't true. The last time he'd bailed from the life and left Lew on his own, the lunkhead had wound up in federal prison.

But it was all just woolgathering. Jonathan could no more leave Lew than he could leave his skin. And when all was said and done, there was one thing he knew he was feeling about this whole situation that he hadn't felt in years—excited.

Jonathan waved to the driver and headed down with his suitcase. He got in, and they headed over to pick up Lew. Less than an hour later, they were both on board The Custodians' private jet at Heathrow.

THE BOEING 747-8 Intercontinental jet liner was capable of seating six hundred people in its uncustomized form. Today there were only eight on board, including the pilot and the copilot. At top speed, they'd reach their destination in just over eight hours. A few guards, with their weapons stowed away, sat near the front of the plane. Fahd was up in the cockpit, talking to the pilots. Jonathan and Lew were seated near the back of the plane. Emily, because of her condition, had stayed home.

Lew was just finishing his second dinner while Jonathan sipped on some green tea after barely touching his. Everything was happening so fast that Lew had no idea what was in store for them, but he'd decided that whatever it was, there probably wasn't going to be much time for hitting a drive-thru. Assuming they even had drive-thrus wherever they were going.

"So what do you think?" Jonathan asked, putting down his teacup.

"A little frozen in the middle, but not bad," Lew said.

Jonathan just looked at him. Lew could tell he wasn't in the mood for playing around. Not that he was either, but it was how he dealt with things.

"You don't think it's all a little convenient? I mean, exactly what we need at exactly the right time? And why us? Our track record hasn't exactly been stellar lately. If it's just the symbol—The Monarch—that they want, why not just start using it themselves?"

"We considered that," Fahd said from behind them. Lew didn't particularly like Fahd. He was shifty and had this weird habit of sidling up to you without being heard. Lew preferred his friends and foes the same way: head-on and in plain sight. Fahd sat down across from them.

"So why didn't you?" Lew asked.

"Modis Operandi," Fahd said. "It's not just you and it's not just him, it's the two of you together. You have a way of working that's unlike anything we've ever seen before. It would be easy to just start drawing symbols all over the place. But duplicating your style and methods is a whole different story."

"We have a style?" Lew said, only half kidding.

"Like no other," Fahd said. Lew could tell from the look on Jonathan's face he wasn't buying it either. "But enough of the compliments. I want you two to get some sleep before we land, so let's go over what we know."

Fahd put a tablet computer down in front of them and swiped the screen open. An image of a huge yacht displayed.

"This is the *Jurojin Maru*, one of the largest yachts in the world. It's almost six hundred feet long, has a crew of over fifty—most of whom are former SAS—and can normally accommodate up to ninety guests."

Lew leaned forward and whistled, more than impressed by the floating city. He could see two helicopter pads, two pools, a tennis court and several decks filled with what looked like lounge chairs. It had to be at least six stories high, not counting whatever lay below the waterline.

"Normally accommodate?" Jonathan said.

"Yes, I'll get to that. The *Jurojin Maru* has two minisubmarines and a moon pool in a pressurized deck at the base of the ship and several high-speed launches. She also has state-of-the-art defenses to protect its guests from pirates and terrorists."

"Defenses?" Lew said. That little tidbit he didn't like.

"Antiballistic and antisubmarine missile systems, paparazzi laser deterrent, armor plating, bulletproof glass, and an armory stocked with everything from machine pistols to RPGs," Fahd said.

"Son of a bitch," Lew said.

"Who owns it?" Jonathan asked. Fahd swiped a new picture into view. A small Asian woman who Lew thought looked to be about a hundred and fifty years old appeared.

"Umi Tenabe, head of the Tenabe Group, one of the richest multinationals in Japan. They're into everything: construction, engineering, pharmaceuticals, electronics—you name it. Aside from running her father's company after he died, a minor miracle in Japan's society, especially back then, she was an incredible philanthropist. Mostly sciences, and for the past ten years, almost exclusively longevity research and life extension."

"I can see why," Lew said, thinking if he ever got that old, he'd eat a bullet, not figure out how to get more wrinkles.

"Was?" Jonathan said.

"Yes, as I said, for ten years she was the major funding source for the science, but six months ago her husband, Mikawa, passed away, and she's mostly disappeared from the scene—along with her money. Umi popped up again a few months ago to host this," Fahd said, swiping. An announcement for a Longevity and Life Extension Conference appeared on the tablet.

"This weekend," Lew said, noticing the date.

"Yes," Fahd said. "My contacts tell me guests have already started to arrive."

"It's all very interesting, Fahd," Jonathan said, "but why do we care about this?"

"Because of this." Another swipe made both Jonathan and Lew lean forward.

On the screen was the unmistakable work of Pablo Picasso. Working with Jonathan, Lew had learned a great deal about art over the years and could even recognize certain styles and artists, but anything beyond that was Jonathan's purview.

"*Le pigeon aux petits pois*," Jonathan said. A moment later, he said to Lew, "*The Pigeon with Green Peas*. It's—"

"A Picasso," Lew said, fighting every reflex to make a French restaurant joke.

"That was supposed to have been destroyed back in 2010," Jonathan said. "The thief confessed and said so."

"And as we both know, thieves never lie," Fahd said with a wink.

"How much?" Lew asked.

"About thirty million," Jonathan said.

"Thirty-two million, at last appraisal," Fahd said.

"Let me guess," Lew said. "The pigeon dinner is somewhere on the super floating death fortress. Yeah, this will be a snap. Forget it, buddy."

"Lew," Jonathan said, with a tone that Lew knew said take it easy. Lew didn't think he was being unruly, but he couldn't always tell. Regardless, this whole thing sounded like suicide, and he was damn sure not going to sit there and quietly drink the Kool-Aid.

"Were you not here for the whole SAS guards, missiles, and lasers discussion? Even if we *could* get on the ship, we'd never be able to grab it. And even if by some miracle we did, we'd end up with an RPG enema on our way home."

"Something tells me we're not going to have a problem getting on board," Jonathan said, looking to Fahd. "You got us passes for this conference, didn't you?"

"Well," Fahd said, looking from Jonathan to Lew. "Yes and no."

"Why do I feel like I was just auctioned off to the lowest bidder," Lew said.

"We were only able to get one pass. Jonathan, you'll be replacing Dr. Chris Hudson, gerontologist from USC," Fahd said, handing Jonathan his credentials.

"And the real Dr. Hudson?" Jonathan asked.

"Terrible case of the stomach flu, I'm afraid. Just a shame," Fahd said.

"Yeah, I'll bet," Jonathan said. "And the fact that I know about as much about gerontology as I do quantum physics won't be a problem?"

"We've prepared some quick notes for you, both on Hudson and gerontology. Ryan, our tech, will be coming around with some equipment for you, one of which is a smart phone. It'll have everything you need on it."

"Gotcha," Jonathan said, looking through his credentials.

"Um, ex-fucking-scuse me. How exactly am I getting on board?" Lew said, feeling like a stepchild. But there was no way he was letting Jonathan go in alone.

"You'll be going in through the moon pool, Lew," Fahd said. "Once on board, you'll mix with the support staff." Fahd handed Lew his credentials.

"I'll be going where-what? Uh, where exactly is this floating fortress docked?"

"It's . . . not exactly docked. It's located off Iwo Jima."

"How far off?" Lew asked.

"About eight hundred miles east of Okinawa."

"So, the middle of the ocean. What the hell is it doing way out there?"

"We're not really sure. It's probably for security. Aside from scientists and researchers, the conference is also hosting some of the most prominent philanthropists funding longevity research today. Even some government officials. We figure that's the reason for all the extra guards. Without them, half of the people on the guest list wouldn't be going.

"But that will work in our favor. While everyone's security staff is bumping into each other, you can locate the painting and figure out the best way to get it."

"You don't know where it is?" Lew said. He was hating this plan more and more.

"Well, we've got some probable locations for you, but as to an exact, pinpoint location—"

"So, no."

"Uh, no. Not exactly."

"Perfect."

"AH, HERE HE IS," Fahd said a few minutes later. Jonathan looked up and saw a heavyset, bearded man approaching. He was the youngest member of The Custodians Jonathan had seen yet and he was carrying a metal briefcase.

"Is now a good time?" the man asked.

"As good as any," Fahd said, getting up. "Jonathan, Lew, this is Ryan, our tech. I'll leave you guys to it. When you're done with Ryan, try to get some shut-eye." Fahd left, and Ryan sat down, putting the metal briefcase on his lap. He smiled sheepishly and opened the case.

"Okay, first things first, I'll need your personal phones and any weapons you have on you," Ryan said. Jonathan and Lew looked at each other, then back at Ryan, making no movement to comply. "You'll get them back when the mission is complete. Don't worry about that."

They continued to stare at Ryan. Jonathan could remember this routine from back in the day when he was prepping for missions, but that was then.

"It's standard operating procedure, guys," Ryan said. "Really, it's no big—"

"Look, kid," Lew said leaning forward. "It ain't gonna happen."

"What's the problem?" Fahd said when Ryan waved him back over. Ryan explained. The men looked at each other for a moment, then Fahd nodded toward the front of the plane. "Can I talk to you for a second, Jonathan?"

He was going to refuse, but Jonathan could feel things heating up, so he got up and went a few rows away with Fahd.

"You have to understand—" Jonathan started.

"Oh, I understand," Fahd said, sounding almost angry. "You'll take our protection, our intel for jobs and, ultimately, our money, but you don't want to play by our rules. I think I understand completely."

"It's not like that," Jonathan said. Or was it? Fahd had kind of hit the nail right on the head. Jonathan knew when they had agreed to become The Monarch again for The Custodians that there would be some concessions. But at the first one, he'd flat-out refused to play along. Maybe he wasn't as ready for this as he thought.

"Look, we'll be outfitting you for the mission with everything we've deemed necessary. And trust me, whatever you guys have on you won't even hold a candle to what we'll provide. But if you're thinking it's all some ploy to get you unarmed, look around you."

Jonathan saw what Fahd was talking about. All of the guards—who outnumbered him and Lew by threefold—were still carrying machine guns over their shoulders.

"If all I wanted to do was disarm you, you would be disarmed. Besides, I disarmed you both once already back in the Complex. Use your head."

"You're right, you're right," Jonathan said, shaking his head.

"Good," Fahd said. "Can you get Lew to play along?"

"Yes," Jonathan said. It was interesting that Fahd had known that the way to defuse this situation was to convince him. And that it would be Jonathan's job to convince Lew, not his. They really had done their homework.

"Now before we have to do this all over again, there's one more thing that you'll need to convince Lew about," Fahd said.

AFTER HE RETURNED to his seat, Jonathan convinced Lew that it was okay and actually in their interest to comply. It took some doing, but this was the easy part.

Jonathan took his ankle holster off and put it and the Walther PPK in it on top of Ryan's metal briefcase. Then he took the folding knife out and put it beside his gun.

"That's me," Jonathan said. He looked at Lew, who was reluctant, but eventually reached in his pockets.

Ten minutes later, the case and the seat beside Ryan were filled with guns, ammo, knives, brass knuckles, a telescoping baton and two leather saps Lew had armed himself with while packing his bag.

"How the hell do you stay upright?" Jonathan said. Lew just grinned and shrugged.

Ryan put as much of it into the case as he could.

"Okay, this is yours," Ryan said, handing Jonathan a smart phone. "And this is for Lew." He handed Lew a similar phone.

"Do we get decoder rings too?" Lew said. Ryan looked confused.

"Ignore him," Jonathan said.

"Hey, this thing is busted. No signal," Lew said.

"They're not real phones. Just data devices," Ryan said. "

"So how do we communicate?" Lew asked.

Here we go.

Ryan pulled something that looked like a space-age gun out of the briefcase. Lew recoiled.

"What the fuck is that?" Lew said.

"This is your locator-slash-comm pellet injector. A little pellet that goes in just behind your ear. You'll be able to talk to each other and us, without anyone's knowing. It also has GPS, so we can locate you. May I?" Ryan said, leaning toward Jonathan.

"Sure," Jonathan said, trying to show Lew that it was no big deal.

This was what they had agreed to. It wouldn't be the first time Jonathan had received an implant before a mission though those were usually RFID and under the skin on his arm, but that was a long time ago. The technology had obviously come a long way.

"Are you nuts?" Lew said, but Jonathan could tell his own reaction was tempering Lew's.

"We've all got them," Ryan said, turning his head and squeezing the skin behind his ear until a lump showed. "It's kind of mandatory."

Jonathan shrugged and turned his head. Ryan placed the injector against his skin and pulled the trigger. It stung for a second, but then it went numb.

"Hold this against it for a few seconds," Ryan said, handing Jonathan some gauze. "Now you."

Lew hesitated, but then reluctantly leaned forward, and Ryan implanted his. When he was done, Ryan took out a laptop and opened it up.

"Let's see if we can find you. Uh, yep, there you are," Ryan said, turning the screen so they could see blips on a map. "Working perfectly."

"And these things work anywhere? Any distance?" Jonathan asked.

"Pretty much, except the signal attenuates under just a foot or two of water. We'll lose you, so just try to stay out of it."

"Of course," Lew said. "Are these things always on?"

"The tracking part is, but the audio is controlled by software. Kind of like a bluetooth device. For instance, for you two to communicate, someone has to use the software to connect or pair your devices. Otherwise, you don't hear anything," Ryan said.

"But you guys can still hear us whenever you want?" Jonathan asked.

"Not on this mission. The ship has a jamming perimeter. Radios still work on the ship, but no signals in or out."

After Ryan left, they reclined their seats and shut off the overhead lights. When Jonathan couldn't sleep, he turned on his data device and started reading through his cover and the tech primer on gerontology. There was a lot to memorize, but he didn't think it would be a problem. It was all superficial information, though. If he got cornered into a real scientific conversation by a couple of actual scientists, he was going to be in trouble.

Jonathan was still fretting about that an hour later when Lew's snoring stopped. He coughed, then looked at Jonathan in the dark.

"Can't sleep?" Lew said quietly.

"It's all a little much and a little fast."

"You don't think they're on the level?" Lew said. Jonathan looked at the guards, who were mostly sleeping, and Fahd, who was talking quietly with Ryan as they looked at a computer screen.

"Nothing to say they aren't."

"Yet," Lew said. He turned over, using his duster as a blanket. "Relax, you get to be a spy again. You're good at it."

Sometimes Lew's insight and awareness took Jonathan by surprise, even after all these years. And he knew that if Lew hadn't been going along to watch his back, he probably wouldn't have been doing this.

"You realize they haven't told us what our cut will be if their intel is wrong and there's no painting on board," Lew said. He reached up and tapped behind his ear where the implant was. "You hear that, Fahd? Lew's gots ta be paid." He chuckled to himself, then was snoring again in no time.

Jonathan smiled and shook his head. He wasn't sure what was ahead of them, but he knew they'd face it together. He put the data device away and rolled over to get some sleep himself. They had a long day ahead of them.

Chapter Fourteen

Jurojin Maru
Saturday
3:00 A.M. Local Time

MAGGIE REYNOLDS WAS pulling her sneakers on in her stateroom when Alex turned on the light and sat up in the makeshift bed she'd set up on her couch for him. It wasn't lost on her that except for a thin sheet, the lothario was naked.

"I'm pretty sure morning needs more light than this, darling," Alex said. "Where are you off to?"

"I'm just going for a run. I'm too wired. Just need to burn off some of this nervous energy. I'll be back in about an hour," she said.

"Want some company?" he asked, starting to pull his sheet off.

"No! I mean, no, no, that's all right. You—you just stay there," she said, pulling his sheet back up over him. "The majority of the guests are going to start arriving tomorrow, and if you're really here to help me, we can figure out a game plan when I get back."

"Running. Game plan. You're exhausting, darling. And there's so many better ways to burn off nervous energy." He smiled as he said it, and she could tell he was taking the piss out of her. He winked at her before rolling over and shutting off the light.

Maggie opened the door, checked to make sure he wasn't looking, then took her gun out of the table by the door and slipped it into her shorts before she left.

Her run couldn't really be called a jog this time. She trotted more than anything else, trying to avoid anyone who happened to be wandering the decks even at this early hour. She didn't want to be exhausted by the time she reached her goal, just in case. Her shorts were tight, and the gun kept trying to bobble out of her waistband, so it took her almost an hour to get down belowdecks, back to where the three men wearing those strange exo suits had been moving that mysterious—obviously heavy—crate.

As she made her way, she kept thinking about the day ahead of her. It was annoying her, but she couldn't help it. Even if it was only a cover job, she had always been a perfectionist. And in only a few hours almost a hundred scientists, philanthropists, heads of state, and even royalty would be descending on the *Jurojin Maru*. Her job as Umi's security chief was a cover, but keeping everyone safe wasn't. And now that MI6's albatross was sleeping on her couch, she wanted—needed—to be faultless.

She eased up to the door the men had been taking the crate through and looked inside. It was a huge hold that contained not only that crate, but dozens of smaller crates stacked around the room. As she edged closer to the partially open door, she heard voices inside. They were speaking Japanese and, oddly enough, English. But voices or not, she had to get a look inside one of those crates. No one was in sight, so she eased into the room and hid between a couple of the crates.

The voices seemed to be coming from the far side of the hold, but the echo of the huge metal room made it hard to be sure. Quietly, she reached up and tried to lift the lid off one of the crates, but it didn't budge. She reasoned that it must be nailed shut but she just didn't have enough leverage to open it reaching up from her crouch. Peeking over the lid of the crate, she could see shadows dancing on the far wall behind the forest of crate stacks, the only light in the room coming from dim emergency lighting on the walls.

She slowly stood up. Keeping her eye on the shadows, she pulled at the lid. It held fast at first, but then started to give way when she wiggled it from side to side. It was almost open enough to allow her to look inside, when one of the nails squeaked its reluctance.

Bollocks!

With no time to shove the lid back down and footsteps approaching, she ducked behind the crate again and took her gun out, hoping no one would notice the askew lid. The footsteps stopped just a few feet away. Maggie peeked between two crates and saw that it wasn't a beefy workman but one of Umi's guards. Technically, one of Maggie's men, but somehow she thought the point would have been lost on him if she revealed herself.

"Clive. What is it?" Another guard called to his companion.

"Nothing, I guess. Thought I heard something."

"Relax, mate. The only things down here are us and the rats."

"I guess you're right," Clive said after a long pause. Maggie was thankful for the dim lighting—until she saw one of the rats they'd mentioned chewing on the edge of a nearby crate. She stifled her desire to jump up and empty her clip into the vermin.

"Get back over here. The others will be returning from the lab anytime, and we've still got a dozen tanks to prepare."

"Roger," Clive said before Maggie heard his footsteps heading away from her position.

Lab?

There was something bigger going on here than a simple smuggling or planned theft. Something too big for one person to handle. She'd have to come back later. With help. She eased her gun back into her waistband and slipped out the door.

Now that she was unsure of the loyalty of most of her guards, that left only one person. She hated the idea of having to owe anyone, especially the albatross, but she didn't have any choice. And regardless of her desires, she was pretty sure she knew how to get his cooperation.

UMI EDGED OUT of the darkness at the end of the hall after watching Maggie disappear around the corner. She had been right not to trust her. But there was another part of her that was impressed by the woman's tenacity. Umi had no idea what Maggie had heard while in the hold, but she could guess. Her guards were all professionals at what they did, but she was asking more of them than even she wanted to. They weren't spies, they were weapons.

The head guard, and Umi's true head of security, Mr. Morgan, stepped out into the hall just then, appearing surprised to find his employer skulking in the darkness in the middle of the night.

"Mrs. Tenabe. Can I help you with anything?"

"That depends, Mr. Morgan. Are we ready for tomorrow?" Umi asked, shuffling toward the man, who towered over her.

"We will be," he said, casting a momentary glance over his shoulder at the door to the hold. "But I've been meaning to ask you. There are nowhere near enough masks for my men."

"Is that a problem?" Umi asked.

"Well . . ."

Umi could tell this was going to be an issue if she didn't handle it right away. "How many men are we talking about, Mr. Morgan?"

"About three dozen."

"Just tell them to go up on deck and stay upwind until the all clear," Umi said, thinking of it that very moment. She wasn't even sure if that would work, but she didn't really care.

"Yes, ma'am."

"And are we clear, Mr. Morgan?"

"Crystal, ma'am."

"Good," Umi said. "Then I suggest you get back to work."

"Yes, ma'am." Morgan turned to head back the way he'd come.

"Tell me something, Mr. Morgan," Umi said suddenly.

"Ma'am?"

"What's your take on our new security chief?"

"Ms. Reynolds? She's competent. Organized. But, as you requested I've been keeping her in the dark as far as the real mission. Has that changed?"

"Not at all. I was just curious. Does she ask a lot of questions?"

"Questions? No, no more than I would if I were in her shoes. She's mostly interested in the safety of the guests as far as I can tell. Is that all?"

"Yes, thank you," Umi said. Morgan nodded and headed back into the hold.

"She can tell," a male voice with a British accent said from behind Umi. Alex lit a cigarette and stepped out of the shadows. Alex had followed Maggie when she'd left her room and reported in to Umi.

"Tell, Mr. Corsair?"

"That she's out of the loop. You need to be careful with that one."

"In what way?"

"Your money won't sway her. She did ten years in a Russian gulag, left there by her government to rot, and when she came out, all she wanted to do was prove to her bosses that she was loyal and still relevant."

"So she's not like you," Umi said. Alex took a drag on his cigarette and laughed, a deep belly laugh. His reaction surprised her.

"You should save your game for someone who gives a shit, darling. I lost my need to be relevant a long fucking time ago. The only way to get under my skin is not to pay me. And trust me, that's not a place you want to find yourself."

Umi just eyed Alex, unconcerned at his veiled threat. After all the subterfuge, backroom deals and broken promises, she actually found someone who was so open refreshing.

"You're sure she shouldn't accidentally fall overboard tonight?" Alex asked.

"Not yet. We need her for tomorrow. Once everyone's on board, you can do whatever you want to her." A darkness passed across Alex's eyes for a moment that even Umi found disconcerting, but then it was gone.

"Thanks, but I'm going to be long gone before your little party starts. At my age, I don't think it would be a good idea to hang around for the festivities." Alex smiled, then put his cigarette out on the bulkhead.

Umi smiled back at him, wondering what he would do if she told him no one was going anywhere. "Yes. Well, my men aren't going to delay her forever, so I suggest you get back to her room before she does. To be safe."

"Safe? Now, darling, where's the fun in that?"

A HALF HOUR later, Maggie eased the door to her room open and tiptoed inside. She'd been gone for what seemed like hours, thanks to those idiots up on deck. She had never seen so many people up and about this late at night before. A squad of Umi's guards had picked tonight to walk patrols between here and the hold. It had taken forever before she could slip by them.

Alex still had his back to the door and was snoring logs as she entered. She put her gun back in the drawer and slipped into the bathroom for a quick shower. Her muscles were aching, and the hot spray felt good. She was exhausted but knew she wasn't going to get much sleep for the next few days.

She tied a towel around her body before she wiped the steam off the mirror. Even with the towel on she could still see the scars—which ached more than her muscles. A swarm of healed cigarette burns dotted her breasts. Knife wounds—she honestly couldn't remember how many—decorated her shoulders and neck. Her legs ached from the bullet wounds she'd received during an attempted escape from the gulag. Her left eye still drooped slightly from the weekly beatings from the guards though the doctors assured her she was the only one who could notice.

Will he even be interested in someone who looks like this?

She shook off the familiar depression, turned off the light, and left the bathroom. She steeled herself, then padded barefoot across the room and sat on the edge of the couch. Alex woke up almost immediately.

"What is it, darling?" Alex asked, rubbing his brown eyes with the back of one hand. They blinked wide when he realized how she was dressed.

"We've got a problem," Maggie said. She told him what she'd overheard down in the hold, about the reference to the lab and tanks.

"What was in the crate?" Alex asked, sitting up with what appeared to be interest. Maggie hoped at least part of that interest was in her story.

"I don't know. I couldn't get the lid off without being seen."

"Well, couldn't the tanks have just been oxygen? We are at sea, after all."

"Maybe, but the way they talked about them—"

"And didn't I read that a huge part of Tenabe's corporation is involved with pharmaceuticals?"

"Yes, but—"

"Darling," Alex said, putting his hand on her bare leg, "I think you might be jumping the gun here, as it were. I mean, you went down there looking to find something. And you think you did, but from what you're saying, you didn't actually see anything except men working through the night. Just before a big event here tomorrow."

Everything he was saying made sense. That wasn't what bothered her—it was how fast he came up with explanations.

"So you don't want to help me," she said, somberly. "Fine." She tried to stand up, but he held her where she was.

"Now take it easy. I didn't say that. We just need to be careful. Umi Tenabe is very powerful. If we make a move—the wrong move—"

"I know, I know. God I hate that woman," Maggie said.

Alex laughed. "She can be a lot to take, that's for sure."

Maggie forced herself to smile back.

"That's better, poppet. Now, what do you need me to do?"

"First, I need you to report in to the Home Office for me in the morning. Things are going to be crazy here, and I won't have time. Tell them I strongly recommend getting some more people here, ASAP."

"Done," Alex said.

"Then while everyone's busy at the opening gala tomorrow, I need you to go down to that hold and find out what's in those crates. There are a couple of junior guards I mostly trust who I can send with you."

"Good. I'll need a lookout," Alex said. Maggie was feeling better until Alex's fingers slipped under her towel. She knew this was the price. She didn't push them away.

"You see, we do make a good team," Alex said. He reached up with his free hand and pulled her down to him. She could feel him hard and ready under the thin sheet.

There were a lot of things going through her mind as she opened her mouth against his, but one thought just wouldn't go away:

When did he meet Umi?

Chapter Fifteen

Atlantis Explorer
8:13 A.M. Local Time

THE RESEARCH VESSEL that Jonathan and Lew had choppered out to from Nagoya's Central Japan Airport flew an Australian flag, but Jonathan doubted that the ship had ever been anywhere near the Down Under continent.

The *Atlantis Explorer* was a big ship, at least two hundred feet long and stark white against the dark green-blue of the ocean and the roiling gray clouds on the horizon. According to Fahd, she was a science ship funded solely by The Custodians, but today she was really just a way station. They had been moving at high speed up until a few minutes ago, getting Lew and him as close as possible to the *Jirojin Maru* without being detected. Their communications-jamming perimeter worked both ways, so they just had to worry about line of sight. They were still several kilometers out, but they couldn't risk getting any closer.

Lew was up on deck somewhere, getting outfitted for his swim, which was starting to concern Jonathan. Lew was strong—

stronger than anyone Jonathan had ever known—but this was one hell of a long swim in brutally rough waters. Lew's military training and certification had been a long time ago, and strength or not, Lew wasn't a kid. Not that he had been showing any concern himself before they'd hurried Jonathan belowdecks for his final preparations and makeover. The only thing Lew had asked was if he could get something to eat before the swim.

Jonathan, on the other hand, had been asking questions nonstop. Which he could tell was starting to wear thin on Fahd and his people. He didn't care. If even one of the answers didn't pass his internal bullshit detector, he'd put a stop to this before anyone hit the water.

As several people dressed him, prepared his luggage, ran over his back story, and pasted a false mustache on him so he more closely matched Dr. Chris Hudson's appearance, Jonathan asked again about the swim ahead of Lew.

"I already told you, it's not so much of a swim as a ride," Fahd said, referring to the swimmer delivery vehicle, a powered sled that would drag Lew through the water. "His dive watch/computer is locked on the *Jirojin Maru*'s location. All he has to do is hang on, and he'll be there in a half an hour. Hell, if the inbound helicopter traffic is what I hear it is, he'll be on board before you are."

"*Would you relax, Mom? I've got this,*" Lew's voice said into Jonathan's head from the implant behind his ear. It was a strange sensation, but he was starting to get used to it. He was even getting used to how different Lew's voice sounded coming from the implant than as sound waves traveling through the air. It was sort of like when you listened to your own voice on a recording and heard how strange it was, but in reverse.

"Fine, but don't come crying to me when you end up in Russia," Jonathan said. Lew laughed, but everyone in the room just looked at him.

"That's not really possible, sir," a young man started to explain before Jonathan waved off the unnecessary explanation.

"Tell me again why no one is going to realize I'm not Dr. Hudson?" Jonathan said.

"We didn't just pick him at random, Jonathan. We've checked the attendees list. No one is even remotely acquainted with him. And if they've seen any pictures of him, our little makeover should stand up nicely," Fahd said, referring not just to the fake mustache but to the clothes and quick blond dye job. "Besides, it's a conference. Everyone's going to be half in the bag ten minutes after they hit the *Jirojin Maru*'s deck."

"Uh-huh," Jonathan said. He didn't like the logic any better now than he had the first time he'd heard the explanation.

"Besides, you're not here to meet colleagues or discuss the lengthening of chromosome telomeres," Fahd said. Jonathan recognized the tech-speak from his gerontology primer. Obviously, Fahd had familiarized himself with the science as well. That made him feel a little better, actually.

"Right," Jonathan said.

"Mix with the crowds, but at your first opportunity, break away and find the Picasso."

Jonathan adjusted his clothing and looked at himself in the mirror. The transformation was a little shocking. He looked ten years younger, which was amazing since he already looked years younger than he really was. It would have been great, but he also thought he looked like a complete douche bag.

He was dressed in a pink button-down shirt, open to the ster-

num, a blue blazer, and tight tan jeans, accented by a black belt
with a gold buckle and a pink handkerchief in his blazer pocket.
On his feet were black leather and suede buckled loafers, his bare
ankles showing above them. They'd hung a gold chain around his
neck with a diamond-encrusted gold pendant, put a few titanium
and platinum rings on his right hand and a watch on his left arm
that had a face the size of a pickle jar lid. His hair was blonder
than he'd expected and full of product that kept it looking to Jonathan like a haircut from the sixties. As he looked at himself, Fahd
slipped a pair of Oliver Peoples Sheldrake glasses on him. They had
thick black frames and blue-tinted lenses with no prescription.

"Perfect," Fahd said.

"This guy is a scientist?" Jonathan asked incredulously. Fahd
showed him the picture they were going by. He had to admit, the
image in the mirror was a dead ringer for the guy in the photo.

"Top of his field," Fahd said. "And he holds more patents than
IBM. It's a brave new world."

"Apparently," Jonathan said. "So what's the exit strategy?"
He had been waiting for them to tell him, but he was starting to
wonder if they even had one.

"Here," Fahd said. He took the pendant from around Jonathan's neck and pulled off the end. He showed it to Jonathan. It
was a USB drive.

"What's that for?"

"This is your ticket out," Fahd said, putting the pendant back
together. "The launches are secured, like most things on Tenabe's
ship, by electronics. Get in one and plug this in. It will unlock the
controls and lower the launch into the water. Just get far enough
away from the ship to avoid the jamming perimeter and contact
us through your implant. We'll pick you up."

"Gotcha."

As they grabbed his luggage—a ridiculous number of soft chocolate-leather bags—and headed out the door, Jonathan stayed rooted to his spot, looking at himself in the mirror.

"What is it?"

"Any way you can get Lew into the water before I get up there?"

TWO MEN IN dark blue coveralls grunted and pulled as they tried once again to get Lew's bulk squeezed into the black wetsuit. One of them swore in Greek, and the other said something in a language Lew didn't recognize. He'd already popped the zipper out of one suit. If this one didn't cooperate, he was going to be in trouble. He didn't want to think about what even a half hour in the cold water would feel like without protection.

Finally, with a joint effort, the suit squeaked up over his massive shoulders. A few inhales later, and he was safely inside his second skin. Lew felt like his muscles were being pushed deeper into his body.

"Told you it would fit," Lew said, though really, he just wanted to get this swim over with so he could get out of the thing. He hadn't been given his exit strategy yet, but he was hoping it involved a cushy helicopter.

The men helped him shoulder his way into his air tank and pulled the hood of the wetsuit up over his head. As he was once again being instructed on how to operate the swimmer delivery vehicle, Jonathan, Fahd, and a few more men in dark blue coveralls came up onto the mission deck at the ship's stern. Lew lost all focus on what he was supposed to be doing when he saw Jonathan. At first he didn't even recognize him, then despite the crush on his abdomen from the suit, Lew's belly laugh echoed out over the deck.

"Wh—what the hell are you supposed to be?" Lew managed when he stopped laughing.

"Shut up," Jonathan said.

Just before Lew could ride Jonathan some more, Lew felt the zipper running up his back split open. He would have sworn, but he was just too happy to be able to breathe again.

A few minutes later, the upper part of his ruined suit had been taken away. He stood on deck in wetsuit shorts that stopped just above his knees, naked from the waist up except for the bulky dive watch on his wrist and very aware that Fahd's men kept staring at his scars. Or, at least, he hoped they were staring at his scars.

Lew, more worried about being left out than having to endure the cold water against his naked flesh, convinced the men to forget the top and just help him on with his air tank. Jonathan joined him as the men reluctantly complied. Lew checked his regulator and nodded when he was sure it was working. He leaned his swim fins and a neoprene duffel bag holding his dry clothes, smartphone, and Custodians-supplied weapon against the sled he'd be riding. The security check on the deck of the *Jirojin Maru* was apparently too strict for Jonathan to bring a weapon, even in his luggage.

It didn't take long for Lew to feel Jonathan's stare burning into his back.

"What?" Lew finally said without turning around.

"You know what I'm going to say."

"Guys, let's give them a minute," Fahd said. With a wave of his hand, the men in the coveralls dropped what they were doing and disappeared belowdecks. "Five minutes, guys," Fahd said to Jonathan and Lew before he left himself.

"It's not that far," Lew said, pretending to fiddle with his equipment still. "I've got this."

"Yeah, so you said before," Jonathan said. Lew didn't want to look at him. Partly because of his ridiculous getup, and partly because he knew if he made eye contact, he'd have to face the fact that Jonathan was right.

"So we agree."

"Lew."

Lew continued fiddling.

"Lew."

Lew finally dropped the bag and turned around, looking Jonathan in the eye. Jonathan slipped off his blue-tinted glasses.

"You can't do this. Being hardheaded isn't going to fend off hypothermia. You're going to have to sit this one out, buddy," Jonathan said. "Besides, it's a cakewalk. George is out of the picture, no one is in danger. It's just about the painting. And look at this," Jonathan said, gesturing at the ship. "And look at me. These Custodians or whatever they call themselves may still be keeping some secrets, but it's obvious they've done their research and have everything figured out. I'll be fine."

Lew kept disagreeing, right up until the chopper sitting on the bridge deck at the bow of the *Atlantis Explorer* took off with Jonathan and Fahd in it. He kept disagreeing, but he knew Jonathan was right. Lew was sure he could make it, especially with the sled, but he'd be in no shape to do much of anything for a while once he got there.

"If it goes south, I'm going to make sure they use a picture of how you look right now for your obituary," Lew said out loud, talking to Jonathan over their implants as they flew away. He wasn't even sure if Jonathan could hear him from that distance. Not at first, anyway.

"I love you too, big guy."

Lew smiled, gave a wave, and turned around. The smile fell from his face.

Two of the larger crewmen were headed toward him, the looks on their faces making it plain they didn't have a fruit basket waiting. He wasn't sure if this was a mutiny or if something bigger was behind their actions, but for the moment he didn't have time to worry about that. Lew was half-naked and still had the heavy air tank on his back, but he didn't have a second to shed the weight. He stepped toward the approaching men, holding his hands up.

"Hey, guys, just take it easy," Lew said. One of the men pulled a small club from his belt. Easy was apparently not an option.

"We've got orders to lock you up until Fahd gets back," the club wielder said. "Come with us, or you'll feel pain."

"Have it your way," Lew said. The man lowered the club, misunderstanding what Lew was saying. When he was close enough, Lew's hands shot out, grabbing the man's neck. Then with one smooth motion, Lew headbutted the bridge of his nose. Blood sprayed his friend as the man howled for a moment before dropping to the deck. Lew relieved him of his club.

"No. Wait," the other man said, his eyes wide.

"That ship has sailed, sonny," Lew said, snapping his wrist in a whipping motion. The sound of the club cracking off the side of the crewman's head reminded Lew of an afternoon at Fenway.

"Jonny! Jonny, can you hear me?" Lew said when the last man was down, looking off in the direction the helicopter had flown. There was no response. Whatever connection they'd had was gone.

Four other crewmen suddenly flowed out the doors on either side of the forecastle crew quarters, and Lew had no more time to worry about Jonathan. He tossed the club at one of them and ran straight ahead between the two groups, jumping up onto the wall in front of him. He climbed up one level and continued on up until he was on top of the pilot house.

It wasn't for his own freedom that he was fighting, of course. Jonathan had no idea what he was flying into—*if* any of what Fahd had told them was even true. All he knew was that he had to get off this ship and help Jonathan somehow.

He ran toward the stern, working his way through the communication towers and antennas before finally jumping back down to the deck behind the pilot house. He lifted his foot to keep running but something caught the tank on his back and pulled him down. As he hit the deck, he saw a crewman had come out the back of the pilot house at just the wrong time. Rolling from his downed position, Lew took the crewman's legs out from under him. The man hit hard, and Lew was on top of him with a few forearm strikes to the side of his head before the crewman could react.

Lew got up and took a few steps but then stopped. Almost a dozen men were heading toward him from the stern. They stood between him and his goal—the equipment at the back of the boat.

Guide wires and communication cables ran from the top of pilot house to the hydrographic winch just above the stern, where these crewmen had been dressing him just a few minutes ago.

"Damn it! I need some kind of . . ." Lew looked down at the unconscious crewman behind him. He grabbed him and undid his belt, pulling it out of the crewman's pant loops. He put the belt between his teeth and climbed back up on the pilot house as the crewmen reached the deck behind him. One of them grabbed his foot as Lew was pulling himself up. Lew grabbed onto the base of one of the antennas to keep from being pulled down, kicking blindly behind him. On the third kick he made contact with something. A crewman grunted, and Lew was free again.

On top of the pilot house, Lew turned and saw that there were now two dozen crewmen coming toward him.

"Seriously?" Lew shouted at them.

He climbed a few feet up one of the antennas, swung the belt over the guide wire, and kicked off, sliding down the length of the ship with his feet lifted so the crewmen he flew over couldn't grab him. He smiled with victory until he realized his ride was coming to an end—at high speed. His instinct was to let go and roll with the impact, but with forty pounds of tank on his back, that would be disastrous at worst and damage the tank at best. The tank he needed.

Off to the starboard side was one of the two rescue launch boats, secured by taut ropes and currently covered with canvas sheets. It would burn the hell out of his hands, but he didn't have any choice. He swung his legs back and thrust them forward, letting go as he reached the swing's apex. The momentum tossed him to the point where the rope ran down to the base of the winch and tied off. He just hoped it was tied well.

Lew grabbed the rope and squeezed tight. The rope burned his palms, and he howled but held on as his body churned through the air. Finally, he let go, slamming down face-first into the rescue boat's canvas, almost bouncing right off the ship and into the water. He pulled himself up and jumped down to the deck, running the second his feet hit the metal plating.

If I can just get to the fins and sled. Then another voice in his head said what if there is no boat out there? He shook that voice away and kept going.

A few yards later, he was back where they'd tried to squeeze him into his wetsuit. He heard metal bulkhead doors slamming open behind him and more footsteps than he cared to count. His plan had to change. There was only time to grab one thing and keep running. He reached down, grabbing the swim fins and mask from the deck, as he heard a gunshot and felt something whiz by over his head. Then he threw himself over the side of the ship.

As soon as he was beneath the surface—his palms screaming from the cool relief—he swam under the ship for protection. Lew put his regulator in his mouth and took a few calming breaths, then he put his mask on, blowing out his nose to clear the water from his vision. He blinked as everything came into stark focus. On either side of the ship, tubes of bubbles shot repeatedly down into the water. Bullets. They were shooting wild, as he'd guessed they would. He slipped on his swim fins and checked the dive computer on his wrist.

He couldn't wait much longer. If the crewmen got their wits about them and threw on some gear to come after him, he was done. He swam the length of the ship, angling down as he did, then turned and followed his computer's heading. The *Jirojin Maru* was the only other thing on the water within fifty kilometers. But even if there'd been alternatives, it didn't matter. Jonathan—hopefully—would be on that ship. The crewmen trying to grab him—and the bullets, of course—was the only reason he was in the water without a full wetsuit. The long swim ahead of him was crazy, but with Jonathan possibly in the same danger as Lew, he didn't have a choice. Lew had no idea what was going on here, but there was one thing he did know—this had nothing to do with a painting.

All Aboard

Chapter Sixteen

Jirojin Maru
9:30 A.M. Local Time

AN HOUR AFTER taking off, Jonathan's chopper touched down on the deck of the *Jurojin Maru*. The flight over had only taken a few minutes, but Fahd's report of helicopter traffic had been dead-on. When they'd arrived in the vicinity, they were seventh in line. The ship wasn't the largest one Jonathan had ever seen, but it was damn close.

The horizon was already darker from the approaching storm than when they'd left the *Atlantis Explorer*, making the midmorning look like dusk. They were in for some serious chop before the day was over.

But weather conditions aside, the location was remote, to say the least. Jonathan thought it was an odd place to have a world conference on longevity. And somehow he doubted it was a coincidence.

As the rotors wound down, hunched crewmen came running over to the helicopter. They pulled the doors open and, without a word, rapidly took Jonathan's bags out. There were even more helicopters hovering overhead awaiting their turn for one of the two helipads on the deck, and the crew clearly wanted Jonathan's helicopter back up in the air as soon as possible.

Jonathan looked past the busy crewman at the frenetic activity on the deck. They were on the fore helipad, and dozens of people milled around outside. Many were obviously *Jirojin Maru* crew members or security staff, the latter identifiable by the weapons over their shoulders. But others were obviously conference guests, everyone dressed to the nines and surrounded by more baggage than most celebrities had, waiting for their turn to be taken to their staterooms.

"And when Alexander saw the breadth of his domain, he wept for there were no more worlds to conquer," Fahd said from the pilot seat.

"Excuse me?"

"Nothing. The extravagance and waste just gets to me sometimes. Anyways, when you step out, you're Chris Hudson until we meet again. Like I said, you'll do fine. Mix and mingle and play the part for a while. And whatever you do, don't lose that pendant."

Fahd had been acting strange ever since they'd left the *Atlantis Explorer*. Not that Jonathan knew him well enough to really have a baseline on his personality, but he just seemed . . . off. But of course, part of that could've been that Jonathan himself felt off being here without Lew.

One of the crewmen banged on the side of the chopper.

"*Iku jikan*," he said at first. Then, "No time. You go." Before either Jonathan or Fahd could reply, he backed away from the chopper and waved his arms up like a magician trying to levitate his assistant.

"That's my cue," Fahd said. "We'll be in touch. Have fun, Dr. Hudson."

"Right," Jonathan said, stepping out of the chopper onto the deck. The warm wind gusting from the clouds on the horizon buffeted him as he adjusted his jacket before jogging over to where his luggage had been put down.

Jonathan watched the chopper rev up, then lift off the deck. As he watched, he felt a hand gently caress his back.

"Hi, I'm Melinda. You look like you could use a drink," a raspy voice shouted over the noise of the chopper.

Jonathan turned around and looked down at about thirty-two pounds of cleavage. Her badge said "Melinda Lacie, Crystasis Foundation." She was barely over four feet tall, smelled of vanilla, hair spray, and margaritas and apparently had an affinity for spandex. Reflexively, Jonathan took one of the drinks she was holding.

"Thanks."

"You're tall," she drawled out. Her eyes seemed to be having trouble focusing. Jonathan looked past her for help but instead saw a line of similar women. They all raised their glasses to him with the same inebriated smile Melinda was wearing.

Oh boy.

Chapter Seventeen

Jirojin Maru
9:57 A.M. Local Time

MAGGIE HAD BEEN welcoming conference guests for the past two hours. She'd designated the bow heliport for all the higher-profile conference guests and was greeting them personally. She was so tired, she thought it was a miracle that she hadn't dozed off and fallen over the side of the ship by now. Especially with the wind buffeting the deck.

The sky was gray, and the wind made the clouds look like the undulating smoke from a volcano. So far the rain had left them alone, but she knew that wasn't going to last. Captain Tanaka had said they were just getting the edge of the storm but warned that could change at a moment's notice. Maggie had a crate of rain slickers and umbrellas off to the side if things shifted, but looking at it just reminded her about that huge crate down in the ship's hold.

All night—first, while clinging convincingly to Alex Corsair's sweating, naked body, and later while attempting to actually get some sleep—she'd drifted in and out of consciousness wondering what could possibly be in that crate. Or any of the crates, for that matter. She was purposely being kept out of the loop, but she felt there had to be a reason. It had to be more than the fact she was new to the ship.

Of course, part of her needed there to be a reason. Not just to her exclusion but to what Dr. Eric Norris's disconnected call had meant. They didn't have any hard facts or evidence, but Maggie had gotten a gut feeling when she's seen Norris's name on the call log. After researching his name, she was sure something was going on here besides a fun weekend in the—currently hiding— sun and a discussion of gerontology.

She was being marginalized—not only on the ship but at MI6 as well. A sensible person probably would have taken the hint and moved on, but after what she'd been through, she just couldn't bring herself to give up. It wasn't in her nature. She would always fight, buck the trends, wade upstream. And she knew there would come a time when she'd be the albatross on someone else's mission. But not today. Today she knew she was right. *Knew* it deep in her gut. And it would take a lot to dissuade her from that opinion. Even more than the disappointment she felt at that moment.

"Empty?" Maggie said into her radio when she answered Alex's hail and heard his report. "That's impossible!" A silver AgustaWestland AW119 Koala Ke chopper slowly touched down behind her. She put one finger in her ear to block out the noise.

"I don't know what to tell you, darling. I'm down here with the lid off, and it's empty," Alex said. She'd left her room while Alex was still asleep. She knew her job and could do it with the best of them—all of it—but she just couldn't stomach starting today by facing his smug, satiated gob.

She wracked her brain. How could it be empty? It had weighed a ton. Even with all her body weight, she hadn't been able to budge it. Maggie looked over her shoulder as the chopper's rotors wound down, and guards started toward the doors.

"They must have emptied it. What about the other crates? The smaller ones," she said, desperate for some sort of validation.

"They're all empty. Come and see for yourself."

"No, no," Maggie said. She didn't have time for this now. "Never mind. Did you call the Home Office? Are we getting any help?"

"I'm afraid I'm nothing but bad news today, darling. They want some proof before they allocate any more resources. They actually tried to recall me, but I fought them on it. Afraid all I can offer you is one old agent for the duration."

"At least that's something. Thanks, Alex. I appreciate it," Maggie said, walking slowly toward the chopper as a couple of diplomats from Italy stepped down to the deck.

"Wish I could have done more. What do you want me to do now?"

"The last few guests are arriving now. I'll find you when I'm done up here, and we'll figure out our next move," she said. She had to see someone else, first. She didn't know what he wanted, but Captain Tanaka had asked her to meet him in a passenger's room as soon as she was available. Problems already, and the conference had just begun. Great.

"See you then."

Maggie put her radio away. It didn't make any sense. Any of it. The Home Office would never have tried to recall him. Was he was lying? For what gain?

Maggie took two welcome bags from the ship stewards standing near the walkway to the helipad, pasted a smile onto her face, and greeted the diplomats.

"SHE DOESN'T BELIEVE me," Alex said from his seat on the huge crate he'd just lied about. He had been telling the truth about the smaller crates. They were all empty, now. "That slack you've been giving her is about to pull taut. I know you're not worried, but I'm not sure you're ready for what will happen."

"No matter, Mr. Corsair," Umi said. "In a few hours, I'll give my welcome speech, and things will be under way. She could be the most naive person on Earth or the savviest, but after that, it simply won't matter."

Alex eyed the old woman. She gave this impression of being . . . not frail, but harmless. Then when you looked at her harder—took a good, long appraisal—what lay beneath her facade peeked out. While you were assessing her, she was assessing you. If you weren't careful, you could find yourself with no escape.

"So you still want to wait," he said finally.

"Let the gas take care of her, along with everybody else," Umi said. Then she slowly turned toward him, at first it seemed because that was as fast as she could move, but Alex knew it was because everything she did was deliberate and calculated, right down to how she angled her head when she looked at you. He knew the only response was to take it, to withstand the glare. Looking away would be your worst mistake.

"What is it?" he asked.

"You've been very useful, Mr. Corsair. I've quite enjoyed seeing how your mind works, but I would have thought someone as old as you would have learned patience and economy of effort by now." She was baiting him.

"I guess I'm not a very quick study," Alex said.

"I think we both know that's not true," Umi said as she started for the door.

While he didn't show it, he was growing tired of her constant probing and evaluating. He could play that game too.

"And the crate?" Alex asked, jumping down. "Should we send it down or leave it here?"

Umi stopped in her tracks. It was the first time Alex had seen her react to something physically. She almost seemed to act her age for a moment but quickly regained her composure. She slowly turned and faced him.

"I don't care where it goes, Mr. Corsair." Umi shuffled a little closer and held his gaze. "But if that crate is ever opened again . . ." She lifted a shaking finger but seemed to regain her composure and left the thought unfinished.

"Understood, darling."

Umi took a moment to steady herself and headed back toward the door.

"And them?" Alex asked, nodding toward the two junior guards Maggie has sent down with Alex. They sat on the floor, up against the wall, their heads resting on each other's shoulders. Their haircuts, builds, and matching uniforms made them look like a couple of twin mannequins, like they weren't even real. Right down to the tight grouping of three bloody bullet holes in each of their chests.

"Do as you will," Umi said without turning around.

Alex smiled. He hated to admit it, but he liked the old bird. It would be a shame if he had to kill her before this was over.

45,000 feet

10:21 A.M.

TATSU SLOUCHED DOWN so hard and fast in her seat, her head bounced off the airplane's window shade. She sucked air in through her teeth and rubbed the side of her head to make the pain go away.

"My goodness, are you all right?" the woman beside her asked in Japanese. Tatsu's quick movements had shocked the woman so, she'd spilled her drink all over her magazine.

"I . . . I'm fine," Tatsu said. "I twitched as I was dozing off, sorry," Tatsu said with a thin smile. She apologized profusely as she helped the woman clean off her tray, staying hidden behind the seat in front of her. Eventually, the woman returned to her soggy magazine, and Tatsu said she should get some sleep while she could.

They were only an hour out from Tokyo International Airport and what Tatsu had convinced herself was karmic good luck had turned out to be just the opposite. She had hoped Per Broden and his horrific arm had taken the earlier flight and spent an hour laying over in Paris. When she hadn't seen Per in Toronto's boarding area, or anywhere else, she'd taken it as a sign she was right. But she'd been wrong.

A few minutes ago she had looked over from watching the less-than-fantastic in-flight movie and seen Per waiting his turn at the washrooms. He'd changed his clothes since she'd seen him outside the motel and shaved his head to hide his burned hair, but it was definitely him. She figured he must have been sitting in one of the sections closer to the nose of the plane, or she would have seen him before this. She was pretty confident he hadn't seen her, but even if she could stay out of sight for the rest of the flight, getting off the plane and through the airport was going to be a chore.

Tatsu peeked between the seats but couldn't see up to the washrooms from there. She leaned back and wondered why she hadn't contacted Umi directly to warn her, yet. Though she was pretty sure she knew the reason. By now, Umi no doubt thought she was dead. But more than that, it had been Umi's idea. Tatsu hadn't really dealt with those feelings, yet. She still wanted to protect Umi—after all, she'd given Tatsu so much—but she couldn't understand why Umi had been so ready to let her die. No, more than that. Had been so ready to *order* her to die.

Of course, Tatsu knew what everyone whispered about Umi: how cold she was, how heartless and merciless. But she'd never been that way with Tatsu. Quite the opposite. And after all these years, she knew it couldn't just be an act. That would take an incredible amount of guile and deception on Umi's part, not to mention an incredible amount of obliviousness on Tatsu's part. And she was nowhere near that foolish.

Am I?

Jesus, am I that easily manipulated? Has my entire life been serving an old woman who bought *me? No, no that can't be true. It can't.*

Tatsu's desire to get to Umi increased tenfold. She needed to know the answer. And she knew that she didn't have much time before there'd be no one to give it to her. But if she had to deal with Per first, she might never get to Umi or the answers she so desperately needed. *Unless . . . unless instead of protecting Nagura, I use him.*

She realized she could use Nagura to delay Per, so Tatsu could have a final few minutes with her. There'd be a price to pay, of course. Nagura was a genius, but his creations aside, he didn't have the skills to fight a flea. Tatsu thought about that for a moment. His well-being aside, Nagura had spent an incredible amount of time over the past six months with both Umi and Tatsu. And he had a keen, insightful mind. If he hadn't noticed anything manipulative in Umi's behavior toward Tatsu, anything Tatsu herself had missed in that time, chances are there was nothing to notice.

But if she had missed anything because of the misguided devotion she felt for Umi . . .

First things first. She texted Nagura and told him to meet her in the workshop behind his restaurant just before the noon show started. And to leave the back door unlocked for her. Ten minutes later, she received a text back telling her that he would and he was looking forward to seeing her. She put away her personal feelings and focused on the next problem.

Regardless of what Per had discovered at Crystasis, he wouldn't know about the workshop. He would no doubt walk in the front door of the restaurant and get the lay of the land, first. He didn't realized how tight a timeline they were on, so Tatsu would have plenty of time to get Nagura's help.

Avoiding Per wouldn't be easy, but she'd certainly done harder things. All she really had to do now was make sure she stayed out of his sight until they landed. She turned toward the window and pulled the blanket over most of her face. As she waited for the hour to pass, she found herself running conversations she'd had with Umi through her mind. She had a great memory and could remember them almost word for word. With each conversation, her conviction that Umi wasn't that self-serving got thinner and thinner.

She had to get to Umi before the gas was released. It was all that mattered, now.

Chapter Eighteen

Jirojin Maru
10:45 A.M. Local Time

THERE WERE ALMOST twice as many people mingling on the deck around the stern's heliport now, but somehow Jonathan still found himself trapped by Melinda Lacie and her friends.

"Seriously, you should come around the top deck tomorrow," Melinda said, exchanging a look with her friends as she spoke to Jonathan. "We'll be suntanning before the presentations start."

"Uh-huh," a redhead towering over Melinda at about four-foot-three, said while she worked the straw of her margarita and nodded. Then Melinda leaned up as if to tell Jonathan a secret. He reflexively leaned down.

"Au naturel."

Jonathan's eyes widened, and he snapped his head back as the women giggled. Then he felt an arm around his shoulders.

Oh, God. Now what?

"Good morning, ladies," the arm's voice said. Jonathan turned and saw that it was a man in a uniform. Above the breast was a name tag: "Captain Tanaka." Despite his Japanese appearance, he spoke perfect, unaccented English. "You don't mind if I steal Dr. Hudson for a few moments, do you?" Tanaka didn't wait for approval but steered Jonathan away from the women and over to the stairs near the back of the deck.

"Oh my God, thank you," Jonathan said. "How did you—"

"Go to your room," Tanaka said, suddenly deadly serious.

"Excuse me?" Jonathan asked, unsure of what he'd heard. The captain looked around as if trying to see if anyone could hear them.

"I'm with Fahd. Go to your room and open your luggage. Right. Now." To send his point home, the captain pushed Jonathan toward the stairs.

Jonathan looked over to where his luggage had been and saw it was gone. He'd been so distracted that he hadn't even seen anyone take it to his room. He pulled his key from his pocket, read the room number, and headed off without another word.

He should have known that The Custodians would have at least one man on board. Though it begged the question why *he* was here. And why hadn't Fahd included Tanaka in his briefing? Jonathan still thought there was something off about The Custodians. He worried that he'd bought into this whole scheme too easily. Lew and Emily's urgings had helped swayed him, but what had really sold him was the idea of Natalie's protection. That and Fahd's apprehension of Canton George. And that was the thing: If someone wanted to perfectly bring down Jonathan's defenses, those were the exact things they could do to convince him. But now with the first chance he'd had to be alone and think, it all just seemed—too perfect.

He headed up the stairs in search of his room. It only took him about ten minutes to find the large stateroom on the upper deck. He unlocked it and went in, locking the door behind him.

The room was immense, the walls paneled in a caramel oak and offset by the white wall-to-wall carpeting. A few white-upholstered chairs and couches were scattered around, but the focus of the room was the massive king-size bed in the center, which faced a huge flat-screen television on one wall. Over top of the bed on the ceiling was a round mirror. Jonathan tried to ignore that.

On the bed was his luggage. He closed the drapes behind the bed and opened one of the bags. It held more clothes in the same style as the ones he was wearing, including more loafers, all in a range of browns. He closed the bag up again and tossed it on the floor. Then he opened a smaller bag and was confused at what he saw. Inside the bag were two gas masks and a note:

"Press the Settings Button on Your Data Device."

He picked up one of the gas masks, inspected it, then put it down on the bedspread, his doubt of The Custodians' validity growing. Then he took out the data device Ryan had given him and pressed the "Settings" icon. An audio recording began playing through his implant. It was Fahd. Jonathan sat on the bed as he listened.

"Hello, Jonathan. I wish I had more time to explain everything to you, but we're coming late to this party. If you're listening to this, then you've met Captain Tanaka. Not his real name, of course, but as you've no doubt surmised, he's our man. Unfortunately, he's not really an operative. He's captained yachts before, and he was the only one we could get in there on such short notice who could work the computer systems that control the yacht. He got us a sample of the gas a few weeks ago, which was crucial, but even that was really too much for him. But I'm getting ahead of myself."

Gas? Jonathan looked down at the masks as he listened.

"First, there is no painting. The Custodians do indeed want to work with The Monarch—aka you and Lew—but your life after being a spy has nothing to do with why you're here, today."

"What the fuck?" Jonathan said. The recording continued.

"We intercepted a call from a Dr. Norris to MI6 a few weeks ago which put all this into motion. The call didn't last long and was short on details, but apparently Umi Tenabe's longevity conference was not as benevolent as it appeared. Lives were apparently in danger. The call was cut off before any more details could be revealed, but it concerned us enough to put our man in there to find out what was really going on, if anything.

"We created a—family crisis for the existing captain of the *Jirojin Maru*, which opened up the space with little time to fill it. When the real Tanaka was contacted to report for duty, we replaced him with ours.

"It wasn't long before Tanaka was able to verify Norris's call, despite the fact that Norris had apparently disappeared the same night he made the call. Tenabe wasn't trying to restart her funding of gerontology research at all. Quite the reverse. She wanted to erase every advancement her ten years of financing and support had brought about.

"But you can't just put the genie back in the bottle, not in today's world with the Internet and information sharing. When borders mean nothing, how do you contain something? Umi Tanabe's solution was elegant and horrifying—invite all the world players to a single secluded location. She couldn't erase the knowledge, but she could erase everyone who knew what to do with it."

"Oh my God," Jonathan uttered, still dealing with the fact that The Custodians were sophisticated enough to get away with monitoring calls to MI6. "She's going to kill them all."

The recording went on for ten minutes, confirming Jonathan's fear. Tanabe's plan was to get everyone in their rooms under the guise of hearing her welcome speech, then the gas canisters that her men had placed all around the ship would release their contents, killing everyone. Then the ship full of corpses would travel on automatic pilot almost a thousand kilometers south, where it would be left for the authorities to find—after several videos were "leaked" to the Internet for everyone to see. Videos telling the authorities where to find the ship and about an experiment gone wrong. There was no experiment, of course, it was all a lie concocted to ensure that the ship of corpses would be a warning to anyone who tried to unnaturally extend life. With a single act, she'd cripple the science.

Umi had no intention of sacrificing herself, apparently, planning on slipping away just before the gas was released.

"With your background and no time to get another operative out there, we knew you were our only choice. Of course, Lew's background is very different, and he wasn't suited to this kind of assignment at all, which is why I've detained him on the *Atlantis Explorer* until you get back.

"Tanaka will give you the timetable and your final instructions. Best of luck, Jonathan. I know I've put our faith in the right place."

Jonathan just stared at the data device, waiting for more information to come out of it. None did.

"This is crazy," Jonathan whispered. He was about to play the recording again when he heard a light rapping on the door.

He put the data device away and put the mask back in his luggage. He answered the door. It was Tanaka.

"I only have a few minutes before I'll be missed," Tanaka said, coming into the room and shutting the door behind him. "You listened to the recording?" he asked, taking out his own data device, which looked just like the one Jonathan had.

"Why?" It was all Jonathan could manage. "Why would she do this?"

Tanaka tapped through several screens on his device. On a final tap, Jonathan heard a click from his implant. "There, our implants are connected now," he said, putting his device away.

"Her husband," Tanaka said in answer to Jonathan's question.

"Mikawa," Jonathan said, thinking back over the notes he'd read on the plane.

"Yes. I've listened over the comms to some conversations she's had with Tatsu Koga. No real relation, but she treats like her granddaughter. Or, great-granddaughter, considering Umi's age. Umi's looking for revenge. A final act."

"Final? Is she committing suicide during the attack?"

"No, she's already dying. She's under a doctor's care. Some kind of cancer. As the gas is released, she's taking all her belongings and her closest guards and escaping to some place called Ashita. It must be close, because they're taking the submarine to get there."

"Ashita?" Jonathan said.

"Yeah, all I can tell you is the word is Japanese for *tomorrow*. Other than that, all we have is the name."

"Why didn't Fahd send in the troops to shut all this down before it got started?" Jonathan asked, but he was pretty sure he knew why.

"The defense system. The loss of life would have been on par with the gas attack. And based on our profile of Umi's dealings over the years, she would have scuttled the ship and everyone on board rather than give up. A surgical strike with a small team was determined to be the only viable option."

"Umi's profile? How long have you been watching her?"

"Not long. Only a few weeks. Their analysis was based on public knowledge and interviews with ex-employees and people she's done business with. It's patchwork at best, yes, but it's all they had."

"Great. But what good are only *two* gas masks? What's the full head count? Looked to be dozens on the heliport."

"Not counting her guards, there are ninety-seven staff and guests on board."

"Ninety-seven? Jesus. When is she releasing the gas?"

"One thirty," Tanaka said.

Jonathan checked his watch. It was almost eleven.

"Are you fucking kidding me? You've had three weeks, and you're putting a plan in action less than three hours before the attack? That's insane! Why did you wait so long?" Jonathan knew he needed to calm down, but he needed some answers more.

Tanaka flipped a latch on the upright lid of Jonathan's luggage and the insert fell out of the way, revealing two injection guns and two bottles of a yellow liquid in glass cartridges. Tanaka took one of the guns out of its Velcro straps, then pushed one of the glass cartridges into its base. It hissed when he did.

Tanaka rolled up his sleeve and injected himself.

"You're pretty trusting," Jonathan said, calming down. "How do you even know that's not just apple juice?"

"Because this isn't my first go-round with The Custodians. I've been an analyst with them for almost ten years. Trust me, if they say something, it's a fact. Now you," he said, holding the gun out.

"Whoa, whoa, hang on just a second," Jonathan said. It was too much too fast. He needed to catch his breath before he made any decision about anything. Especially about shooting something into his body. Of course, he hadn't hesitated about letting them inject a communication implant into his neck. Why had he given in to that so easily anyway? Not just given in, but convinced Lew to give in too. Had he actually missed this life that much?

And what about Natalie? Would they protect her if he backed out, assuming he even could back out? Not to mention the almost hundred people whose lives were now depending on him. The downside was just too great. It had been so long since he trusted anyone besides Lew. Then he thought about what Lew would do if he was in this situation, and he knew what he had to do. He rolled up his sleeve and held out his arm.

"Do it."

Tanaka injected him. It didn't hurt much. Tanaka put the injection gun back in the case.

"Why do we need masks if we've got the antidote?"

"The best they could do on short notice. The injection renders the poison into just a knockout gas. Without the masks, anyone who is inoculated is still out cold. Even us. "

"Hang on. There's no way you've got masks on board for everyone. Are you telling me—"

"You've got two and a half hours to inject everyone on board, or they're dead," Tanaka said. "While keeping the guards from seeing you or starting a panic, of course."

"Of course," Jonathan said. "This is nuts. It's impossible for one person—"

A knock at the door shut Jonathan up. Tanaka smiled. "I got you some help."

"Some help? Who?"

"Uh . . . I think it's best if I just show you. Go ahead and answer the door."

Jonathan looked at Tanaka and another knock sounded. With a slight scowl, he walked to the door and opened it. Jonathan felt like he'd been kicked in the gut. For a terrible second, he thought he was having a reaction to the injection, but it only took a moment to realize that wasn't what he was having a reaction to. She was older and seemed a little less soft around the edges, but that was to be expected. He could tell from the way she opened her mouth and gasped for breath that she was having a similar reaction.

"Jesus, Maggie?" Jonathan said, his chest heaving.

Maggie's eyes seemed to be welling up, but then she launched herself into the room and into his arms. They kissed hard and deep. Jonathan squeezed her in his arms, like he was trying to make her part of him. She tasted like coffee and gum. It was the best goddamn thing he'd ever tasted.

Tanaka cleared his throat loudly, bringing Jonathan back to Earth. Somehow he found the strength to break away from her and stepped back to look at her again. As he did, all the emotions of their time together on that mission came flooding back. But now there was a different look in her eyes. It had been over twenty years, but it felt like it had only been twenty minutes. And he knew that look all too well; she usually saved it for a Russian she was about to coldcock.

"Now, Maggie. Just hang on—"

Her left cross was just as powerful as ever, and it sent Jonathan rolling down onto the carpet.

"You bloody son of a bitch!" Maggie said.

"Whoa, what the hell?" Tanaka said. "Fahd said you two knew each other. And the kiss. I don't get it."

Jonathan sat up and leaned on the bed, touching the back of his hand to the bead of blood in the corner of his mouth, smiling. Now he understood the other reason Fahd had chosen him for this job.

"Oh, we know each other, all right," Maggie said, her arms crossed. "Now who the hell is Fahd?"

"Captain, I'd like you to meet my fake wife."

Chapter Nineteen

Russia, 1994

"SITREP, CANARY," JONATHAN said without taking his eyes away from his night-vision binoculars. His voice-activated throat microphone picked up his larynx vibrations and automatically transmitted them across the expanse of frozen scrub and dirt to the seemingly lifeless hunting shack almost five hundred yards away. It was too far for his liking, but it couldn't be helped. The ridge of trees where he was crouched was the closest possible cover.

"Almost done, Peddler," Maggie's response came back in his radio earpiece. "On the road in five."

"Copy that, Canary. Don't dawdle. Ivan's on his way." Jonathan actually had no idea if the Russian squad was returning, yet, but he wanted her out of there. Another sign things had gone too far, Jonathan thought.

"Copy that."

He knew that even if the troops were walking in the door, Maggie wasn't about to leave until she found what they were looking for. It had been almost three months, and this was the first opportunity they hadn't blown. He understood perfectly from a logistics point of view, it was the feeling of helplessness he hated. At this distance, if the squad that usually manned the hunting cabin-turned–listening post decided to abruptly return, by the time he covered the distance between him and Maggie, it would be too late. He kept trying to tell himself that he was just being a nervous Nellie, that other concerns were coloring his judgment, but he'd had a bad feeling in his gut since this night had started. On any other op, he would have listened to his gut and called it off, but things were different this time. He couldn't trust his instinct the way he usually did. And that scared the hell out of him.

Whitewash was a joint American/British mission to remove message codes from a listening post just across the Finnish/Russian border. They were codes the Russians didn't even know they had, yet, and the mission was meant to keep it that way. Security was light, thanks to most of the Russian forces being busy with their impending Chechen War. Two three-man Russian squads rotated shifts every two weeks. In any other political climate, the data would have been sent to Moscow for analysis months ago, but Ivan's internal strife had been Britain and America's gain.

But with the squads living in—and rarely even going outside—the cabin, their only hope for undetected access was during the shift change. A few times there had been as much as an hour when, for whatever reason, the current squad left before their replacements arrived. That's where Jonathan and Maggie came in.

Posing as newlyweds, they had been sitting across the border in a cabin for months, waiting for their chance. The cabin had a single twenty-inch television with no reception, a laser-disc player, and no discs. Now and then they'd turn on the set just to watch the snow on the screen instead of the snow on the windows for a while. Then on one of their sojourns into the nearby town,

Jonathan found a single laser disc for sale in a bin of used books—the complete *Star Wars* collection. The disc had all three original movies and a ton of interviews and behind-the-scenes documentaries. Jonathan was in heaven. Maggie hated it, but they watched that thing over and over.

By this point, there had actually already been two chances to complete their mission, but they'd missed them.

On the first occurrence, they had been in town getting supplies. To keep up appearances for their cover, they would periodically go into town and be very "newlyweddy" in public — holding hands, laughing loudly, kissing and groping in the little shops. It was typical spy craft and they'd each done it on numerous occasions on other missions with other agents. But after two months of this, the act started to become real. It broke every rule in the book, but they couldn't seem to help themselves. Nor did they care to try.

The second occurrence happened while they were slick and naked and lost in each other. They didn't even realize they'd missed a chance until much later when they were exhausted and spent. It took hours explaining—lying—to each of their handlers about what had happened and that the mission was still viable. When they'd both finally succeeded in perpetuating the lie, they'd fallen on each other again to celebrate.

It was a whirlwind romance, and, Jonathan knew, one destined for disaster.

When the current opportunity finally occurred, Maggie was the one to go in, as planned. He was there, among other reasons, because he spoke Finnish. Maggie was fluent in Russian. From the very beginning, she was the one who would have to go into the lion's den. At the time, he hadn't thought anything of it. Now, it was killing him.

"Canary, do you have it or . . ." Jonathan's transmission trailed off as he heard the unmistakable sound of a truck's gears grinding across the field. *Shit.*

"Listen carefully, Peddler," Maggie buzzed in his ear. And he knew. The second she spoke the first word, he knew. Her tone was different—resigned. They were blown.

Jonathan got up, grabbed his rifle and started running, commanding every cell in his body to ignore his training and get his ass across that field. His breath puffed in and out in steamy cold pulses under the new moon overhead. He fell into the crunchy grass and snow hard. Fighting for his wind, he jumped back up and started running again, barely fifty yards from where he'd started.

"Canary. I'm. Inbound," he managed as he ran. "Find a defensible corner. Just keep firing. I'll shoot from here and draw their—"

"Peddler."

"—fire. Should be. Able to draw—"

"Jonathan, don't."

"—at least. One of them. Out into. The—"

"AGENT HALL, STOP!"

Jonathan stopped dead at the command, panting, his lungs on fire, his legs aching. He wasn't even halfway.

"Maggie," was all he could manage. He knew she was right. He tried to blink his eyes clear as he brought the binoculars up and looked at the tinted pale green horizon. It was the replacements. Five of them, this time. They were laughing and pushing each other like boys on a playground. He could just make out a bottle being passed around. They didn't know she was there, yet. She had maybe two minutes before they tired of the rough-housing and went inside. If she was lucky, a minute after that before they found her. Then they'd be out of the cabin and searching the area for him. He barely had enough time to run back to cover.

He didn't move.

"I knew the risk. Not your fault, baby," Maggie said, her voice would have sounded strong to most people—to him a few months ago. But now he knew her inflections. She was terrified. So was he, for her.

"Jesus, Mags," Jonathan said, frustration making him punch his hip as he paced back and forth. More than half of him wanted to keep running toward her, but he knew what she was doing. She was letting herself be taken so he could get away. He couldn't let what might be her last act be in vain.

"We'll always have Hoth," she said. Jonathan laughed, despite himself.

"Maggie, I—" A door slam rattled in his ear, and he knew they were inside the cabin.

"Go!"

He turned and ran, ran hard. It would be a miracle if he didn't catch a bullet in the back. What did hit him hurt more. His earpiece buzzed one final time.

"I love you too."

Chapter Twenty

Jirojin Maru
11:15 A.M. Local Time

BREATHING SO SHALLOWLY that he was on the verge of passing out, Lew Katchbrow reached up from the murky depths toward the rectangle of light above him. It shimmered like a mirage, and it wouldn't have surprised Lew at all if it turned out to be a figment of his waterlogged imagination. With what little energy he had left, he kicked and slowly rose toward the light.

After things turned out not to be at all what they appeared on Fahd's ship, Lew had feared that the *Jirojin Maru* might not have even had a moon pool, but there it was. Or, at least, he hoped it was there. As he rose, the rectangle grew. The moon pool was about the size of an in-ground backyard swimming pool. Shimmery colors and objects came into focus as he got closer, various cranes and hoists seeming to be the equipment of the day.

And then, finally, his water-wrinkled hand broke the surface and felt air for the first time in hours. With shaking limbs, he managed to pull himself up and over the lip of the moon pool onto the grating of the walkway around the edge. Lying facedown, he reached up and pulled the rebreather out of his mouth and the mask off his head. He lay there panting for a while, only finally moving because he started violently shivering.

They were right, Lew thought. Half a wetsuit *was* a dumb idea.

He kicked off his fins and shouldered his way out of the oxygen tank before trying to stand up. He fell right back down. Back when he'd first been trained, he would have jumped up and been ready for another dive by now. But there were just too many years between to think about anything except getting warm and finding Jonathan.

Using the ship's bulkhead wall, he pulled himself up to his feet, steadying himself for a minute until the room stopped swirling.

"Excuse me," someone said behind him, tapping his shoulder.

Crap. Busted five seconds after getting on board.

Lew turned around, trying to think up an excuse for why he'd just climbed aboard a ship in the middle of nowhere, but his worries were allayed when he saw a well-dressed black man swinging a pipe at his head.

"Wait!"

The pipe slammed into the side of Lew's head, and he drowned in blackness.

"HANG ON," JONATHAN said, tapping behind his ear and turning away from the others as if it would help him hear better. It was crazy, but he could have sworn he heard Lew for a second. *Wait. He'd said wait.* Was that his imagination, or was his conscience taking on Lew's persona to get his attention? When almost a minute passed with no other sound, Jonathan turned back to Maggie and Tanaka, who were looking at him like he'd just spoken in tongues.

"You all right?" Maggie asked.

"Yeah, yeah, sorry. Thought I heard someone in the hall. You were saying," Jonathan said, covering. He didn't feel like explaining who The Custodians were or that he had a communication implant in his neck. From the look on Tanaka's face, he didn't want that either.

They had told Tanaka a very brief version of their mission in Russia. Neither one of them really wanted to relive the finer details. Jonathan had been wondering how Tanaka knew Maggie, but as it turned out, he didn't, really. Once she'd established her cover on the *Jirojin Maru* as the new security chief, they'd only had passing contact. Fahd was the only reason Tanaka knew anything about Maggie and Jonathan's history as spies—information exchanged before the communications blackout had gone into effect.

"So she was captured?" Tanaka said. Jonathan and Maggie looked at each other.

"Let's stay in the present," Jonathan said.

"This Fahd is your handler?" Maggie said, obviously agreeing with Jonathan. Tanaka had told Maggie that they were with the CIA. She seemed to be buying it. Jonathan hated lying to her, especially after all this time, but it was just more expedient.

"Yeah," Jonathan said. He needed to get things moving. He understood now why Fahd had sent him in. They needed Maggie on their side, and they didn't have time to convince her. Fahd was relying on Jonathan's history with Maggie to get her on board in the shortest possible time. Having her help was a gift, but if he was going to get almost a hundred people inoculated before the gas was released, they didn't have time for long-winded explanations. "You're back with MI6?"

"Yes," she said.

"Okay, I'm going to assume you were sent in here for the same reason Tanaka was, Dr. Norris's phone call. Fahd sent me in because of what Tanaka found out." Jonathan quickly told Maggie what Tanaka had just told him. Then he opened his suitcase and took out a mask and the injector gun, holding them up in front of him.

"We've got less than two hours to inject every person on board, or they're all dead."

"YOU'RE NOT SURPRISED?" Jonathan asked.

"No, not after what I've been seeing around the ship," Maggie said. She explained about the hold below where she'd found all the crates and heard guards talking about tanks.

Jonathan stepped forward and injected Maggie, partly because he wanted her protected, but he was also curious just how far she trusted him.

"Thanks," she said quietly.

"You need to be careful," Tanaka said. "If you double-dose someone, you're going to do Umi's job for her."

"What?" Jonathan said, shaking his head. "Look, this is never going to work. We'd be lucky to get half the ship done without a repeat, if that."

"So half the people still die? No, that's unacceptable," Maggie said. Jonathan could tell she felt the same way about that as he did. It wasn't an option. Tanaka, on the other hand, was more open-minded.

"They're still good odds. Half the ship saved is still over fifty people alive," Tanaka said.

"No. It's almost fifty people dead," Jonathan said, tossing the injector gun on the bed. "You might as well walk around and shoot fifty of them in the head. We need to come up with an alternative."

"And fast," Maggie said. They only had ninety minutes, now.

"Umi's going to have the guards escort everyone to their rooms at twelve thirty you said," Jonathan said to Tanaka.

"Yes, that's the plan. At first, I thought it was because there wasn't anywhere on the ship big enough to hold everyone for her welcoming speech, but now I think it has to do with the gas. It would just dissipate on the open, larger decks. The canisters are probably set up to flood all the rooms. More efficient," Tanaka said.

"Right, and as soon as her speech is over, she's going to release the gas. That's not enough time if we wait for them to be in their rooms before we go door-to-door to inoculate them. We need to get them into their rooms sooner. Then we might have a chance of getting through the ship without killing anyone," Jonathan said.

"You mean killing any passengers. Umi's guards are going to be everywhere making sure the guests stay put," Tanaka said. "Until they realize they don't have enough masks, and Umi isn't letting them off the ship either.

"How many guards have masks?" Jonathan asked.

"From what I can tell, less than ten," Tanaka said.

"Great, add another forty corpses to the body count," Jonathan said. "But before they realize they're doomed, they're going to make inoculations even harder to complete."

"Unless they're busy elsewhere," Maggie said. Jonathan looked at her, recognizing the gleam in her eye.

"You got something?" he asked.

"Maybe. But first things first," she said, looking at Tanaka. "She'll never listen to me, but she'll listen to you."

"Huh? Now, wait. I told you, I'm an analyst, not an operative. The only reason I'm here is because I could pilot the ship, and I was close. What you're talking about—"

Maggie put her hand on Tanaka's shoulder. "Today everyone is an operative. Besides, look at all the information you've gathered on your own."

"That's different. All the intercoms go through the communications array on the bridge. All I did was push some buttons and listen."

Jonathan put his hand on Tanaka's other shoulder. "I got news for you buddy, that's called being a spy."

"Goddamn," Tanaka said. He looked around the stateroom like he was trying to find a secret door that would take him out of this nightmare. When he didn't find one, he sighed. "What do you want me to do?"

Jonathan straightened his captain's hat. "You're the captain. Just be the captain."

ALEX CORSAIR HAD been ordering Umi's guards around for months, both on the ship and when he took some of them down to Ashita with him, so when he asked three of them to come with him, they obeyed without question. He led them down into the hold, where minutes ago he'd carried the intruder's limp body. Unconscious, the huge, half-naked man weighed more than Alex could have imagined. If not for the exoskeleton suit, he never would have been able to carry him on his own. Which would have meant providing explanations to what he considered expendable henchmen. Thankfully, the body was neatly tucked into Umi's huge crate, the lid once again securely in place.

"That one," Alex said, pointing at the crate. "Mrs. Tenabe wants it taken down immediately. You'll need the exoskeleton suits."

While they donned their strength-enhancing rigs, Alex lighted a cigarette and thought about what he'd seen in the crate. He'd looked in it before, of course, but it was still a wonder to see them again. No wonder Umi wanted it kept sealed, he thought.

Though Alex was paid generously, he'd also served Umi well over these past few months. His expertise in the intel community had been invaluable, and unlike Tatsu, there was no explanation needed when she wanted him to be ruthless or deadly. But now that his usefulness was no longer required, he could already feel Umi moving on and cutting him out of the loop. He was starting to see how Maggie must feel, but unlike her, he wasn't about to just sit and take it. First, he'd have a little fun, then he'd take care of business. While he wouldn't be there to see it, that brute's popping out of the crate in front of everyone down there, revealing her darkest secrets, would be his pièce de résistance. Unless the idiot died in the box. He'd hit him pretty hard with the pipe. No matter—when she saw the crate down there, it would have the same effect.

With the aid of the suits, it only took the guards ten minutes to get the crate loaded on the submarine in the moon-pool room. Alex ordered them to take it down, then get back as soon as possible. He watched as the huge crane and winch moved the sub over the water and lowered it into the sea. A few minutes later, and the sub was gone.

"Morons," Alex said, tossing his cigarette into the moon pool. His prank in place, he turned his attention to fleeing the ship before all hell broke loose.

Chapter Twenty-one

IF THE OTHER staterooms were luxurious, Umi's suite was palatial. The treasures decorating the ten-room space were alone worth millions. But they were just things, she didn't even see them anymore when she moved from room to room. And since losing Mikawa, the place just seemed incredibly empty. She didn't even like being there anymore, instead spending most of her time in her tiny office several decks down. But today was different.

Umi struggled, but with the aid of a chair, she knelt before her antique bamboo bookcase. On the wall over the bookcase, above her eye line even when she was standing, was her Shinto shrine. She thought most religion of any sort was nonsense, but Mikawa hadn't. They'd always had a shrine in their homes around the world, but Umi had just viewed them as knickknacks.

Above this shrine, however, she had placed a picture of Mikawa. In an ornate box at the base of the shrine were a few of Mikawa's ashes. And on a clean white plate were a few squares of chocolate, Mikawa's favorite food. Her eyes welled, and a tear snuck out of her control and ran down her wrinkled cheek. She missed Mikawa so much.

"It won't be long, my love," she whispered. "We'll be together soon. But there is much to do first."

Umi knelt in silence for a few minutes, her knees aching, but she ignored the pain. She thought of happy times with her lost love. Simple things like having her staff prepare a wonderful dinner, then dismissing them so it was just the two of them.

Her thoughts were interrupted by a rapping on her door. She tried to ignore it, but it repeated harder and faster. Finally, a voice accompanied the intrusion.

"Mrs. Tenabe? It's Captain Tanaka. I need to see you immediately. It's important."

Umi struggled to her feet, brushed her slacks clean, and went to the door. As she walked, she swayed with the ship. *The storm's getting worse,* she thought.

"What is it, Captain? What couldn't wait?"

"I . . . I just wanted you to know that I've ordered the guards to take the passengers to their rooms now," Tanaka said.

"*You* ordered? Since when do you order anything, Mr. Tanaka?"

"Yes, I know. It was a little presumptuous of me. But since they were going to be taken there anyway soon, I thought it prudent," Tanaka said, swaying slightly in the hallway. "As you can see, because of the storm, there's a safety issue."

"Fine. Just clear it with Mr. Morgan."

"Yes, ma'am," Tanaka said.

"And Mr. Tanaka, let's be clear. You don't order anything on this ship without checking with me first. Understand?"

"Yes, ma'am. Apologies."

"Oh, and tell Mr. Corsair to contact me if you see him."

"I will, ma'am."

Umi closed the door. When she was alone, she allowed her disappointment to show. With everyone in their rooms, there was no longer a need for the pretense of a speech. She had worked hard on what would have been her final speech. It would have been a fitting cap on her career, but now Tanaka's concern for the passengers had taken that away from her.

Some people are so selfish.

11:35 A.M.

"I THOUGHT YOU said the storm was moving away? How did you convince her it was getting worse?" Jonathan said to Tanaka into a radio Maggie had gotten for them from the armory. The radio was for show so they didn't need to explain their implants to Maggie. And since Maggie didn't have an implant, the radios were useful, but the gun that sat snuggly in his waistband made him feel better as he sat on the edge of the bed in his stateroom.

"You said be the captain. I set the automatic pilot to be a little . . . choppy," Tanaka's voice said, sounding positively elated.

"Nice," Jonathan said. "All right, head back to the bridge and stand by."

"Roger."

"Well, that's step one. It's up to you now. Care to share how you plan to thin the guards out?" Jonathan said to Maggie.

"A girl's got to have her secrets," Maggie said. "Oh, and I need this." She took the second injector off the bed.

"You're the boss," Jonathan said.

"And don't you forget it," Maggie said with a smile, then headed for the door.

"Listen, Mags," Jonathan said. He hadn't even meant to talk about this now, it just sort of slipped out while he was looking at her.

"Don't," Maggie said without turning around. But she didn't leave.

"I thought you were dead. You have to believe me. I need you to know. I tried, but no one would tell me anything. I . . . I thought you were dead."

Silence dragged out as they both stood there. Finally, Maggie turned and looked at him, her eyes moist.

"I was."

11:40 A.M.

"You burk!" Alex cursed at the idiot who had sabotaged the launches. It was the last one, and they had all been wrecked, their instrumentation smashed to bits. Most likely that Morgan bastard, Alex thought. He probably put one of those exoskeleton suits on and played whack-a-mole with the dashboard controls. Whoever had done it, had also punched bowling-ball-sized holes in the hull. And with no choppers on board, Alex was well and truly trapped.

The old cow really doesn't want anyone escaping her gas, Alex thought.

He had a mask back in his cabin, so he could survive the attack, but then what? Get caught on board with over a hundred dead bodies? The other option was to go down in the sub with everyone else, but the idea of being trapped on the bottom of the ocean did little to entice Alex.

He had his money, and now he just wanted to go spend it. And that meant getting off the ship. But how? He'd always had the famous Corsair luck keeping him safe through his long career, never taking even one sick day from injury. No matter how tight the spot he got into, he always found a way out. But where was that luck now?

"*Corsair-san?*"

Alex spun around, stopping just shy of pulling his gun and shooting. A steward stood on the deck looking comical in his white uniform.

"What is it?" Alex said, calming himself. Then when the steward didn't respond, he repeated the question in Japanese.

"Miss Reynolds is looking for you. It's rather urgent. She said that you could find her in Hold C in the control room." With his message delivered, the steward bowed and turned to leave.

"What's the hurry?" Alex asked.

"I don't want to miss the speech. I have to get back to my quarters."

"Right," Alex said, knowing the steward and the rest of the ship staff didn't have a single mask between them. "Say, how did you find me?"

"Miss Reynolds sent out ten of us across the ship to find you." Alex nodded, and the steward bowed again, then hurried away.

Alex smiled. He was pretty sure he knew what Maggie wanted. Hold C was a smaller, rarely used hold. Nice and quiet. Practically romantic. But he'd have to hurry. She was a great shag, but she wasn't worth dying for.

Chapter Twenty-two

Tokyo
11:45 A.M. Local Time

IF GOD WERE a mechanic, Tatsu supposed that this is what creation would have looked like. Dozens of limbs hung from the ceiling of the warehouse-sized workshop. Some shone in gold and silver high-polished finishes, some were duller grays and blacks, and others were even dressed in eerie analogues for human flesh. They were in varying degrees of repair—some sparkling and new, others worn and lightly dented. Some were demolished—nightmares of gashes and gouges ripped into them—most still slick with the fluid of defeat. Many of the latter were sticking out of a huge barrel in the corner of the workshop, like a futuristic bin of baguettes.

None of this bothered Tatsu. They were just machines and parts, but what did bother her were all the heads. They were lined up along the wall behind several of the tables scattered with tools and electronics, seeming to stare at her accusingly. *Why weren't you here to help us?*

In her earlier visits, it had bothered Tatsu that there didn't appear to be any torsos around. She'd learned later that the torsos were still in service, either in the restaurant show or in various robot battle competitions around the world. Nagura would just strip the damaged limbs or heads off and switch them for new or repaired ones, sending the units right back into service as if no battles had ever occurred.

Tatsu had envied that.

And then she saw him, and her heart fluttered slightly—or maybe an organ a little lower did. Nagura was hunched over a workbench in the corner, working on a disassembled head with a soldering iron, wisps of thin, blue smoke rising up into the air every now and then. She remembered months ago when she'd first met Nagura. From Umi's description of him, Tatsu had expected him to be almost troll-like, looking close to the eye engineer in *Bladerunner,* but nothing could've been further from the truth. Nagura was beautiful—tall, with jet-black hair, strong features, and a well-trimmed body. Just the way God should look, she thought.

"Tatsu!" Nagura yelled when he saw her standing in the entrance of his shop. He put away his tools, wiped his hands, and came running over to her. Her breath caught as he threw his arms around her. "It's so good to see you! I was so excited when I got your text."

"And you, as well! How's the restaurant business?" she asked, trying to sound as blase as possible. She was sure he'd noticed how long she'd lingered in his embrace. And how she kept staring at the healing burn marks on the side of his face.

"Wonderful! I wasn't sure how I'd like it, but I think I could do this for the rest of my life. The looks on the faces of the visitors as they watch the shows is so gratifying."

Nagura had created the robotic equivalent of the Medieval Knights restaurant franchise. While people sat in the restaurant and ate, his robots performed and fought in front of them. People came from all around the world to see the show.

"This is all possible because of Mrs. Tenabe, of course. I'll never be able to thank her enough," he said, as Tatsu followed him deeper into the workshop. Then his face seemed to drop slightly, and the brilliant smile that had been there shrank. "I'm still devastated over what happened."

"We all are," Tatsu said. "But you shouldn't feel bad. You did what you were supposed to. Your creations matched the specs supplied to you to the letter. The fault didn't lie with you." She had told him pretty much the same thing every time she'd seen him since the tragedy, but it didn't seem to help anymore.

"Still. How is she? She hasn't changed her mind, has she? Because I'd be happy to—"

"No." Her answer was abrupt, but it was all that needed to be said. And her tone made it plain that she didn't want to talk about it.

"Of course." Nagura said, then, after a moment, his smile was back where it belonged. "Now, you didn't come here to chitchat, I'll bet. What can I do for you?"

"We're in a bit of trouble, and we don't have much time," Tatsu said.

"We?" Nagura said.

Tatsu quickly told Nagura about Per—a watered-down version, of course. She'd managed to avoid him at the airport and grab a waiting taxi, but she had no idea if he was here yet or not.

"My goodness!" Nagura said when she was done. "What can I do?"

"I need you to delay him. I've got a chopper waiting to take me to the *Jirojin Maru*. I just need time to get to it without his follow-ing. But you need to be careful, Nagura. This man is dangerous," Tatsu said though she knew she was downplaying the danger. It was instinct and the right call to achieve her goal, but with everything she'd experienced in the past few days, it made her feel awful.

"Consider it done," Nagura said, picking up a remote-control unit off the workbench. "And don't you worry about us, we'll be—careful," Nagura said. He worked the remote and one of his battle-bots rolled out, wielding a chain saw for an arm.

THE RUNWAY WAS over fifty feet long, lined on either side by makeshift fences of thick chains, meant to give a sense of danger and foreboding. Behind the chains were three tiers of glass and chrome tables festooned with confetti, half-eaten sushi, and multicolored glow sticks that patrons waved in an effort to be part of the show. Over every inch of the walls were huge television screens blasting flashing colors and dazzling images into the restaurant.

Crisscrossing the ceiling—some stationary and some running on tracks—were every color and kind of flashing, strobing, and spotting lights. Set into the corners of the ceiling were massive speakers that blasted patrons with decibels of driving pop music and electronic beats, in case they had any awareness left after the light shows got through with them.

Per found it all annoying but sat stone-faced, even raising the glow stick in front of him to try to blend in with the huge crowd.

Every few minutes, a new act would roll out of the curtain on one side of the runway. They'd perform their part of the after-noon's show, passing in front of the dining audience, then exit through the curtain on the opposite end of the runway. As far as Per could tell, the theme was a combination of sex and robots. Every attraction found some way to incorporate several mostly naked women, who somehow found a way to decorate what little clothing they wore—bikinis, thigh-high leggings and headgear—with neon rope lights and flashing strobes. From what he could discern, half the robots were actually performers in robot costumes. The other half—Per's kindred spirits—were actual robots, some humanoid but most platforms, devices, and ridiculous creatures sprung from Japanese culture.

What little interest Per had had in the show passed when he noticed the tall, dark-haired man in the corner staring at him. When the man called a few of the larger bouncers over and whispered to them while looking at Per and pointing, that was all he could take.

The next attraction rolled out. It was another huge platform decorated like a Matisse nightmare. Sitting atop the platform and driving it with a joystick was a young woman who Per thought looked like some sort of video-game sex worker. Hanging on both sides of the platform were two performers in shiny silver robot costumes approximating the Cylons in *Battlestar Galactica*, their big blocky heads bopping left and right to the music. They hung on to the platform with one arm and waved neon strobing swords in their free hands at the audience, who howled and waved their glow sticks in response.

As the platform stopped in front of his table to perform their antics, Per took the opportunity, stepping up on his table and vaulting over the chain fence in a single motion. People screamed, some laughed, but most used their phones to capture this new part of the show. To Per's surprise, the performers just played into it. One of the robots let go of the platform and started to dance with Per. Then he realized what the performers were doing. They were trying to occupy him until the bouncers arrived.

Per reached up on the platform and pulled the girl off, tossing her on the floor. The tone of the audience changed from elation to confusion, some of them starting to stand up themselves. Before she finished rolling away, Per was in the driver's seat. Only ten feet away, the bouncers were yelling in Japanese and waving for him to get down. Per ignored them, but the audience didn't. Others stood and several started talking amongst themselves and heading for the exit.

A hand grabbed Per from behind. Without looking, Per knew it was the third performer and reached up with his robotic arm, tossing him not only off the platform, but over the chain fence and onto a table in front of several customers who hadn't figured things out yet. That sparked everyone to life, realizing at last that this was not part of the show. In the next moment, everyone jumped up screaming and fighting for the door.

Per grabbed the joystick and slammed it forward. The platform took off with surprising speed, mowing down the bouncers, who had no chance to get out of the way. And he kept going.

A few seconds later, with people tossing glow sticks and sushi at Per, he blasted through the curtain at the other end of the runway and left the sensory overload of the show behind him. It took his eyes a moment to adjust to the dim backstage. In that time, another two bouncers showed up and managed to pull Per off the stationary platform. Per stayed on his feet and blocked their blows before he delivered strikes of his own. Per saw the tall man in the corner of the backstage area watching.

Enough foolishness.

He swung his robotic arm back and forth, knocking the

bouncers down and out. Per looked down and saw a gun in a holster under one of the unconscious bouncer's jackets. Per grabbed it and headed for the tall man, whose eyes were still wide from watching Per's attack.

"Nagura! Don't move!" Per shouted as he marched toward him.

Of course, Nagura immediately turned and ran through a door marked "Private."

Per followed.

He found himself in some sort of workshop. He ignored the robotic parts hanging around him and searched for his quarry. Per moved up and down the aisles between the tables, looking under them and swinging the gun around each corner. Suddenly, there was movement behind him. Per spun around and was facing two battle robots advancing on him.

They were each about five feet tall and designed to take pieces off other equally hardened robots. Human flesh would not be a problem. One had a chain saw for an arm, and the other had a spinning radial saw swinging back and forth on a pendulum coming out of its chest.

Robotic arm or not, Per couldn't take on both of them at once without ending up with a need for many more replacement parts, so he fired a few shots at one. The bullets sparked off its metal body and did little else. Per retreated around the corner.

A slamming noise behind him made him spin around. Another robot, this one with swords for arms and another sword sprouting from its chest, was taking turns stabbing each of them into the ground in front of it. Chips of the hardwood floor flew up into the air. And it was moving toward him.

Per turned away and calmly thought. These weren't self-driven robots, they were machines that needed someone to control them.

Nagura, no doubt. Per scanned the back of the workshop and saw something sticking up and moving above one of the workbenches. He realized it was the end of an antenna.

Per looked around the workshop, then up at the robotic limbs and appendage weapons sticking out of the suspended grating overhead. The grating was attached to the ceiling by metal guidewires collected into a single pulley. As the three deadly machines moved in on his position, Per swung the gun up and emptied the clip into the pulley. When the gun's hammer clicked against nothing, the limbs were still hanging in place, though swinging back and forth. The pulley was ruined but somehow still hanging on.

Per jumped out of the path of the stabbing swords, grabbed one of the robot heads off the bench and, using his robotic arm, hurled it at the pulley as hard as he could. The head exploded in shards and rained down. And then, finally, the guidewires snapped out of the pulley and all of the limbs and weapons slammed down behind the workbench where Nagura was hiding.

After a howl, the three attackers on either side of Per fell silent. When he was sure they were dormant, he stepped over them and headed for the workbench. Coming around the corner, Per saw his carnage. Nagura was fighting for breath. A jagged sword had pierced his leg, and blood slowly oozed out onto the floor. That was survivable. But a mace with razor-sharp points had impaled Nagura through the middle of his chest. He didn't have much time left. Per knelt beside him and looked at the wounds, tilting his head to the side, momentarily fascinated by the damage.

"Do you speak English?" Per asked.

Nagura nodded. "Y . . . yes."

Per reached down and put his hand on the jagged sword piercing Nagura's leg. "Tell me about Dead Lights."

I SHOULD HAVE killed Nagura, Tatsu thought as she sat in the chopper and waited for takeoff.

The thought shocked Tatsu. It came from a part of her brain she didn't want to use anymore. Ever since she killed Hank back in Toronto, her mind had been constantly churning through all the things Umi had asked her to do over the years. Not the least of which was kill herself.

In hopes that Umi hadn't had time to notify anyone else of her supposed demise, Tatsu had used the normal transportation channels and called for a helicopter. It had taken some time, but when it showed up on the roof of one of Umi's buildings on the east side of Tokyo, she knew she'd been right.

As the pilot filed their flight plan, she relaxed, knowing that soon she'd be on her way back home. Home. She found it a little odd to think of the *Jirojin Maru* as home, but that's what it was.

Logically, killing Nagura made perfect sense. He was a loose end. But Tatsu knew that in a few hours it wouldn't make any difference. She was one of the few people who knew Umi's endgame. Only her, Alex Corsair, and Mr. Morgan knew what was coming. And Dr. Reese, assuming he was still alive. Besides, she was the one who had nicknamed the things Dead Li—

Her thoughts were interrupted as someone yanked the door to the chopper open. Tatsu turned to see who it was.

It's not possible.

"Room for one more?" Per said as he got in and closed the door, the gun in his hand keeping Tatsu and the pilot pinned to their seats.

Where's Nagura? And more importantly, what does Per know? As terrible as it was, her first thought—her instinct—had been exactly right. If she'd killed Nagura, Per would've been running around Tokyo in vain. But Nagura knew the transportation channels and had no doubt pointed Per right to her.

"I want you to understand something," Per said. "*You* killed your friend. The same way you'll kill the pilot if you don't tell me exactly what I want to know. I'm a reasonable man . . ."

"Tatsu," she said. There was no point in hiding any longer.

"I'm a reasonable man, Tatsu. But I will not be deterred. I am going to find out what Dead Lights means. That is a fact. You have no control over that," he said, leaning in until the barrel of the gun was only inches from Tatsu's face. She could still smell the burned gunpowder of its recent firings. "But you can control *how* I find out."

Tatsu's mind raced. Her options were few. She could achieve Umi's last request—and protect her—by forcing this man's hand and taking a bullet. But he wouldn't stop there. What he'd just said wasn't hyperbole—she could tell that from his deeds and the look in his eyes. At the very least, the pilot would die. More likely, Per would torture both of them for information, only letting them die when he was sure they weren't useful anymore.

"I can see you're trying to decide how to react. Maybe this will help you; my employer hired me to kill you. I could have done that back in Toronto."

"Why didn't you?" she asked.

"Because I don't care what he hired me for. It was just a way for me to get access to resources I needed. Resources to help me find out what "Dead Lights" means. Nagura didn't know, or if he did, he didn't tell, but I highly doubt that. Tracking the missing Dr. Reese was again just a way to find what I wanted. I don't care what happened to him. I'm telling you all this because I want you to be fully aware that what happens next is up to you. I want to be clear about what I want. I know you're the Dead Lights bomber. What I don't know is if you even know why you were doing what you were doing."

Is he actually being honest?

"Why do you need to know what 'Dead Lights' means so badly?" she asked.

"Call it . . . a personality quirk. The reason doesn't really matter, does it?"

"I suppose not, no."

While they spoke, she continued to wrack her brain for a solution. She could try to fight him, but in these close quarters, she didn't have a chance. And again, she and the pilot would die. She wondered why she cared so much about the pilot. She didn't even know his name. He was just one of the thousands of people who worked for Umi. But maybe that was the point. It wasn't who he was but what he represented. If she was really going to succumb to Umi's bullying, she'd wait until they were in the air, then kill the pilot, in turn killing them all. That was her instinct talking again. But she was more than her instinct. She wasn't just a thought-less animal, she had a mind and she could reason and think—she could choose.

So she did.

"I do know what 'Dead Lights' means. And I can even show them to you."

"You . . ." For the first time, Per showed emotion. He was even at a loss for words.

"But the only way I'll do that is if you help me. I need to get to Umi Tenabe on the *Jirojin Maru*—the ship where the conference is being held—before . . . before 4:45 P.M.," Tatsu said, only partially lying. If she was right about Umi, Tatsu was going to need help getting to her. Help getting through the guards and getting past Mr. Corsair and Mr. Morgan. If they didn't get to the ship by 1:30 P.M., Umi wouldn't be there. But it was a way station they had to use to get to where Umi would be.

"Deal," Per said. "Your friend told me about this Umi—what he did for her and what happened. If true, it's a remarkable story. I'm looking forward to meeting her. And Mikawa, especially."

Jesus, Nagura told him everything! Now she knew for a fact he was dead. There was no other way Per could know what he obviously knew.

"I don't think meeting Mikawa would be such a great idea," Tatsu said, a quake and underlying warning in her voice. They were going to have to be in Mikawa's vicinity to get to Umi, that was unavoidable, but she didn't want to think about that right now. And she didn't like the way she was starting to think of that . . . *thing* . . . as Mikawa. That was only partly right. Mikawa— the Mikawa she had known—was dead. She'd prefer it if he stayed that way.

Per put the gun away, and, a few minutes later, the chopper lifted off and rose into the air. After swinging along the coast, it banked and headed out to sea. Tatsu looked at the afternoon sky in front of them, the dark, roiling clouds seemingly readying themselves for something tumultuous. Tatsu did the same.

Chapter Twenty-three

Jirojin Maru
12:38 P.M. Local Time

WITH THE TRAP set, Maggie hunkered down in the shadows of the control room of Hold C and waited. Thanks to Tanaka's intel on the number of masks, she knew that all but a half dozen guards were destined to die with everyone else on the ship. After gathering the ship's staff in the dining room, she had injected them all and given them a final assignment.

At least *they* listen to me, Maggie thought.

She'd sent all but ten of them out to find the unlucky guards and tell them Mr. Morgan wanted to see them in Hold C for a final briefing before the speech. It was risky, but she didn't have a choice. The guards wouldn't have responded to the request if she used her own name. Even the two junior guards who did listen to her had disappeared though now she had a pretty good idea what had happened to them.

Hold C was more than just a hold. Months ago it had been redesigned with automatic locks, a surveillance system, and a control booth with a separate entrance. The control booth had a wall of glass allowing the occupants to observe what was happening in the hold. Maggie didn't know why it had been renovated, but it made the perfect stage for her deception. She checked her watch. Jonathan should be well into his injection rounds by now. She started to think about Jonathan—and that kiss—and was grateful her wonderings were interrupted as the first few guards started to show up.

"How are the injections going?" Maggie said quietly into her radio while she waited for the rest of the guards.

"Good," Jonathan's voice said after a moment. "I've had a little resistance, but the flu story seems to be working on almost everyone."

"Almost?"

"A couple of the scientists wanted a better explanation than I had. I handled it," Jonathan said.

"Roger that," Maggie said, smiling. She knew there were now a couple of scientists tied up and no doubt scared, but inoculated. "No problem with the guards?"

"Negative. There were a few at first I had to dodge, but they seem to have all left now. Whatever you're doing, it appears to be working."

"Roger."

"Just get here as soon as you can. I'm going to need some backup when I get to the upper decks."

"I will. Out," Maggie said, putting her radio away as the hold continued to fill. The guards were milling around each other and quietly talking. They seemed to be pretty much ignoring the small crate in the middle of the room.

Maggie scanned the crowd and saw that no one was carrying a mask. Even if her invitation had managed to reach a guard with a mask, she knew he'd be unlikely to bring it along, where the others could see it. She counted heads. Most of them were here. This would have to do. Time for the show. She reached up and threw the locking switch on the control panel. Magnets slammed the door shut and locked it. Everyone turned toward the clang, and the murmurs got much louder. She snapped on the lights and stood up in front of the control room's microphone.

"Please quiet down," Maggie said. When the guards saw her, at least half of them rolled their eyes and whispered to each other, some of them laughing. She steeled herself. "Gentleman, please quiet down, I'm trying to save your lives."

The murmuring eased, and the guards moved in closer to the window. Not all of them, but more than a few unsnapped the holster covers on their belts.

"Where's Morgan!"

"Why's the door locked!"

"I'm going to answer all your questions if you'll just quiet down and listen," she said.

The room got deathly quiet.

"That's better," Maggie said, reaching into her pocket and pulling out her ID. She held it up to the window. "Some of you have heard that I have an MI6 background, but what you don't know is that I am an active MI6 agent and was sent here to uncover the real reason behind this conference. With the CIA's help, I've done that. There's no time for all the details right now, so I'll cut to the chase. In less than an hour, poison gas is going to be released on this ship in an attempt to kill everyone on board."

A few guards tried to make light of the statement and whisper to others, but were told to shut up. Even more of the guards had a kind of slow realization come across their faces, followed by fear.

"Some of you have been involved in a project placing canisters around the ship. You may or may not have known what they were for, but I can guarantee you that Mrs. Tenabe had no intention of letting anyone get off the ship before she released the toxin. You may have also noticed that some guards aren't here, including Mr. Morgan. That's by design. Anyone not here has been supplied a gas mask to survive the attack."

"How do we know this is true?" a few shouted.

"Do you have any masks for us?" Even more shouted. Maggie relaxed a little. She was starting to get through to them.

"I don't have any masks for you—" The crowd erupted into shouts before she could finish, and some began trying to open the door.

"Please! Calm down!" But the crowd was getting away from her.

Something thumped on the glass right beside her head and she flinched. For a second she thought someone had thrown something from the crowd, then she looked beside her and saw that Alex had entered the booth behind her and had slammed his own ID against the glass.

"Quiet down! NOW!" Alex shouted.

The crowd slowly responded, moving back in front of the window.

"That's better. Agent Reynolds is telling the truth. I'm with MI6 as well. If you want to live, listen to her." Alex backed away and nodded for Maggie to continue with a wink. "All yours, darling." Maggie was grateful but found it more than a little curious how fast the guards responded to Alex. She chalked it up to misogyny and continued.

"In the crate behind you is an injection gun. In it is an anti-toxin that will protect you from the gas," Maggie said, leaving out the part about them still being rendered unconscious for hours. A couple of the guards fought for the crate and ripped it open, one of them pulling out the injection gun.

"Bloody animals," Alex muttered.

"You need to be careful! A double shot of the toxin will be just as deadly as the gas. Form a line and inject everyone in turn. Once I see that everyone is inoculated, I'll open the door." To her relief, the guards slowly formed a line and began rolling up their sleeves, another guard acted as the nurse while everyone moved past him. Maggie switched the microphone off.

"Where the hell have you been?" Maggie asked Alex.

"Keeping tabs on Umi, like I said I would," Alex said. "Are you really going to open the door once they're all injected?"

"No," Maggie said.

"I think that's prudent, darling, but how do we get inoculated with the injection gun locked in there?"

"I've already been injected. There's another injection gun inoculating all the passengers right now. "

"All of them? But how did—Ahh, that's why everyone was ordered to their rooms early. Tanaka?"

"He's with us," Maggie said, leaving the booth. Alex followed. "Come on, I'll bring you up to speed on the way. Jonathan—the CIA agent with the other injector—needs our help on the upper decks."

"And help him we shall," Alex said.

12:50 P.M.

JONATHAN WAS EXHAUSTED. Not physically, but all the lying and conning and stress was taking its toll. He thought about Lew and wished he was here. Lew wasn't great at the finesse part of things, but you could guarantee if the passengers had seen him standing behind Jonathan, nobody would have said boo about getting a shot. But it was more than that; without Lew, Jonathan didn't have a sounding board, someone to bounce ideas off and someone to call him on his bullshit. He hadn't realized how dependent he had become on that until now.

Jonathan looked at his clipboard. Not counting the staterooms on the upper deck that he needed help with, he had just nine to go. He was about to knock on his next door when the radio on his hip beeped.

"Go," Jonathan said.

"Guards are all tucked in," Maggie said. "We're on our way to you now."

"Roger that. Wait, *we're* on our way?"

"I'll explain when I get there," Maggie said. "Say ten minutes."

"Copy that. I'll try to be ready for the upper deck when you get here."

"Copy. Out."

Jonathan put his radio away and knocked on the next door. Maybe these last few will go fast, he thought. He felt otherwise when the door opened.

"Hello, stranger." Melinda, the cougar from the arrival deck said, still sipping on an apparently endless supply of margaritas. "Did anyone order a bucket of yummy?" she said mockingly to her roommates, two other wide-eyed drink-sippers who seemed to be having trouble getting to the door. Jonathan was going to blame the endless drinks, but then he felt the ship list, himself.

"C'min c'min," Melinda said, stepping out of the way. Jonathan stood his ground, afraid if he went in there he'd lose more than time.

Think, Hall, you don't have time for this.

He reached inside the messenger bag hanging from his shoulder and held up the injector gun. Their eyes got even wider, which seemed impossible.

"You guys want to party?"

After promising to return after the speech with a couple of buddies, Jonathan had injected the trio. He guaranteed them the trip of their lives from his home-brewed psychedelic. They couldn't stick their arms out fast enough.

"Hurry back," Melinda said, waggling her fingers at him as he backed down the hall.

"I will," Jonathan said in the same singsongy way.

When the door finally closed, Jonathan shivered and marched toward the next door.

Maybe he was glad Lew wasn't here, after all, thinking of the ridicule he'd be getting lambasted with right now if he were.

Miraculously, Jonathan moved through the rest of the rooms on the deck in record time. As he came out into the hall from the final room, Maggie and a tall, well-dressed black man came around the corner of the hall junction.

"Jonathan Hall, this is Alex Corsair, MI6. He's been helping me. Alex, this Jonathan Hall, CIA. He's . . . an old colleague."

Jonathan shook Alex's hand. He had a strong handshake but a strange look in his eye. Almost like the situation was amusing him.

"Where are we?" Maggie asked Jonathan.

"That's the last down here. I've still got the two upstairs to do, but when I checked earlier, the hallway still had about a half dozen guards who didn't look like they were going anywhere anytime soon."

"That's Morgan's inner circle," Maggie said. "His most loyal guards. And the most experienced mercenaries on the staff. It makes sense they'd be posted up there. Those suites are for the dignitaries."

"Dignitaries?" Jonathan asked.

"The big money, darling," Alex said.

"Money and government officials who can approve grants," Maggie said. "If Umi wanted to wipe out the gerontology research field, she'd pretty much just have to take them out."

"Right. Cut off the supply line, and the scientists have nothing to work with," Jonathan said.

Just then, three guards came around the corner, practically bumping into them. Jonathan started to reach for the gun in his waistband, but Maggie stopped him.

"Everyone back to their . . . oh, it's you," the lead guard said.

"Just making some final preparations," Maggie said. "You better get to your quarters before the speech starts."

"Right. Let's go guys," the guard said. The others were glaring at Jonathan pretty hard, but eventually they left.

"I suggest we hurry before we run into anyone else," Alex said.

Something was bugging Jonathan. The guards seemed to listen to Maggie, but they had actively ignored Alex. The way they'd blatantly ignored him reminded Jonathan of when Natalie used to not look at him when she'd been caught doing something she shouldn't.

"Right," Maggie said. "Ideas for getting past the guards upstairs?"

"Why don't you two head up this way, and I'll head up the stairs at the other end of the corridor," Alex said. "I'll create a disturbance to attract their attention, and you can take care of our distinguished guests. Then we can figure a way off this ship."

Jonathan and Maggie shared a glance, and he realized Alex wasn't fooling her. She was playing him for some reason.

"Sounds good," Maggie said.

Jonathan and Maggie were in position up at the top of the stairs, waiting for Alex's diversion before he said anything.

"I don't trust that guy."

Jonathan peeked around the corner down the hallway. Two guards were posted at each of the two doors. Even if they came out shooting, it was doubtful they could take out all four without their getting a shot off. And the guards had machine guns slung over their shoulders. This was bad.

"That's because you're smart," Maggie said.

"Then what are we doing here?" Jonathan asked as Maggie looked at her watch.

"Just giving him enough rope," she said.

1:10 P.M.

ALEX PEEKED AROUND the corner again to be sure he hadn't been followed. He had to get this message to Umi without being seen. Maggie might actually be able to get Alex off the ship if he helped her, but Alex had never been one to put all his eggs in one basket. If he could get back into Umi's good graces, she'd be able to get him off the ship as well. Granted, that would mean going down to that death trap on the bottom of the ocean, but one step at a time.

"What do you mean 'forget about my speech,' Mr. Corsair?" Umi demanded over the radio. "And where have you been for the past hour?"

"I'm only going to say this once," Alex said. "Things are not what they appear. Your little plan has been upended. Maggie isn't ex-MI6; she's here on assignment."

"Assignment? What assignment?" Umi asked, sounding more than a little alarmed. "How long have you known this?"

"She's onto your plan, or part of it, at least. And she's got the CIA involved," Alex said. "Guarantee me passage off this death trap, and I'll help you. And I don't fancy spending the rest of my life on Ashita."

"There's no way the CIA could be on board without my knowing about it, I assure you," Umi said.

"They're not only on board, they're steering your bloody ship!"

"Tanaka? That fool? That's not possible," Umi said. "The storm—"

"Is easing. He played you with a rigged automatic pilot. And your figurehead of security is running around—"

Alex felt the cold steel of a gun barrel against his neck.

1:15 P.M.

JONATHAN PRESSED THE barrel of his gun harder into Alex's neck, then reached over him and took the radio out of his hand. He frisked Alex with one hand, taking the gun he found and sticking it in his belt.

"I always wanted to be a figurehead," Maggie said, holding one of the zip ties that Jonathan had been using to "convince" the passengers who didn't buy the flu story. She snapped it taut in front of Alex's face as Jonathan kept his gun against Alex's neck and relieved him of his cell phone.

"Suits you," Jonathan said with a smile. He liked bantering with her. It felt familiar, but they didn't really have time for this.

"It's not what it looks like," Alex finally said, seeming to get his composure back after being caught red-handed.

"Then why don't you—"

Alex made a move to disarm Jonathan while he was talking with a back-swinging elbow, but Jonathan easily dodged it. Then, to his surprise, Maggie punctuated the escape attempt with a punch to the side of Alex's face that came from her knees. Alex crumpled to the ground, out cold.

"Jesus," Jonathan said.

"Now *that's* what a proper figurehead would do. God, that felt bloody good," Maggie said, rubbing her knuckles.

"You pulled your punch back in my room," Jonathan said. He put his gun away, rolled Alex over, and put the plastic tie on his wrists.

"Not really. He just pissed me off more. What's our time like?" Maggie asked.

"Less than fifteen minutes. Maybe," Jonathan said.

"What do you mean, 'Maybe'?"

"If Umi didn't know you and Tanaka were onto her before, she sure as shit does now. If it's an option, she could release the gas early," Jonathan said as they muscled Alex's body into a storage closet.

"Nothing we can do about that now. Let's get these last four people inoculated, then we can worry about us," Maggie said.

"*It is on a timer,*" Tanaka said from Jonathan's implant. "*I listened in on a conversation Umi and Morgan had. Being on a timer is the only way they can make sure all the gas gets released simultaneously. And you have exactly thirteen minutes left.*"

"Right," Jonathan said to both of them. He was still wondering what Alex had meant when he'd said to Umi, "*She's onto your plan, or part of it, at least.*" What was the other part?

"So now that we don't have a diversion, any ideas?" Maggie asked.

"No way we can take them from a single point, but if we came at them from both ends of the corridor at the same time . . ."

"Brilliant," Maggie said. "I knew you weren't just a pretty face. You head down the other end. Let's synchronize our watches."

"I'll give you two minutes. And mark."

"See you in two," Jonathan said, hurrying down the hall. When he was far enough away from her, he tapped behind his ear. "Tanaka, you there?"

"*It's an implant, Jonathan. I'm always here.*"

"Right. Then you heard our plan. I've just got a minute. Alex said something about the gas just being *part* of Umi's plan. Any idea what he was talking about?" Jonathan reached the end of the corridor and took up position, keeping his eye on his watch.

"*At first we thought the ship assault was her whole plan, but conversations I heard made it clear there was something else— something big—that comes after the gas attack. No specifics, though, sorry. If I hear anything else about it, I'll let you know,*" Tanaka said.

"All right. Watch yourself. Umi knows you're with us, now. She doesn't seem like the kind of woman who forgives betrayal easily."

"You're right about that. But in our favor, she's got an ego bigger than her ship. I doubt she thinks anyone can beat her in anything."

"Let's hope she's wrong," Jonathan said, taking out his gun. He pulled the slide back and loaded a round into the chamber. Then he watched the final seconds tick by and rolled once so he was flat on the ground with the gun in both hands pointed down the corridor.

He squeezed off two shots at the two guards closest to him. One hit the first guard in the shoulder and the other caught the second guard in the hip. They both howled and dropped, but were still trying to raise their guns. Jonathan heard other shots but stayed focused on his targets.

"Drop your weapons! Now!" Jonathan shouted. The guard with the ruined hip complied, dropping his gun and falling back in agony. The other guard ignored the order and started firing. The ground around Jonathan erupted in destruction as the machine gun carved a path across the carpet toward him. The rapid-fire echoes stopped just before they reached him. The guard flopped forward with a gaping hole in his forehead, Maggie standing behind him, her gun still smoking.

Jonathan looked farther down the hallway and saw that Maggie's guards were lying motionless on the ground, bullet holes in their foreheads, as well. He got up and moved down the hall toward the guard he'd wounded. Maggie was lining up a kill shot as he did.

"No, wait!"

Maggie stopped. "Why?"

"I've got some questions for this one," Jonathan said, relieving the wounded man of his machine gun.

"Why would he tell you anything?" Maggie demanded.

"Look around. They don't have masks with them," Jonathan said. "He's going to tell us everything we want to know. Because if he doesn't, we're going to tie him up right here and let the gas have him."

"What? You wouldn't do that. Come on!" the guard said in English between winces over his wound.

"Try me," Jonathan said, turning to walk away.

"Wait! Fine, I'll tell you what you want to know. Anything. Just don't leave me here!"

"So much for seasoned mercenaries," Maggie said.

"Look at him. He's a kid. I doubt he's ever seen any action before," Jonathan said. The guard didn't correct him. "The others are the same. Look."

Maggie looked as confused as Jonathan felt. "If these guards aren't Morgan's inner circle, then where the hell are they?"

"My money is on wherever Umi and Morgan are. Sub, maybe? But first things first, you go take care of these last four passengers," Jonathan said, handing Maggie the injection gun.

"Why me?"

"They were locked in their rooms under guard and they just heard gunshots outside their doors. Even if they would have listened to me before, they sure won't now. But they'll listen to you. You vetted them, reassured them of the security measures and safety of the conference. They know your face."

"Right," Maggie said. She headed for the first door, knocked and in less than thirty seconds was inside talking with the dignitaries. Jonathan crouched beside the wounded guard.

"What's your name?"

"Darren Pirkl, sir," the kid managed.

"Okay, Darren, tell me about Ashita. And I'd make it fast if I were you," Jonathan said, tapping his watch with his gun and making a face like he was choking. Darren didn't find it funny at all.

"They don't tell me much," Darren said, wincing. "I know the old lady is going down there before the gas attack."

"*Down* there?"

"They've been taking stuff somewhere with the subs for months. Someplace called Ashita."

"There's more than one sub?"

"Well, there used to be. One of them broke down. It's off to the side of the moon pool behind some partitions. You'd have to know it was there to even see it. They've just been using the other one, lately."

"You haven't been down there?"

"No, only Mr. Morgan's elite guards go down."

Maggie emerged from the stateroom.

"Two down, two to go," she said hurrying to the other door. "You get anything out of him?"

"Oh, yeah. We've learned that a sub is broken and there might be a place called Ashita 'down' somewhere."

"In other words, nothing," Maggie said. The next two dignitaries finally opened the door but it took Maggie almost a full minute to get them to let her in.

"You heard her, kid. You're not telling me anything that's going to make me want to get you out of here."

"That's all I know! I swear!"

"Have it your way," Jonathan said, standing up and heading away.

"Wait! Uh, the big guy. I saw some big guy climb out of the moon pool wearing scuba gear!"

Jonathan's chest tightened, and he felt the hairs on the back of his neck stand up. "What big guy? Describe him."

"He was big, like I said. And blond. Only wearing wetsuit shorts after he took off his gear. And he was . . . all scarred up."

"What else did you see? Where did this guy go?"

"He didn't go anywhere. He looked real tired. Then Mr. Corsair snuck up behind him and hit him with a pipe. Knocked him out. Or killed him. I don't know, which."

Jonathan couldn't believe what he was hearing. Lew? On board?

"How'd you see all this?" Jonathan asked. He partly wished the kid was lying but also knew that if Alex had seen the kid, he'd probably be dead by now. Darren looked away, like he didn't want to say any more. Jonathan lunged at him, grabbing a fistful of his uniform. "How'd you see it!"

"Okay, okay! Me and a couple of the other guards used to go into the busted sub to smoke weed. We made a bong out of one of the rebreathers. And the sub keeps the smell from getting out. We were in there when we heard the big guy flop out of the moon pool. I stuck my head out and peeked around the partition. I saw the whole thing."

"Where is he now? The big guy."

"Mr. Corsair put him in a big crate, then had a couple of the other guards load him in the working sub. He told them to take him there."

"Take him where?"

"To Ashita. If he's alive, the big guy is on Ashita. That's all I know. After they left, we took off and swore each other to secrecy. We knew what Mr. Corsair would do to us if he found out we were there."

"Do to you? What exactly is Corsair's job?" Jonathan said. The guy was obviously not MI6, or if he was, he was dirty. But the way Maggie had talked, Corsair had only been on the ship as long as she had.

"I don't know about official job, but he's Ms. Tenabe's enforcer. You do something to cross him, and you disappear. One of the guards told a story about seeing Corsair on deck with one of the scientists a few weeks ago. He shoved a knife in his neck and tossed him overboard like he was flicking a cigarette butt away. He's crazy."

"How long has he worked for her?"

"He was here before I was. At least a year. Now how about getting me out of here?"

"Corsair," Jonathan said between clenched teeth. He let go of Darren, stood up, and headed for the end of the corridor just as Maggie was coming out of the final suite.

"And we're done. Hey, where are you going? Jesus, what's wrong, Jonathan?" Maggie said.

"No time. Zap the kid. I'm going to have a little chat with our asshole in the closet," Jonathan said.

He grabbed the door to the closet and threw it open. The closet was empty. Alex was on the loose.

"Fuck! Tanaka, did you get all that?"

"*Jesus, yes,*" Tanaka said.

"Can you get a message out to Fahd? Find out if Lew left the *Atlantis Explorer*?"

"Not possible. Like I told you, I don't know anything about the communications jamming equipment. And anybody who does is locked up in a room waiting to be gassed."

"Goddamn it! Jonathan shouted, slamming the butt of his gun into the bulkhead.

"Uh, who are you talking to, Sport?" Maggie asked, eying Jonathan like he'd lost his mind.

"*Jonathan. Jonathan!*" Tanaka shouted.

"What?"

"*You've got less than five minutes before the gas is released. We can deal with this after the gas clears. Right now, you've got to get your mask!"*

"No time," Jonathan said, knowing there was no way he could get to his room in time. And it wouldn't help Maggie anyway, there was only one mask there. Tanaka had the other. If they didn't want to spend the next twelve hours asleep, they had to get out of there. And fast.

"Shit," Tanaka said. *"Okay, get your asses up on deck and as far away from enclosed spaces as you can. The wind's coming from the west. I'll turn the ship. Get to the starboard helipad. And I mean right to the fucking rail. Go!"*

Jonathan dropped the messenger bag and started to run, but realized he had no idea where the starboard helipad was. Then Maggie grabbed him and slammed him up against the wall.

"Stop fucking around, Jonathan! You're scaring me. I need you here right now."

"I am here," he said pushing her away. "I don't have time to explain. Just trust me. We need to get to the starboard heliport. We've got maybe four minutes before the gas is released."

"Four . . . but how do you—"

"Maggie!" Jonathan shouted, and this time he grabbed her by the shoulders. "Which way?"

"Uh, down here, across the ship, then up to the deck."

Jonathan grabbed her hand and ran. He tried not to think about Lew, but it was impossible. If the kid was wrong about the crate, and Lew was on board somewhere, he was about to die.

Abandon Ship!

Chapter Twenty-four

Above the *Jirojin Maru*
1:25 P.M. Local Time

"THERE IT IS!" Tatsu said with relief. Because of the wind, the flight had taken longer than expected. She had been starting to worry they weren't going to find the ship. Though part of her thought that might be the best scenario.

"What's he waiting for? Tell him to land," Per said into his headset.

"I don't know," Tatsu said. She spoke to the pilot in Japanese.

"We can't land!" The pilot shouted to her. "The storm was moving away, but now it's swung back again. The wind sheer will slam us onto the deck!"

"Well?" Per said when the pilot stopped talking.

"He says the storm is still too strong. He can't land."

"I suggest you encourage him."

Tatsu looked at her watch and knew that in the next couple of minutes, the only thing on that ship would be corpses.

She argued with the pilot—not for Per, but for herself—but he wouldn't change his mind.

"He won't land. Says he couldn't even if he wanted to. He's not being defiant, it's the truth. I've seen landing accidents in weather a lot milder than this."

Per looked at the pilot, then back at Tatsu. He seemed to be trying to work something out. Then he looked down at the ship.

"The wind is coming from the west. Tell him to come in from the back of the ship and to get as low over it as he can."

"And then what?" Tatsu asked, already knowing the answer.

"And then we jump."

It took some doing, but she finally convinced the pilot to try.

"Get ready! We're going in," she shouted. Maybe Umi will get her wish after all, Tatsu thought as she worked to keep her mind from envisioning a fiery helicopter death.

The helicopter banked to the west to ready its approach, the wind rocking them back and forth like some kind of crazy pendulum in the sky. They swung around, and the pilot aimed the nose of the helicopter at the deck far below them, shouting something over and over.

"What's he saying?" Per asked.

"There's no real translation. The closest is 'this is fucking crazy.'"

And then, for the first time she could remember, Per smiled.

JONATHAN FELT LIKE he'd been climbing stairs forever. They'd run into a couple of straggler guards, without masks and doomed to die in the next few moments. Jonathan had disarmed them, but before he could inoculate them, they ran off. Against Maggie's protests, they had chased the guards down into the bowels of the ship. They finally managed to catch up to the guards and inoculate them, but not before losing precious time.

Maggie, on the other hand, didn't seem winded at all. She was obviously in better shape than he was. They'd run half the length of the ship and started climbing all the way up to the top level, the equivalent of running up a seven-story building.

Too long. It's been too long.

He couldn't believe the gas hadn't been released yet. A tiny voice in his head said maybe it's all a hoax, but he knew that was foolish wishing. The kind of thinking that gets people killed.

"There!" Maggie shouted as they reached the top level and turned down a final corridor. At the end of it was an opening where they could see the heliport. It was pouring rain out, and the way it was whipping across the opening made it obvious the storm had swung around again.

She grabbed his hand, and they ran. "Told you we'd be . . . all right . . ."

Up ahead, six feet before the opening, white-blue vapor began pouring from the air vents in the corridor bulkheads. Maggie and Jonathan came to a stop and turned around. The same vapor was pouring out vents ten feet behind them. They were trapped.

Maggie collapsed against Jonathan's chest as they both watched the slivers of their escape cloud over. Time seemed to stand still. He listened to the sound of the rain and wind at the end of the corridor, the hiss of the gas all around them, the heaving panting of their exhaustion.

He tried to take solace in the fact that they'd saved everyone on board, but it wasn't enough. He kept hearing Corsair say "part of it" over and over. What was the rest of Umi's plan? Who would die then, while he and Maggie were sleeping? Jonathan thought about Lew, who might or might not be dead already. And then, oddly enough, he thought about that kiss Maggie had laid on him back in his stateroom. And he decided.

It wasn't time to give up. Not yet.

"Come on! Take a deep breath and cover your eyes!" He shouted over the roar of the weather outside. He expected her to say it was a waste of time, but she did just as he asked.

And then they ran faster than they had before, not breathing and blind. They bounced off the bulkheads a few times but finally felt the wind and rain peppering them. They were outside. Jonathan let out his breathe and dropped his arm from his eyes.

"We made i—Jesus, Maggie look out!"

THEY WERE OUT of control. The helicopter had caught a pole mounted to the deck on its first approach, sheering it off and flinging it into the ocean, a foot-high, three-inch round stub the only thing left to indicate that something had once been there. The rotor was damaged, the pilot was fighting with the stick between screams, and they were spinning like a tether ball on a string. Somehow, the pilot was keeping the bird from slamming into the deck, but just barely.

Tatsu looked out the window and saw the tail almost mulch two people on the deck. She recognized one of them as Ms. Reynolds, the security chief Umi had hired, but she didn't recognize the man. She watched the man shout, then dive and knock Reynolds out of the way of the spinning tail just in time.

The real problem was that they couldn't open the door to even try to get out. The centripetal force was pinning it shut. Per took his jacket off to free his robotic arm from the cumbersome material and instead of grabbing the handle of the door, as he'd been trying to do, he grabbed the hinges and ripped them from the metal. Then he punched the door with his arm, and it flew away from the chopper, far into the ocean.

The storm was inside now, rain pelting them so hard, they could barely keep their eyes open.

"Grab onto me!" Per yelled. She could barely hear him over the shrieking of the wind, but she did as he said, wrapping her arms around him. And then they jumped.

As they flew through the air, Tatsu waited for the spinning chopper to slam into them and cut them to shreds. But pushing off as they had had unbalanced the chopper, and it warbled away from the ship and into the ocean. They were falling incredibly fast, but Per caught one of the upper deck's metal cables in his artificial hand, and they jerked to a stop for a moment. The force was too much even for that incredible device, though, and soon they were falling again. They slammed hard onto the deck beside the other two people lying there, barely missing the jagged pipe stub sticking out of the deck.

Tastu heard Reynolds say her name in astonishment, then she passed out.

MAGGIE WATCHED THE wounded helicopter skip across the surface of the rough sea a few times before the tail dug into the water, the force snapping the chopper in half. A second later, a ball of fire exploded in the sky, the heat searing even from this distance. She turned away until the blast subsided, and when she turned back, the helicopter was all but gone. Maggie looked back at Tatsu and the strange little man who had jumped from the helicopter with her on his back.

"Who the hell are you?" Maggie asked.

"Per Broden."

"How do you know—" Maggie's question was cut short as gunfire strafed along the deck between them.

Everyone looked up at the source. Two stories up, Alex Corsair straddled the railing wearing a gas mask and firing a machine gun in short bursts at them. He'd shed his suit jacket and was a stark figure against the dark, roiling storm clouds that seemed to be trying to engulf the entire ship. Maggie knew despite everything else, Alex was a crack shot. The listing of the ship was the only thing that had saved them. Maggie drew her gun and took aim but before she could fire, Jonathan knocked her arm down and her shot embedded into the bulkhead.

"Jonathan! What are you doing?"

"I need him alive," Jonathan said. Then they heard more shots, but not aimed at them. Someone in a guard's uniform was similarly straddling the railing two decks above Alex, wearing a gas mask and firing at him.

"It's Morgan!" Maggie shouted. She knew why Morgan was still here and trying to kill Alex; Umi didn't want any loose ends. But Morgan hadn't counted on their ragtag group being scattered around the deck of the ship.

They watched as Alex tried to turn, but his focus was taken by trying to keep his balance. Then two pink clouds bloomed on his right arm and shoulder as Morgan fired again.

"No!" Jonathan shouted, opening fire on Morgan.

A second later, Maggie joined in. The listing of the ship threw their aim off as well, bullets dancing across the bulkhead all around Morgan. He ducked and took off. Alex stood wavering, two more red flowers on his crisp, white shirt. He seemed to be trying to raise the machine gun for another shot, but his arm wouldn't obey. And then he toppled over.

The machine gun clattered down beside Jonathan, then Alex landed on his back, blood shooting up into the air like one of those timed fountains in Vegas. Maggie saw why. Alex had landed on the jagged piece of pipe sticking out of the deck, impaling him through his abdomen. His mouth worked as he tried to grab this foreign thing sticking out of him, but his blood-slicked hands just slid off it, over and over.

"COVER ME," JONATHAN said to Maggie as he rushed to Alex's side.

"Corsair. Corsair!" Jonathan said. Alex just stared at the sky, blood bubbles coming out of his mouth, staining his brilliant white teeth a ghastly red. He was laughing, or trying to. Jonathan pushed up Alex's mask, grabbed his head in his hands and turned it so they were looking at each other.

"B . . . better talk quick, darling," Alex said, blood staining his crisp, white teeth.

"The big guy you hit with a pipe by the moon pool. Did you kill him? What did you do with the body?" Jonathan asked.

"Not sure. Bastard bent the pipe. Glad I didn't have to go toe to toe with him," Alex said, then he fought a violent coughing bout. "I sent him down to Ashita. My gift to the iron bitch. Wish . . . wish I could watch him pop out down there and reveal her secrets."

"What secrets?" Maggie asked, moving beside Alex.

"I'm sorry I used you, poppit. You've got a good heart, even after all you've been through," Alex said. "And you were a great lay, darling." Jonathan's head snapped down and looked at her. She seemed to ignore it.

"Alex, what secrets? What exactly is Ashita? Some kind of

underwater habitat, like a science station? If we go down there, what can we—"

Alex grabbed her arm, his eyes wide with fear.

"Don't go down there, Maggie. Whatever you do," Alex said in a harsh whisper. "She's not done. This is just the start. Thought I could take my money and run. Not meant to be."

"What the hell does that mean?" Jonathan said.

Jonathan looked up at Per Broden and the young girl apparently named Tatsu a few feet away. The man had pulled her into his lap, almost like he was protecting something he needed. Tatsu was still out, but she was moving—alive.

"Mikawa but not Mikawa. Ashita will kill for her," Alex said. It made no sense to Jonathan.

"Alex. Alex!"

"Tatsu knows. She was there at the start. Ask her," Alex said, grabbing both her arms to try and sit up. *Ask her!*"

And then he fell back to the deck. Lifeless.

"What happened?" Tatsu said, coming around. She looked at the dead, bloody man a few feet away, then at the damage around the heliport.

"We were just about to ask you the same thing," Jonathan said.

Chapter Twenty-five

Unknown

LEW FELT LIKE he'd been on a weeklong drinking binge. Every muscle in his body ached from his swim, and his head throbbed from where the well-dressed stranger had tried to knock his melon out of the park. When he'd woken up, he'd had the terrifying thought that he'd been buried alive. He'd reached out in the darkness and felt his wooden prison, about the size of a large coffin, complete with sealed lid. He'd pushed on it as hard as he could in his current state, but the invisible barrier wouldn't budge.

As terrifying as that had been, what was working harder on his psyche at the moment was that he didn't seem to be alone in his box. Beneath him, he could feel at least two bodies. Or what *felt* like bodies because there was something odd about them. Lew had experience lying with corpses—in Iraq, hiding under a pile of them had kept him alive. But this was different.

First, there was no smell. The smell that would live in Lew's nightmares until his dying day was unmistakable—and missing. And what he did smell was foreign to him—a kind of plasticky, burned smell. But not burned flesh. That too—unfortunately—he had experience with. Still, they definitely felt like bodies. But not bodies. They were too cold and hard, even for corpses. Lew knew the only one way to find out what was going on was to get out. Unless, of course, he really had been buried, and there was nothing outside his box besides a ton of dirt.

Lew convinced himself that didn't make any sense. The closest dirt to where he'd been laid out with that pipe was hundreds of feet under the ocean, or many kilometers to the east on the island of Iwo Jima. He worked to calm himself, then drew his knees up to his chest and kicked out at the lid to his enigma. If nothing else, being in an oversized coffin meant he had enough room to get some momentum.

At first, the lid refused to give way, but after a few more hits— each one sending a spike of pain through Lew's aching head—the nails around the edges of the lid began to give a little with loud squeaks. Relief filled Lew's chest when the slight cracks allowed brilliant light into the box. There was enough that he could have turned to see who—or what—he was lying on, but he knew it was a better idea to wait until he was free to do that. He was still dangerously close to a freakout.

Four or five more kicks, and the cracks turned into troughs of light. He squinted against the harsh brightness. He could see deep blues and bright whites outside his prison. And then, with a final kick, accompanied by a strength-empowering yell, Lew kicked the lid completely off the box. Without waiting to even register where he was, he fought his muscle aches and climbed out, his bare feet slapping down on the cold, white cementlike floor. He stayed hunched over for a few moments, catching his breath. When he finally did look around, it took his brain a while to comprehend what he was seeing.

"What the shit?"

He was in a large, mostly white room filled with crates of varying sizes, furniture, and steamer trunks. The ceiling was about twelve feet high, and all but one wall was nothing but stark white. It was the fourth wall that was playing with his mind. Made out of several large triangles fitted together, each as tall as him, the panes were transparent. It had to be some pretty thick Plexiglas, Lew reasoned, because on the other side of the glass was the ocean floor. The light, both in the room and for about twenty yards beyond the glass, seemed to be coming from the triangles themselves.

Lew slowly padded over to the triangle wall, shivering now that he was out of the warm confines of his box. He leaned forward and looked out the glass, feeling like he was at some kind of reverse aquarium. Sealife was everywhere outside—plants waving gently back and forth in the invisible current, strange-looking fish braving the light and periodically approaching the triangles before abruptly turning and shimmying away. The ocean itself was filled with a kind of cloud of plankton and sediment drifting through the light, like dust in a sunbeam.

Lew reached out and touched the glass. To his surprise, it was warm not cold, as he'd expected. He slid his hand over to the triangle's edges. It was smooth and strong, but definitely not made of concrete or any other building material he'd ever seen. Hugging himself for warmth, he tentatively made his way back to the crate and looked inside.

"What the fuck are you?" Lew said when he saw what was inside. He was just reaching into the crate when a voice made him spin around.

"Help me."

Ashita

2:10 P.M.

UMI CLIMBED OUT of the submarine, pushing the guards' hands out of her way. She didn't need their help, and she resented the fact that they thought she did. Ignoring their apologies, she stepped onto Ashita's lower docking port. Though she had been there many times before, this time was different. She would never leave this place again.

"Take everything up to my residence. I'm going to the nineteenth floor," Umi said, making her way toward the tower and the elevators. "Send the sub back to the ship."

"Where's Mr. Morgan?" one of the guards asked. Originally, there weren't supposed to be any further trips between Ashita and the *Jirojin Maru*, but the interference on the ship had required an adjustment to the plan.

"He's taking care of a few final details for me. Nothing you should be concerned about. Get the sub unloaded and send it back up for him. He'll be with us shortly."

When fully functioning, the subs didn't need anyone to pilot them, similar to the fly-by-wire system used by passenger jets in case anything happened to their pilots during flight. In fact, there were only two or three people on her staff who had been manually trained to pilot the subs.

"Yes, ma'am," the guard said, then to the other guards, "Come on, lads. Get the exo suits. Some of these final crates are bloody heavy. Move!"

The final crates and cases were filled with Umi's treasures— items she had gathered over the past sixty years. She was a collector in all areas of her life: from people, to art, to information.

Unfortunately, she'd had to leave some things behind—like her Picasso collection and Tatsu. Not that it really mattered; even the treasures she had brought with her were destined to be left behind once she crossed over. Still, she couldn't stand the idea of someone else's having her prizes.

Or getting the better of her.

Being triumphant in the business world meant never letting anyone better you. And if by some chance of fate they did, never letting their moves go unanswered. It was one of the reasons for her success. When most other companies heard they were up against the Tenabe Group, more often than not they dropped out of the fight. They knew what would happen if they did something insane like win a deal away from her. Not only their financial lives, but their personal lives would be put on the block. And Umi was consistent to the end.

Morgan had been sent to finish what Umi felt were incomplete transactions. Mainly, to kill Tanaka, Ms. Reynolds, and anyone who had helped them interfere with her plans. Alex Corsair was on the list, as well. He had served her well over the past year, but he knew far too much about her business practices and what would come next.

And if by some accident Morgan failed and got himself killed, that would just save her the trouble of doing it later. But right now, it was time for a reunion.

Chapter Twenty-six

Jirojin Maru
2:15 P.M. Local Time

RAIN SLUICED DOWN onto the heliport, washing away the blood and debris. The storm continued to intensify with every passing moment. The sky overhead was black with clouds, turning day into night, save for the periodic flash of lightning, the following thunder deafening and palpable. The sea was tossing the *Jirojin Maru* around like a toy in a hot tub filled with ink, the huge waves starting to break over the deck.

Jonathan was the only one on his feet, and staying there was more than a little difficult. The gas had stopped billowing out of the vents, but no one knew how long it would be before the ship's innards were traversable without risking unconsciousness for some, or death for the others. And they only had one mask—still sitting on Alex Corsair's lifeless forehead.

"What's happening, Tanaka? Things are getting really fucking hairy back here," Jonathan shouted. He'd explained the implant to Maggie and the others, fending off their questions about it as government secrets.

"*The storm is getting stronger,*" Tanaka said.

"Yeah," Jonathan said, looking out to sea. "Tell me something I don't know."

"*When the gas stopped, I went into a few staterooms and checked out the guests. The antitoxin seems to be working as described. Everyone's out cold, but alive.*"

"That's great, but we're going to be just the opposite if we don't get off this deck like five minutes ago," Jonathan said, fighting for his balance after another rocking wave.

"What's he saying?" Maggie asked from her position beside Alex.

"He says the storm's getting stronger."

Maggie rolled her eyes.

"I know, I know," Jonathan said. Then, "Tanaka, give me something, or we're going to have no choice but to head in."

"*Don't! Some of the hallways up here are still thick with vapor. You won't get fifty feet without passing out.*"

"Fuck!"

Maggie looked at him.

"Gas is still too thick to go inside."

"If we can get to the moon-pool room, we'll be okay," Tatsu said. She'd been less than forthcoming when asked what Alex's dying words had meant, saying she didn't know any more than he had. Less even. Jonathan didn't know if he believed her or not. He didn't know enough about her to make an evaluation.

"What do you mean?" Per asked.

"The room is pressurized to keep the water in the moon pool from flooding the ship," Tatsu said. "If it's keeping the water out—"

"It'll keep the gas out," Maggie completed. "But we're still four decks up and half a ship away."

"One of us should take the mask and try to find some other ones. Then come back and we can all get to this moon-pool room," Per said.

Jonathan wasn't sure what to make of this guy. And he had no idea how the two of them could possibly be alive after that jump from the helicopter.

"*Great idea, but anyone with a mask has already left the ship,*" Tanaka said. Apparently that had been Umi's original plan; Tanaka had seen her sub depart on the sonar. It had disappeared once it reached the jamming perimeter. Jonathan had already shared the information with the group.

"Not everyone," Jonathan said. "I've got one in my room."

"Wait, what about Tanaka?" Maggie said. Jonathan instantly knew what she meant, slapping himself in the forehead. If Tanaka was on the bridge, he was seconds away from Jonathan's room.

"Tanaka, did you hear that?"

"*Yeah,*" said Tanaka. "*But since Morgan's wandering around with a gun, I don't like the idea much.*"

"If you don't hurry, you're going to have the deaths of four people on your hands. I'm betting you'd like that even less."

"*You're right,*" Tanaka said. "*But I—hang on!*"

"What is it?" Jonathan asked.

"*The sub. It's coming back!*" Jonathan relayed Tanaka's message to Maggie.

"Great, so we've got more guards to deal with?" Maggie asked. Tatsu explained how the sub didn't need to be piloted, so they might have sent it back just to get Morgan.

"But you don't know that," Jonathan said. Then after a moment, "Ah, it doesn't matter if it's empty or if there are ten guards on board, this is the only plan we've got. Tanaka, get over to my room, grab the mask, and get out here. We can buddy breathe with two masks down to the moon-pool room."

"I'm almost to your room now. See you in ten."

"Make it five," Jonathan said. He turned his attention back to the others around him. "He's on his way."

"Unless he runs into Morgan," Maggie said. Jonathan ignored her and knelt in front of Tatsu. For a second, Per looked like he was going to intervene. Jonathan didn't know what this guy's real deal was, but let that go for now.

"Tatsu. In another situation, I'd be tactful and very clever, but I don't have time for that. You're lying. I know you're lying, and so does everyone else. If you don't tell us the truth, we're going to leave you and your friend when Tanaka gets here."

Per made a motion to protect her again.

"And unless you're faster than a bullet, I'd stay exactly where I was, mister," Jonathan said as Maggie pulled the slide on her weapon back and let it go to emphasize his point. He looked for frustration and anger in Per's eyes, but there was nothing there. Even so, Per finally moved away from Tatsu.

"I won't interfere," Per said. "I just want answers. We're on the same side."

"Sure we are. Now, Tatsu. What was Alex talking about?" Jonathan said.

Tatsu seemed to assess their situation, heave a sigh, then finally give in to the inevitable.

"I don't know everything," Tatsu said, "despite what Mr. Corsair said. But I do know how this all started."

"UNTIL MIKAWA, UMI'S late husband, came along, all she cared about was the bottom line, the next deal. She had just turned ninety when she met Mikawa, twenty-two years her junior, but neither one cared about their age. Except for the fact that finding each other so late in life meant their days together truly were numbered," Tatsu said.

She couldn't believe she was telling this story to a bunch of strangers. For so much of Tatsu's life, she'd trained herself to keep secrets. But things were different now. And even if they weren't, there was very little anyone could do to Umi now.

"Everyone thought Mikawa was an opportunist, but they didn't know him. He was the kindest man with the biggest heart that I ever met." Tatsu said, glad the rain was pelting her face, and no one could see her tears. Her whole life, she had felt like she owed Umi, and that's why she'd done the things she did for her. But Mikawa had shown her compassion and love, expecting nothing in return. She'd loved him like a father.

"Through their years together, he kept his job as a tailor and never took a single dime from Umi or her company. No one knew or cared about that, though."

"That's a lovely story, but what does it have to do with our current situation?" Maggie asked.

"I'm getting to that," Tatsu said, as lightning flashed, and a wave broke over the side of the ship, washing over everyone.

"Get to it quicker," Jonathan said.

"It was about then," Tatsu continued, "that Umi took an interest in gerontology, the study of the aging process. She wanted more life, both for her and for Mikawa, who was showing his age far more at seventy than she was at ninety-two. She was afraid she was going to lose him, and Umi couldn't stand the idea that there was something affecting her life that she had no control over. So she did what she does best; she took control back. It was the biggest influx of capital investment the science had ever seen. No matter how far-fetched or fringe the research, she dumped ridiculous working capital into it. But even that was mild compared to the change in her behavior six months ago."

"What happened six months ago?" Jonathan asked.

"They ran out of time. Mikawa, who had survived several battles with cancer thanks to Umi's research and money, was under attack again. But this time, the cancer was frighteningly aggressive. Before they could treat it, it metastasized into every system and organ in his body. He had days, if that, to live.

"Umi called in every team that was even remotely close to a solution. But the science simply wasn't ready. The treatments would have killed him faster than the cancer or his age. All, save one. Or two, actually. The two most likely projects combined."

"You're talking about Nagura and Dr. Reese," Per said, more to himself it seemed than anyone else. When Tatsu nodded, everyone looked at Per. "I said I wanted answers, I didn't say I didn't have any."

Tatsu thought most people would have punctuated something like that with a sarcastic smile. Per just blinked, stone-faced, waiting for more of her story. Jonathan shook his head.

"For those of us who didn't just destroy a helicopter, who the hell are Nagura and Dr. Reese?" Jonathan asked.

Tatsu explained Nagura's robotic fame, both in the battling-robot rings and in the field of robotics.

"Robotics?" Maggie said. "Sorry, I know what robotics are, I just don't see . . . how . . ." Tatsu could tell by the dawning in her eyes that she had made the connection.

"Dr. Reese worked for CRYSTASIS," she continued. "A company fighting almost as hard as Umi to find the secret to life extension. Reese specialized in neural net computers and artificial intelligence, heading up a special project. Very special.

"It was all still a long shot, the longest shot Umi had ever taken in her life, but it was all she had. And she's not one to give up, no matter what the odds are. Six months ago, long before Dr. Reese's research was ready for application, she invited the two teams here and gave them carte blanche. Whatever they needed they got. And the teams had just enough hubris to think that was all they needed. Everyone's spirits rose, even Mikawa's. Until the accident."

Chapter Twenty-seven

Six months ago

"DR. REESE, WE need you in the control room." Nagura stepped back from the microphone and looked through the large window at Reese, who was moving from one bank of machines to another.

Tatsu thought his swirling lab coat made him look like he was dancing. She had never seen machines like these before, the displays and flashing lights looking like some kind of science-fiction movie to her. Hold C had been set up in remarkable time, the machines constantly arriving over the past few days. Tatsu had spent most of it with Umi and Mikawa, just sitting and holding Mikawa's hand sometimes. She felt so helpless.

They were set up on the *Jirojin Maru* because of the legality involved with human trials of technology that wasn't anywhere near ready for that stage. That and the fact that if they were successful, Umi and Mikawa couldn't very well wander around the mainland in their new bodies.

Reese waved at the control-room window without looking, like he was shooing a gnat. He stood between the two operating-room tables set up in the hold, bending over the one with Mikawa on it. Mikawa wanted to be awake as long as possible, but he'd been having some rough days, and he didn't look like he was going to make it to lunch, never mind be able to withstand the procedure.

Tatsu had thought they were crazy when they'd first told her they were going to try to transfer Mikawa's mind into a robot—Nagura actually called it a *cipher*, which apparently meant a robot body with no one inside it yet—but she forced herself to be positive when she saw how much Umi was hoping and praying this would work. And it was his last chance. She knew he wouldn't live beyond the week, crazy ideas or not.

Mikawa was wearing an EEG brain cap that looked to Tatsu like an old-style swimming cap except for the hundreds of thin, fiber-optic cables running out of it. They joined up just behind his head; and then the futuristic ponytail connected with a bank of machines against the wall. A mass of other wires ran from various body parts into the workstation on wheels that sat between the two tables. The monitor on top of the workstation table showed all of Mikawa's vital signs across several windows. The center of the display showed an animated, colored representation of Mikawa's brain, various quadrants lighting up orange and red briefly before falling back into a cool blue.

"Reese, you've checked and rechecked the readings a hundred times," Nagura said into the microphone again. "If he's not ready now, he's never going to be."

Also in the control room were Umi Tenabe and Alex Corsair. Everyone else on the ship had been forbidden to come down to this area until further notice. Tatsu thought Umi looked as if she were going to pass out at any second. Tatsu kept asking her to sit down, but Umi just ignored her and stared out the window. Alex, on the other hand, looked bored.

"We've only got one shot at this, Nagura," Reese said. "If our calculations are off by even a—"

"They're not," Nagura said, his voice full of confidence.

But Tatsu had seen Nagura bent over the occupant on the table beside Mikawa for most of the night, so she knew he wasn't as confident as he pretended to be. Which was understandable. It was his baby. He had created it. Created *them*, actually. There were two humanoid robots in the room, but only one was connected and part of this procedure. The other one, the robot for Umi, was lying dormant in a large crate against the far wall.

When Umi had first seen the robots, she'd balked and almost canceled the project. Nagura had reassured her that the appearance of the robots—now merely humanoid with white, almost translucent "skin"—was temporary. Function had to come before form. Once the procedure was successful, they'd have all the time in the world to dress them up. Nagura promised that these sexless drones would not stay that way. They would look and feel like any other human, except that they would last for hundreds of years. More, maybe.

Tatsu watched Reese make a few more adjustments to Mikawa's skullcap, then touch the screen display on the workstation and manually adjust some settings. When he was done, he backed up, and his eyes darted around the room, giving everything one last check.

"Okay, we're ready. Initiate the start-up sequence," Reese said, seeming reluctant to leave his patient and head up into the control room.

"About bloody time, darling," Alex said to Reese when he entered. Reese ignored him.

Inside the control room were even more monitors and controls set into the console desks. Nagura had explained to Tatsu that the procedure was designed to run on its own, but they had the option of jumping in and making adjustments as they went.

"Give him a break, Corsair," Nagura said. He was just about the only one on board who ever stood up to Umi's dark shadow. "The human brain has over one hundred billion neurons. Each of those can make over a thousand connections. Conservatively meaning there are one hundred terabytes of data to manage."

"A hundred what?" Alex asked. Nagura shook his head, but Tatsu could tell he was enjoying this distraction while they waited for the start-up procedure to initialize.

"Look, imagine a pickup truck filled with books," Nagura said.

"Ah, okay, well that's not that—"

"Now imagine one hundred thousand of them."

"Bugger me."

"*Start-up initialized. Administering focal protocol,*" the computer said in an electronic, but feminine voice.

"What's happening now?" Umi asked. It was the smallest voice Tatsu had ever heard her use.

"He's being given drugs that will focus his mind and increase the blood flow to the brain," Reese said.

"*Initiating test transfer.*"

"This is the first big hurdle," Nagura said. "We're sending a sample piece of data from Mikawa to the cipher's processing unit. Then we'll do a checksum—a test—to make sure the data transferred successfully. If it passes, we'll increase the speed of the transfer slowly over several tests and eventually introduce compression algorithms—uh, ways to make the data smaller. It sounds complicated, but the whole test will only take a minute or two."

Everyone stood quietly as they waited. Tatsu thought even Alex seemed pensive.

"*Test complete. Stand by for data transfer at the highest possible data rate.*"

"This is our last chance to abort, Umi. We can stop it now and aside from the drugs in his system, he'll be just as he was," Nagura said.

"Carry on, gentlemen."

Reese and Nagura looked at each other with bright eyes.

"Here we go," Nagura said.

Tatsu walked over and put an arm around Umi. They hugged each other as they watched.

"Well?" Reese asked Nagura ten minutes later as Nagura stared at the readings on the equipment embedded into the console desks.

"It's working," Nagura said. Reese smiled wide and practically bounced. "It's working!" The men hugged while they laughed in relief. Umi and Tatsu hugged tighter.

"I'll be damned," Alex said.

But the joy was short-lived.

"*Catastrophic failure. Preparing to abort. Catastrophic failure. Preparing to abort.*"

Nagura's face dropped. He let go of Reese and checked the readouts.

"No, no, no." He looked through the window. Tatsu followed his line of sight and saw the representation of Mikawa's brain on the display completely lit up in bright red, yellow letters blinking across the screen: "Data Corruprion."

"What's happening?" Umi yelled. "I thought you couldn't abort now!"

"We can't," Reese said, running out of the control room.

"Is it aborting or not?" Alex asked.

"It's a computer. It doesn't understand that an abort will kill him. It just knows the transfer is failing, so it wants to abort to save itself."

"Save itself? Stop it!" Tatsu shouted.

"I can't! The only thing I can do is delay the abort and increase the speed of the transfer," Nagura said, punching buttons and typing into the keyboard without waiting for Umi's okay.

"Well?" Umi asked.

"It . . . it seems to be working. If we can keep him—oh shit!" Nagura yelled. He grabbed the microphone. "What the fuck are you doing, Reese!"

"What is it?" Tatsu asked.

"He's disconnecting the cipher!" Nagura said before he ran out of the control room. Tatsu followed him.

When they got to the lab, Reese was yanking out fiber-optic cables by the handful. Nagura yelled and leaped on him. Reese was no match for him—a few blows and a kick to his head, and he was down.

"Watch him," Nagura said to Tatsu, pointing at Reese's moaning form on the floor, and he began frantically reconnecting the cables between the cipher and the machines. As he did, Mr. Morgan and one of his guards showed up. Tatsu yanked Reese to his feet and shoved him at Morgan, who grabbed the bloody and disoriented scientist.

"Get him out of here," Umi said, without looking at Reese, her voice practically a whisper.

"Yes, ma'am," Morgan said, as he and the other guard grabbed Reese under the arms and dragged him out of the hold.

A few moments later, Nagura finished reconnecting all the

cables. He checked the connections to the cipher, then he examined Mikawa.

"Will it still work?" Tatsu asked, as Umi came in to join them. Tatsu could feel Alex sitting up in the control room, watching them.

"It has to," Nagura said. "Mikawa's in bad shape. He won't survive another attempt." Nagura stepped to the machines, and Tatsu watched his hands fly across the controls like a concert pianist.

"Is . . . *it* okay?" Umi asked, motioning at the cipher. Tatsu knew she wanted to ask about Mikawa, even run to his side, but she would never do that in front of all these people. It wasn't her way. But more than that, Tatsu noticed how Umi had trouble referring to the cipher, and she really wondered what Umi's reaction would be if this actually worked.

"I think so. The disconnection was a shock to the artificial synapse, but the buffers seem to have retained all the data. Now it's flowing . . . wait. Damn it. It's flowing too fast."

"I thought you said it had to go fast?" Tatsu asked.

"Not this fast. The cipher won't—" Nagura suddenly looked like he was trying to remember something, his nostrils flaring. "Do you smell something burning?" he asked, as if he were afraid of the answer.

Tatsu stepped closer, and a smell like burning plastic hit her sinuses. She looked down and saw the side of the cipher's head seeming to come alive, wriggling before her eyes. Blue smoke wafted up from the shifting flesh analogue, and she realized what was happening.

Jesus, it's melting!

She tried to warn Nagura, but she was too late. The side of the cipher's head bubbled, cracked, then shrank away from the metallic skull underneath. Nagura watched it all.

"No, no, NO!" Nagura yelled as sparks started shooting up from the charring metal, the room filling with smoke.

Tatsu suddenly realized that the smoke could be toxic. Umi! She ran back and tried to drag the old woman from the danger, but she wouldn't budge, then actually slapped Tatsu across the face. In shock, Tatsu let go and touched her burning cheek. If anyone else had tried that, they'd already be dead. But she just stared at Umi like a scolded child, watching the old woman's eyes flick from Mikawa to the cipher and back again.

Sparks and smoke sprayed out of the cipher's head, then suddenly the head exploded, the blast knocking Nagura to the floor. Tatsu ran and helped him up, but Nagura pushed away from her, coughing and wincing from minor burns to the side of his face. He grabbed an extinguisher and put out the flames that were licking across and melting the rest of the cipher's face.

"It's destroyed. Reese's neural net couldn't handle the data," Nagura said, waving fumes away from his face.

"Can you fix it?" Umi said weakly.

"Not in time. The robot will be fine. I've got a dozen parts back at my workshop that could fix it in a few hours. But the neural net—the brain—is toast."

"What about—" Umi's question was interrupted by a high-pitched whine, and Mikawa suddenly began convulsing violently. Nagura ran to his side. As he did, the convulsing stopped, and the brain image on the screen went white.

"Oh my God," Nagura hissed.

"Is he . . . dead?" Umi asked.

"Yes, but that's not . . . Reese didn't shut down the process before he started yanking the cables. It kept going. It emptied Mikawa's mind completely. He didn't die from the cancer or the strain of the procedure. He died because . . . he's not *here* anymore," Nagura said, waving his hands over Mikawa's body.

"Oh my God," Tatsu said, putting her arm tentatively around Umi, who was looking pale and like she might pass out. "Was he . . ." She motioned at the burned cipher.

"No, the transfer never passed the checksum. He's . . . he's still in the buffer," Nagura said, turning and looking at the machines behind him.

"You mean he's *in* the machine?" Tatsu asked incredulously.

"He's alive?" Umi asked.

"Yes, but . . ." Nagura stepped to the machines and checked a few readouts. "Damn it, I was afraid of this."

"Afraid of what?"

"The buffer isn't designed for long-term storage. Especially the amount of data we're talking about. It's . . . it's starting to degrade. Flush itself."

"Flush itself?" Tatsu said.

"These machines are very sophisticated. Just like before, it's trying to save itself. It's dumping Mikawa, bit by bit. We're losing him."

"What about the other robot?" Tatsu said.

"We'll never initialize it in time. The buffer will be completely empty by then."

"There's got to be something we can do!" Tatsu pleaded.

Nagura ran his hand through his hair and paced. Tatsu was sure all was lost, when suddenly Nagura stopped and looked at Umi.

"What is it?" Umi asked.

"It's a long shot, but there's only one networked system close by that could handle this amount of data."

"Is that possible?" Umi asked. Tatsu realized what they were talking about.

Ashita.

"Maybe. But we have to decide now. We've already lost eight percent of him."

"Umi, maybe we should—" Tatsu didn't get to finish.

"Do it."

Chapter Twenty-eight

Unknown

"WHO'S THERE?" LEW said again. The voice had been so small and brief, he was starting to think he'd imagined it. Just as he was about to give up and get back to what was in the crate, he heard it again.

"Please. Help me. It's trying to kill me."

Lew zeroed in on the source of the strange voice. It was coming from behind a stack of boxes. He stared at them, trying to see who was in the room with him. Finally, he saw a single eye staring out at him from a crack between two crates.

"What's trying to kill you?" Lew asked, edging forward. "Come on out from behind there. I won't hurt you." Whether Lew would actually hurt him or not depended on what the voice did next, but Lew needed answers. And clothes, he thought, shivering.

Slowly, a thin, shaking man stood up behind the crates, his bloodshot, wide eyes rimmed with thick black circles. As he stood up, his gaze flicked left and right, like a squirrel in the park being offered a peanut. Lew had seen that look before. On detainees in Kuwait. This guy was sleep deprived. Sleep deprived times ten. The soldiers interrogating them would wake them up whenever they fell asleep—play loud music, hose them down with ice water—whatever it took to keep them from getting any rest. After days or weeks of this, they got this same look—and started to hallucinate. If it went on much longer, they'd literally lose their minds. This guy wasn't far from there.

"That's it. All the way up. Who you hiding from, buddy?" Lew said in an almost singsong voice, like he was talking to a child. Lew was holding his hands up too, so the man could see he wasn't armed.

"I'm hiding from . . . *him*," the man said, practically hissing as he pointed up at the ceiling. There was nothing on the ceiling but more white.

"What's your name?" Lew asked. The man was dressed in an oversized lab coat, filthy to the point of being brown. He kept glaring up into the corners of the room.

Crap. This guy isn't going to be any help at all.

"It wasn't my fault, you know."

"Of course it wasn't, buddy. These things just happen sometimes," Lew said.

The man stood up straight and just looked at Lew. Then he started nodding and crying. "Yes. You understand. It wasn't my fault. But I'm the only one they put down here. How is *that* fair?" he said, coming out from behind the crates.

"It's not . . . I'm sorry, I forgot—What's your name again?"

"*Reese*," he said in an even lower whisper.

"Hey, Reese. I'm Lew. Do you think you can help me, Reese? I'm kinda freezing here."

"Where are your clothes?" Reese said, seeming to notice Lew's lack of attire for the first time.

"*It* took them," Lew said, hoping if he played along, he'd get further. Direct questions weren't doing much.

"I knew it! We need to stick together Lew. Maybe . . . maybe you can stand guard while I get some sleep? I'm so tired."

Bingo.

"I know you are, buddy. Now, clothes. A T-shirt, a blanket—anything."

Reese's focus came back to the room for a moment. He stepped over to a steamer trunk and swung it open. Inside was a mini wardrobe. Shirts, underwear, socks, shoes—the works. The shirts were too small for Lew, but he found a grubby football jersey that fit him. He slipped it on. Everything else was too small, but this would do for now.

"Do you know anything about that?" Lew asked, pointing at the triangles and the ocean beyond.

"It's the ocean," Reese said matter-of-factly. "We're on the bottom."

"Uh, the *bottom*? Exactly how far down are we?"

"Not . . . not my specialty. They told me about five hundred meters. Not the bottom-bottom, we're on a ridge."

Jesus. Lew did some quick calculations. Five hundred meters. About sixteen hundred feet. Somewhere around fifty-one atmospheres. But he didn't feel it. *Of course. The atmosphere must be normalized. We're on some sort of specialized submarine.* Lew knew from his time in the military that submarines had gone a lot deeper than this.

"Do you know anything about these?" Lew said, walking over to the crate he had been in.

Reese walked over and looked inside. On the bottom lay two human-looking robots, one with a damaged head, blackened like it had been burned. Impossibly, Reese's eyes got larger than they already were. He started panting like he couldn't catch his breath.

"No! You're with them! You're with it! Get away!" Reese was blathering, backing away from Lew like he was the plague.

"Easy, easy. I'm not with anyone."

"No! You're lying! You want to kill me!" Reese threw one of the small crates at Lew. While he was ducking, Reese pressed a panel on the wall and a door slid open. He ran out, straight into a couple of guards who stood outside. Lew stayed in a crouch and eased back behind the crate.

"There you are, Reese," one of the guards said. "We've been looking for you."

"No! He's with you! You all want to kill me!"

"Reese, settle down! You want me to use my Taser again?" one of the guards said, pulling a Taser out of his belt. Reese immediately stopped thrashing.

"No. No, I'll be good. No more tasing."

"Attaboy. Now, the boss lady wants to see you. Pronto. Let's take a little walk, and maybe she'll let you sleep tonight."

"I'd like that," Reese said, as the trio moved away.

Lew waited a few more minutes before he came out from his hiding spot.

What the hell was going on here? And where the hell was Jonny? He tapped behind his ear a few times.

"Jonny? You there, buddy?"

Only silence.

He didn't have a choice. He'd have to try to find him. But if he started lurking around a submarine dressed the way he was, it would be almost impossible to keep from being spotted. Unless they'd gotten their hands on something like a Typhoon-class submarine with it's massive multifloored layout. Even then. And where the hell would they get—

"*Hello, Lew.*"

Lew looked around for a second, then realized it had come from his implant. It wasn't Jonny, though.

"Hello? Is that you, Fahd?" Lew thought about how much he would love to get his hands on that little bastard.

"*No, we are not Fahd.*"

We?

Lew got up and moved to the door. Staying in one place like this was too risky. He had to get moving. He peeked around the corner of the door and felt prickles crawl up his back and into his neck from what he saw. His mouth fell open as he looked around and up . . . and up and up and up. He was definitely *not* on a submarine.

"If you're not Fahd, then who the hell are you?" Lew managed.

"*Our name is Mikawa. And we have a proposition for you, Lew.*"

Chapter Twenty-nine

Jirojin Maru
2:30 P.M. Local Time

BEFORE ANYONE COULD react to Tatsu's fantastic story, a powerful wave broke over the starboard side and slammed down onto the already waterlogged group sitting on the heliport pad. Tatsu, the smallest and lightest of them all, was almost washed away by it, but Per grabbed her in time.

"Here comes another one!" Jonathan yelled. The foursome huddled around Alex's body and grabbed onto each other. They weathered the onslaught, but just barely.

"If they keep getting stronger, we won't be able to take much more," Maggie said, huddled into Jonathan's side.

"Tanaka! Where the fuck are you?" Jonathan yelled into the air. There was a slight buzz from his implant, but he couldn't make it out with the storm raging over him. "Say again, Tanaka?"

"*I'm . . . I'm almost . . . there,*" Tanaka said louder, sounding strained. A minute later, Tanaka emerged onto the heliport, and Jonathan saw why his speech was halting.

"Tanaka!" Tatsu said.

Tanaka had been shot; deep red, almost black, blood oozed from a stomach wound in his pristine white uniform. His mask was pulled down around his neck, and he held another mask in a bloody hand. As soon as he reached the heliport, he fell to his knees. Jonathan got up to go to him.

"Tanaka! What the hell—" But then he looked starboard and saw a monster wave bearing down on them, bigger than the last two combined. "Grab onto something!" But there was nothing except each other. Tanaka was alone, kneeling, and wounded. Jonathan dove at Tanaka just as the wave crashed down.

Jonathan felt like someone had dropped a building on him. His senses were obliterated for a terrifying moment. Nothing but the roar of the storm. When they returned, he was sliding. Somehow he'd managed to grab Tanaka, but from the looks of it, he was out cold. Deadweight. And dragging Jonathan at incredible speed toward the port side.

Jonathan could hear Lew's voice in his head—*Let go, stupid!*—but he hung on. If he let go, Tanaka was a goner if he wasn't already. A tug on his leg made him look back. Per was hanging on to him as the three of them slid toward, then over the side.

Jonathan distantly heard Maggie and Tatsu screaming. He opened his eyes and saw that he still had ahold of Tanaka's hand, but the two of them were well over the side of the boat, staring down at the dark, roiling ocean forty feet below them. He looked back and saw that Per had grabbed onto the railing and was having no trouble at all hanging onto it, but he was struggling with his other arm's load.

How is he— Then Jonathan saw how Per was able to hold so much weight—now and when he'd jumped from the chopper. Per's sleeve had pulled up to his elbow, or what should have been an elbow. In its place was a mechanical joint. *He's part machine!*

"Let go of him!" Per yelled. "You can't save him, and you're going to kill us both!"

No way am I letting go of the poor bastard.

"Jonathan! Let . . . let me go," Tanaka managed. "He's right." Jonathan looked down and saw that Tanaka had come around, but his pupils kept trying to roll up under his eyelids.

"No! Nobody dies!" Jonathan shouted.

"He's already dead!" Per answered.

Then Lew's voice in his head again: *Jonny, think of Natalie. Think of Maggie. Hell, think of me!*

A sound built in Jonathan's throat like a rising roar. He looked in Tanaka's eyes, which seemed hooded and vacant.

"I'm sorry," Jonathan said, as he let go and watched Tanaka fall like a rag doll. He hit the surface and disappeared under the dark waves.

"*Fuck!*" Jonathan howled at the storm as Per hauled him up. They fell back on the deck, panting. They looked at each other and after a wordless moment, Per nodded. Per put out his human hand, and Jonathan grabbed it, each pulling on the other to stand. "Let's get out of here."

Jonathan marched past Per, ignored Maggie and Tatsu, and walked right through the doorway into the ship. Tanaka's mask had been around his neck, not on his face, and—not counting his bullet wound—he'd been fine. Jonathan headed down the hall to the first junction and took a deep inhale. When he exhaled and felt normal, he ran back to the doorway.

"Let's go!"

"What about Alex?" Maggie called.

"Leave him," Jonathan said. "Let the fucking sea have him."

Everyone ran inside, entering a little tentatively but continuing when the air didn't lay them out.

When the foursome reached a Y in the corridor, they stopped. Everyone was shivering.

"We need to get out of these clothes," Per said.

"There's a maintenance room just down this hall," Maggie said. "There should be some coveralls or something."

A few minutes later, they were all dressed in gray coveralls that said "Tenabe" on the back. The coveralls were baggy but fit Jonathan's lanky frame. Everyone else had to roll up the legs and sleeves, including Per. Jonathan thought they looked like the worst moving company in the world. The thought—and nonchalantly seeing Maggie strip down to change—had lightened his mood.

Maggie had dumped the messenger bag, thanks to the big pockets in the coveralls. She and Jonathan had guns in their pockets, and Jonathan carried the machine gun they'd taken off Alex slung over one shoulder.

"Now what?" Maggie said.

"Head to the moon-pool room," Jonathan said.

"Why?" Maggie said.

"To hopefully get to the sub before Morgan does and get down to Ashita."

"Again, why? Who is this Lew that Alex hit with a pipe and sent down there?"

"He's my partner. There's not enough time to explain everything, but I'm not with the CIA," Jonathan said.

"You don't say," Maggie said. Jonathan looked at her, not really that surprised. "The implant made me suspicious, but if you were CIA, no bloody way would you have run around the ship trying to save a bunch of scientists. That was all Jonathan."

"Look, just show me where the moon-pool room is; you don't have to come down. I know you—"

"I'm coming," she said flatly.

"Don't take this wrong, I need the help and then some, but why? Even if I can get down there, the odds of a return trip are not promising," Jonathan said.

"Jonathan, you just saved a hundred lives. Lives that, technically, I was responsible for. Without you, even if I had discovered Umi's plan on my own, they'd all be dead. Including me."

"Per and I are going, too," Tatsu said out of the blue.

"Whoa, what?" Jonathan said. Maggie would be helpful, and he'd actually been hoping she'd come down with him. But these two? Per had saved his life, and no doubt that arm of his would come in handy, but Tatsu? She was practically a kid though she did have the inside track on this whole plan of Umi's.

"I've got my own score to settle with Umi before she dies. Which means I don't have much time. And I promised to show Per something down there in exchange for his help."

"Show him something," Maggie said, disbelief evident in her tone.

"Rest easy. I have no intention of interfering with your search for his friend. I simply want information. That is all," Per said.

"But will you help if it's needed?" Jonathan asked. "If you've got some kind of death wish—"

"Yes, of course I will," Per said. "And I have no intention of dying anytime soon." When Jonathan couldn't detect any deception in Per's eyes, he shrugged at Maggie.

"So, it's a party," he said.

"J . . . Jonathan."

He spun around but realized no one around him was saying anything. It was his implant. Tanaka was still *alive*.

Then all Jonathan heard was coughing, gasping and grunting. Jonathan imagined the wounded Tanaka fighting to tread water in the violent seas. With his last breaths he was trying to tell him something.

"Tanaka?" Jonathan said. The shock on everyone's face was evident.

"He's still alive?" Tatsu asked.

"What's he saying?" Maggie asked.

Jonathan waved them all quiet.

" . . . *SB*," Tanaka said, followed by thick swallowing noises. " . . . *ata dev . . .*"

"Tanaka, you're not making any sense," Jonathan said, but what could he do? Tanaka would be lucky if he had two minutes left. Whatever he had to say was crucial, or at least Tanaka thought so. If he was ever in the same situation, Jonathan wondered if he'd be saying anything besides "help" and Natalie's name.

" . . . *database . . . virus . . . dead lights . . .*"

What the hell? He'd heard those words completely, but they didn't make any sense. Maybe Tanaka had already lost too much blood. Maybe—

"*Destroy Ashita!*" Tanaka screamed. Jonathan hoped it was only in frustration at getting his point across. Regardless, Jonathan couldn't do that. Never mind the loss of life of whoever was currently down there, that might include Lew.

"*USB . . . device . . .*" then gurgling. Tanaka fell quiet and didn't speak again. It was over. Jonathan looked at the others and shook his head. He wasn't sure what he'd heard or if it was even what Tanaka had wanted to say, but he kept it to himself for now.

With Tanaka gone, they continued their trek to the moon-pool room, albeit a little more somberly. They came to a large metal door with a wheel on it. Maggie spun the wheel on the door and yanked it open. Inside was an air lock, a small chamber with a similar door on the other side.

"There's only room for two of us at a time," Jonathan said. "Maggie and I will go first. You guys come in after." Before anyone could complain, Jonathan shoved Maggie inside, stepped in, and pulled the door shut behind them.

"Press that button there," Maggie said. Jonathan did, and they waited for the indicator over the inside door to turn green.

But it wasn't an accident that Jonathan had gotten in there with Maggie alone. As they waited, he told her what Tanaka had said.

"What the hell are dead lights?" Maggie asked.

"I have no idea. I was hoping you'd know."

"Not a clue. But until we do, I think you're right to keep it from our companions."

"See, we always did, um, think . . ." Suddenly Jonathan was very aware of the tight quarters and how close he was to Maggie's body.

" . . . alike," Maggie said, her voice softer than before. The air seemed electric. She licked her lips, and Jonathan could feel himself unable to resist leaning in. But just as their lips were about to touch, something occurred to him.

"Of course, *data* device!" Jonathan said, routing through the pockets of his coveralls.

"That is the oddest rejection I've ever gotten," Maggie said.

"That door will keep them out until we leave and shut this door, right?"

"Uh, yeah. The pressure has to equalize before they can open theirs. Why? What's a data device?"

"This," Jonathan said, pulling out the data device Fahd had given him. Maggie looked thoroughly unimpressed.

"It's a phone."

"Let's hope it's more," Jonathan said. He reached up and pulled the end of his pendant apart, revealing the USB plug. "Cross your fingers."

Jonathan inserted the USB drive into his data device. For a terrible second, nothing happened. Then the device came to life, a light on the USB drive blinked, and Jonathan could hear Fahd's voice through his implant. He quickly explained what was happening to Maggie and asked her to be patient.

"*Welcome to phase two, Jonathan. Your real mission,*" Fahd said, the display of the data device coming to life. An old woman's face was displayed.

"*This is Umi Tenabe. You've no doubt been told quite a bit about her, by now. She's deadly. Don't underestimate her, or it will be the last thing you do. In cooperation with certain factions of the Japanese government, she's built this.*" The data device now displayed a geodesic dome under the sea, huge white triangles all across its surface.

"*It's called* Ashita—*Japanese for* tomorrow—*and is a self-sustaining deepwater city capable of housing almost five thousand people. In tourism mode, it can house twenty-five hundred people and host hundreds of others as guests. Or, that was the plan given to the Japanese government. Our intel, while not corroborated, says Umi has reneged on their deal and is holding Ashita hostage, if you will, threatening to expose sensitive information about key government personnel if they should try to take it back by force.*"

"*Which brings us to your target: Umi's database,*" Fahd said. A metallic briefcase displayed on the device. "*For sixty years, Umi has done business with some of the largest and most important corporations on earth, including defense contractors, governments, and even DARPA. During every transaction, every deal, she either made information part of the terms or made arrangements to steal information. What she has now is the most complete and dangerous database of scientific research and military design ever compiled. If any one government were to get their hands on it, the balance of power in the world would change forever.*

"*Our intel says that the database is on Ashita. Umi had her scientists incorporate the data into the city's advanced AI control computer, but one of the scientists is now with us. He was sent in from some company called Crystasis, but once he was in place, we approached him. He made a copy of the database and hid it. It is imperative that you contact him and, primarily, get the database out, but also retrieve our man, if possible. His name is Dr. Reese.*"

Jonathan recognized the name from Tatsu's story as one of the scientists who had tried to save Mikawa.

"Dr. Reese?" Maggie said. Jonathan had been relaying a précis version of what he was hearing for her.

"*. . . main objective, but we underestimated Umi's desire for revenge. A biologist named Dr. Norris worked for her for a while but disappeared a few weeks ago. We don't have much beyond that, as the communications perimeter went up shortly after. According to what we could piece together from Tanaka and Reese, Norris was developing a virus for her—a virus she was going to release into the food chain. Originally called Project Threshold, it apparently was recently renamed Project Dead Lights. Near as we can determine, it was designed to shorten telomeres on human chromosomes. I'm* *afraid that's all we received. Our counsel is to make the database your priority and look into Dead Lights if there's time. There's no guarantee that Norris completed his work or what the real outcome of shortened telomeres are, but I wanted you to have all the information we do.*

"*In Reese's final report, he said one of the sub's automated systems had broken down. Since you might need it to get down there, we've incorporated our version of those systems into your data device. It's not as sophisticated, but it will get you within sight of Ashita. Good luck.*"

The recording ended abruptly. Jonathan spun the wheel to open the door to the moon-pool room. Per and Tatsu were no doubt getting antsy about why it was taking so long. He swung the door open and felt his heart sink even further.

"The sub," Maggie said.

It was gone.

"Do you think this implant of his is for real?" Tatsu said.

"No reason not to," Per said.

"You think he's telling us everything?"

"Highly unlikely," Per said. "Much the same way your story left details out."

Tatsu felt her skin flush. She'd always been a terrible liar. She wondered why she cared if Per knew she was leaving things out or not.

"I don't know what you're talking about," Tatsu said, finally.

"Of course," Per said, not seeming to care one way or the other, "as long as you follow through on your promise, I don't care what you tell them."

The light over the air lock changed to green, indicating the inside door had been shut and the room had pressurized to match the ship's normal pressure. Per spun the wheel on the door and pulled it open.

"And you promised to help me get to Umi before she . . . before it's too late."

"And so I shall. Getting us to Ashita is the only thing that matters, now."

"Which means what? You'll kill anyone who gets in your way?"

"You're not really one to talk about killing, Tatsu. In the short time I've known you, you've left bodies for me to find. Twice. And I think I've proved that I don't intend anyone any harm, as long as I get what I want."

"Proved?"

"I've saved both your and Jonathan's life since we got here. There have been a ridiculous number of times I could have hurt or killed you all. Yes, proved," Per said, as they stepped into the chamber, and he pulled the door shut behind them. When the door was secured, Tatsu hit the button to start the pressurization process.

"And I suppose pointing a gun at me back at the helicop—" Tatsu stopped talking as Per handed her his gun.

"Take it."

Tatsu took it slowly, unsure of this game.

"Shoot me."

"What?"

"Go ahead," Per said, grasping the barrel and placing it against his forehead. "Shoot me."

Tatsu thought about it for a minute, looking in Per's eyes. What little emotion she could find there seemed to say he was serious. She put her finger on the trigger and applied a little pressure, the hammer easing back ever so slightly. Time seemed to stand still, the only sound the slight hiss of the chamber's pressure changing and the blood pounding in her ears. Finally, she flicked the magazine eject button with her thumb and caught the clip that slid out of the gun's grip. It was empty. No bullets. She took the gun away from his forehead and pulled the slide back to see if a round was waiting in the chamber, but it was empty too.

"You unloaded it," she said, though when she thought back to being on deck when both Alex and Mr. Morgan were shooting at them, Per hadn't fired a shot.

"It was never loaded," Per said. The light changed to green, and he spun the wheel on the door.

They stepped through the door, leaving the empty gun behind them. Jonathan and Maggie were standing by the edge of the moon pool. The empty moon pool.

"Where's the sub?" Per asked.

"Morgan," Maggie said.

"Is there another way we can get down there?" Jonathan asked, stepping over to Tatsu. Everyone was looking at her.

"Maybe."

Chapter Thirty

Ashita

2:45 P.M. Local Time

LEW HAD NEVER had such a surreal experience in his life. He was almost a kilometer under the ocean walking barefoot through a massive, deserted park. Lush green grass stretched for as far as the eye could see, and from its feel underfoot, it wasn't artificial. Groves of trees were sporadically placed here and there, with picnic areas complete with picnic tables, water fountains, and barbecues in large supply, some of them with huge, ivy-covered trellises over their entrances. But even with all that, the place felt . . . wrong.

There were no birds, no kids screeching, not even any squirrels darting here and there. Lew felt more like he was on a spaceship than under the ocean.

The walls, all pristine and white, curved gently around the perimeter, with doors that led to mechanical rooms, storage areas, and even public washrooms. And in the center of it all was a massive conical tower rising up to the ceiling of the sphere half a kilometer over his head. Lew just wanted to run away from this madness, but for the time being, Mikawa was his best option.

"*Please hurry, Lew,*" Mikawa's voice said.

"You say this place is called Ashita?" Lew asked as he headed around the perimeter of the park.

"*That's right.*"

"How big *is* it?" Lew asked.

"*How big?*" Mikawa said, seeming almost confused. Then a moment later: "*It has 196,428.5714 square meters of surface area. 8,184,523.8095 cubic meters of volume, a displacement of—*"

"Whoa, whoa," Lew said, getting dizzy. "What are you, a scientist?"

"*Something like that,*" Mikawa said.

"Okay, something a normal person can understand. How many floors in the tower?"

"*Thirty-eight.*"

"See, wasn't that easy?" Lew said, looking up at the top of the tower and whistling. "So where are you?"

"*We are exactly 125.2—*"

"Uh, uh, uh," Lew chided.

"*Yes. Normal. We are halfway up. Floor nineteen,*" Mikawa said.

"There ya go," Lew said. "We'll have you de-geeked in no time, Mickey. So how many people are in Ashita?"

"*Currently there are eight people in Ashita.*"

"And you can track where they are? I mean, I don't have to worry about running into any, right?"

"*Only Dr. Reese is wearing a tag we can track. Our other calculations are arrived at through visual identification. And your communication implant.*"

"Is mine the only communication implant?" Lew asked, hope edging his voice.

"*Yes.*"

Crap. Jonny, where are you?

"Do you know who they are? The other people in Ashita?"

"*Some of them.*"

"Tell me who they are and their current locations."

"*Umi Tenabe is in her residence on the top floor with four guards. We only recognize their uniforms. Dr. Reese is in the research facility on the main floor with two other guards.*"

Tenabe. Lew remembered that name from the briefing on the plane.

"*Dr. Reese, huh?*"

Lew was sure he was talking to a computer of some kind, but it seemed to get confused just like a person would yet adapted incredibly well. Like when he gave it a nickname, it didn't even react. It just adapted. Lew wasn't sure what the deal was down here, but he did know one thing—he was in the middle of a serious shitstorm. And, with no weapons, he was in no shape to take on six guards.

Mikawa's proposition was a simple one: He'd get Lew back to the surface if Lew did something for him. Mikawa wanted the undamaged robot body from the crate Lew had been in. But they apparently weighed around four hundred pounds each. Lew needed something called an exoskeleton suit in order to lift the robot and transport it. So now Lew was on his way to the docking port, where apparently there were a couple of these exoskeletons. Lew still hadn't determined if helping Mikawa was such a wise thing to do, but Lew was picking his battles. If he didn't push too hard, Mikawa seemed compelled to answer direct questions. And the one thing Lew needed more than anything right now was information. Well, and to get out of his wetsuit shorts before his balls shot out his nose.

"Why don't you tell me about Dr. Reese, Mickey," Lew said.

"*Dr. Chris Reese. Born April 15, 1985 in London, Ontario, Canada. He has a PhD in machine learning and another in computer science, both from the University of Toronto. He most recently worked for the Crystasis Foundation before coming to Ashita six months ago.*"

"Six months in this place did *that* to him?" Lew said. The last thing Reese looked like was a doctor of anything but crazy.

"*No, we have been . . . we have been . . .*"

"You okay, Mickey?" Lew thought he sounded more confused than before.

"*There were orders to keep him from sleeping,*" Mikawa finally said. Usually that torture technique was to break a subject so they'd cooperate. Reese had looked well past that point, like someone had just been punishing him.

"Notify me of everyone's movements, Mickey."

"*Affirmative,*" Mikawa said.

Just then a small robot came whirring around the corner. It traveled at a good clip, but when it got close to the wall, the robot turned and whirred away.

"What the hell was that?" Lew asked.

"*Maintenance robot. All of Ashita is automated. They clean, make repairs, and the drones deliver things.*"

"Drones?" Lew said, looking up. He hadn't noticed them before, but there were several quad-copter drones flying around high overhead, each with a small box underneath them. "Huh. What are they delivering and to who?"

"*Some are just cameras. Others are delivering things to other robots.*"

"Well, it's definitely a Japanese underwater city," Lew said to himself.

"*Please repeat, Lew?*"

"I was just saying all you need are some sushi restaurants and an indoor golf course."

"*Restaurants and shopping will be on level fifteen to twenty-five. They are still under construction.*"

"So no golf," Lew quipped.

"*There are a few dozen golf simulators on the entertainment level. Three are functioning if you would like to play.*"

Lew shook his head. "I'm good, thanks," Lew said as he continued toward the docking port. "Tell me something, Mickey."

"*Tell you . . .*" Mikawa stumbled on Lew's colloquialism.

"Sorry, I was just wondering, why me? Why do you need my help? And why not get one of the other people down here to help you? They're all on Umi's payroll already."

"*That is why, Lew. We need to do something Umi Tenabe does not want us to do. You are the first anomaly since Nagura to come down here. We have lost contact with him. We didn't choose you, you were the only option.*"

"Don't sweat it, Mickey. You wouldn't believe the number of times in my life where that's been the case."

Chapter Thirty-one

Jirojin Maru
2:51 P.M. Local Time

JONATHAN STOOD BESIDE Maggie watching Tatsu work the crane that ran on tracks in the ceiling as Per waved his arms and guided her toward the water. The disabled sub from behind the partition was in the jaws of the crane. It wasn't like any submarine Jonathan had ever seen. Two huge glass balls sat nestled in a pocket of bright yellow metal.

"You're not really going to let them come with us, are you?" Maggie said quietly. He'd been having his own tug-of-war about that.

"Per hasn't shown himself as a threat," Jonathan said. "Just the opposite."

"It's not him I'm worried about. Tatsu and Umi are close. She's been sending the kid out on missions for months. "

"To do what?"

Maggie didn't answer. Jonathan looked at her.

"You don't know, do you," Jonathan said.

"That's not the point. I don't know what Tatsu's experienced out there the past few weeks, no, but to think it has resulted in a complete one-eighty on her loyalties seems like a foolish bet."

"Or the perfect time to turn her into an asset," Jonathan said. "You know the drill better than I. If she's doubting her loyalties, this is the perfect time to use her. So what—"

"I don't care what she said, she knows the rest of Umi's plan." Maggie turned and faced him. "In detail. We're walking blind into who-knows-what down there, and I'd bloody well like a little more idea if we're coming back."

Jonathan watched Tatsu move the sub over the moon pool with Per's help and lower it into the water. After moving the crane jaws out of the way, Tatsu jumped down. There was something in the way she jumped, control and fluidity. Jonathan, trained in Kenjutsu himself, had seen people move like that before. It betrayed their training, their balance, and their lethality.

"All right," Jonathan whispered as Per and Tatsu walked toward them. "Back my play when the time comes." Maggie nodded.

"Can this thing go deep enough?" Maggie asked.

"And then some," Tatsu said.

"How is it disabled?" Per asked.

"The automated systems malfunctioned," Tatsu said.

"Automated?" Jonathan asked.

"Ashita sends out a constant signal—a heartbeat. The automated systems on the submarine lock on and follow the signals to the docking bay on Ashita. There's no real piloting, usually."

"How do you know all this?" Jonathan asked.

"When Ashita was first completed, Umi would take me with her quite often. Sometimes we stayed down there for weeks at a time. It's really beautiful. But to answer your question, Umi does everything for a reason. At the time, the automation wasn't perfected and would frequently cut out—or she would make it cut out, I'm not sure which. She trained me on how to manually control the sub so she'd have someone to get her out if need be."

Jonathan had made up his mind. He stepped back and brought the machine gun to bear on Tatsu. Maggie stepped behind him.

"Per, don't get any ideas. Just move away," Jonathan said. Per calmly raised his hands to show he was no threat and moved off to the side.

"What's going on?" Tatsu asked, sounding truly surprised.

"I've got nothing against you, Tatsu, and I really hope I'm making a big mistake, but you're not going down there without giving us more information. I'm not sure if I buy the shift in your loyalty to Umi, but one thing we do know is that you know whatever she's planning down there. To the letter. It's why you keep saying we don't have much time. You've got sixty seconds to come clean, or we're going to leave you here."

"But . . . you need me. How else are you going to find—"

Jonathan showed her the display on his data device, a blinking light showing where Ashita's signal was coming from.

"But you don't know how to pilot—"

"We're smart," Maggie said. "We'll figure it out."

"You need me to find Dead Lights!" Tatsu said to Per.

"I want to find them, yes, but I don't want to die doing it. If there's a timetable or other danger down there, we need to know what it is," Per said. Jonathan wasn't sure if he believed Per's allegiance, but he knew how to get him to behave.

"That's a moot point," Jonathan said. "*I* know what Dead Lights are. I can show them to you." Per looked at Jonathan like he'd just sprouted a second head.

"You're lying!" Tatsu said.

"I am? So, Dead Lights has nothing to do with, oh, Dr. Norris and the virus he created to shorten telomeres," Jonathan said. He was trying to be smug, but he was just glad he had pronounced the word right. Whatever it meant.

"But how?"

"Alex told me last night in bed," Maggie said. Jonathan thought that was risky since they really didn't know what Corsair knew—and he had just started to put the image of Corsair mounting Maggie out of his mind—but it seemed to work. Tatsu's shoulders bowed, and she physically slumped. Now the question was what she knew and what she was truly willing to share. If Jonathan sensed any deception at all, sub piloting or not, he would indeed leave her here.

"Umi will be technically dead at 4:45 P.M.," Tatsu said. "If I don't talk to her in the next ninety minutes, I never will."

"Technically dead?" Jonathan said.

"She's going to transfer herself into Ashita's computer—merge herself with the AI and Mikawa. Her body will be lifeless, but her plan is to live on.

"And the virus? How does she plan to use it?" Jonathan said, hoping he wasn't tipping their hand.

"It's on a timer," Tatsu said. "At 5:15 p.m., thousands of tons of infected algae will be released into the ocean currents using the escape pods. As it drifts, fish and crustaceans will consume it and in turn be infected. And then it will move up the food chain. Umi told me that in six to eighteen months, seventy percent of humans will unknowingly carry the virus."

"Jesus," Jonathan said.

"The telomeres," Maggie said. "What does shortening them do?"

"It's a theory," Tatsu said. "It might not work. The alteration might not do anything."

"But if it works?" Jonathan asked, lowering the machine gun's barrel.

"No human will live past eighty years ever again."

KNOWING THE TIME constraint they were working under now, Jonathan made his decision as fast as he could. Tatsu was far from harmless, but he needed everyone, in one way or another, for this journey to have a round-trip. Even so, Jonathan and Maggie searched Per and Tatsu before they got into the sub. It was unlikely that they had any weapons on them after everyone had changed into coveralls, but they had to be sure. No weapons were found, and Jonathan convinced Maggie to trust Tatsu, for now. Which was easier when he pointed out that it was he and Maggie who were now keeping secrets from the others.

While they were talking, Jonathan also told her about Per's arm. As it turned out, she had already noticed that there was something odd about Per's gloved hand.

But what he didn't like more was that he still hadn't come clean with her about being The Monarch for all these years. He wondered how she was going to react when she found out he and Lew had been art thieves while she'd been cooling her heels in Russia. Not to mention how she'd view the hidden agenda if she knew it came from a clandestine group called The Custodians. Suddenly, he was very glad they didn't have time to discuss things any further.

With Jonathan and Maggie in one of the sub's transparent bubbles and Per and Tatsu in the other—where the steering mechanism was—they sank beneath the waterline and headed for Ashita. Jonathan called out course corrections from his data device's screen as they descended even farther. Other than that, the occupants were almost silent.

The visibility under the water was incredible. With two solid glass bubbles and no struts, their view was unobstructed and breathtaking. They could even look down between their feet though the ocean was so deep that their view just sort of faded into black.

"Wow," Maggie said, looking around.

A mere three minutes later, they were already one hundred fifty meters down. Tatsu angled their descent based on Jonathan's instructions, and they cruised almost silently toward the blackness below. Every now and then, they'd pass sea creatures momentarily curious, then apparently terrified when they saw the surface dwellers inconceivably floating in their world. They sank deeper and deeper, but their piece of atmosphere appeared unchanged. The water around them rapidly darkened as the light from the surface found it harder and harder to stretch down so far.

A sudden flash made Jonathan snap his head around. But it wasn't Ashita. It was Maggie with her cell phone. She was trying to take pictures of the life outside the skin of the sub. They exchanged a smile and just for a moment, life wasn't on the line. They were just tourists miraculously in an alien world. And like he'd done so many times since that night on the Finnish/Russian border, Jonathan wondered what life would have been like if he hadn't failed her so many years ago.

"There it is!" Tatsu called out suddenly, breaking the spell.

"Holy shit," Jonathan said, as Tatsu turned the submarine and headed directly for the glowing orb. They were still a couple of hundred meters out, but Ashita filled their view, like some kind of glowing volleyball.

"How much time do we have, again?" Maggie asked. "Because I think it would take three days to find *anybody* in there."

Jonathan hadn't been ready for the sheer immensity of the underwater city, either. Maggie, as usual, had great foresight. Jonathan wondered what would happen if their time ran out, and he still hadn't found Lew. He closed his eyes and shook his head, trying to make that idea go away.

"Maybe there's a—UHN!" Something slammed into the back of the sub, thrusting Jonathan and Maggie out of their seats. Jonathan rammed face-first into the inner shell of the transparent bubble, and Maggie collided into his back, grinding his face harder into the wall. Then they collapsed on the floor of the sub.

Jonathan spit blood, and Maggie got up and looked at Tatsu. Per's crazy arm had apparently kept him in his seat, and the pilot's chair was wedged in behind the other seats in their side of the sub, so both Per and Tatsu had managed to avoid injury. Maggie was groaning but appeared okay.

"What the hell was that?" Maggie yelled.

"He's over there," Per said. They all looked and saw a larger sub, a single window in the front of the tubular design. Inside the window, they could see the pilot who had just rammed them coming around for another swipe.

"Morgan," Jonathan said.

LEW HAD RETURNED wearing the exo suit in half the time it had taken him to get over to the dock. He had been skeptical at first, and it had taken Mikawa several minutes to walk him through how to even put the thing on, but Lew couldn't believe how the contraption made him feel. He rarely mentioned them, but after years of abuse, there were few muscles and joints in Lew's body that didn't ache on a daily basis. But now, almost all of the pain was gone as the suit supported his weight, doing the work his muscles usually had to do. He felt like a kid again, like he could run faster and jump farther than he had in years.

Once back in the storage area where he'd woken up, Lew picked up the burned robot with one hand and tossed it aside like it was made of styrofoam. He couldn't help but laugh at the act. Then he reached in and picked up the remaining body. He slung it over his shoulder.

"Where to now, Mickey?" Lew said, thinking maybe he shouldn't be in such a rush to leave this place. It was devoid of the most annoying thing Lew endured on the surface—people. The air was fresh, and the artificial light sure felt like sunshine. If they had cheeseburgers and Guinness, he might be home. And clothes, he thought, still shivering a little.

Mikawa directed Lew to the main tower rising in the center of the landscape. Despite carrying four hundred pounds over one shoulder, Lew started toward the tower and soon found himself trotting through the grass, his feet leaving deep footprints in the turf. It only took him a few minutes to make the journey.

Lew entered the tower through the main lobby. Despite being on the ocean floor, it looked like any other building lobby up on the surface: large open space, smooth shiny surfaces everywhere, a reception desk and two elevators. Lew walked over to the desk, examining a directory and map on display.

"Where are Reese and the two guards now?" Lew asked.

"*They are still in the research lab, in Dr. Norris's office.*"

"Dr. Norris? Tell me about Dr. Norris," Lew said, walking around the reception desk. He spotted a door marked "Authorized Personnel Only" and made a beeline for it.

"*Dr. Eric Norris. Born May 31, 1975 in Chicago, Illinois, USA.*

PhD in biology from Duke University, specializing in algal studies. He most recently worked for the Tenabe Group."

"Algal studies?"

"*The study and application of biological interactions of ocean algae. We can find and cite several of his papers on the subject if you would like.*"

"No, that'll be fine," Lew said. "If he worked for Tenabe and has an office down here, where is he?"

"*Dr. Norris, along with most of his team, has been missing for three weeks, ever since completing the Dead Lights Project. We made inquiries but received no answers.*"

Dead Lights? Nothing like a creepy project name. Lew was going to ask more about it, but he'd reached his goal, and that would have to wait for the moment.

He put the robot down and opened the "Authorized Personnel Only" door. Inside, he found a short hallway with several doors lining it. The door that interested him was marked "Security." It was locked, but with a little Lew finesse—Lew's nickname for his shoulder—he coaxed it open, an effort equal to doing the bump on the dance floor thanks to his exo suit. Inside, he found an equipment room. He went in and switched on the light.

"Hello baby," Lew said. The room was filled with guard uniforms of all sizes, complete with socks and shoes. Lew stepped out of his exo suit, then stripped down, fighting with his wetsuit shorts, which were becoming a part of his flesh. He groaned with pleasure as he took a moment to let his parts breathe and return to their normal size. "Drink it in, boys."

When the cramp finally left his side, he slipped into one of the uniforms. There was a weapons closet as well, but all it had in it were Tasers and nightsticks. He'd never liked Tasers, so he took two nightsticks and stuck them on either side of his uniform's belt.

He caught himself in a mirror for a second. It was the first time he'd put on a uniform in over twenty years. He didn't like the feeling it gave him, so he looked away. He stepped back into the exo suit, which was a breeze this time, and went back out to the lobby. He picked up the robot and slung it back over his shoulder.

"Now, where were we," Lew said. But Mikawa didn't respond. "Mickey?"

"*Lew, there appear to be two submersibles impacting each other one hundred thirty-two meters to the northeast,*" Mikawa finally said after a few minutes of silence. "*It should be known that this could interfere with the optimum dispersal.*"

"The dispersal of what?" Lew asked, knowing somewhere in his bones that Jonny was out there in one of those submersibles. Then Lew remembered what Mikawa had said about Norris.

"Tell me about Project Dead Lights, Mickey."

JONATHAN TRIED TO hang on as Tatsu flipped their sub nose-up, and Morgan barreled toward them. They were almost all the way around his trajectory when his nose caught the metal tail of their sub with a loud crunch. The little submersible flipped wildly end over end several times before it came back under control.

"Is everyone all right?" Tatsu yelled.

Jonathan had taken the worst of it. The flip had sent him slamming into the ceiling and back down onto the seats, smashing his face on the hard plastic armrest. Blood was gushing out his nose, and he was having trouble focusing, feeling like he was going to pass out.

Maggie was massaging her neck from the whiplash. Per seemed

to be status quo, but Jonathan was pretty sure you could break off one of his fingers and his face wouldn't show it.

"More or less," Jonathan said nasally, spitting blood into the bottom of the sub.

"He's batting us around like a Ping-Pong ball," Maggie said.

"And if he'd caught one of the bubbles with that last run, we'd be . . . well, it wouldn't be pretty," Tatsu said.

Jonathan looked around for something to help them, but they were sitting with their ass hanging out. Below, he could see the glowing ball of Ashita. *So close. If only. . .*

"Where's the docking port down there?" Jonathan asked.

"There are two," Tatsu said, spinning her head around to watch Morgan make a long, arcing turn. "One on the top and another at the base."

"What are you thinking?" Maggie asked.

"He can't maneuver like we can in that tub. How's his speed?" Jonathan asked.

"He's slower than us, but not by much," Tatsu said.

"Okay, next run, wait until the last moment and dive under him. Go as fast as you can toward the lower docking port."

"Yes, very good," Per said.

"What good will that do? We'll never dock in time. He'll slam into us when we slow down to engage the seal," Tatsu said.

"I believe he doesn't intend for us to slow down," Per said.

"Right," Maggie said. "We've got the maneuverability. He doesn't. We pull up at the last second and—"

"And Morgan eats it," Jonathan said.

"That's crazy," Tatsu said. "I'm not an expert pilot. What if I time it wrong?"

"You won't," Maggie said.

Tatsu rolled her eyes. "But what if I do."

"I don't believe it will matter, Tatsu," Per said. When everyone looked at him, he looked down. They followed his lead. The bottom of the sub had about an inch of water in it.

"Oh my God," Maggie said.

"It's got to be a system leak," Tatsu said. "If either bubble was cracked, the pressure change would have imploded us almost immediately."

"Comforting," Jonathan said, tenderly touching his nose.

"Is it broken?" Maggie asked.

"Oh yeah," Jonathan said. "But on the bright side, this next flip will probably snap it back into place." He tried to smile, but it hurt too much.

"Here he comes," Tatsu said.

Jonathan looked out the bubble and saw Morgan's sub racing toward them. He sat down, and this time grabbed onto his chair like Per and Maggie were doing.

Jonathan felt her hand reach out and take his. Jonathan looked into her eyes and nodded. "Let's play some chicken."

Morgan, with a look on his face like that of a comic-book villain, flew toward them. When he'd halved the distance, Tatsu started forward. He reacted and seemed confused for a minute, but then he bore down, the subs flying at each other. The distance shrank incredibly fast, twenty meters, fifteen, ten, then it was time. Jonathan felt Maggie squeeze his hand, and he squeezed back, closing his eyes.

"Here we go!" Tatsu said as she slammed the stick forward. They rocketed down, the runners under Morgan's sub screeching as they glanced off the top of the little sub. "We made it!"

But Jonathan didn't get as excited as Tatsu. That was only

step one. Freezing water sloshed around Jonathan's ankles as he opened his eyes and saw their target far below. The docking port was a ten-meter-long tunnel, sticking out from Ashita's curved base like a foot.

"Ease up," Jonathan said as he looked back and saw Morgan making the turn. If they got to the port too soon, the plan wouldn't work. Jonathan watched as Morgan came out of his turn, his mouth yawning open like he was yelling something. And then he was closing on them.

"Go!" Maggie yelled.

As they flew deeper and deeper, the water got darker and darker. Jonathan looked up, but he couldn't see the dim light of the surface any longer. He thought about Natalie. How much he missed her and how he couldn't bear the idea of dying without seeing her face one more time, holding her in his arms and telling her it would be all right.

They passed the top of Ashita and flew down past the triangle windows that made up its incredible structure. He could see inside the dome now, a giant tower rising in the center like a space-age skyscraper, the lush lawn and trees lining the base floor. Was Lew in there? Would he see him again?

"He's almost on us!" Maggie shouted. "Faster!"

"This is it!" Tatsu shouted back. The sub was shimmying. Jonathan didn't know if it was from the speed or the depth, but it didn't really matter. He wanted to close his eyes again but forced himself to keep watching. The port grew in size and he could see the door that led inside the behemoth, wondering what would happen if the plan worked, and Morgan slammed into the port.

"Now!" Tatsu shouted, yanking back on the stick.

The sub shot up over the port and continued to rise, water

racing around the bubble from the gees they were pulling. The freezing water fell back on them, making everyone's breath catch. Jonathan wiped the stinging seawater from his eyes and looked back. Morgan was desperately trying to mimic their maneuver, but the lumbering sub couldn't match their little vehicle's arc. With the nose pulled up, the tubular sub slammed belly first into the roof of the port, ripping open like a Christmas cracker. For a brief second, Jonathan saw Morgan raising his hands over his head, his open mouth shaped into a different kind of scream, then the pressure of a half mile of water slammed down on the broken sub, crushing the tube into a rough ball of metal, a sea of bubbles rising.

They watched the ball bounce onto the seafloor and roll to a stop. Jonathan checked the docking port, waiting for the worst to happen, but aside from some scrape marks across the roof, the port held. Whatever it was made of was stronger than steel.

There were no shouts of victory. No sighs of relief. They'd watched a life end in one of the most horrible ways possible. Everyone was silent, and Maggie and Jonathan stopped holding hands, Jonathan's aching from her grip. Everyone fought to catch their breath and deal with what had just happened as Tatsu slowed their ascent and banked over the top of the sphere.

"There's the other port," Per said solemnly. Though he seemed to say everything solemnly, this time was slightly different.

Jonathan checked his watch as Tatsu maneuvered into the upper docking bay. Eighty minutes. He stared at the vastness of Ashita below. They had named it right. *Tomorrow.*

Today wasn't ready for any of this. Not by a long shot.

Chapter Thirty-two

3:45 P.M.

"WHAT THE HELL was that?" Lew asked after the entire sphere began vibrating all of a sudden.

"*One of the submersibles has had a catastrophic depressurization. Shall we continue?*" Mikawa said, referring to the explanation of Project Dead Lights he was running through for the second time with Lew.

"Crap. Where's the other sub?" Lew asked as he continued to climb the stairs toward his goal on the nineteenth floor, the robot over his shoulder swaying with each step. He figured summoning one of the elevators would be like sending off an "I'm over here" flare. He wasn't really sure anyone was looking for him, but he wanted to keep it that way.

"*The remaining submersible has berthed in the upper docking ring. Shall we continue?*" Mikawa said.

"Yes, fine. Continue," Lew said. He then mumbled to himself, "Not like it will help." The first run-through had made about as much sense as a giant sphere at the bottom of the ocean. He'd asked for a repeat, but in simpler terms.

"*Project Dead Lights—originally Project Threshold—was started six months ago. The main goal was to limit the human life span.*"

"Limit? Limit it to what?"

"*Eighty years.*"

"You need a virus for that? How many people in the world are even older than eighty?" Lew asked.

"*Approximately seventy-five million.*"

"Jesus. So, this virus would make seventy-five million people drop dead?"

"*I've already answered that question. Shall I continue?*"

"Yes, continue."

"*Dr. Eric Norris was asked to implement the project using an algal delivery system. This vector was achieved in computer model four weeks ago. The Threshold virus was completed three weeks ago. The optimal launch date was selected and entered into the launch computer. Dr. Eric Norris disappeared later that day.* "

Lew stopped climbing. "Algal delivery system? Simplify, Mikawa," Lew said, mostly understanding this time.

"*Algae designed to be released into the ocean's currents for worldwide dispersal.*"

"*Mother.* Is the launch sequence still running?" Lew asked.

"*Yes, Lew. And the vector has grown to sufficient capacity, as outlined in Dr. Norris's charter.*"

"What is the launch date, Mikawa?"

"*Today.*"

"When today?"

"*Sixty-nine minutes and forty-two seconds from now.*"

"Of course it is," Lew said. "Where is Project Dead Lights?"

"*Doctor Norris's lab.*"

"Can you control it? Stop the launch?" Lew asked.

"*No, the launch controls are on a discrete system. We have no way of interacting with it.*"

"How are the algae being launched?" Lew asked, reasoning that virus or not, algae were living things, and if they just tried to squirt it out into the ocean from down here, the cold and pressure would end their little experiment before it started.

"*A few dozen escape pods were installed in case of emergency when Ashita was first brought online. They have since been repurposed as algae-delivery capsules.*"

"Where are the escape pods?" Lew asked.

"*At the top of Ashita. There's an access hatch in the visitor center that leads up to the escape annex.*"

Lew opened the door a crack and looked out from the stairwell into the hallway that led to Dr. Norris's lab. Ten meters up the hall, two guards stood outside a door. Every now and then, Reese would stick his head out and say something to the guards. One of them would touch the Taser on his belt, and Reese would disappear back into the room.

"*Lew, you've stopped climbing. Is there a problem?*"

"No problem, Mickey. Just a detour. I'll be on my way up to you in no time."

"*Good. That is good. We knew you were not like the others. We can trust you,*" Mikawa said. The change in Mikawa's tone concerned Lew, but he didn't have time to psychoanalyze a bunch of circuits right now.

"We're buddies, Mickey. You can count on that," Lew said.

"*Yes, count on that. Also, Lew, we have an update. There are now twelve people on Ashita.*"

"Four more from the other sub?"

"*Yes. And now that it is docked, we have run a diagnostic. It*

would be unsafe to use the sub again in its current condition. Would
you like us to initiate repairs?"

"Uh, sure," Lew said. Then he thought of something else.
"Does anyone on Ashita besides me have a communication implant now?"

"Yes, one of the new guests has a similar implant, would you like
us to activate it?"

"You can do that? I mean, yes! Activate it!"

"Communications activated."

Suddenly, Lew felt nervous, a very unusual feeling for him. He
forcibly calmed himself.

"Jonny?"

Ashita

Chapter Thirty-three

JONATHAN LOOKED OVER the edge of the walkway that led from the docking ring to the top of the central tower. The thirty-eight-story drop was dizzying. The only thing between them and the ground level was another walkway about halfway down. He stepped back from the edge, which was protected by a half-finished railing, nothing but a few spines sticking up out of the walkway.

"What's inside that door?" Maggie asked, as they approached the central tower.

"The orientation area," Tatsu said. "Mostly open space with a few automated information kiosks providing tourist information about Ashita."

"Tourists were going to come here?" Jonathan said.

"I know it's hard to tell, but Ashita isn't finished, yet. Most of the floors are still under construction. Or were, six months ago. The work crews continued for a while after Mikawa was transferred into the computer system. But over time . . ."

"Over time what?" Jonathan asked. He'd figured there were

still some things Tatsu hadn't shared. The question was, now that they were down here, where would her loyalties lie?

"Accidents started to happen. Almost a dozen construction workers were killed over a two-week period. Then the crews stopped coming. You couldn't really blame them," Tatsu said, a faraway look in her eye.

"Something tells me these accidents weren't really accidents," Maggie said.

"You've come this far, Tatsu. What happened after Mikawa was transferred into the computer?" Jonathan asked gently. Tatsu looked at him, then at the others staring at her, waiting. Her eyes were moist as Jonathan guessed she was reliving those days.

"At first, nothing out of the ordinary. We started to doubt whether it had even worked. All computer functions, including the AI programming, continued as before. But it *had* worked, and Mikawa was merging with the AI program, insinuating himself into every system. But this wasn't really Mikawa. By the time the transfer was made, twenty-five percent of the data taken from Mikawa's brain had degraded and corrupted. What was left was almost a paraphrasing of him. Like someone describing Mikawa who didn't really know the deep truth of his being. Like that game telephone, where one person whispers something to the next person, and so on down the line. Until the last person says what they heard. The data started out as Mikawa, but in the end it was barely recognizable."

"What happened then?" Per asked.

"The first signs were small things. Maintenance robots and drones seemingly going off program. It was Mikawa exercising his power, seeing what he could control. That's how the first few accidents happened. At first, maintenance robots would move unexpectedly, tripping workers. Later, closed-circuit video showed robots and drones cutting safety harnesses and loosening scaffolding bolts. Then the reprogramming became more blatant. Video showed drones literally knocking men off platforms to their death."

"Oh my God," Maggie said, looking down over the edge of the walkway.

"The day the construction crews stopped coming back, four men were working on malfunctions in the docking tunnel," Tatsu said.

"No," Jonathan said, already knowing what was coming.

"Mikawa sealed them in and opened the outer doors," Tatsu said, now not just tearing up, but crying. "The . . . the pressure kept them in the tunnel. When we got the outer doors closed and reopened the inner ones . . ."

Jonathan covered his mouth and felt his own eyes welling up.

"Alex ordered some guards to . . . clean up. They did it, but then they left in the night, and we never heard from them again," Tatsu said.

"Why didn't you shut the computer down?" Per asked, matter-of-factly.

"Don't you think we tried? It's impossible! Mikawa, if he still has any kind of discrete identity, is the only thing that could possibly extract itself from the computer. We can't turn the AI off, it controls everything. The air, the heat and light, even the pressure—everything."

Maggie moved closer to Jonathan.

"And now Umi is going to join the AI and Mikawa," Maggie said quietly to Jonathan.

Jonathan looked up in the air, movement catching his eye. A

drone flew over them and disappeared around the back side of the tower. They needed to get out of there as soon as they could. Assuming Mikawa let them.

"Does Mikawa know we are here?" Per asked Tatsu.

"Possibly. Some of the drones have cameras," Tatsu said.

Now everyone was looking up.

"Just standing here is probably a bad idea," Jonathan said. "Let's get moving."

"Agreed," Maggie said.

"Meet back here in a half an hour," Jonathan said to Per and Tatsu. Tatsu nodded, then she went with Per into the tower.

"What's our plan?" Maggie said when they were gone.

Jonathan exhaled and looked around the vastness of Ashita again.

This is hopeless. What am I supposed to do, just start shouting Lew from the—

"Jonny?" Lew's voice said.

Great, I'm imagining hearing his voice again.

"Jonny, are you there?" Lew's voice said again.

The hairs on the back of Jonathan's neck stood up as he started to believe what he was hearing.

"Lew?"

"Sure, we can try to find him first, but look at the size of this place," Maggie said, misunderstanding.

"No, I'm hearing Lew's voice on my implant! Lew, are you there?" Jonathan said.

"*Welcome to the party,*" Lew said. "*That sub's imploding out there your handiwork?*"

"You could say that," Jonathan said. "Where the hell are you?"

"*Second floor, bottom of the tower. Where are you?*"

"Top of the tower. Stay put, I'm on my way," Jonathan said, grabbing Maggie's hand and rushing to the elevators.

"*Watch yourself, there are still four of Umi's guards around up there,*" Lew said.

"Umi? How do you know . . . never mind. We're on our way."

"*We?*" Lew said.

Jonathan quickly explained about Maggie.

"*Great, I'm getting coldcocked with pipes, and you're picking up chicks,*" Lew said. Jonathan smiled.

"What did he say?" Maggie asked.

"Nothing," Jonathan said. The elevator doors opened, but Jonathan stopped short of getting in. After Tatsu's story, he thought better of it. "Feel like getting some exercise?" Jonathan said, nodding toward the door marked "Stairs."

"You read my mind," Maggie said. They got into the stairwell and trotted down as fast as they could.

"Taking the stairs, Lew," Jonathan said.

"*Copy that.*"

When they were halfway down, Maggie said: "You haven't told me where you guys were partners. Was it at the CIA?"

"Uh, a little after that," Jonathan said, picking up the pace so they'd be too winded to talk. A few minutes later, they pushed through the exit to the second floor.

"Whoa!" Maggie said.

Lew was standing only a few feet from the door, wearing an exo suit and carrying a robot over his shoulder. Under his exo suit, Jonathan saw that Lew was wearing a guard uniform.

"Man, have I got a story to tell you," Lew said. Jonathan thought he looked like a robot, himself. He knew of exo suits from his intel days, but he'd never seen one like this. And, of course, he'd never seen one on Lew. If Lew needed strength support, that thing over his shoulder must weigh a ton. But Lew wasn't the only one with a story to tell.

"Back atcha, brother," Jonathan said.

3:53 P.M.

TROIS GYMNOPEDIES: NO. 3 by French composer Erik Satie echoed across the red and gold furnishings in what would have been Umi's drawing room, where she would have entertained royalty, artists, and scholars alike. In the coming years, the world would have heard about the wonder of Ashita. At first a spectacle and even a curiosity, but after she saved Japan from overpopulation and enhanced the oceanic sciences, it would have been viewed for what it really was: evolution. There would have been many spheres built around the world. A kingdom under the sea. With Umi and Mikawa as their immortal king and queen.

Would have. While it was the dream, as it turned out, it had never been true. They had played her. With all of her subterfuge, half-truths, and outright lies, she hadn't even seen it coming. The player had been played. Umi had tried to save face by telling Tatsu and a few others that it was she who had reneged on their deal, and she was the one holding Ashita hostage, but even if they all believed her, it was little solace for what was really happening.

Umi raised a trembling, wrinkled hand and placed it on the floor-to-ceiling window, looking beyond the space outside, at the ocean held back by her creation. The same way she'd tried to use technology to hold back the march of time. But in the end, time won out.

Her eyes focused on her reflection only inches away. She'd been a fool.

Her eyes flitted from her reflection to that of the incongruous technology behind her—the machines, cables, and hospital bed she'd had Nagura set up weeks ago. She checked her watch. It was almost time. Soon, she would join her beloved. They would be one in Ashita's central processing unit. Entwined so no one could tell one from the other. *Who would have thought that Umi Tenabe would end her flesh-and-blood life as a romantic,* she thought. No one except Mikawa. He'd seen in her things that no one else had. Things even she didn't see. She missed him so.

But Mikawa is dead.

She shook the idea away though it was more fact than idea. It was true that some of Mikawa was gone forever. For a start, his body had been buried at sea. The body that had betrayed him. In the same way that Umi's body was now betraying her. Though at a hundred and two years of age, it wasn't so much a betrayal as an inevitability. But it was all relative. When people are in their thirties, fifty seems old, but when they're in their sixties, fifty seems young. To Umi, dying at eighty, as Mikawa had, was far too young.

She was getting upset, and she tried to calm herself. But in truth, it wasn't her thoughts that were upsetting her. The visit with Mikawa on the nineteenth floor had upset her. Try though she might, he wouldn't talk to her. She knew he had the capability of talking from their past conversations. Conversations that had upset her far more than his silence today.

But none of it mattered. Soon they would meld as one. They would have many lifetimes to reconcile any differences. The important thing is that they would be together. Forever.

And all it cost was fifty million lives and the future of the human race.

TATSU AND PER had easily gotten past the guards outside Umi's residence, but now she was wishing that perhaps they had been turned away. What if Umi wasn't happy to see her but angry? What if she called the guards in to do what Tatsu had failed to do in Toronto?

As they walked through the residence, peeking around corners and into rooms, looking for Umi, Tatsu briefly thought about Toronto again. The man beside her had tried to kill her, and she had tried to kill him. She had aches and pains from being hit with that arm of his, but he was bald and sporting a limp thanks to her. Yet here they were, halfway around the world, ostensibly on the same side. It had definitely been a strange day.

They reached the drawing room. Umi was sitting on the hospital bed beside the machinery Tatsu had helped Nagura carry up here. She didn't like the way she felt when she thought about Nagura, so she put him out of her mind for the moment.

She and Per entered quietly. She had noticed that Per had let her take the lead from the guards until now. He didn't make any suggestions or speak at all, really. For that, she was glad.

Umi was looking out the window, hunched and appearing . . . sad. It was difficult at first for Tatsu to identify the sadness since she'd never seen Umi look that way before in her life. Even when Mikawa died, she'd seemed more shocked and angry than sad. Now, the old woman seemed to really be showing her age. And in that single moment, Tatsu realized that Umi wanted to die. This wasn't about being with Mikawa or moving on to the next plane of life, she just wanted it to end. And so did Tatsu.

"*Obasan?*" Tatsu said softly. Umi turned and looked at the intruders in her doorway, seeming to take a moment to even realize who Tatsu was.

"Tatsu? What are you doing here?" she asked. Looking at Per, her eyes widened, then narrowed. "Have you come to kill me?"

"If I had, you would be dead, madame," Per said.

"Then why—"

"Don't do this," Tatsu said, cutting the distance between them in half. Per remained where he was. "Come back with me before it's too late. We can find another doctor who can help you."

"Oh, child," Umi said, sounding disappointed. "Is that what this is about? Is that why you've disobeyed me? Why you've brought a dangerous stranger to my bedside in my final moments?"

"They don't have to be your final moments. Stay away from the machine. Stop your revenge. It's so ugly, and I know the face you show the world isn't your true face. Give up this insanity before it's too late!"

"Child, it was too late the moment you took my hand all those years ago, back at the institution. And I'm not taking revenge on anyone," Umi said as she struggled to stand. She appeared to be more hurt than angry. "Is that what you think of me? That I'm so petty, all I want is revenge and death?"

Tatsu felt like she'd been hit with a club. What was Umi talking about?

"I . . . I don't understand. The gas attack on the ship. The virus you're going to release—"

"*I'm* going to release? I've got nothing to do with it!" Umi yelled so loud she coughed afterward.

"But . . . but . . . Dr. Norris developed the virus. He worked for—"

"The Japanese government! Or a faction of it, at least. Norris didn't work for me, he was foisted on me. I couldn't stop the virus release if I wanted. And even if I could, there's an attack submarine sitting twenty kilometers away with a torpedo aimed right at the heart of Ashita. What do you think the deadlines are about? If I interfere with the launch of the virus, or if they don't detect a launch at exactly 5:15 P.M., Ashita will be destroyed."

"But, why would the Japanese government want to kill people?"

"To save the ones who will be left. Japan has a population problem, but not the one most of the world thinks it does. Our aging population outweighs all other nations on Earth. If everyone was like me, it wouldn't be a problem, but they're not. They're a burden on society. Almost twenty percent of Japan's population is over eighty years old. And more than fifty percent is over sixty. It's a problem now, but in the coming years, it will cripple our country.

"And Japan's not alone. The same problem is happening all around the world. Japan is just feeling the brunt of it first. Too many years without war and disease has put the planet on a collision course with a disaster of a different kind. One that we won't recover from unless someone does something about it. Now."

"That's what you believe or that's what they told you?" Tatsu asked.

"Both, but solving the world's problems down the road is not really what concerns someone of my age."

"Then why—" Umi stepped faster than Tatsu thought she could move until she was nose to nose with her.

"I'm trying to save Mikawa, you idiot girl!" With that, Umi pushed Tatsu, and she fell back into the arms of the guards who had come up behind them. Tatsu realized Umi had pressed her panic alarm.

Two of the guards grabbed Per, but he launched one of them into the air. Before he could do anything else, the other guard zapped him in the neck with his Taser and Per went down like a sack of machine parts. Tatsu struggled, but a moment later she felt pain in her neck and smelled flesh burning.

She was out before she hit the floor.

Chapter Thirty-four

4:00 P.M.

"REESE?" LEW SAID when Jonathan told him Reese was the key to finding the hidden database copy. "We're fucked."

Jonathan motioned for Lew to be quiet. Lew had brought Jonathan and Maggie up to date on what he had learned about Mikawa and Project Dead Lights. And then Jonathan and Maggie had brought Lew up to speed on everything Tatsu had told them. But not verbally. With both of their implants not only connected, but no doubt monitored by Mikawa, they quickly decided against sharing their information out in the open. Once they checked that no cameras could see them, they used Jonathan's data device to type messages back and forth. And with Lew's lack of typing skills, it was taking a frustratingly long time.

When Jonathan had finally gotten to the real mission for The Custodians, Lew had been unable to contain himself and spoken out loud about Reese.

"Is everything all right, Lew?" Mikawa asked, his odd voice coming out of Jonathan's implant as well. Jonathan typed what Mikawa had said for Maggie. They both looked accusingly at Lew.

"Uh, sure, Mickey. I was . . . I was just telling Jonathan a joke."
Jonathan rolled his eyes.

"*Time is getting short, Lew. We think you should get moving
again if you want us to help you get back to the surface.*"

"Sure. Almost done, Mickey. I'm going to head up in a minute."

"*Very good, Lew.*"

Then Lew typed something that almost made Jonathan speak
out loud:

He doesn't just listen. Tracks my position. Using implant. Need
to cut it out. Both of them. Take them up to him for me. I get Reese
and find database. Keep Mick busy.

Jonathan shook his head, but Maggie tapped his shoulder and
nodded. She agreed with Lew. *Great, two against one.*

Lew was already out of his exo suit, and he held up a finger,
indicating they should wait. Then he took off down the hall. A
few minutes later, he was back with a first-aid kit. He opened it
up and took out a knife. After pouring antiseptic on the blade, he
gave it to Maggie. She did the job without even making a face, first
cutting Lew's out, then Jonathan's, patching them up as best she
could with what was in the kit. Jonathan wrapped gauze around
the implants and put them in his pocket.

"We should be okay to talk softly," Jonathan said, barely above
a whisper.

"Good," Lew said. "Now get up there and see if there's any
chance of shutting Mickey off."

"Probably not, but worth a shot," Maggie said.

"You know this is only going to work for a few minutes," Jonathan said. "If he's trying to talk to you now, he's probably already
onto us."

"So get going," Lew said.

"What about that?" Maggie said, pointing at the robot body slumped against the wall.

"Do NOT bring that up there," Lew said.

"I agree," Jonathan said. "I think we can guess what he wants it for. Last thing we need is him walking around."

"When I get Reese and the database, we'll head up to the sub," Lew said, turning and heading away.

"Lew."

"What?"

"Watch the time. It's already quarter after. If you can't find the database by quarter to, you and Reese just haul ass up to the sub."

"Oh, really? Why?" Lew said, blinking to punctuate his sarcasm. Lew laughed and disappeared around a corner.

Jonathan was going to apologize for him, but when he looked at Maggie, she was smiling.

"What? He's funny," Maggie said.

"Let's go."

They headed for the stairs at a trot and were soon on their way up.

4:15 P.M.

A MINUTE AFTER everyone had left the hallway, a maintenance robot shaped not unlike a metallic loaf of pumpernickel whirred into the corridor. It looped around to be sure the hallway was indeed empty, then it approached its target, coming to rest at the foot of the robot body. The tiny camera on the front antenna wiggled back and forth for a moment. Then, as abruptly as it had arrived, it whirred around and angled its way out of the corridor.

The robot body, now alone, sat unmoving, like a knight in shining armor on display at a museum. Soon, other sounds filled the space. A buzzing and humming. Then the transport quad-copter drones came around the corner. Four of them flying in formation. They stopped in midair and hovered for a few moments. Then two of them moved forward and, being careful of each other, dropped down, each latching onto a foot.

The weight was too much to lift off the ground, but they easily dragged the body down the corridor as the other two copters allowed them to pass. Once out in the open, the two waiting drones moved in and each latched onto a wrist. They slowly rose until the body left the ground, ever so slightly. They were pushed beyond their maximum. This was as high as they could get their payload.

A signal was sent, and soon another, larger drone descended from high above. It slowly moved into position and secured its clamps around the robot's neck. The extra lifting power in place, the five drones lifted their package up and up and up.

When they reached the midlevel walkway, they set the robot down. Three of the drones, including the larger one, disengaged and flew away for other tasks. The two remaining craft proceeded to drag the body inside toward their target.

The nineteenth floor.

Chapter Thirty-five

LEW PEERED AROUND the corner and confirmed that Reese's chaperones were still guarding and tormenting him. He checked their belts and saw that the only weapons they had were the Tasers. He figured some sort of directive must have gone out about not using firearms when you were living in a dome under the sea. Made sense. Even so, he wished he had that machine gun Jonathan was toting around. But the fact was that Jonathan was probably going to need it a lot more than he.

Lew thought of several scenarios that would make his success against two trained soldiers more likely, but he didn't have time for any of that. He needed to get past them, pronto, and get Reese somehow lucid enough to remember where he hid that database. Which meant handling this with Lew's natural state: the direct approach. He figured he was already dressed like them; it couldn't be that hard to act like them. He took out one of his nightsticks and waited for Reese to distract them again before he made his move. It wasn't long before Reese stepped out into the hall again. As he did, Lew nonchalantly turned the corner, swinging his nightstick like a 1920s flatfoot, and whistling. He walked right toward them, all smiles.

"Hey! Stop right there!" one of the guards said. The other guard shoved Reese back into the office before joining his partner. They headed toward Lew, both with their hands on their Tasers, but apparently unsure if he was worth using them. Lew had counted on that.

"Relax, boys. The old lady told me to come down and give you a message," Lew said.

"What's that?" the younger guard said. Unfortunately, Lew wasn't fooling the closer, older guard.

"Who the fuck are you, mate?" the guard said, pulling his Taser. But it was too late. Lew was close enough.

"The message is: I'm checking Dr. Reese out, boys. You can turn and run now or eat carpet." Lew swung his nightstick at the guard nearest him, hitting him in the wrist that was holding his Taser. A crack, then a howl equally loud echoed in the hallway as the Taser hit the ground.

Lew pulled his other nightstick out and struck the hand again as it tried to come up at him, almost simultaneously striking the guard in the side of the head with the first nightstick. And like that, the guard was down and out.

"Whoa, hang on," the second guard said, raising his hands when he saw what had happened to his partner.

Lew didn't have time to tie him up, so he struck at his head as he had with the first guard, but the kid deflected the stick with his hand and in the same motion pulled his own nightstick. The kid was scared, but he was crazy fast and obviously skilled.

You couldn't just tie him up?

The kid blocked Lew's next hit and swung one of his own,

which was what Lew wanted. He took the hit, immobilized the club under his arm, and spun around until he was behind the kid and had him in a headlock. It wasn't long until the kid was asleep from lack of blood to the brain. Lew was going to have a huge bruise under his arm, but now he could get on with things.

Lew stepped into the dimly lit office space. Several cubicles with computers in them sat to the left, and to the right were some storage cabinets and a door marked "Dr. Norris." Inside the glassed-in office was a single desk, papers spread all over. Like everywhere else in Ashita, it was all deserted.

"Reese," Lew said. "Where are you? It's Lew."

"You're dressed like one of them," Reese's voice said from behind a partition. Lew walked over and peeked around the edge. Reese was crouched under the desk, literally shaking with fear and exhaustion.

Bastards.

"It's a disguise. I fooled them."

"R . . . really?"

"Really," Lew said, gently taking Reese by the shoulders and helping him up. He didn't know what Reese had done, but nobody deserved this.

"It's a good disguise," Reese said, his eyes flitting back and forth uncontrollably.

"Thanks. How'd you like to go home?"

For a second, Reese looked shocked, like he was waiting for the punch line. Then he started crying, the tears pouring out of his dark, hooded eyes. He nodded a few times and grabbed Lew in a tight embrace.

Lew patted him on the back. "It's okay, buddy. It's okay." Lew let him cry for a bit, then gently pushed him away. Reese sniffed and wiped his nose with his sleeve.

Lew sat Reese down before grabbing some power cords from under one of the desks. He went out into the hall and tied up the two guards. Then he noticed they each had two-way radios on their belts. He took them both and clipped them to his belt before he headed back into the offices.

"Can we go, now?" Reese asked.

"Pretty soon. I just need you to do something for me, first," Lew said.

"What?" Reese said, twitching and looking behind him like he'd heard something. Lew saw a scar on Reese's neck in the same place Lew and Jonathan now had bandages. They'd found his implant and removed it. Awhile ago, based on how the scar had heeled already.

"I need that copy of Mick . . . of the computer's database that you made. The one for Fahd. Do you remember where you hid it?"

"Database . . . database . . ." Reese mumbled, running his hands through his hair. "Are we going home now, Lew?" He was too far gone. Lew needed a way to make Reese alert, if only long enough so he could tell Lew where he'd hidden the database copy. He knew a way to do it, but Reese wasn't going to like it.

When Lew was in the service, they'd used a field phone's charge to shock themselves awake. It was like getting a pot of coffee poured down your throat in a few seconds, and it hurt like hell. Of course, he didn't have a field phone. Lew looked around and saw that one of the computers had a USB cable hanging out of it. He figured someone must have used it to charge his phone and just left the cable.

"Wait here," Lew said. He rooted around the desk and found a pair of scissors. Then he cut off the end of the USB cable, baring the wires. After licking his thumb, he grimaced and touched the exposed wires. Pain shot up his hand and he yelped, dropping the wire.

Lew picked up the wire again and got Reese to sit in the chair. He moved behind Reese.

"What are we doing, Lew?" Reese asked.

"If this works, we're all going home," Lew said. He put one hand on the side of Reese's head to brace him, then jammed the wires into the opposite side of his scalp. The smell of burning flesh permeated Lew's nose almost immediately. He counted to five, holding Reese as he squirmed and yelped, then let him go.

Free, Reese jumped up out of the chair, shaking his head and arms. Lew knew he was shaking off the tingle.

"I'm sorry, buddy. I had to—"

"Whoa, what a rush!" Reese said, the slur gone from his speech. Lew could see his eyes were much more focused now, but he knew it wouldn't last for long. "Did Fahd really send you to get me out?"

"Uh, sure. Sure he did. Well, for you and the copy of the database you made." Lew said.

"Great. Let's go, then," Reese said, heading for the door.

"Hang on, where is it?" Lew said, afraid Reese would crash again before they got wherever they were going.

"I put it where they'd never think to look but where I could be guaranteed a quick exit. If the old bitch hadn't made me her pet project, that is."

"And that's where?"

"You're going to love this. It's under the pilot seat in the submarine. Pretty rad, right?" Lew closed his eyes and slapped his palm to his face, shaking his head.

"Which submarine?" Lew asked around the edge of his hand.

"Which? There's only one functioning sub. I put it in that one."

"Perfect."

4:25 P.M.

JONATHAN AND MAGGIE pushed through the double doors on the nineteenth floor, not sure what to expect. Jonathan had visions of giant walls of computers with flashing lights and a million knobs and buttons. Or, at least, he'd hoped for something like that, something that he'd be able to unplug or damage. But in the end, they were faced with something very different.

Like most of Ashita, the floors, ceiling, and inner walls were bone white, and a large, double-paned window in the far wall provided the only source of light. That wasn't really a shock, but the vast emptiness of the floor was. There was no furniture. No devices. No electronics that they could see at all. The only thing in the room was what looked like a—again, white—bathtub.

Jonathan spun around, looking this way and that. Nothing changed. The movement caused a sudden pang in his broken nose. He sucked air through his teeth and gently touched it as he and Maggie slowly walked toward the only thing there.

"Still hurts?"

"Oh, yeah," Jonathan said.

"You know, if you let me, I could fix that for you."

"Ha! No thank you. I still remember the yoga stretch you

tried to teach me that strained my back when we were . . . you know."

"Yes, I do know. I was there. And you were just a big baby."

It was nervous banter, helping them deal with the intense anxiety of the situation, but it also made Jonathan realize that even after all this time, they'd easily fallen back into their old rhythms.

As they got closer to the tub, they saw that it was filled with a thick, pink paste. It reminded Jonathan of a science show he'd seen where they'd mixed water and cornstarch together creating a different state of matter called a suspension—neither liquid nor solid, but both. If left alone, it behaved like water. If touched or put under pressure, it became a solid. The difference was, this pink stuff seemed to be moving on its own, alive with electricity. Flares, like miniature lightning, flashed and sparked all throughout the substance. Jonathan thought it looked a lot like animations of neurons in the human brain firing.

"Hello, Jonny," the tub said, light flashing as it spoke. Both Maggie and Jonathan took a few steps back.

"Hello, Mikawa," Jonathan said.

"We are sorry Lew could not be here," Mikawa said. "We were so looking forward to meeting him. He is a very . . . unique human."

"You have no idea," Jonathan said. And at that moment, Jonathan was hoping he'd given Lew enough time to get Reese out and put his hands on the database. But he was also wondering how Mikawa knew Lew wasn't there. If he was tracking the implants, he should have thought Lew was in the room, since both implants were still in Jonathan's pocket.

"Who is your companion?" Mikawa asked, confirming that he was seeing—or, at least, sensing—them. Jonathan looked at Maggie, then nodded toward Mikawa.

"Uh, hello there," Maggie said. "My name's Maggie Reynolds. Nice to meet you." She reached down and gently patted the surface of the paste. It wobbled and glowed even more.

Silence followed their exchange, all the while the pink material continued to flash and sparkle, like it was working on something. Jonathan was starting to feel uncomfortable.

"I'm sorry we didn't bring the robot body for you, Mikawa. You probably can't understand this, but we were—"

"Afraid," Mikawa said.

"Do you understand what that means?" Jonathan asked. He was stalling for Lew, but he was also fascinated by this thing. Was it just a collection of programming, or could it actually think?

"I understand everything."

"Everything? That's a very grandiose statement."

"It is simply a statement."

"It's a false statement. You can't possibly understand everything. Do you understand how small your world is here? And how vast the rest of the world is, both in size and complexity?"

"As I said, I understand everything."

Jonathan was in awe. Either this thing ran on hubris, or it truly was sentient, and it was purposely trying to intimidate them. But why? "Are you self-aware, Mikawa?"

"I am aware of myself, yes. 'I think, therefore I am,' I believe is the human colloquialism."

"Do you have emotions?"

"No."

"Do you want to have emotions?"

"Emotions are chemical reactions. I am not chemical. I am mechanical."

"What is the meaning of life, Mikawa?"

Maggie eased up behind Jonathan and whispered, "What are you doing?"

Jonathan ignored her. He took the machine gun off his shoulder and handed it to her, then he walked around the other side of the tub. He found it curious that Mikawa hadn't answered yet. All the other answers had come very fast.

"What is the meaning of life, Mikawa? Answer the question."

"To live forever."

A section of the wall suddenly separated from the rest of the tiles and slid open. A tilted table slowly rolled out into the room, and Jonathan saw why Mikawa hadn't cared whether they had brought the robot body or not. He already had it.

"Jesus," Maggie said, stepping back from the tub and pointing the machine gun at the robot.

Jonathan jumped back as well, but his fascination kept him closer than her. The table came to a stop.

Then the robot moved.

At first the head turned from side to side and the hands flexed open and closed, like someone waking up from a very deep sleep. But soon, almost all of the joints were moving. And it wasn't long before it pushed itself up off the table and stood before them, still flexing and testing its parts. The robot's lidless eyes—really, just advanced camera lenses—whirred and dilated.

"Mikawa?" Jonathan asked tentatively. The robot's head swiveled up then right until the lenses were pointed at him.

"Hello, Jonny. It's nice to be able to see you."

Jonathan fought for his voice. "Why have you transferred yourself into that body, Mikawa? It can't have near the capacity of where you were."

"You are correct, it does not."

"Then why?"

"It is necessary."

"Necessary for what?"

"To leave Ashita. To be in the world." Jonathan and Maggie traded a look of concern that bordered on fear.

"How were you able to transfer into the robot, Mikawa? Nagura and Reese were unable to—"

"They are flawed. I am not."

"Are you saying that you are perfect?" Jonathan asked, moving back by Maggie. As he passed, he whispered in her ear for a moment.

"By human definitions, yes."

"But if you're Mikawa, then you were human. How can you be perfect if you're human?"

"Because now I'm more."

"Do you matter more than human lives?"

"Human lives are transitory. And by definition flawed and inconsequential."

"But humans made you, Mikawa. How could that be?"

Mikawa didn't respond.

Jonathan said: "If humans are flawed and they made you, logic dictates that you are also flawed." More silence followed as Mikawa chewed on that idea. Distracted by the thought puzzle, this was their chance to get past Mikawa's lightning defenses, but it wouldn't last long.

"Now!" Jonathan shouted, rushing Mikawa. Jonathan leaped

into the air toward Mikawa. He doubted that he'd reach his target, but that wasn't the point of the attack. His fingertips had just grazed the robot's shiny torso when Mikawa reacted. Jonathan yelped as Mikawa grabbed his forearm in one of his powerful hands and flung him aside like an annoying insect. The pain in Jonathan's wrist was soon surpassed by the pain of crashing into the wall and crumpling to the floor in a heap. But Jonathan had just been a distraction. He tried to cover up as Maggie opened fire on the robot, bullets ricocheting everywhere off Mikawa's skin. After a long burst, Maggie stopped firing. When the smoke cleared, Mikawa was still standing, barely dented, and now he moved toward Maggie.

Not only had the attack failed, it had managed to turn Mikawa's attention away from Jonathan. Anxiety clawed at his guts as Jonathan tried desperately to think of a way to get Mikawa's attention, or at the least to keep that thing away from Maggie. But there was nothing in the room. Not even a chair to throw. Abandoning his search inside the room, Jonathan looked out the window and—

That's it!

"Shoot the window!" Jonathan shouted from the ground, holding his wrist to his chest. He was pretty sure it was broken.

Maggie fired again, glass exploded, and air from outside wafted into the room. Jonathan winced and struggled to get to his feet. His wrist might have been the only real damage he had so far, but the rest of his body screamed from the collision with the wall. The second he got to his feet, Jonathan took a few steps and launched himself into the air before Mikawa could swivel to face him. This time he reached his goal unimpeded, drop-kicking the robot. Jonathan howled as he dropped back to the floor, right on top of his busted wrist. Squeezing tears from his eyes, he looked up in time to see Mikawa topple backward and out the broken window.

"You're insane," Maggie said, as she helped Jonathan to his feet.

"No argument there," Jonathan managed, every movement of his body feeling like a new injury being inflicted. He leaned on Maggie and they shuffled over to the window. Nineteen floors down, Mikawa lay on the grass below. They smiled and laughed slightly, but stopped suddenly.

"Look!" Maggie shouted. Mikawa was moving.

"That's . . . that's impossible," Jonathan said as he watched Mikawa get up off the ground. The robot looked up at them and headed out of sight.

"Jesus, Lew's down there!" Jonathan said, realizing that they had no way to warn him. "Come on!"

4:30 P.M.

"REESE! STOP!" LEW called, trying to catch his breath. Even with his nap in the crate, Lew hadn't had time to recover from his swim to the *Jirojin Maru*, yet. His body ached, and his head was still splitting from that crack with the pipe.

When he'd told Reese what had happened to the sub—and his hidden database—the scientist had lost his shit. Lew could understand why. After everything the guy had been through on this mission and down here in Ashita, to find out the main reason you'd done it all was simply gone was more than he could take. Reese had shouted that he didn't believe it and run out of the office.

Lew had run after him, only pausing by the stairs for a minute to leave a radio for Jonathan if he came down looking for him, but that minute had given Reese a crazy head start. Lew knew where he was headed: to the dock to see for himself. Though it didn't make much sense, Lew knew the guy wasn't running on sense right now. And if he kept exerting himself like this, he was going to crash any minute.

"Reese!" Lew shouted when he saw him dart around a grove of maple trees. Lew dug deep and ran on. As he rounded the trees, he saw Reese standing against the transparent wall of the dock, both his hands and nose pressed against the glass.

When Lew arrived, he came to a stop and put his hands on his knees to catch his breath. If they were going to stop the virus from launching, they didn't have time for this nonsense.

"Y . . . you're killing me, buddy," Lew said, but when he looked up, Reese wasn't standing against the glass anymore. For a terrible second, Lew thought he'd run off to check the upper dock, but as Lew stood up, he saw that Reese was lying on the ground. He walked over to him and saw that Reese wasn't just on the ground, he was out. Lew knelt and pressed his fingers against Reese's carotid artery. There was a pulse, but it was thready. Even if he'd been able to, this guy couldn't take another shock. And he sure as hell wasn't walking anywhere. He was going to have to carry him.

"Goddamn it, Reese," Lew said. Reese didn't weigh four hundred pounds, but Lew was out of gas. Over at the side of the dock, Lew saw his answer: another exo suit.

Lew put on the suit, a breeze now that he'd done it a few times, and stood up. Most of his body pain disappeared. He felt such relief, he would have worn the suit even if he didn't have someone to carry.

Lew picked Reese up and put him over his shoulders in a fireman's carry. He caught his reflection in the glass.

"I wonder what the rest of the Avengers are doing tonight."

Lew turned and started back toward the tower. He took out his radio and tried to raise Jonathan on it, but no one answered. He was wondering what Jonathan was doing when he saw someone fall out a window at the top of the tower and slam into the ground.

"Oh, shit," Lew said, starting into a trot. When he was halfway there, he saw the figure get up and realized it was no person. The artificial light gleamed off the robot body, making it obvious even from this distance what it was. Mikawa had gotten the robot body somehow, and he was out of the computer. Out and apparently impervious since he'd just walked away from a four-hundred-foot fall.

"L . . . Lew . . ." Reese managed from Lew's shoulders. Lew stopped and put him down on the grass.

As he knelt beside Reese, the scientist's eyes flickered open.

"Lew . . . the . . . database," Reese managed. Lew could tell by the way his pupils kept sliding up under his eyelids the consciousness wasn't going to last. Even if Lew had something there to shock him again, he didn't think the guy could handle it.

"Don't worry about that now," Lew said. "We've got bigger problems." Lew told Reese about Mikawa's being in the robot body, hoping that there was still enough scientist left in Reese to offer some kind of advice on how to deal with it.

"The head," Reese said weakly.

"What about it?"

"The . . . the head will contain the same information as my database backup. Get . . . the head."

"Oh, is that all? Take the killer robot's head off? Gee, thanks, Reese," Lew said. "Any idea on how I kill it without destroying the head?"

"Con . . . control unit in chest . . ." Reese's eyes rolled up and closed.

"Reese," Lew said, shaking him. "Reese!" His eyes fluttered open, and his pupils darted around like he didn't recognize where he was. Lew was out of time with this guy.

"Sorry . . . the head is just mass storage. Like . . . a hard drive. Not like the human . . . brain. The system controls are in his ch . . . chest," Reese said before closing his eyes again.

"Reese!" Lew shook him, but he wasn't coming around again. He'd gotten all he could.

If what Jonathan had told him about Umi's database were even half-true, whether he liked it or not, he had to try.

4:35 P.M.

JONATHAN AND MAGGIE reached the main floor and almost ran right by the radio Lew had taped to the wall for him. He ripped the masking tape with "Jonny" written on it off the radio and immediately hit the talk button.

"Lew! Lew!"

"Jesus, you're alive," Lew said.

"Barely," Jonathan said. "Where are you?"

"Heading back. Reese freaked when he found out the database copy was destroyed, and I had to chase him down. I'm about two minutes out."

"Destroyed? Shit. Never mind that right now. Mikawa got the robot body somehow, and he's out of the computer."

"I know. I saw him do a swan dive off the tower and walk away without so much as a dent," Lew said. He then told Jonathan what

Reese had said about the robot's head. "Let's make that Plan B, right after getting the hell out of here," Jonathan said.

"Works for me. Where are you?" Lew asked.

"Right where you left the radio."

"Good. Get that exo suit on and get out here. It's our only chance."

"Roger. On it," Jonathan said. They ran around the corner to where the exo suit still lay on the ground.

"You're not really going to fight that thing, are you?" Maggie said. "Even with those suits and the two of you, odds are—"

"Not me. You," Jonathan said, painfully raising his broken wrist to send his point home.

"Me? Whoa, there's no bloody way."

"It's our only chance, Maggie," Jonathan said.

"Our only chance at what? Getting killed?"

Chapter Thirty-six

4:40 P.M.

UMI, WEARING THE silk pajamas Mikawa had bought her for their wedding night, complete with robe and slippers, walked to the sound system. She put *Adagio for Strings* on, the violins echoing off her high-ceilinged home under the sea. She closed her eyes and listened for a moment, feeling the music more than hearing it.

She had thought about going back down to the nineteenth floor to try to talk to Mikawa again, but she didn't want to end this life with frustration. Although Tatsu had made that all but impossible. After everything she had done for that girl. *But no, don't let it upset you. Not now.*

Mikawa hadn't spoken to her for weeks, now, so getting upset about that was pointless. Umi liked to think that he simply wasn't able to speak. That had been the case after he was first transferred in, after all. She hoped that things would be different for her. Though communicating outside of the world she was about to enter seemed like it would hold little interest for her.

She opened her eyes and shuffled over to her bed. She took off her robe and neatly folded it before placing it on a chair. Then she stepped out of her slippers and climbed onto the bed. When she was comfortable, she picked up the EEG brain cap and slipped it over her gray hair, tightening the strap under her chin.

The readout on the machines behind her showed two minutes and thirty seconds until the transfer would start. She wasn't going to get to hear the end of Samuel Barber's masterpiece. Not in this body, anyway.

She wondered if the virus about to be released on the world would be ascribed to her. But, really, she knew that it would be. The same way the attack on the ship would be. Even though from Morgan's last report, somehow no one had been killed on the *Jirojin Maru*. Well, that wasn't quite true. He said that he had taken care of Tanaka and Corsair. That made her feel better. After all these months of working under the direction of the government, having things done solely for her seemed appropriate at the end of her physical life. Even though, to save face, she'd been acting like it was all her idea from the beginning.

She wondered why she had told Tatsu the truth. Especially with Per Broden standing right behind her. But she knew, Broden notwithstanding and with Mikawa gone, Tatsu was the only one she considered family. Not that it mattered now.

Umi lay down and closed her eyes, the strings reaching a crescendo. One hundred two years were about to end. The wail was appropriate.

4:40 P.M.

PER OPENED HIS EYES.

He was lying on the ground, the side of his neck still aching from the Taser shock. Every muscle in his body was sore, and his head was pounding. He forced himself to sit up and saw they were in a large open area, a sign on the wall said "Visitor Center." Several kiosks were scattered around the welcome area. But what caught his eye was Tatsu, lying beside him, still out.

He wondered why they had just been left there and not even handcuffed. He checked his watch—it was already fifteen minutes past when they were supposed to meet Jonathan and Maggie on the walkway by the dock. He didn't know which was worse: the idea that they'd left without them or the idea that they hadn't and didn't know about the torpedo aimed at Ashita.

"Tatsu. Wake up," Per said, jostling her. She came to and took a swing at whoever was waking her. Per ducked it easily.

"What? Where are we? What time is it?" she asked, sitting up. He answered both her questions and forced himself to his feet, staggering slightly. Then he helped Tatsu up.

"Come on." Per shook his head to clear it and headed toward the doors. He noticed a ladder and hatch in the ceiling against one wall. "Does that lead up to the escape pods? Where the virus will be launched?"

"Uh, yes," Tatsu said, obviously trying to shake the fuzz out of her own brain. "Why didn't they tie us up?"

"I am not sure," Per said. "But I doubt it is a good thing."

As they walked by each of the kiosks, their motion activated prerecorded messages.

"Ashita," the announcer's baritone rumbled. "Your home under the sea. Jules Verne created the *Nautilus*, and the Tenabe Group, in association with the Japanese government, now give you Ashita. The city of Tomorrow. Self-sufficient, renewing, and capable of housing and employing over five thousand people."

As they passed a few more kiosks, Per noticed that some were broadcasting in different languages: Japanese, English, Urdu, and more.

They pushed through the doors leading to the walkway, which swirled around the tower and up to the docking port. Beyond it, Per could see the small submarine—backing away from the docking ring.

"We're too late," Per said.

"No! No! Wait!" Tatsu yelled, running toward the air lock. Then she stopped and took a step back, seeming confused.

Per saw why. It wasn't Jonathan or Maggie in the sub, but four of Umi's guards. Now he understood why they'd just been left on the visitor center's floor. The guards, after hearing Umi's revelation to Tatsu, were running for their lives. He could see that Tatsu had worked it out, as well.

"Coward!" she yelled. As the sub turned and headed away, most of the guards avoided eye contact with them. But one did. He smiled and gave the V symbol with his fingers, palm inward. A final "fuck you."

And then the sub, which—if not for the cowardly guards—would have held them in a short time, cracked and imploded. In a wink the vessel was nothing more than detritus, a wall of bubbles rising up in its place.

"Oh my God," Tatsu said quietly.

"Mikawa," Per said. "His maintenance drones, no doubt." They hadn't been repairing the sub, they had been sabotaging it.

And then, as if on cue, a drone fell out of the sky and hit the walkway a few feet from them, before it slid over the edge.

"What the hell is happening?" Tatsu said. They walked to the edge and looked down. What they saw sent Per running toward the doors. "Hey!"

Per stopped in the doorway. "Stay up here. You're the only one who knows how the escape pods work." He checked his watch. It was 4:45 p.m. They had thirty minutes.

"The torpedo. They don't know about the attack sub!" Tatsu yelled after him. "You have to tell them. They have to get up here, NOW!"

"Of that I am aware," Per said. "But I believe something else is occupying them at the moment."

Bridge of the JS *Hakuryū*
20 Kilometers West of Ashita
4:43 P.M.

HIROSHI NISHIDA, THE sonar operator, stood behind the row of men seated at the navigation wheels, pressing the cups of his headphones tight to his ears. He was sure he had heard it again, but now there was nothing but the normal background sounds of the ocean.

The men, dressed in the usual all-white, short-sleeved uniform of the Japan Maritime Self-Defense Force, were used to the tight confines of the Sōryū-class submarine. They were even used to their captain's gruff moods. What they weren't used to was sitting still in the water for hours with no real orders.

"Captain on deck!"

Hiroshi spun and saw that Captain Makoto and his shadow were on the bridge.

"Situation report, Mr. Nishida!" the captain barked.

"*Hai!* I heard it again, Captain," Nishida said, pulling the headphones down around his neck. "Definitely a pressure wave.

Approximately twenty kilometers to the east." Nishida had heard the first pressure-wave echo, almost identical in modulation to this new one, just over an hour ago from the exact same spot.

"And it's the same as the first?" Captain Makoto said.

"*Hai!* Shall we set headings for the area?"

"Negative! I'll give the orders, Mr. Makoto!" the captain shouted.

"*Hai!* Of course, my apologies, Captain," Nishida said. His excitement at having something to do making him belligerent.

The shadow, a man dressed in a dark business suit who had accompanied the captain everywhere since they'd shipped out, leaned forward and whispered something to the captain. Sailors had been instructed not to speak to him or ask his name. In fact, they were not even supposed to look at him. When he was done, the captain nodded.

"What do the sensors show?" the captain said. They had been monitoring a set of sensors on the surface of the ocean in approximately the same area as the origin of the echoes. The crew hadn't been told what they were monitoring the sensors for, just that any change at all should be reported.

"No change, Captain!" another sailor responded.

The shadow closed his eyes and shook his head. They weren't going anywhere.

"Continue your vigilance. Report anything out of the ordinary. We'll be in my quarters," the captain said, promptly leaving the bridge, his shadow right behind him.

Nashida stared after them, wrestling with himself. Nashida's father had always said he wouldn't amount to much in the military—he asked too many questions. Most of his fellow crewman were happy to just follow orders, never wondering why. Nashida, on the other hand, had lost rank twice and been beaten more times than he cared to remember for asking why he was being asked to do something. His mother always defended him, of course, saying he wasn't a poor follower but a born leader. Nashida didn't think he was either.

Finally, he gave in to his nature, put down his headphones, and headed after the men to try and find out what was going on. As he walked the tight passageway, he nodded to a few fellow crewmen as he passed. He reached the short T in the passageway that led to the captain's quarters. Nashida swallowed thickly and eased up to the door. Then he did what he was good at. He listened.

"How can it mean nothing?" the captain said.

"You have your orders, Captain. I suggest you concentrate on them and stop allowing yourself to be distracted," the shadow said.

"I still don't even know where these orders come from!"

"You do not need to know, Captain. Your job is to follow them. I can trust you to do that, correct?"

"Of course! In over twenty years, I have never disobeyed an order. But I've never had an order like this."

"There is still a possibility you won't have to fire. Your concerns could all be for nothing."

"Or I could have to fire on a civilian target."

"It's not a civilian target. It's a Japanese government target."

"Which arm of the government? I don't even know what agency you work for!"

"*Enough!*" The shadow yelled so loud, Nashida jerked his head back from the door for a moment.

"Fine," the captain finally said.

"Just follow your orders and stop asking so many questions. If the sensors don't detect an algae bloom by 5:15 P.M., fire the torpedo. Do we understand each other?"

"Perfectly," the captain said, his voice laced with disgust.

A chair scraped the floor, and Nashida moved away from the door. A moment later, the shadow came out, mumbling to himself, and headed for his quarters. Nashida made his way back to the bridge.

"Where were you?" one of the navigators asked when he returned to his station.

"Nowhere," Nashida said. He performed his duties, listening intently, but now he couldn't take his eyes off the readings of the station a few feet away—the one monitoring the sensors.

Or off the torpedo's firing controls.

4:45 P.M.

TATSU HAD TO see her one last time.

She entered the palatial residence to classical music blasting. She moved into the huge drawing room, where the music was coming from, and shut it off. Her breath caught as she turned around. Umi was in the bed against the wall where Nagura's machines sat. Lights still flickered slowly on the displays.

Tatsu stepped to the console and saw that the main screen was blinking something.

Sōsa kanryō. Operation complete.

She'd done it. She'd actually gone through with it.

Tatsu moved to the side of the bed. Umi looked so small and frail laying there. She not only looked her age for the first time since Tatsu had known her, but she looked even older. Tatsu reached out and gently touched the side of Umi's neck with two fingers. No pulse. She was gone. Tatsu leaned forward and gently kissed her wrinkled cheek.

"Good-bye, *Obasan*," she said through tears. Whatever motivations there had been in life didn't matter now.

Tatsu was doing something good, now. She had a long way to go to make up for all the bad, but at least she had started. She left the residence and headed for the hatch to the escape pods. She had to be ready.

In case anyone got out of this alive.

Chapter Thirty-seven

JONATHAN STOOD OUTSIDE the base of the tower, machine gun at the ready. He was scanning the trees, trying to spot Mikawa for Lew and Maggie. Lew was fifty meters to the left, leaning on a tree. He'd already been knocked through the air twice, and each time he got up more slowly. Maggie was twenty meters out right in front of Jonathan, watching him for signals. She'd dodged Mikawa's attacks so far, but he'd jumped away again, and they had no idea where his next attack would come from. Something came running out of the doors beside Jonathan, and he quickly raised the gun toward it. At the last second, he realized it was Per and refrained from firing.

"Where the hell have you been?" Jonathan said, returning his attention to the field in front of him. He thought he saw metal flash up above one of the trees, but then he realized it was another drone falling. He pointed, and Maggie sidestepped just as the drone slammed to the ground, kicking up dirt.

"Things have changed," Per said. "You've only got a few minutes."

"What? Why?"

Per told him about Umi's confession, the torpedo, and the loss of their sub as fast as he could.

"Jesus, you're nothing but good news, aren't you?" Jonathan had his own bad news, though, and brought Per up to speed.

"You're trying to get his head?" Per said.

"That was the plan, but it's not working out so well."

"This is a valiant endeavor, Jonathan, but you simply don't have time. If we don't leave immediately, we won't be able to."

"Why not?" Jonathan asked.

"If the virus launches, there won't be any escape pods left. We need to leave before 5:15 P.M."

"Right. And Mikawa knows that, so . . ." Jonathan stepped out farther from the building and looked up. Sure enough, there was Mikawa, the light reflecting off his metallic body. He was climbing the outside of the tower.

"He's on the tower!" Jonathan shouted, pointing up for Maggie and Lew. "He's trying to get to the escape pods!" He raised his gun, but Per knocked it down. "What are you doing?"

"Let him climb. We can run up the stairs and beat him. We need to be up near the escape pods anyway. And from what you've said, it's going to be vastly easier to fight him in close quarters than out here where he can keep striking and jumping away."

"Shit, you're right," Jonathan said. He called Lew and Maggie in. After talking Lew out of trying to climb up after Mikawa, they grabbed Reese, who was still asleep, and headed up the stairs.

"Hang on!" Lew shouted. He gave Reese to Maggie and ran around the corner.

"What the hell is he doing?" Maggie asked, putting Reese over her shoulder.

A minute later, Lew returned with a tied-up guard over each shoulder. One was still out cold, but one had come around and wouldn't shut up.

"You want another club to the head?" Lew asked. The guard shut up. "That's what I thought. Now, let's go." Jonathan shook his head, and they all headed up the stairs as fast as they could.

They reached the visitor center, and it quickly became obvious they weren't going to be able to get up the ladder and through the hatch with the exo suits on. With little choice, Maggie and Lew took them off, and they all climbed up, handing up the guards and Reese.

The area had a low ceiling and much less floor space compared to the other areas since it was close to the top of the sphere. There were no windows and, as was the style of Ashita, all the walls, which curved around the room, were white. Against one wall were twelve escape pods, each looking like a bright orange space capsule, the color making them easily identifiable when they reached the surface. Tatsu had the door to one of them open and was fiddling with the controls.

Jonathan looked inside and was surprised how roomy they were. They were only going to need about two pods to get out. And with little time left, Jonathan convinced them to launch one pod right away. They put the guards and Reese inside.

"So how do you launch these things," Lew asked.

"I've already run the power-up diagnostics and primed the oxygen tanks. Once the power-up completes, you just shut the door, secure this latch, and hit the red launch button," Tatsu said.

"That's it?"

"That's it," she said. "But with Reese out and them tied up, somebody has to go with them."

"Get in," Jonathan said to Tatsu.

"Me?" Tatsu said.

"There's no time to argue," Jonathan said. "If this doesn't work, between you and Reese, you can give the authorities enough data to fight this thing."

Tatsu stepped into the pod and turned around.

"Oh, and here," Jonathan said, handing Tatsu the removed implants. "This will help them find you."

"If you see a guy name Fahd, kick him in the nards for me," Lew said before she shut the door.

Tatsu quickly explained how the virus would pump up from the lab on the main floor in large green pipes and fill the remaining escape pods just before launch time if they didn't stop it.

They stood back and, after hearing the door latch, a glass enclosure slid down from the ceiling. It quickly filled with water, and, with a *whoosh!*, the pod shot up and out of Ashita. The opening in the ceiling slid shut, the water drained out, then the glass rose again. It took less than a minute, and there was no sign the pod had ever been there.

Jonathan, Lew, Maggie, and Per turned and looked at each other. It was silent except for the *chunk-scrape*, *chunk-scrape*, *chunk-scrape* of Mikawa climbing up toward them.

"Any ideas?" Jonathan said.

"Cut the pipes that feed the virus up here. It'll buy us about fifteen minutes," Maggie said. "Of course, we have no idea if the virus has to be ingested. If it's also airborne . . ."

"If anyone wants out, take a pod and go. No judgments," Jonathan said.

Nobody spoke.

"I saw an axe in the fire-hose case in the visitor center," Per said.

"I'll help," Lew said.

Mikawa wasn't getting off Ashita in one piece.

And in all likelihood, neither was anybody else.

4:57 P.M.

"IF THERE'S ANYTHING in this pipe, it's a pretty good bet we're both about to get our telsmears shortened," Lew said, getting ready to hack at the only green pipe that ran beneath the escape pods.

"Telomeres," Per said. "And I know that you know the difference."

Lew pretended he didn't hear Per and released his frustration by hacking into the PVC. It only took a few whacks before the pipe was severed about three feet above the floor.

"One supervillain plan disabled," Lew said, bending the pipe sticking out of the floor away from the piece leading to the pods, in case the flow still came and at a good clip.

"Why do you do that, Lew?" Per asked.

"Do what?" Lew asked, wedging the pipe behind some others so it would spew anything that came up toward the elevators.

"Pretend that you are . . . not dumb, but that you get details wrong. When clearly you do not."

"I don't know what you're talking about," Lew said, holding the axe head up between them. "But I've got a real fucking dislike for robot parts right now, so maybe you want to get away from me."

Per stared at him a little longer, tilting his head a little and sucking at his teeth.

"As you wish."

"I wish."

5:03 P.M.

JONATHAN WINCED AS Maggie gently wrapped gauze around the temporary splint she had rigged up for his wrist. They were alone up in the annex where the escape pods were, standing against the far wall. Jonathan, a head taller than Maggie, looked down at her while she worked on his wrist. She pulled the gauze tight, and he sucked air through his teeth.

"Don't be such a baby," Maggie said, without looking up from her operation.

"Don't be so rough," Jonathan said. He leaned down and inhaled the scent coming from her hair. Maggie abruptly looked up.

"Did you just smell my hair?"

"What? Don't be ridiculous. I just sniffled. Lotta pollen down here," Jonathan said.

"Uh-huh," Maggie said. She had been about to say something else, but Jonathan would never know what that was. A surprise even to him, he leaned down and kissed Maggie. She responded immediately this time, dropping the gauze and reaching her arms up around Jonathan's neck.

Finally, regretfully, he pulled himself away from her mouth. Her head moved with him at first, but eventually she let him break away. Her arms were still around his neck as she leaned back against the wall.

"This is not a good use of our final moments, Mr. Hall," Maggie said quietly.

"I think it's a fine use, Ms. Reynolds," Jonathan said. He tried to kiss her again, but she leaned away. Jonathan laughed and puffed a sigh that he, at least logically, agreed with her. He stood up, albeit a little awkwardly, so she could finish wrapping his wrist. The operation was completed in silence though they both seemed unable to get the smiles off their faces.

"There. Good as new," Maggie said.

They heard someone coming up the ladder and parted completely.

"To be continued," Jonathan said.

"Count on it," Maggie said, as he turned and walked toward the hatch, examining his patched-up wrist.

A second later, the entire wall behind Maggie collapsed on her.

5:06 P.M.

JONATHAN WAS ON the ground. He shook off the disorientation and turned to see what had hit him. A massive hunk of the wall had collapsed into the room. Then he saw some blond hair and bloodied hands sticking out from under the rubble.

"Mag—" Jonathan didn't get to finish. Mikawa, dented and seeming angry, despite his unmoving facial features, stood in the hole he had just kicked in the wall, the bright light behind him silhouetting his artificial form.

Jonathan turned to yell for help and saw Per halfway out of the hatch.

"Lew! It's Mikawa! He's broken through the wall!" Per yelled down into the hole before he climbed up and ran to Jonathan's side. He helped him up as Mikawa stepped into the room. They were between him and what he wanted—escape.

"Lew, get up here!" Jonathan shouted, taking up a position beside Per. They had to keep him from getting to the pods.

Maggie started groaning and moving. She coughed blood onto the ground as she tried to raise her head and get up, but there was too much rubble on her. Then Mikawa put his foot on the rubble lying on Maggie's back, and she screamed.

"Out of my way," Mikawa said, the gears and pulleys in his leg tightening, and he leaned forward, obviously putting more weight on his foot to send his point home. Maggie screamed again.

"I'll fucking tear you apart, tin man," Jonathan said, but he knew he was helpless.

"Jonathan. He'll kill her," Per said. Jonathan flexed his good hand in frustration, desperate for any other solution besides letting this thing get what it wanted. But there wasn't any. And Mikawa knew it.

"Get off her, and I'll move," Jonathan said. "Back up and let me help her, and you can have whatever you want."

Mikawa stared at him with his optics, tiny motors in various parts of him whirring and adjusting. Then, to Jonathan's surprise, he complied. The easing of pressure caused Maggie just as much pain, as she screamed again when he removed his weight.

"I knew love, once. It's a weakness. A disease. Even now, it's killing you. You'll pull her aside, and I'll leave this tomb. And you? You'll have one more moment—if she survives—before a torpedo pulls you apart, like dust in a high wind. Here, save her. You're all dying anyways."

As Mikawa rambled on, Jonathan and Per carefully moved

rubble off Maggie and, being as gentle as they could, dragged her to the side, a streak of blood painting the floor behind her.

Then Maggie closed her eyes and was silent.

"Maggie. Maggie!"

"You see?" Mikawa said, moving into the room again. "Wasted. You could have run. The logical thing would have been to run for an escape pod. Your emotions betrayed you."

Jonathan stared at Maggie's unmoving body as he clawed at the rubble-strewn ground with both hands, ignoring the pain from his damaged wrist. Using it, really. He panted, taking deep breaths as his exhales blew dust clouds up from the floor. He wasn't sure if he was fighting for control or bracing himself for the loss of it, not that it mattered. He grabbed a hunk of stone in his good hand and raised himself, but before he could launch himself onto Mikawa, he was frozen where he stood by what he saw. Behind the monster, dressed in his exo-suit, was Lew, a look in his eye Jonathan had only ever seen once before.

"Betray *this*, fucker!" Lew grabbed Mikawa from behind and heaved them both out through the hole he'd come in.

"LEW!"

5:11 P.M.

LEW AND MIKAWA slammed into the walkway halfway down the tower like a sock filled with nickels hitting a prison rat, pieces of Mikawa spraying into the air. Lew, riding Mikawa down, had taken the brunt in his exo suit, but it could only do so much.

He rolled off the robot and fought to get to his feet. He could taste blood, and his leg was in agony, but the exo suit had kept him together. Upright, he shook off the ringing in his ears and turned around. Mikawa was on his feet too, but he'd seen better days. His left hand was still on the ground, an eight-inch equivalent of an ulna bone sticking out of its wrist. His right foot was twisted outward, and his head seemed to be lolling to one side.

Part of Lew wanted to turn and run. He knew time was ticking down, and they only had minutes before the torpedo took Ashita off the map, but his mission wasn't complete. Lew rolled his neck and raised his fists. If robots could look surprised, Mikawa was flabbergasted.

"Let's go, Pinocchio," Lew said.

"I wish is wasn't you, Lew. I genuinely liked you. Of all the humans I've met, you're the most—"

"Pissed," Lew said, moving toward him.

Lew slammed his right fist, protected with the suit's metal, into Mikawa's head. The robot stumbled back. Then Lew hit him with his left. And then again. And again and again. But aside from pushing him back, he wasn't damaging the thing.

"My turn," Mikawa said, his leg coming up insanely fast, hitting Lew in the midsection and sending him sprawling on his back, almost sliding right off the walkway. Mikawa, unable to balance on his twisted foot, fell backward onto the ground as well.

Lew struggled up to his feet and, again, raised his fists as Mikawa got up, but he had to think of a new attack. Angrily smashing his fists into the part of Mikawa he needed wasn't such a great idea. And then he remembered what Reese had said—Mikawa's control unit was in his torso, not in his head. His head was just a big hard disk. Lew needed to calm down. Think rationally. Stay in control.

Lew faked a left, then, interlocking his fingers, clubbed his fists into Mikawa's shoulder, shoving him aside. The robot stopped well short of falling off the walkway, but when he turned back, Lew was behind him. He grabbed Mikawa in a headlock. Unfortunately, he'd never be able to choke him out, and while Mikawa was incredibly strong, so was Lew and the suit. Lew drove him to his knees and held on.

"You're wasting time," Mikawa said. "Just throw yourself off the walkway, Lew. End things on your terms. I'll allow you to do that. You will never beat me. All things being equal, a human can never better a machine. Even with the aid of machinery." Mikawa's voice not being strained from Lew's squeezing where his throat should have been was wholly unsatisfying, but that wasn't Lew's plan.

"There's one thing you forgot," Lew said.

"And what is that, Lew?"

"Humans don't fight fair."

Lew used all the power the suit could muster and rammed the mechanical ulna from Mikawa's detached hand through his back and out his chest. Sparks and some sort of liquid sprayed out of the hole.

"LEwuuuuuuuuu . . ."

The dead lights in Mikawa's eyes dimmed, then went out.

When he was sure the thing was dead, and he'd caught his breath, Lew grabbed Mikawa's head in his hands and pulled. He howled as he separated it from the mechanical body. Finally, Lew stepped back and let the headless body fall over the edge, crashing to the forest floor below.

Chapter Thirty-eight

CAPTAIN MAKOTO WAITED while Hiroshi Nishida, the sonar operator, verified his readings. He wanted to be absolutely sure. Had to be. As far as the shadow was concerned, the enigmatic, nameless government operative, they should have fired the torpedo by now.

"There was definitely some sort of launch at the top of the hour," Nishida said.

"And nothing else, since?"

"No, sir."

"What about the sensors?" the shadow said. Everyone turned and looked at him. It was the first time he'd spoken to anyone besides the captain. Then everyone looked at the crewman monitoring the sensor readings.

"Nothing, sir. I've checked multiple times. Nothing has been released into the water at that location."

The captain sighed. He exchanged a look with the shadow but resigned himself to his duty.

"Fire torpedo, mister."

"*Hai!*"

The torpedo tube flooded, and the Type 89 torpedo launched at Ashita, its screws churning through the water at almost seventy knots. The torpedo would impact its target in just over nine minutes.

The captain turned to say something to the shadow, but he was already gone.

"Take us home," the captain said as he left the bridge.

Ashita
5:17 p.m.

LEW KEPT THE exo suit on as he climbed the stairs to the top of the tower. He was exhausted, and most of him just wanted to lie down and go to sleep. His body ached even with the suit's support, but he could tell that if he took it off, he wasn't going to make it twenty feet, never mind almost twenty floors. Under his arm, he carried his prize. He kept waiting for the head to start talking to him. If it did, he was going to use what little energy he had left to punt it off the top of the tower.

Per met him on the stairs halfway up. He took the head off him and let Lew put his arm around him for extra support. Lew tried to not think about the robotic thing Per was using to hold him up.

"Maggie?" Lew said as they rounded the thirty-fifth floor. Per shook his head. "Fuck. Jonny?"

"Your partner won't leave her side. We may have a problem," Per said.

"Like what?"

"She's still breathing, but she's lost all feeling in her legs. From the look of it, her back and possibly her neck are broken. We never should have moved her in the first place, but if we move her again . . ." They exchanged a look. "If we try to put her in a pod, it will probably kill her."

"If we don't, she's going to die anyway," Lew said, wincing as they rounded the final set of stairs. "How are we for time?"

"You should probably stop asking me questions."

"That bad, huh," Lew said. They hobbled over to the ladder.

Per helped Lew get the suit off and, on his first step, he collapsed.

"Fuck," Lew said, doing a poor job of taking the pain. "It's my leg."

Per knelt beside him and ran his human hand up and down Lew's leg.

"I don't really think this is the time for—AH!" Lew's sarcasm was punctured when Per twisted his foot back and forth. "Son of a bitch!"

"Definitely broken," Per said. Lew fought for breath as sweat broke out on his forehead from the pain.

"Your bedside manner sucks, Per," Lew managed. "Get me over to the ladder. You can heave me up with your can opener."

Per sat him at the base of the ladder, and then climbed up through the hatch. Once there, he turned around and reached down with his robotic arm. Lew climbed the ladder using one arm, dragging the exo suit along.

"What are you doing?" Per asked, as Lew passed him the exo suit. It wouldn't fit through the hatch while being worn, but it could fit on its own.

"What I do best—something dumb. Just take it."

Per took the suit and pulled it up, then he reached down and pulled Lew up to the escape-pod annex.

"Do you want me to help you put it on, again?" Per asked.

"It's not for me. Go get the escape pod open and put our friend inside," Lew said, nodding at Mikawa's head. Per nodded and headed to an escape pod. Lew grabbed the suit and dragged himself across the floor over to where Jonathan was on his knees beside Maggie.

"Hey, buddy," Lew said.

Jonathan looked up, seeming a little confused. "Lew? Should have known you were indestructible."

"I'm feeling pretty destructible, to tell the truth. Listen, Jonny, we gotta go."

"I can't. Look at her. If we try to move her—"

"I know, Per told me," Lew said.

Maggie, who had been out, opened her eyes. "You're alive?" she said, swallowing thickly.

"Nice to see you too, Maggie. Listen, you need to tell your boyfriend here to let me move you, or we're all about to have a real bad day."

"Can't . . . can't feel my legs. Neck feels . . . weird."

"I told you, Lew, she can't."

Lew hated what he was about to do, but he didn't have a choice.

"Per!" Per came out of the open pod and joined them. "I need you to get Jonathan in the pod and keep him there. Now."

Without a word, Per grabbed Jonathan with his robot arm and hauled him to his feet. Jonathan resisted and even reached for the machine gun that was on the floor, but Lew pushed it out of his reach.

"Lew! What the fuck are you doing! You'll kill her!"

"Go," Lew said, and Per dragged Jonathan away.

"You'll kill her, you bastard!"

"Maybe," Lew said to himself.

Maggie opened her eyes again. "Are you going to leave me here? I know I should be brave and say that's what you should do, but I'm so bloody scared, Lew."

"We're going to try something. It's probably going to hurt, but it's all we've got." Lew said. He worked his way around her so she was between him and the exo suit.

"I get it," Maggie said when she saw how he'd lined up the suit.

"Scream if you have to," Lew said, slipping his hands under her neck and tailbone.

"I'll be okay."

"I wasn't talking to you."

She laughed, and as she did, he lifted her off the ground with nothing but his upper-body strength. Then he wriggled himself forward so she was over top of the suit. Trying to ignore her screams and cries, he lowered her into it. When everything was latched and secured, he activated the suit.

Maggie's eyes rolled back in her head, and she heaved a sigh of relief that was almost sensual. She swallowed and started to breathe normally. Lew worked his way up onto his good leg, then reached down to help her up, but as it turned out, she didn't need his help.

"Are you good?" Lew asked.

"You're bloody brilliant, Lew."

"Good, in that case, can you help me into the pod?" She laughed again and put her arm around him. They shuffled over to the pod.

Jonathan, who was being held inside by Per and uttering crazy threats against everyone, eased up and stared in amazement when Lew and Maggie got into the pod. They slammed the door behind them. Lew fell down onto the bench seat, which wrapped around the pod's perimeter. Maggie sat down beside Jonathan and took his hand. Per let go and sat back himself.

"Jesus, Lew. God, I'm sorry, man."

"Just shut up and push the button."

Epilogue

WHILE THE *ATLANTIS EXPLORER*'s aft crane was lifting the first escape pod out of the drink and onto her deck, their sonar detected the trail of the JS *Hakuryū*'s torpedo moments before the massive explosion on the ocean floor filled their screens. For a terrible five minutes they couldn't detect anything else, and they thought the worst. Finally, a few hundred meters off their port side, another escape pod broke the surface.

The *Atlantis Explorer* pulled alongside the bobbing pod and again used one of her aft cranes to lift it out of the roiling ocean. The storm had headed off north again, but its remnants were still being felt.

The Custodians' medical crew checked everyone out. They set Jonathan's busted nose and gave him a better temporary splint and sling for his broken wrist. They gave Lew an inflatable splint for his leg and a pair of crutches. Maggie was left in her exo suit but given painkillers and saline. They didn't have the facilities to treat her on the ship. Per was uninjured, or at least he refused to let anyone examine him.

Everyone from the first pod was fine, including Reese, who apparently was still asleep.

Once they were checked out, they all sat on the foredeck of the *Atlantis Explorer* with gray blankets over their shoulders. The Custodians' medics wanted Maggie to lie down, but she said as long as she kept the suit on, she was fine. She was sharing a blanket with Jonathan.

After Lew's last experience on board the ship, he was a little reluctant to stay put, but there wasn't much choice at the moment. Fahd and several members of The Custodians crew had already apologized to him profusely. Jonathan was trying to accept the miscommunication story, but if Lew hadn't been Lew, not only would he probably be dead, so would just about everyone else. Not to mention, the Dead Lights virus would have been released into the ocean currents.

The Custodians personnel were combing the *Jirojin Maru* and evaluating the situation over there. From the reports so far, all of the guests and crew were still out cold but alive and well. The medical staff didn't expect anyone to wake up for another seven or eight hours. The guards in the hold were out cold, as well, but they all had plastic-tie handcuffs on them now. Including the two who had come up in the first escape pod. Apparently The Custodians were working with the Japanese government, who were swearing up and down that they had nothing to do with this whole debacle. They had agreed to help the Japanese ferret out the responsible parties within their ranks. The Custodians would handle the debriefing of all of Tenabe's people when they reached the mainland. When that was completed, they'd determine who would be set free and who would be turned over to the authorities.

They weren't cuffing her, but Tatsu would have to answer for her part though Fahd assured Jonathan that her actions on Ashita would be taken into account. Everyone said they'd vouch for her, but apparently there was evidence linking her to several bombings in the States.

"We tracked Tanaka's implant and picked up his body a few kilometers east of here," Fahd said, standing near Jonathan. Jonathan and Maggie nodded somberly.

"He was in so far over his head, it wasn't funny," Jonathan said.

"Couldn't be helped," Fahd said. "And don't fault him for keeping things from you for so long. He was under my orders."

"I don't, and I know," Jonathan said, his disdain clear.

"Look, I don't blame you and Lew for being pissed," Fahd said. "I know you'd both probably like to take a swing at me right now, but we have a way of doing things. If you're going to be part of it, you need to get okay with that."

"Yeah, about that," Jonathan said, but Maggie interrupted him.

"What about Alex Corsair's body?" Maggie said.

"We looked. He must have been washed overboard. There's no sign of him on the deck. Even the blood washed away," Fahd said.

"Are you going to go down and check out Ashita?" Per asked.

"We've had an ROV down there for a half an hour," Fahd said.

"A what?" Maggie asked.

"A remotely operated vehicle. A little unmanned sub with cameras on it, tethered to the *Atlantis Explorer*," Fahd said.

"And?" Lew said.

"It's going to be hard to verify the story you guys told. There's some debris on the ridge, but it looks like whatever was left after the torpedo hit rolled over the edge to the bottom of the Japan Trench. Over ten thousand meters down. There will have to be a review to determine if it's worth investigating further."

"If it's worth it?" Lew spewed, getting up on his feet. Jonathan got up quickly and stepped between him and Fahd.

"Take it easy, Lew," Jonathan said. Then he turned to Fahd. "About our future with The Custodians. There isn't one. "

"That's up to you, and I understand, but I think you're making a mistake. Take some time to think about it. I told you, we're the good guys even if we do use unorthodox methods."

"Good guys," Lew said. "You sent Jonny in blind and almost got everyone killed. Not to mention using amateurs like Tanaka and Reese. Tanaka is dead, and what Reese went through . . ."

"Sir?" One of Fahd's men came over carrying a satellite phone. He handed it to Fahd. "It's Mr. Valmont." Jonathan noticed Fahd's demeanor change, and his Adam's apple clicked up and down.

"Excuse me," Fahd said, turning and taking a few steps away so he could take the call in private. Jonathan watched Fahd's body language, which seemed more submissive than he'd seen him act so far.

"What's that about?" Lew asked.

"Not sure. But if I had to guess, I'd say our friend Fahd isn't as high up on The Custodians' food chain as we thought." After a few more minutes, with a lot of gesturing by Fahd, he handed the phone back to the crewman and rejoined Jonathan and Lew.

"I've been asked to extend The Custodians' formal apology to you, Mr. Katchbrow," Fahd said, his facial expression betraying his true feelings.

"*Mr.* Katchbrow?" Lew said. "Damn, you done fucked up, son!" Everyone tried to hide their smiles.

"Um, yes," Fahd said. "And Ms. Koga, I've been asked to extend The Custodians' hospitality to you. And to ask you if you would be interested in joining us. You don't have to answer now, it's a standing invitation."

"What about the authorities? The bombings?" Maggie asked.

"If the Americans come for you, we'll do all we can mitigate the charges."

Tatsu smiled. Fahd turned and looked at Per.

"I've also been asked—"

"No thank you," Per said. His tone told Fahd it would be pointless to press him.

"As you wish."

Per exchanged a look with Lew, who winked at him, before Per looked back to Fahd. "I wish."

"CAN I TALK to you for a minute?" Tatsu asked Per, gesturing for them to step away from the main group. Per nodded and followed her to the ship's railing.

"What is it, Miss Koga?"

"You can call me Tatsu," she said.

"Fine, what is it, Tatsu?" Per asked.

"Things didn't really turn out the way we expected down there, but we had a deal. You kept your part, but I didn't get a chance to keep mine."

"True."

"Well, I can't show it to you anymore, but I can tell you about it," Tatsu said. She explained that Project Dead Lights was the virus they had just defeated.

"I see."

"Are you disappointed?"

"No. I was just thinking, even though we destroyed the virus, most likely the data on how to make the virus was sent to the Japanese government before Norris died."

"I . . . I never thought of that." Tatsu and Per looked out to sea.

"I'm not so sure we stopped anything."

THE CHOPPER TOUCHED down on the mainland, and the doors of the limousine waiting by the landing pad opened almost immediately. Jonathan, Lew, Per, and Maggie, still in her exo suit, stepped down onto the tarmac. Tatsu was on another chopper headed to some sort of interview process with The Custodians. Jonathan wasn't sure how he felt about that. Reese had still been sleeping on the ship the last time Jonathan saw him.

Emily stepped out of the limo and waved. Jonathan smiled and looked at Lew.

"Told you we were the good guys," Fahd said from behind them. "Natalie's in the car too." Then he headed into a nearby building.

Jonathan watched Lew move faster than he thought he could on his crutches. When he got to Emily, he dropped the crutches and grabbed her. He picked her up and swung her around, hopping on one foot.

"Your friend's quite a guy," Maggie said. The chopper was winding down behind them, but the noise still forced them to speak loudly. Jonathan looked at Emily and Lew kiss, then back at Maggie.

"Listen, there's something I need to tell you," Jonathan said.

"It's okay," Maggie said, but he could tell from her tone that it wasn't. He hadn't told Maggie anything about his life—not about being The Monarch or about being a dad. There hadn't been time. Until now. He wasn't sure he'd ever tell her about the art-theft side of his life—she was still in MI-6, after all. But there was a part of his life he knew he wanted to share. He owed her that, at least.

"After I knew you weren't dead, and you were released, I wanted to contact you. I even dialed a few times. But, I was in a different place. I had someone who needed me. All of me. I couldn't . . . God, this sounds lame."

"No it doesn't," Maggie said, looking down. "I get it, I do. We were great, but we were then. You moved on. I would have done the same thing."

"You're not hearing me," Jonathan said. "I'll be right back."

Natalie stepped from the car. Jonathan meant to run to her, but the sight of her sapped the strength from his legs. It was the first time he'd seen his daughter in over a year, now looking like a tall version of her mother. The realization hit Jonathan by surprise, and by the time Natalie had run over to him, his tears were flowing. He held her tight and kissed the crown of her head.

After a long embrace, both of them laughing and wiping tears away, he looked over at Maggie. She was more than a little confused. Jonathan put his arm around Natalie and led her over to the chopper.

"Maggie, I'd like you to meet my daughter, Natalie."

Acknowledgments

THANKS TO ALL my friends and family for their love and support, especially Barb Einarsen and Kiersten Soderstrom.

Thanks to all the readers, bloggers, reviewers, librarians and booksellers who not only enjoy books but seek them out and prop them up.

Big thanks to Dan Mallory, Joanne Minutillo, Danielle Bartlett and the entire Witness Impulse team for getting the word out about my books.

Huge thanks to my editor, Chelsey Emmelhainz, who helped me take this book from title to completion. Your expertise, patience and threats of bodily harm cannot be highlighted enough in this process. May you dream of Lew.

And special thanks to Tasha DiZazzo for everything else.

Want more Jonathan and Lew?

Keep reading for an excerpt from Jack Soren's
debut international thriller

The Monarch

Available now wherever ebooks are sold.

The Monarch

JONATHAN WATCHED EMILY BURROWS clumsily answer questions from the reporters about The Monarch—a situation he found more than a little surreal—when he heard his name. He saw Lew ignoring Miss Burrows and looking up at one of the huge displays overhead. When Jonathan saw what Lew was looking at the hairs on the back of his neck prickled.

" . . . *a photographer from Tallahassee, Florida. It's not yet known what motivated this mild-mannered family man to take up a ritualistic killing spree. Again, for those just tuning in, the killer known as The Monarch has been identified by the FBI as Jonathan Hall . . .*"

A fist slammed into Jonathan's face just below his right eye. The world swam, and Jonathan was only peripherally aware that someone grabbed him and dragged him away. Even in his delirious state all he could think about was Natalie. If that broadcast wasn't nationwide now, it would be in minutes. Soon, everyone in Tallahassee would see it. He'd lose her for sure.

As more and more of his senses returned, Jonathan knew he had only one chance. Get to Natalie as soon as he could. If he could just explain things, maybe she'd understand. Either way, they could run. Whether that was any kind of life for an eleven-year-old would be something he'd anguish over later. Right now he needed to stay out of a prison cell.

"Get your shit together, Jonny," Lew said. "We've got to get you out of here."

Jonathan's vision returned as Lew led him toward the door. He looked down at Lew's hands gripping his arm and noticed they were bloody and bruised. He looked back and saw two men with earpieces lying on the ground, bloody and broken. Past them, he saw that four armed men had jumped out of the crowd and up onto the raised platform by the podium. The FBI agent called Wagner and the NYPD chief of police were on the ground, not moving. Two of the men had their guns pointed over the crowd, and were intermittently shouting and firing into the air.

Two other men had Emily Burrows and were dragging her out like they'd tried to drag him. If not for Natalie, he might try to help her, then a thought occurred to him. He got his feet under him, shook off the remaining bells in his ears, and pushed Lew off him. A few more bullets thunked into the ceiling and pieces of cement crashed around them. They raised their arms over their heads to deflect the debris, the crowd screaming and running every which way. Jonathan's was the only face up on that screen right now. They—thugs and cops alike—would only be after him right now. He had to keep it that way.

"What the hell are you doing?" Lew asked.

"Get Burrows. She's in danger."

"Who the fuck isn't? Come on," Lew said, trying to grab Jonathan's arm. Jonathan's wits and reflexes were back and he slipped out of the grab easily.

"I'm serious, Lew. Go help her. Something's fucked up here and I'll be damned if I'll let one more person get hurt in our name," he lied.

Lew hesitated for a second, then said, "Aw, fuck!" and ran over to help Emily.

Jonathan turned and pushed his way through the crowd out of the building and into the concourse. He had to get out of there and as far away from Lew as he could.

He dodged through the people in the plaza, fighting off the odd person who made the connection between the images on the big screens mounted overhead and this lunatic running by. It wasn't hard, but if the crowd got too thick he wouldn't have room to maneuver. It would be pile-on-the-serial-killer, and he knew there wouldn't be enough left of him to pour into a jar for a court date. But even if he got through them and to the street, he'd still be up shit's creek.

I need a diversion.

Just then the front windows of the federal building exploded in a mass of noise, smoke, and glass, the blast wave hitting Jonathan in the back and knocking him to the ground. His senses dulled by the concussion, he distantly heard screams of pain and panic, bodies both slamming and flopping to the ground around him like someone had opened a window high overhead and alternately pushed and thrown them out.

By the time he raised his face off the pavement again, his ears were ringing just slightly louder than the sound of all the car alarms around him going off.

He got up, shaking the dust and glass off himself. He had been far enough away from the blast seat that the crowd had blocked the worst of the projectiles from him. Then he saw the carnage. It was horrific. Half the people who had been standing in the plaza—the people he'd just run through—were all on the ground, either deathly still or writhing in moist pain. Blood was everywhere. The glass had cut them to shreds. He knew the people inside the concourse were probably worse off, but smoke still filled the enclosed area and he couldn't see anything.

"Lew!" Jonathan called, jumping up on one of the serpentine benches, trying to see inside. "Lew!" He waited, fearing the worst. After what seemed like forever, a dusty and bloody figure stumbled out over the bodies wearing a duster. *Thank God.*

"There he is!" Two men over to the side started toward Jonathan. Their appearance and unwounded state said they hadn't been here for the explosion. It still wasn't safe to be around him. Knowing Lew was alive, Jonathan turned and ran.

When he got to the street, a limo came screeching to a halt in front of him. The back door flew open and a man with a gun inside said, "Get in or you're dead."

Jonathan kicked the door closed, turned, and ran up the sidewalk.

LEW TRIED TO run but he was still too fuzzy and just ended up falling onto someone on the ground. He pushed himself up and looked into a woman's panicked eyes. Glass from the explosion had sliced into her face and neck. Blood gurgled out of her wounds as she fought for breath.

"Help . . . hel . . ." And then she was gone. The dead and dying littered the plaza. He shook his head and got back up to his feet.

When the windows exploded he'd been standing behind the company directory. The initial fireball had eaten all the oxygen in the area and sucked in more hungrily, slamming him headfirst into the structure. He reached up and touched the pain in his head and his fingers came away warm and wet. It wasn't the first time he'd cracked his skull, but it always hurt like a mother.

Through the smoke he saw Jonathan kick a car door closed and take off up the sidewalk. Then the car peeled out, jumped the curb, and drove after him. Lew was running before he realized it, cutting across the plaza, stepping around the human obstacles scattered before him. He had no idea where the Burrows woman had been during the explosion, but he didn't care anymore. Whoever had done this was after the closest thing to a brother he had.

But he only had one emotion right now, and it was pure rage. He didn't know who all was involved in this despicable event, but he knew some of them were in that car.

He left the plaza and sprinted across the road, his lungs screaming. He hadn't run full-out in a long time. He'd let the only thing he'd ever really been able to count on atrophy over the past few years, but he still had the skills to put the pain into a corner of his mind and lock it away. His heart would have to explode before he'd stop running.

He rounded the corner and saw Jonathan turn around just as the car caught up to him. He thought it was going to run him down, but at the last moment it swerved and a door on the car opened, slamming Jonathan to the pavement like a ragdoll. Lew kept running.

Someone got out and scooped Jonathan up, carried him over to the car, and tossed him in. The man looked up and saw Lew coming like a locomotive. He pulled a gun and fired a few wild shots as he backed into the car after Jonathan. And still, Lew kept running.

The door closed and the car pulled off of the sidewalk, but had to stop as traffic cut it off. Horns blared and people shouted. The limo slammed into the car blocking its exit, then backed up so it could take off using the space it had created. Lew reached the car just as it was backing up and before it could take off, he leaped onto the roof.

The car sped away through the gap it had created with Lew on top. He gripped the sides and hung on, wishing he had any weapon besides his hard head. He'd be shaken off if the car ever got out of the lunch hour traffic, so he balled up his fist, wound up, and slammed it into the driver's door window. The window exploded into the car and Lew felt the bones in two fingers break. He put that pain away too.

Someone shouted and then two bullets fired up through the roof from inside the limo. They missed him and went through his duster. He rolled to the side as two more shots blasted through the roof where he had just been a moment ago. Then he heard a shot inside the car and the shooting stopped. Lew was even more frantic, but his busted hand was making it hard to hang on. As if they'd heard his thoughts, the limo start careening from one side of the street to the other, bouncing off the parked cars as it went.

On the third bounce, Lew lost his grip and found himself airborne. He slammed into the side of a parked truck and felt consciousness slip from him before he landed on the pavement.

JONATHAN, WEDGED DOWN on the floor of the backseat of the limo, plastic ties around his ankles and wrists, watched Lew fly off the roof of the car. Beside Jonathan lay the man who had grabbed him and tied him up—dead with a bullet through his forehead.

While he'd been shooting at Lew on the roof, Jonathan pulled his knees tight to his chest and kicked out. The shooter turned, rage in his eyes, and pointed his gun at Jonathan. A second later, without even turning his head, the driver had swung a gun around and killed his accomplice.

"That's a hell of a guard dog you've got there, mate," the driver said now. He had an Australian accent, but not a thick one, like he'd been away from home for a long time.

"You have no idea," Jonathan said.

"Just sit back, be quiet, and we'll have no problems," the driver said.

"No *more* problems, you mean," Jonathan said. The driver didn't physically react, but his silence told Jonathan he was right. This little operation might have netted him, but it hadn't played out as planned. "Relax, I know how missions can go sometimes. You can't foresee everything. I'm sure your boss will understand."

"I'm not going to tell you again, mate. Shut it." Jonathan was getting to him. He was taking a bigger risk than he normally would, but after seeing the driver kill his partner for threatening him, he'd lay odds he was wanted alive and well. Then he remembered, just before all hell had broken loose, a couple of thugs going after Emily Burrows.

"No problem," Jonathan said, and then after a beat, "Miss Burrows probably wasn't that important to him, anyways."

"You were warned," the driver said, swinging his arm back with the gun gripped in his fist.

"Wait—" Jonathan had forgotten alive and well didn't necessarily mean conscious. The gun slammed into the side of his head and a bright explosion in his mind radiated out until his brain overloaded and everything went dark.

About the Author

JACK SOREN was born and raised in Toronto, Canada. Before becoming a thriller novelist, Jack wrote software manuals, drove a cab, and spent six months as a really terrible private investigator. His debut novel *The Monarch* was nominated for the Kobo Emerging Writer national book award and the Silver Falchion Reader's Choice Award. He lives in the Toronto area.

Discover great authors, exclusive offers, and more at hc.com.